THE
PRIZED
GIRL

Amy K. Green was born and raised in a small New England town where she was once struck by lightning. She was a practicing CPA before leaving the corporate life to work in film production, write, and wear fewer high heels. She now lives in Los Angeles but spends as much time as she can in Boston.

THE
PRIZED
GIRL

AMY K. GREEN

ONE PLACE. MANY STORIES

HQ
An imprint of HarperCollins*Publishers* Ltd
1 London Bridge Street
London SE1 9GF

This edition 2020

1
First published in Great Britain by
HQ, an imprint of HarperCollins*Publishers* Ltd 2020

Copyright © Amy K. Green 2020

Amy K. Green asserts the moral right to be
identified as the author of this work.
A catalogue record for this book is
available from the British Library.

ISBN: 978-0-00833-447-5

MIX
Paper from
responsible sources
FSC® C007454

This book is produced from independently certified FSC™ paper
to ensure responsible forest management.

For more information visit: www.harpercollins.co.uk/green

Printed and bound by CPI Group (UK) Ltd, Croydon CR0 4YY

THE
PRIZED
GIRL

CHAPTER ONE

VIRGINIA

Five Days After

WHEN MY HALF SISTER, Jenny, was killed, it was all over the news—national news, not just the local paper that had to use an offensively large font to fill its pages. Strangers drove great distances to be part of the fanfare. Reporters and their vans lined the street in front of the church hosting her funeral. I parked my dented Jetta along the side of the road about a quarter mile away. There was no reserved parking space for me.

St. Bernard's Cathedral was the only church aesthetically pleasing enough for my stepmother, Linda, to hold the funeral in. It was too large for the community; even Christmas Eve Mass couldn't fill more than half the pews. Not today, though. Today, the local police were turning people away.

Men and women were milling around crying, consoling each other. No one was smiling, not even the polite forced smile you use to mask pain. Just hordes of people looking truly devastated by Jenny's death. I didn't recognize any of them, and I highly doubted they had ever set foot in this town before.

A dopey uniformed officer named Brett stood at the base of the church stairs. We went to high school together. It was the type of town where no matter the age, it felt like we all went to high school together in some shape or form. He looked exhausted, and his buzz cut was useless to sponge up the beads of sweat multiplying across his forehead. He just let them grow until they dripped off and splashed onto his shirt.

Brett was a bouncer without a list, making gut decisions about who he could let into the church. I was fourth in line, an actual line that I had to wait in patiently to attend my own sister's funeral. It was my choice. I didn't deserve special treatment. I was not a good sister.

I watched Brett turn two people away before recognizing the couple in front of me and allowing them inside without hesitation. When I stepped up for my turn, he looked up carelessly, locked on my face, processed who I was, and straightened his spine.

"Virginia . . . hi. I'm very sorry for your loss."

"Thank you," I said.

"This is crazy, huh?" He finally wiped his brow, altering the trajectory of his sweat beads.

"Was I supposed to RSVP?" I joked. I probably shouldn't have. No jokes at funerals.

"Of course not," he said, too nervous to get it. "Please go on in." He stepped aside and extended his arms with such flourish it was as if I had the last golden ticket.

IT WAS LOUD INSIDE. Churches were supposed to be quiet. The noise was unsettling. A group of sobbing women who must have gotten in just before Brett took the helm filled the last two rows. They looked like they were attending the Kentucky Derby. Are funeral hats a thing?

The next few rows were a mixed bag of strange faces and town staples. It was easy to tell who the out-of-towners were because they ignored me. The people from town gave me intrusive pitying looks followed by immediate avoidance of continued eye contact. It was the same way when my mother died.

Wrenton was one of those old New England towns where the founding families all spawned from some combination of people from the *Mayflower*, and for a long time it was just the same names swapped around over and over again. Even though there were a lot more surnames now, it still felt to me like we were all from the same litter, destined to live and die where our ancestors had. Someday, I was going to leave and never look back—just not today.

I could see Linda in the front row amidst a few distant relatives of hers. Her outfit wasn't as on point as I'd expected. Her black skirt was wrinkled in the back, and her pleated blouse was, dare I say, frumpy. She hadn't touched her curling iron, which was a real shocker. Linda always curled her hair for events. Instead, the blonde strands, too long for her age, just fell flat against her back.

I watched her face contort and quiver as people whispered things to her with delicate smiles. I knew she was hurting, but I was struggling to muster any sympathy. Jenny was her only child, her favorite little trophy, and Linda was a parasite. Every activity was a calculated move to help Linda feed off her daughter and reinforce her fragile ego.

It was never more apparent than with the beauty pageants. From ages five to twelve, Jenny won more Grand Supreme titles than anyone else in New England. I was told about it quite often, and Linda wasn't going to let anyone in this church forget it. Gigantic glamour shots of Jenny surrounded the coffin. In each one, a dead-behind-the-eyes little girl was dressed in a slightly provocative costume with enough makeup for a roadside hooker.

You would think my half sister had been some angelic being. There were just so many stories about the pageants, and her beauty, and how big her heart was. *Her potential!* These people were delusional. Jenny would have been fourteen in three weeks. She hadn't done a pageant in months and was becoming a nosy little twat.

I took a seat away from Linda next to an elderly couple who smelled like a forgotten attic. I didn't know them, and they didn't know me. The elderly strangers in the church seemed less creepy to me than the younger people attending the funeral of a child they didn't know. Old people just like to go to church.

From a private door in the front, my father, the esteemed Calvin Kennedy, entered the church and joined his wife. I knew he was a suspect. The father was always a suspect in these sorts of things. Part of me hoped he was guilty. I found solace in fantasizing about all the horrible drop-the-soap-type prison clichés.

I was not one for being out in public for extended periods of time. In Wrenton, everyone knew everything about everyone, or tried to at least. In the minutes it took me to pay for my gas I could learn five to seven intimate facts about my neighbors. World news didn't resonate. A good story was one you had to whisper for fear that the very person you were shit-talking could be lurking just around the next corner.

My skin was crawling. I could feel the eyes on me. Suddenly, I was relevant again and my secrets were fair game. I had to get out of that church. I slipped out of the pew, kept my head down, and made my way to the exit. Another A-plus decision for Virginia Kennedy.

———

JENNY'S FUNERAL LASTED a little over an hour. I waited outside, among the hedges to the left of the church doors. If I smoked, I'd have been smoking. Instead, I just chewed at my fingernails, trying to gnaw them even, each bite making it worse.

I could hear everything. Linda's cousin read a poem she had written that rhymed, some of Jenny's perfect little friends from school sang a song, and the priest talked forever about God choosing special children to stand by his side in heaven. The verbiage was particularly disturbing given she was raped and murdered, left to die in the woods. Seems like he could have *chosen* her with a lightning bolt or something.

When I heard pews creak and feet shuffle, I knew it was my time to fully commit to bailing. I hustled to my car, keeping my head down and praying I wouldn't cross paths with anyone who would attempt to engage. I didn't go to the cemetery. It was a selfish thing to do, but Jenny wouldn't know. She was too busy being God's personal assistant now.

I went home to my tiny apartment, where I could pretend nothing had happened. I could pretend nothing had happened to Jenny, or to me, or to the world. I could embrace some sort of delusional existence where I wasn't a piece-of-shit person or a piece-of-shit sister. It would be harder to hide now, now that Jenny was gone.

CHAPTER TWO

JENNY

Five Weeks Before

THE SCHOOL BUS was late on the first day, and Jenny leaned against the remnants of a rock wall, shifting her weight back and forth, bored, anxious. It was her first year in high school. Technically, she was only in eighth grade, but the student population was small, and long before she was born, the district voted to convert the former middle school building into town offices. The students were displaced. Seventh graders were crammed into the elementary school, and eighth graders moved into the high school. It was normal procedure now, but no less jarring for those making the transition. Last year Jenny had shared the halls with kindergarteners; now there was a guy with a mustache waiting for the bus.

The other students huddled together across the street from Jenny in a small area deemed to have the best cell phone reception. She wished her parents would let her have a cell phone, but there was no way they would give her one after what had happened.

Jenny was the only one who seemed to care when a faint whistling came from up the hill. She gazed toward the bend in Sanford Hill Road, anticipating the source of the sound. A lanky teenage boy in an oversized camouflage jacket, baggy jeans, and combat boots marched around the corner. Jenny recognized what he was immediately: a new kid. He looked older, maybe a junior. She stared at the stranger until it was obvious he was walking toward her, then averted her eyes, pretending to look for something in her backpack.

He sauntered over and joined Jenny at the rock wall, but left a comfortable space between them. He took a deep breath and rubbed at his thighs, preparing for an interaction she didn't care to initiate. She fidgeted with her bag, like maybe she was so enthralled with it that she hadn't noticed him. Surely he would understand because whatever she was looking for was important. Where was the freaking bus?

"Want one?" the boy asked, reaching into his coat pocket.

Jenny paused her frantic searching to look up and see him pull out a packet of cigarettes. "No, thank you," she said, even though her brain pulsed with the opportunity to do something so forbidden.

"Eh, that's good. These things are disgusting." He pulled one from the pack and returned the rest to his pocket. With his other hand, he grabbed a lighter from his jeans and lit up. "I'm hooked." He smiled as he turned his head to blow the smoke away from her.

Jenny debated going back into her bag. Would he notice that she had just given up this all-important search? Why did she even care?

"What's up with this school?" he asked. "I hate new schools. Either they assign me some hyperactive pep squad bitch to show me around, or no one knows I exist."

"We don't have a pep squad."

"Good, maybe I'll be left alone then."

"Maybe" was all Jenny could muster. He had engaged her, but now he wanted to be left alone. Mixed signals.

"Where's the bus?" he asked.

Jenny shrugged.

"You just have all the answers," he teased.

Jenny's reciprocating smile was cut short as a car came speeding down the hill, tearing through the gravel, and sliding to a stop in front of them.

Christine Castleton rolled down the window of her hand-me-down Nissan. "Hey, Jenny," she said, as if they had interacted more than zero times in the past. "I have one seat left. Are you interested?" She intended for the question to be rhetorical. Of course Jenny would want a ride. Christine Castleton was a special brand of popular. After a knee injury her junior year derailed her promising athletic future, she went from golden child to intoxicating rebel. At some point over the summer, she had even dyed her hair a bright magenta, unheard of in this town.

It meant something that she was talking to Jenny. It meant something to be chosen, but Jenny froze. Her summer had been long and full of painful isolation. Her mother had made sure of that. Jenny wasn't ready for the Christine Castletons of the world. It wasn't just a car ride. It was an initiation.

"I'm going to wait for the bus," Jenny answered, trying to be casual about it, but Christine hit the gas and blew through the stop sign at the end of the road, evidencing her disapproval.

"Must be some bus," the boy she had momentarily forgotten about said before smirking. He took one last long drag from the cigarette, tossed it to the ground, and stomped it out with his combat boot. "Day one, can't wait."

The sound of diesel in the distance was the most welcome noise Jenny had ever heard. They both slid off the rock wall, and she was unsure if she should walk with him or leave their interaction at that.

She took the lead, and he followed just enough behind her to show he wasn't sure either.

"I'm JP, by the way. If you cared."

"Jenny," she said, hoping this wasn't a mistake. It was her first day of high school; she hadn't even boarded the bus yet and had already rejected Christine Castleton and attached herself to a weird nobody.

JP reached out to symbolically hold the bus door open for her, and as her foot left the ground, a voice yelling in the distance demanded their attention.

"Jenny! Jenny!" her mother screamed in no particular direction as she came barreling down their driveway, running parallel to Sanford Hill Road and all too visible from the bus. Linda was in her silk bathrobe, hair wet, arms and legs flailing. "Jenny!" She spotted the bus and began a targeted sprint.

Jenny stared in shock before jumping off the bus, pushing JP out of the way. "Mom, what? Stop."

Linda threw her arms around her daughter and squeezed. "Oh my God, I didn't know where you went. I was so scared."

Jenny shoved her off. "Jesus, Mom, this is so embarrassing. Please go."

"You're right, OK, I'm sorry." Linda backed away. "Have a great first day. I love you."

Jenny rolled her eyes and headed back to the bus. Doomed.

CHAPTER THREE

VIRGINIA

THE FUNNY THING about death is how hard everyone strives for normalcy in its wake. If we could all just pretend it didn't happen, these horrible feelings would go away. Only a week had passed since Jenny's murder, and we were having Sunday dinner. The weekly ritual was something none of us enjoyed to begin with. Now, it was unbearable.

I pulled into the driveway around six, awaking several reporters who had been parked across the street for the past three days. They flooded from the vans but couldn't step on the property, and I was grateful for the long driveway. I slipped into the side door attached to the garage. Once I was inside, they went silent and retreated to their vehicles like zombies resetting in a haunted house. They would lie dormant until I resurfaced later that night.

I entered the kitchen from the garage. It smelled like Italian. I peeked in the oven and saw a lasagna. It was store-bought, Costco probably. Linda always cooked extravagant Sunday dinners, but since the murder, doctors had her on something close to horse tranquilizers.

"Hello?" I yelled out into the house.

"In here," said my father from the living room.

He sat in a brown leather chair and clung to his phone, typing with purpose. He looked up after a second. "Virginia, come, sit."

Linda was curled up on the couch, leaving plenty of room for me to join her. She was put together, but wrapped tightly in an old afghan that her late mother had knitted for Jenny, and rocking so subtly one could miss the motion if they weren't looking for signs of insanity.

I lowered myself down onto the couch, afraid if I created too much movement she would break. "How are you doing, Linda?" I asked.

She smiled at me. "I'm doing well. Thank you. How are you?" Her voice was affected. Linda always spoke with misguided energy, but now she was deflated, giving a canned response that was totally inappropriate given the circumstances. *Jesus Christ, Linda, just admit something really horrible happened and you aren't one hundred percent. I won't tell anyone.*

"You know . . ." I trailed off. "A lot of reporters out there."

"A bunch of vultures who don't think of us as real people," spat my father.

"They just want to help," Linda tried.

"Help who? You think they're out there to help us? They're out there waiting for us to do something that they can use to say it's our fault. Proof we weren't good parents, proof we didn't do enough to protect our daughter. It's what they always do."

That upset Linda. She rested her head down on the arm of the sofa, a physical sign of surrender.

"Do the police have any leads?" I asked my father.

"It was that man from the pageants. Had to be. A truly disturbed man. Evil."

Linda met this with a labored moan. "Can you please stop? Can we just have a nice family dinner?"

"Christ, Linda, what else do you expect us to talk about?" he grumbled.

I didn't expect compassion from my father, even in this extreme circumstance, but it wasn't any easier to witness. Even *I* wanted to offer Linda a hug, something my father only did in front of the cameras. She just looked so fragile. I almost forgot how much I disliked her.

The timer went off in the kitchen, and Linda unwrapped herself from the blanket and announced, "The lasagna is ready."

MY FATHER SAT at the head of the table. He brought his phone with him, something that always agitated Linda. I sat in my normal chair to the left. The extra leaves were still in the table from the wake, resulting in three empty chairs instead of just one, Jenny's.

Linda entered with the lasagna and placed it in the center of the table. She had removed it from its packaging and set it into a casserole dish, hiding the evidence. Such a poor misguided woman to think anyone would care that eight days after the death of her only child she didn't make a homemade lasagna.

She took the chair to the right of her husband, then reached out and took his hand, pulling it away from the phone in an affectionate way. He obliged and set it down on the table. A small victory for Linda.

"I would like to say something before we eat," she announced.

"We don't need to be dramatic. Can we just eat?" asked my father.

"Calvin, I want to say something."

He leaned back in his seat. Another Linda win. She interlocked her hands, thinking about her words. "Jenny was such a beautiful girl. She had a bright future. She could have been Miss America, but she was taken from us by a monster. I hope that once they find that man and bring him to justice, we will be able to find peace." She nodded like she had finished grace and reached for the knife, slicing into the lasagna.

Linda's obsession with pageants was nauseating. It had long been one of my triggers. I knew what it was like to be my father's child. It came with such pressure to be successful that I had long ago snapped, revolted, and practically been disowned. That poor child saved me. She became the focus so that I could slip away. It worked for everyone until it stopped working for Jenny. For the past few months, she had not been behaving as required. It was not addressed, and it was ignored to the point that even now Linda was talking Miss America. I could feel my temperature rising. I had to say something.

"But don't you think the timing was odd? I mean, if it was this Benjy guy, why now? She wasn't even doing pageants anymore. Don't you think he would have found a girl, you know, more *perfect*?" I knew the last part would sting. That was the point.

"She *was* perfect," Linda snapped.

"I just mean, I think too much emphasis is being put on her pageant life. The pictures everywhere are these disgusting glamour shots. I think it's just creating a false story. She wasn't a doll. She was a teenager."

"That's enough," my father commanded.

It felt empowering to get that out even if I was alone in thinking it. I was a lousy sister, and this felt like the least I could do. Someone had to stick up for her memory, not the memory her parents and the media wanted portrayed, the memory she would want.

I left right after dinner. They wanted normal and that was normal. I didn't like those people. I hadn't realized how much of a buffer Jenny had been between me and my father and Linda. I always thought they used her to ignore me. Apparently I used her too.

I stepped outside and awoke the zombies.

They kept yelling questions as if I would stand at the top of the driveway and yell answers back down to them. The narrative was already clearly established: Jenny was a beautiful, pristine child raped and murdered by a pedophile obsessed with her. A murder that rocked a perfect town and a perfect family. I would watch that *Dateline* episode. It was time to shake that image up a bit.

When my car reached the end of the driveway, the reporters parted to allow me access into the street. They surrounded the car, trying to get a good look at me. I rolled down the window to help them. Then I raised both middle fingers and announced, "You're all so fucking stupid," before hitting the gas and driving off.

CHAPTER FOUR

JENNY

IT WAS AN uneventful first day thus far as Jenny walked into the bustling lunchroom. Eighth graders were separated into two class blocks, and she found herself in the B block without any of her friends.

Mallory Murphy, Jenny's best friend since kindergarten, waved at her from a table of pretty girls in the center of the room. Mallory was stocky but fit, with blonde ringlets and a reputation built around having a tryout with Olympic gymnastics coach Bela Karolyi once.

"Oh my God, Jenny, I can't believe you aren't in our block," Mallory said before Jenny could even sit. "You have to tell your mom to call. It's so stupid. They'll switch you."

"Yeah." For the first time, Jenny realized she had enjoyed the peace of her morning. She felt bad. These were her best friends.

"There's a new kid," Mallory announced.

"I know," said Jenny.

"You know? Did you meet him? He's in our block. How do you know?"

"He's in our grade?" Jenny questioned.

"Yeah, he's old, though. He's already sixteen. Like, he stayed back a bunch. He must be dumb, but he's kind of hot."

"Ew, Mallory," Nora, one of the skinny teens flanking Mallory, spoke up.

"Whatever," Mallory negated the girl's opinion and switched subjects. "Christine Castleton gave me a ride to school this morning." She paused for a reaction that Jenny wasn't going to give. Poor Mallory, unaware of her sloppy-seconds status. "She told me there were three spots open on the varsity squad and all the freshmen are chubby losers."

Cheerleading, Jenny's current destiny. Mallory was a shoo-in; her gymnastic skills were set to give the small squad a legitimacy it had never experienced. Heck, Christine Castleton could barely jog on her busted knee and was somehow still the captain.

"I can't believe you even have to try out," Laura, another flanking groupie, gushed at Mallory.

A shift had taken place over the summer. Linda had kept Jenny on lockdown after she quit the pageants, and Mallory had eased herself into the alpha role in the group. Jenny searched her brain for jealousy, but could find only relief.

THE ONE CLASS Jenny was unable to hide out in was geometry. It was a high school course offered every other year to students who passed a certain test the school administered at the end of seventh grade. Jenny was ecstatic last year when she found out she'd passed. Now, as she took her rightful seat next to Mallory, she was less thrilled.

"Have you seen Mr. Renkin?" Mallory leaned over and whispered.

Jenny shook her head.

"He's gorgeous."

Almost on cue, Mr. Renkin stepped through the doorway. He had toned arms and broad shoulders, but a small stomach that bunched just a bit over his belt, a flaw that made him real. His eyes were a unique shade of green highlighted by thick black eyelashes, and Jenny thought maybe if he wore one of those veils that covered the rest of his face and body, she could have mirrored Mallory's infatuation. Superficiality aside, his best quality was his playful demeanor, which had long awarded him uncontested status as everyone's favorite teacher.

He dropped the textbooks he was juggling on his desk with a thud. "All right, geniuses, come grab one."

The eight students slid out of their desks like they were disembarking a plane—most filed into an appropriate order; one asshole pushed ahead. Mallory was that asshole. She shoved this poor kid Dirk almost back into his desk. In her defense, he didn't really exist in her mind.

She paused as she placed her hands on the textbook and gifted Mr. Renkin extended eye contact. "I'm Mallory," she said, then waited for him to faint. The teacher nodded, and Mallory headed back to her desk cataloguing the interaction as a victory.

As the rest of the students grabbed their books, Mr. Renkin turned to the whiteboard and wrote his name in large letters, a useless thing to do. All that kids do before school starts is compare their teachers and classes.

"I'm Mr. Renkin," he announced for those who couldn't read, or speak, or think.

He leaned down to squint at the roster list on his desk. "Raise your hand when I read your name."

"Laura?" Hand.

"Krystal?" Hand.

"Dirk?" Hand. He did exist!

"Brian?" Hand.

"Mallory, we met." He grinned, mocking the girl.

"Nora?" Hand.

"Samuel?" Hand.

"And last but not least, Jenny?"

Jenny raised her hand, surprised to be last, defying the laws of alphabetization.

Mr. Renkin placed both hands down and leaned onto the desk as he looked at her. His actions could be those of a man who had reached the end of a list, but the stare felt deeper. Mallory, whose senses were on high alert, turned to look at Jenny in the millisecond before Mr. Renkin looked away and before any other student noticed. When Mallory wouldn't let it go, Jenny gave the best explanation she could—a light shrug.

THE BELL RANG at 3:10 and the swarm of kids around Jenny jumped from their seats. Jenny didn't rush, happy to let them all go first. It was time to grab her bag, walk to the locker room, change into tiny spandex shorts and a tank top, and earn her spot on the squad. It was stupid. It was easy. It made sense, but she didn't want to do it. She didn't know why. Was she being a brat? Was she being lazy? Maybe she was jealous of Mallory after all.

She got on the bus and went home. One action to bear a million consequences.

She wasn't looking forward to facing her mother and explaining why she didn't go to tryouts. If the gods were on her side, she would already be passed out. Linda had developed a nice little wine-drinking habit in the last few months, meaning she drank it by the bottle whenever Jenny left the house. She had debilitating separation anxiety, which only heightened after Jenny quit the pageants, dissolving their special bond. With her husband in New York during the week and Jenny back in school, Linda was buying wine by the case.

Jenny climbed the carpeted stairs to her bedroom and shut the door. The room wasn't her at all, not anymore. Stuffed animals and dolls stared at her from a corner shelf. They looked much more foolish to Jenny than they had the day before. She was officially an eighth grader now.

She opened her closet door and began tossing the animals into the back, one at a time, until the shelf was clear and the closet was a gruesome pileup of beady-eyed carcasses. She flopped down on the bed and gazed up at the sheer princess canopy above her. That would have to go too, but she couldn't bring herself to get back up. She would rip it down later.

So much had changed in the past few months, and she didn't know who to blame. Maybe her dysfunctional family, maybe herself? She couldn't blame Benjy. It wasn't his fault.

CHAPTER FIVE

VIRGINIA

I PARKED ON THE STREET in front of the police station at half past one. I made sure to schedule any appointments in the middle of the day so as to feel the most productive. I usually slept until ten, and if I could manage to stay out until at least three, that was only four hours until it was dark and I could go to bed again.

I found myself recently unemployed due to having quit my job. I was a temporary person. It was the only way I could get out of bed in the morning, knowing it wouldn't be like this forever. It was *hope*, I guess—really mutilated, beyond recognition, *hope*. It was something I definitely didn't inherit from my mother. She had no hope.

My father married my mother when they were both nineteen. They were high school sweethearts out of convenience. The town didn't produce many attractive people, so the ones who existed tended to couple up. They had me one year later and at least four years earlier than my dad planned on procreating.

He was in college studying some business bullshit. He became a big-time finance asshole, but back then he was a kid from a small town with a lot of ambition and a hot wife. They were two kids who got out of Wrenton. They were living in New York City, but when I was born, my mom brought me back with her to be near her sister. My dad took the train home from the city every weekend. He still did.

My mom became extremely paranoid that my dad was cheating. I doubted it. He was not a passionate man. She turned into a belligerent screamer and a drunk. She was small-town, very small-town, and resented her big-city husband. It got ugly. Monday through Friday she would go to the bowling alley with me in tow and drink until the owner put us both in the county's only cab. He would give me a lollipop. I do vaguely remember the candy.

My father would get home sometime after I went to bed on Friday, and by Sunday, they weren't speaking. That included speaking to me. It sounds like a horrible childhood, but it wasn't that bad. Some of my friends at school had these overbearing mothers who would show up all the time and bring them sweaters and kiss them in front of everyone. Ten is the very important age when you start to realize that parents aren't cool and if you have any chance of being cool, they need to back the fuck off. By eleven, I was one of the most popular kids in my class. That lasted for about six months until my mom killed herself.

I lived with my aunt for two years before my father met Linda, got her pregnant, and tried this whole family thing again. Everyone would have been happy for me to stay with my aunt, but when she got sick, I had to go home—a new home with Linda and baby Jenny at the base of Sanford Hill. Everyone really enjoyed the constant reminder I provided of all the terrible shit they were trying to forget. At least I didn't have to change schools; it would have been a real shame if I had to start high school without all that carefully cultivated baggage.

It was the same high school Jenny attended, fully equipped with her own baggage. She had only dipped her toe into those waters when she met her demise. If I could switch places with her, I would. Not for her to be alive now and for me to be dead like some selfless act of love. It's just, if I had died a few weeks before *my* fourteenth birthday, it would have prevented everything.

I FIRST SPOKE to the police on the day they found Jenny's body. Chief Garrety was geriatric, with a physique that couldn't catch a paraplegic criminal. He was sweating profusely that afternoon, and part of me worried we might have a second dead body on our hands. I guess that's why they brought in the big guns. A detective from Hartsfield would be taking over. Hartsfield wasn't much of a city, but they had detectives, so they were bigger than us.

I entered the station to an unmanned reception counter. Being alone made it somehow better and then somehow worse. I didn't want to make small talk, but at least it would be a distraction. Instead, I stood in front of the empty bull pen that seemed to shrink when I felt claustrophobic and expand when I felt small. I could hear some gruff man talk coming from the back, so I rang the bell on the desk like I was picking up dry cleaning. Then I rang it a few more times before Chief Garrety finally poked his head out from the kitchen.

"Oh, Ms. Kennedy, hello." He brushed some crumbs off his shirt and came to meet me. "How are you doing today?"

"You know . . ." I trailed off. I didn't know how long I would have to wait before I could answer "Good" to that question. Death is a funny thing. Murder is worse.

"Yeah." He nodded, then leaned in and hushed his voice. "Look, this guy thinks he's a real hotshot. Solved some big case once. Don't let him push you around, ya know? Just answer his questions and smile a lot. You're a pretty girl."

That wasn't comforting at all and possibly insulting. I couldn't tell. "I'll do my best."

Chief Garrety was convinced. "Follow me."

The chief showed me into the interrogation room and it put me on edge—steel table, two matching chairs, a mirror spanning the wall, dim lighting.

"I'll grab the detective," he said. "And remember . . ." He guided the corners of his mouth up with his fingers into a creepy grin. If I smiled like that, I'd be suspect number one in all murders ever.

I took a seat on the chair facing the door and settled in. The wait was rubbing me the wrong way. *I came in on my time. This is your job. Get it together.* I decided to believe this hotshot detective was taking a shit, a nervous shit because this was the biggest case of his life. I didn't want to be all annoyed when he finally came in. This made him more sympathetic.

I had bitten off three of my fingernails by the time he came in. He sat at the table with a file folder in his hands, staring down, fixated on its contents just like on television. He glanced up and reacted like he hadn't known I would be there. This guy was a trip.

"Hello, Ms. Kennedy. Thank you for coming in. I'm Detective Colsen." He extended his hand and we shook. So formal. He was attractive enough. No traits in particular were anything to fawn over—thirties, twenty-dollar classic haircut, acceptable face shape, average height. Still, he was a stranger, and there was something inexplicable about him that made me nervous.

He helped himself to the other cold, hard chair and fanned his sacred file out on the table. Right away a picture of Jenny's dead body appeared. I hadn't seen it before; I'd only heard what happened. She was covered in leaves and dirt, cemented to her by the early morning rainstorm. There were splotches of blood on her nightgown where the knife had entered. Cuts and bruises were everywhere. Her blonde hair was chopped to pieces, eyes closed, face devoid of color. Her hands were placed so peacefully together over her stomach, I imagined that's how they were now, inside the coffin. I couldn't stop staring. A dead body. A kid. My sister.

Images flashed in my head. Memories of Jenny as a clumsy toddler. My brain's defense mechanism showing her to me at her most innocent, back when I lived in the house and saw her regularly, often letting her sleep on my chest because she couldn't string enough words together to bother me. Back when she was a blob—before she was a person, before she was a performer, before she was my replacement.

The detective caught me staring. "Oh, I'm sorry." He quickly covered the picture with his notes. It wasn't convincing. I knew he wanted to see my reaction.

"Am I a suspect?" I asked.

"Right now, everyone's a suspect, but I wasn't particularly thinking it. Should I be?"

I smiled as instructed in an attempt to subvert the implication.

"Why don't you tell me where you were the night of the murder?" he asked.

"At home. In my apartment."

"Alone?"

"Yes."

He jotted down some notes. He wrote more than seemed reasonable based on how little I had said. "Your parents were home alone that night too," he stated.

"Is that abnormal? I think most people are home alone in the middle of the night. What were you doing in the middle of the night on Saturday?"

"And how was your relationship with your sister?" He ignored me.

I shrugged. "Pretty limited."

"Care to elaborate?"

"I only saw her on Sundays for dinner." That was a lie. I had seen her more recently. Two times to be exact. It was a sad state of affairs that I could so easily count how many times I had seen my sister outside of Sunday dinner. "I don't really get along with my stepmother, and Jenny is, *was*, thirteen years younger than me. We didn't have much in common." Nothing I could share about my sister seemed relevant. It also didn't seem like his business. It's kind of sick how, since my sister was dead, it was acceptable for this stranger to pry into my personal life.

"You don't get along with Linda?" he plucked from my statement.

"*Linda?* You guys on a first name basis already?"

He looked up for a hot second, acknowledging my point without fueling the fire.

"Linda has always found me to be a burden and I've always found her to be incessantly annoying," I explained. "Over time, we have worked out a comfortable groove of avoidance."

"How was her relationship with Jenny?"

"Super."

"Meaning?"

"I don't know. She thought Jenny was the bee's knees."

"And your father? How was his relationship with Jenny?"

"Fine, I guess. He likes her much better than me and nobody killed me, so I guess you can take him off the suspect list."

"And who do you think should be on the suspect list?"

"Isn't that your job?"

"I suppose so," he answered, charmingly unoffended by my obnoxiousness. "Let me ask you something," he said as if I had to give him permission. "I'm going to show you a picture, OK?"

I nodded. It was nice of him to warn me this time.

He slid out another picture of Jenny's body. This one was zoomed in on her neck, her face and body cropped out. "Does this necklace look familiar to you?" he asked, pointing at a small gold pendant in the shape of a heart, the thin chain it hung from caked in mud across her collarbone.

"No," I answered.

He slid the picture back into the folder, nodding. "No one seems to recognize it."

"Kids have secrets," I said, shrugging.

"What do you know about Benjy Lincoln?" he asked, transitioning flawlessly.

"Same thing that it probably says in the file." And a smile.

"Indulge me?" Then he smiled. Too much smiling was happening.

"I don't really know the details, just what I've heard from my father and Linda."

"Do you think he abused her?"

"I wouldn't know. We weren't close like that . . . or at all, really." I waited patiently to be judged, but he just nodded.

"Families are tough," he offered.

I wasn't sure what the point of this interview was, but I knew it wasn't to be my personal therapy session. "Are you arresting Benjy or what?"

"We're trying to find him."

"He's on the lam? Seems suspect."

"I don't know if he's on the *lam*, per se. He left his home a few weeks ago. We're trying to track him down." He leaned back in his chair and stared at me like I would have an answer.

"Well, you should try harder."

He closed the file. "Yes, thank you for coming in, Virginia." He'd graduated to my first name without my offering it. I was on par with his close friend Linda now.

"That's it?" I asked.

"That's it. I just like to meet with the family, create a relationship to move forward with. I want you to feel comfortable coming to me if you think of anything." He pulled a business card from his pocket and handed it to me. I shoved it into my pocket to be destroyed the next time I washed these pants.

We stood in unison, and he guided me out of the room, putting his hand on the small of my back. "I apologize for not saying this sooner, but I'm very sorry for your loss."

"Thank you." One last smile couldn't hurt. He reciprocated.

I walked out of the station and straight to my car. I hoped it was Benjy Lincoln. It felt like an awful thing to hope for, but she was already raped and murdered. Would hoping it was someone else be any better? I just wanted it to be over. That fucking picture. Now I had five hours to spend thinking about it before it would be dark again.

CHAPTER SIX

JENNY

JENNY'S LAST PAGEANT was on April 19, and almost five months had passed since then. It wasn't her biggest competition, not even close. She would have won the Grand Supreme title with ease if she had gotten that far.

She hated pageants by this point. It had been years since she actually enjoyed them, but it was Linda's obsession. Even her father embraced the pageants. He told her it was a real opportunity for her to become something. She wasn't sure what.

With success comes fans. Even a child beauty queen from a small town can have fans, obsessive ones. Her biggest fan was a grown man with a child's IQ named Benjy. She started noticing him when she was nine. He was at almost every pageant. He sat alone, watched the entire show, and always gave a standing ovation during crowning.

When she was ten, he gave her a birthday card. She was walking from the stage to her mother in the back of the ballroom when he stopped her. He was bashful and wouldn't make eye contact. The card was homemade with ten balloons individually cut out from different pieces of construction paper. The message was simple: *Happy Birthday, Jenny. You're the prettiest of all the girls. Love, Benjy.*

Jenny made it a point to say hi to Benny at every pageant after that, always when Linda was out of sight. She wouldn't understand.

Sometimes he would bring her small presents, usually something from a vending machine. Her parents felt strongly that presents were for birthdays and Christmas only, which gave it an added thrill. Occasionally, Benjy would give her letters. They were short and harmless, usually about something she did in a pageant that he liked. Jenny would squirrel the letters away in her pocket, feeding off keeping a secret from Linda.

On April 19, Jenny came to the pageant with her own letter for Benjy. It was one page of notebook paper about how she didn't want to do pageants anymore. She wrote it down so she could get it out, and then realized she didn't have anyone else to share it with.

It was a glitz pageant, Jenny's least favorite kind. It required hours of prep time, with Linda poking and prodding at her hair and face. The pageant had an Easter theme, and the irony of having all these slutted-out children dress as bunnies was lost on the starry-eyed parents. Linda was still in the back, adding last-minute sequins to the tail, when Jenny took the opportunity to give the note to Benjy.

He was sitting in the fourth row, and she waved him over to the corner of the ballroom. He bumbled over to her. "You looked very beautiful onstage. You look beautiful now too, I didn't mean . . . I just . . ." He tripped over his words, worried he had offended her, shifting from one foot to the other.

She grabbed his hand to calm him down. "Thank you, Benjy. You're so sweet."

He steadied his feet. "You have to go change. They don't give you a lot of time here for this one."

"I know, I just wanted to give you something." She reached into a slit in her costume and pulled out the note, folded up into a small square.

"A note for me?" He beamed.

"Yup." She handed it over. "Don't read it yet. Wait till after the show, OK?"

"OK."

"'K, gotta run."

"Good luck," he said as she ran backstage.

LINDA PULLED JENNY'S HAIR back so tight under the bunny ears she thought she might cry. Not an emotional cry, but an uncontrollable release of pain. Large pink satin bunny ears were affixed firmly to her head with about twenty bobby pins. Whiskers were drawn on her face with a thick eye pencil, then highlighted with sequins. One more light pass of translucent powder over Jenny's face and Linda was satisfied.

"Perfect." She glowed.

FROM THE WINGS, Jenny caught a glimpse of Benjy, two rows back on the far aisle. He was staring down into his lap. Benjy usually never took his eyes off the stage. She wasn't even sure he blinked. Jenny nudged forward to get a better look.

It was her note. She should have just let him read the note when she gave it to him. Linda could have waited another five minutes. He began unfolding it.

Another girl finished smiling, waving, and bunny-hopping around the stage. Jenny was next. She edged closer to the curtain without taking her eyes off Benjy as he read. His face twisted, and then he was out of his chair, head tucked down, running for the exit.

In a split second, Jenny was running backstage. She excused herself through her peers, who were shocked to see the one to beat bailing in a panic. She slipped out into the hallway just in time to see Benjy close himself in the janitorial closet down the hall.

She ran toward the closet, heels clacking on the tile floor. As she reached the door, she heard her name announced onstage. She hesitated only a second. She was going to be disqualified. Linda was going to have a panic attack.

Jenny knocked softly on the closet door. "Benjy, it's Jenny. Can I come in?"

"Go away."

"It's going to be OK. I'm coming in."

She slowly opened the door. Benjy was sitting in the corner next to a mop bucket, his arms wrapped around his knees. Jenny knelt down beside him and put her hand on his shoulder. "I didn't want to make you upset. I just wanted to tell you, because you're my friend."

"We're friends?"

"Of course," she said.

"You're so good at pageants. Why do you want to stop?"

"I don't like it. It's almost every weekend on the road with only my mother. They're all the same. I just want to try something else."

"Your mom's gonna be real mad."

"I know. Now give me a hug and let's go finish this one." She wrapped her arms around him. His hug was soft and encompassing.

Jenny felt calm and quiet for the first time in a long time until the door flung open. She lunged away from Benjy, but it was too late. They'd been seen.

Linda's scream filled the hall. The sound was piercing. "Get away from her!" she screeched. "Someone call the police!" Linda grabbed Jenny by the arm, pulling her like a rag doll out of the closet. She slammed the door closed, trapping Benjy inside.

"Mom, stop! He's harmless." Jenny tried to pull her mom away from the door to free Benjy, but her solid thighs were too much. Linda didn't budge.

"Call the police!" Linda screamed again.

Benjy was banging on the door from the inside.

"Let him out! You're scaring him." Jenny punched her mother in the stomach, her satin bunny ears flopping back and forth.

A crowd gathered around. No one was sure what to do. Jenny was pageant royalty, her mom the queen. The pageant director pushed through the spectators. He grabbed Jenny by both arms and pulled her from her mother.

"Linda, what's going on?"

"Call the police. A pervert was attacking my daughter and I've trapped him in here."

"No! She's lying." Jenny flailed in the director's arms and he tightened his grip.

"Take Jenny away. I'll handle this," he said to Linda, and they exchanged prisoners, Jenny for Benjy.

Linda squeezed her arms so tight her fingernails broke Jenny's skin. She dragged her daughter toward the exit while Jenny scrambled her feet, unsuccessfully trying to regain control of her body.

"I hate pageants!" Jenny screamed toward the gawkers. "You're the perverts, not him." Jenny had never acted like this. She was a rabid animal. "I'm never doing one of these ever again. Do you hear me?" And with that, Linda shoved her out the door. Jenny's last pageant.

JENNY AGREED TO see the school guidance counselor, Ms. Willoughby, as a compromise with her parents for skipping cheerleading tryouts. Linda thought with a little counseling Jenny would change her mind. Her father didn't care so much about cheerleading as long as Jenny replaced it with some sort of extracurricular activity. His exact phrasing was, "I won't let that school cultivate your lack of ambition like it did for your sister," which was his pretentious way of saying Virginia had done nothing then, so she did nothing now, as if a semester of volleyball was the solution.

The most interesting thing about Ms. Willoughby was that she was dating Mr. Renkin, and the halls echoed with rumors of students catching them hooking up. Jenny sat outside Ms. Willoughby's office waiting for her turn, but when the door was flung open, it wasn't another misguided student; it was the man himself, Mr. Renkin.

"Jenny . . ." He stopped in his tracks.

"Hi."

"Hope you aren't in any trouble," he said, winking as if the idea were impossible. That was annoying. He didn't know anything about her. She just looked at him, no need for further conversation. He brushed it off and continued on his way.

Jenny stood and poked her head into Ms. Willoughby's office. It was depressing; there wasn't even a window. She sat at a small desk, rubbing her forehead and staring blankly at the papers on her desk.

"Ms. Willoughby?" Jenny said, not sure if she should be interrupting.

The counselor looked up. "Oh, Jenny, come in."

Jenny took a seat as Ms. Willoughby shuffled the papers away.

"So, what brings you to see me?"

"My parents wanted me to. I skipped cheerleading tryouts and now they're worried I'm becoming a delinquent."

"Are you?"

Jenny couldn't help but laugh. "My mother thinks you're going to convince me to do it."

"I'm not here to convince you of anything. I think you should only do what you feel comfortable with. I'm just here to help."

"Were you a cheerleader?" Jenny asked, wondering if the pretty blonde woman in front of her had walked in her shoes and survived.

"Not quite." Ms. Willoughby glanced down and smiled, slipping momentarily into her own memories. "You're at a difficult age. How old are you? Fourteen?"

"Next month."

"Some people are exactly who they are from the day they're born, but for most of us, we change, and that's completely normal. Don't be afraid to change, even if other people give you a hard time."

"My mom's not going to like that advice."

"Well, sometimes it's hard for a parent to look at their own child objectively. Just know that someday you're going to move out of that house. You'll be on your own, and if you let your parents make all your decisions, you won't be prepared."

This woman was basically telling her to disobey her parents but in a totally alluring way that made it seem not only appropriate but also a sign of maturity. Jenny was into it. None of her friends talked like this. Their idea of the future was next semester.

"Nothing that you do right now has to be a life sentence," she continued, like Jenny's desire for her to keep talking was palpable. "Try new things. Let old things go. Whatever feels right to you."

Jenny only heard what she wanted to hear. It was a green light, permission to trust her own instincts.

THE HOUSE WAS pitch-black as Jenny crept down the stairs from her bedroom into the living room. She hadn't heard a peep from Linda in over an hour, and her father was in New York. She ran her hand against the wall until she reached a small accent lamp on the closest end table.

The lamp gave off just enough light for her to see her way around the living room. Behind the couch, along the wall under a large bay window, was an alcohol cabinet. It stretched the five-foot length of the window and doubled as a table for Linda's expansive Christmas village during the holidays. The rest of the year, Linda kept the top barren, like nothing else was worthy of such prominent display.

This was Jenny's first attempt at sneaking out, and she had a new-found appreciation for the almost wall-to-wall carpeting in the house. She slid the cabinet open, revealing an assortment of bottles that she couldn't distinguish. She pulled out the first one, a dark brown color, bourbon. She unscrewed the top, took a whiff, and gagged. She returned it and opted for a much less offensive bottle of peppermint schnapps.

Her bag was too small, and the end of the bottle poked out from under her arm as she slid through the kitchen and out the garage door, the exit farthest from her mother's bedroom.

THERE WERE NO STREETLIGHTS, but the moon was full and it adequately lit her path. JP was waiting at the bottom of the hill where they had agreed on. When he saw her, he flicked his cigarette behind him.

"Did you have any trouble?" he asked.

"No, my mom is dead to the world."

"She's not going to come down the road screaming, is she?"

"No." Jenny laughed, praying it was the truth.

"You wanna go to my place?"

"Is your uncle going to be there?" Everyone knew JP's uncle Boomer. He was a local celebrity, a harmless old drunk with splotchy red skin who always wore shorts, even in the dead of winter.

"Nah, he's gone. I don't know where he went. Been a couple days."

"OK," she agreed, ready to take the next step in her rebellion and follow him up the hill.

THE TREES LINING the dirt road seemed taller at night. The woods weren't particularly dense, serving more as privacy than an unforgiving maze, but that didn't make them any less scary at night. She sped up to walk closer to JP, causing the liquor in her bag to slosh around.

"What do you got in there?" he asked.

"Oh, I took this from the house." She pulled the bottle out and presented it to him.

"What are you going to do with that?" He laughed.

"I just thought we could have a couple drinks."

"You don't have to try and impress me, you know?" he said without looking back at her.

"I'm not."

"Drinking is no good. Makes you do bad things."

"Not all the time. Sometimes it's just fun."

"Says who?"

"I don't know. Everyone."

"That's my house," he announced, pointing through a patch of trees and changing the subject.

BOOMER'S HOUSE WAS, as she'd expected, in shambles: old worn furniture, empty beer cans, a distinctive stale smell. "We can sit out back," JP insisted as soon as they were inside, leading her around a stained plaid couch to the sliding door to the backyard.

As they stepped outside, a motion-sensor floodlight lit up the overgrown lawn. There were two rusty lawn chairs, a cooler, and a lot of cigarette butts. Jenny had zero interest in sitting on one of the rusty chairs but didn't want to seem high-maintenance. Maybe she would get tetanus, but she was sneaking out to hang with a boy. Bad things were supposed to happen.

He reached into the cooler, sifted past a few beers, and pulled out a Sprite. "In case you get sick of the schnapps."

Jenny took the soda, relieved she didn't have to drink the alcohol. "You like living here?" she asked.

"It's OK. Better than my grandma's place." He cracked open a Sprite of his own.

"You think you'll stay here for a while?"

"I bet you'd like that." He smirked. "You ever get out of this town?"

"I used to travel a lot for pageants." She cringed as soon as she said it.

"Pageants? Are you a little beauty queen?"

"Not anymore."

"Fair enough. I got a cousin in Mexico. You ever been there?"

"No. Not even close."

"I'm gonna go there. Soon. Once I get the money."

"How much money?" She hoped for an insurmountable amount that would keep him there with her forever.

"Probably like a few grand. My cousin can get me a job once I get there. I'll just do that until I'm eighteen. Then I'll come back and join the marines. What about you? You got a plan?"

"I'm only thirteen."

"So what? You gotta have a plan. That's how you know you're living your life and not someone else's. You make the plan, then you stick to it. If you can't follow through, then what's the point?" JP chugged the rest of his Sprite, crushed the can, and threw it into the tall grass. "You wanna see something?"

"Sure."

He hopped up and led her toward the edge of the lawn, where the woods began. Jenny was not a fan of the woods at night, but she had to make a choice. Was she going to be a little girl who ran back home, or was she finally going to experience something?

He slowed to a stop as he approached the rock wall bordering the first trees and she was relieved. That is, until he reached behind the wall and pulled out a knife.

Jenny retreated, and he seemed to regret not prefacing it. "It's

OK, don't worry," he said. "It's just a machete." He laid it across both hands and presented it to her in a nonthreatening way. She inched closer to inspect the weapon.

"Why do you have that?" she asked.

"Gotta have a weapon. In case anyone fucks with you." He stepped back from her as he gripped the handle and waved the knife around with calculated precision. "There's lots of bad people out there, Jenny." He whacked the machete into the closest tree. "You know what happened to my mom?" he asked.

"What?"

"Killed. Ex-boyfriend. Beat her to death." He pulled the knife out of the tree. "I was pretty young. I don't really remember it. I kind of remember hiding, but I don't know. Maybe I just think I remember." He inspected the surface of his weapon, brushing off a sliver of bark.

Jenny wasn't sure what to say. His story was so personal and so terrifying.

"I was too young to do anything, you know? Only four. It's not like I could have stopped him."

"Yeah, of course," she said when she realized her silence was causing him some discomfort. It wasn't her intention. Not at all. She wanted to comfort him, but she couldn't find the right words and he didn't seem receptive to a hug, standing there gripping his machete. "What happened after?"

"I had to move in with my grandma. She sucked. She always talked so much shit about my mom, but I know most of it wasn't true. I think she was just pissed to be stuck with me. Boomer says my mom was really nice."

"I'm sure she was."

"Yeah, doesn't matter now. Now it's just me. But see, that's why you need a plan. So you don't end up like her." He slid the machete back behind the rock, and Jenny was happy to see it go.

"C'mon, it's getting late," he said, giving her permission to run home.

CHAPTER SEVEN

VIRGINIA

DETECTIVE COLSEN STOOD in my doorway two hours before I was ready to get up and start the day. He was already in a suit; I was in an oversized T-shirt and boxer shorts. He shoved a newspaper in my face and maneuvered past me and into my apartment uninvited.

It had been a long time since I held a newspaper and even longer since a man was in my apartment. I thought newspapers were a lost art, but there I was with my blurred-out middle fingers on the cover juxtaposed nicely with one of Jenny's glamour shots. The subtle headline read, *Jealous Sister Disrespects Dead Girl.*

"You want to explain this?" he asked.

"Which part?" I threw the paper down on my makeshift coffee table that was technically a TV stand and flopped down on the couch.

"This is not the kind of attention we need right now." He shook his head and helped himself to a seat next to me. It was too close for comfort, but my apartment didn't have any other real seating.

"You can't blame me for this. It should have said, *Grieving Sister Hates Asshole Reporters.*"

"They're saying it because you skipped the funeral."

"I made an appearance."

"It rubbed people the wrong way. And now, the only time you visited your parents since the murder, you stayed for one hour, then reacted like this." He pointed back to my cover photo.

"So what? I don't like them. What do you want me to do?"

"Look, I know who did it. You know who did it. Everyone knows who did it, but the longer it takes us to find him, the more people get restless. They need to have something to talk about, to keep the story going, to point out other suspects."

"So, now I'm a suspect?"

"No, no, you're not a suspect. I'm just saying—"

"Why not? I could have done it. A lot of people could have done it. I think putting all your eggs in one basket is pretty shitty detective work." I was only half awake and not in the mood to be scolded.

"Look, Virginia, I know you like the attention, but this is what I do, and when your antics interfere with me doing my job, we have a problem."

"Attention" was such a weapon word, a grenade thrown out to get under my skin. I wanted to inform him I was perfectly capable of dying alone in a bunker, but regardless of my intentions, I was getting attention, and I didn't like it either.

"What do you suggest?" I asked with as little sarcasm as I could manage.

"Just lie low. Look sad when you go outside. Visit your parents more. No bullshit."

"OK," I said and waited for him to leave. He didn't budge.

"Do you have any coffee?" he asked, almost settling in.

The question caught me off guard and I think I made a stink face. I wasn't sure what had just happened. The authority under which he arrived was blurring into something personal. I couldn't ignore the invasive permission he granted himself because, what? I had smiled at him a few times? "I don't have any coffee."

"Oh, right, I'm sorry," he said, standing. He seemed genuinely enlightened and subsequently embarrassed, and then I just felt bad. Maybe his intentions were not as seedy as I had been eager to assume.

"I think I have some tea?"

"Yeah?" he timidly confirmed the offer.

"Mm-hmm," I mumbled.

The problem with a studio apartment is that it's difficult to excuse yourself from a situation. In a regular apartment, getting the tea would have been a welcomed momentary escape into the kitchen. Instead, I stood and walked four feet to the kitchenette as he watched me the whole way.

I took a mug from next to the sink, filled it with tap water, and stuck it in the microwave.

"So, what do you do around here for fun?" he asked, raising his voice over the hum of the microwave.

I shrugged. "There is a bowling alley about twenty minutes away."

"You like to bowl?"

"No. Did you mean *me* specifically? I thought you meant 'you' as in 'you people.'"

"I mean *you* specifically."

Anything I said he was going to turn into something we could do together. In a different world, maybe even just a different time, I suppose his interest could be welcomed.

"I don't know. It's hard to think about now, after Jenny." I was going to hell for using Jenny's death as a diversion, but it did the trick.

"I understand," he said as the microwave went off.

I pulled open a drawer full of ketchup packets and plastic utensils and riffled around for a tea bag.

"Sorry, I can't find any tea bags. I thought I had a few, but they aren't in here." I shut the drawer and looked at him, unsure of what to do next.

"It's OK. Next time, maybe."

"Maybe."

He nodded and smiled without looking directly at me before excusing himself out the front door. Before it closed, I saw what I was too groggy to see when he first got there. The news vans were now parked on my street.

I would listen. I would lie low as instructed. I couldn't afford to be part of the story. There was too much that I needed to stay hidden.

CHAPTER EIGHT

JENNY

THE FALL KICKOFF DANCE was a noble tradition. The school moved the tables out of the cafeteria, hired a DJ, and charged all the eighth and ninth graders twenty-five dollars to occasionally dance, but mostly huddle in groups and whisper rumors about each other.

Jenny stepped through cheap streamers hanging from the doorway onto the tiled floors built to easily mop up the sticky remnants of two hundred teenagers a day. The overhead lights were off, and two spinning lights from the DJ table projected moving color streams over the young faces.

"Jenny!" Mallory screamed across the dance floor. The sea of inferior students parted at the sound of her voice, giving Jenny direct access to join her friends.

"You're late," Nora chimed in from behind Mallory.

"Yeah," Mallory took over. "We had to come in. We couldn't wait for you outside all night."

"Sorry," Jenny said, lacking all sincerity. "Did I miss anything?"

"Not really. Laura already called dibs on Josh, so don't even consider him," Mallory dictated.

"OK."

"And Krystal, I really think you should go flirt with Chris Hodges. You two would look good together. He's tall like you."

"Chris is so dumb, though," Krystal protested. "They're pulling him out of English."

"So what?" Mallory objected. "You're not getting married. You just have to get experience and he's cute enough."

"What about you?" Jenny asked Mallory, buying time before she inevitably saddled her with a match.

"I'm into older guys. Christine Castleton says there are so many seniors talking about me. Even Kevin Neary." She beamed.

"I'm into older guys too," Jenny insisted, hoping there was room for two in that excuse.

"Bullshit," Mallory scoffed. She had the kind of natural intelligence that would get her far in life without trying and make her unstoppable if she ever did. Everything came easy, which gave her a lot of free time in that mind of hers. Romantically pairing her peers was her current obsession, running scenarios to calculate the most interesting combinations to her and then orchestrating them into existence.

"Don't be scared, Jenny. Just relax and have a good time. Let's dance," she commanded before leading her gaggle to the center of the dance floor.

Mallory and Nora began grinding on each other for the benefit of a group of boys leaning, arms crossed, against the wall. The boys didn't even pretend to look away as Mallory and Nora rotated between duck faces in their direction and giggling with each other.

Laura and Krystal began their own form of seduction before merging with Mallory and Nora. Jenny tried her best to just sway back and forth, under the radar, praying for a chaperone to bust up this pretend orgy so she could retreat to the snack table, but that wasn't going to happen. The sorry excuses for chaperones were a group of overachieving high school volunteers, Ms. Willoughby and this girl Karen's mom, who were selling the tickets out front, and two teachers who must have pulled the short straw. Mr. Cole, the assistant gym teacher, was eating all the snacks, and Mr. Renkin stood guard by the DJ table. He was the only one paying attention to what was happening on the dance floor, but he didn't seem bothered at all by what was transpiring and wouldn't be coming to Jenny's aid anytime soon.

"C'mon, Jenny," Mallory said, reaching out and pulling her in. Jenny glanced over at the boys, their arms crossed, elbowing each other and smirking. Her eyes met those of a kid named Carter. He was the younger brother of a popular senior and a bit of a ring leader among the ninth grade boys. The unintended eye contact was enough to put the boys on the move.

"Ooo, Carter," Mallory whispered into Jenny's ear. Her breath was hot, and Mallory let her lips brush Jenny's ear before she pulled away. It was an unprecedented intimacy, not for Jenny's benefit but for those fast approaching. Jenny wanted nothing to do with it. As the girls rotated to welcome the boys, Jenny used that as her escape.

"I have to go to the bathroom," she said under her breath as she backed away from her friends and walked out of the cafeteria at a pace just short of a run.

JENNY BURST THROUGH the heavy glass door that led from the back of the cafeteria into a small courtyard where remedial students tended to a small garden as a course of study. She had held her breath as she left the cafeteria, praying a hand wouldn't grab her by the elbow and yank her back into the pelvis of one of her friends or, worse, Carter. Once the door closed behind her, she let herself breathe, the first gasp of air heavy and overdone. It wasn't much of a plan. Hide in the courtyard for two hours until it was time to go home? That would raise more questions than if she had just stayed home in the first place.

The anxiety was new for Jenny. Last year she would have craved an event like this. Something changed the day she quit the pageants, the day she watched her mother snap and imprison Benjy in that closet. She could see the fear in his face whenever she closed her eyes, feel his fists pounding against the door whenever she was too still, hear his screams whenever it was too quiet.

Jenny strained to hear the music, heavily muted but still audible in the courtyard if she focused hard enough on it. The grinding anthem transitioned to a slow song, and she was eternally grateful to not be standing in the center of the cafeteria at that moment, watching her protective ring of friends get picked off one at a time until she had nowhere to hide.

Once the slow song hit its second chorus, Jenny figured it was safe to go back inside. Any guy who hadn't found a partner in the first thirty seconds had surely retreated to his fellow unsuccessful friends. She would take a spot by the snack table, and if she got desperate enough, she'd spill soda down the front of her shirt. Mallory would certainly understand how devastating that would be and excuse her long absence as she ran back to the bathroom.

Jenny grabbed the door handle and yanked it back. Her elbow almost popped as the door budged a centimeter before catching the lock and halting to a stop. Why was the freaking courtyard door locked? It was completely enclosed within the confines of the big brick school. Did they think someone would scale the walls, run across the roof, and rappel down into the courtyard to access the unlocked door?

She didn't have many options. The music was too loud and the dance floor too far away for anyone to hear her bang on the door. Panic swept through her as she envisioned Linda coming to pick her up, only to find that her daughter was not among the hormonal creatures waiting on the curb. The cops would be called within minutes. Linda would be screaming. Jenny would finally be discovered by FBI helicopters circling the building with massive spotlights. SEAL Team Six would slide down ropes in seconds to scoop Jenny up and return her to the arms of her devoted mother.

Hyperbole maybe, but the panic was there all the same. She scanned her surroundings, setting her sights on a window across the courtyard she prayed would be unlocked. It was dark on that side. The cafeteria lights didn't stretch much past the door, and with the rest of the school dormant, there wasn't a lot to guide her way.

She shuffled forward with enough caution to keep her from doing any real damage to herself or the plants, but before she could reach the window, she froze. The volume of the music spiked, and she knew the courtyard door had been opened.

JENNY ROTATED SLOWLY to see who was there. As she turned, she crouched a bit to make herself more invisible in the pitch-black edge of the courtyard.

Ms. Willoughby stumbled forward from the fully lit doorway

into the subtler shade of the courtyard. She was playfully fighting the advance as two hands gripping her waist scooted her forward. The hands were Mr. Renkin's, which was obvious even before his green eyes peered over her shoulder. He kicked a rock over to keep the door from shutting all the way. Not his first rodeo.

Mr. Renkin was a notoriously "cool" teacher, and Jenny loved Ms. Willoughby. All she had to do was step forward into the light and announce her presence. They would ask if she was all right. She would say yes and make some excuse about having asthma or something that didn't make sense, but they wouldn't care, and she would scurry back to spill soda on herself. But she didn't move. She didn't speak. She watched.

"OK, OK." Ms. Willoughby smiled, acquiescing to her boyfriend's insistence on her going toward the nearest wall.

Mr. Renkin swiveled Ms. Willoughby's body around, guiding her to the side of the courtyard and giving Jenny a view of both their profiles. He leaned in and kissed Ms. Willoughby, their choreography needing work as he pushed her against the wall, the contact separating their lips unexpectedly and leaving them both kissing air for a beat before reconnecting.

Ms. Willoughby wove her hands in between their bodies until she could place both on his chest and push him back. The shove was gentle, and when their lips parted, she was smiling. "We can't do this here," she whispered.

Mr. Renkin grinned. His torso pushed back against her hands, which weren't putting up much of a fight, and kissed her again, this time so intense that it smacked her head back against the brick wall.

Ms. Willoughby winced and pulled her face away while reaching for the point of contact. "Ouch, damn it."

"Sorry, baby," Mr. Renkin said while pecking her cheeks with military precision until she recovered, dropping her hand from her head.

"What's gotten into you?" she asked. "Let's go back inside. We can finish this at home."

Mr. Renkin puckered out his lower lip, pouting. She reached her hand to his cheek and gave him a simple kiss, but he took it as a green light and shoved his tongue back into her mouth. Ms. Willoughby practically choked as she pulled her head away.

"I'm serious," she insisted. "If we get caught out here, we'll both be fired."

"I know," he whispered into her ear before lowering his face to kiss her neck. Ms. Willoughby closed her eyes as her protest waned.

Jenny knew where this was going and knew it was too late to speak up now. She closed her eyes and did her best to stay perfectly still in the crouched position she found herself in.

She tried not to listen.

She tried to put her mind somewhere else.

Then her legs began to shake.

She held her squat for as long as she could, afraid to move, until she lost the battle and shot upright to avoid falling to the ground. She heard the wood chips beneath her crackle and adjust under her shifted weight. She opened her eyes, staring down. Was the sound as loud as she thought? Was it only in her head? There was only one way to know.

Jenny looked up.

Mr. Renkin's eyes were on her.

Or so she thought at first. Could he see her? She couldn't tell. He didn't blink, but he didn't stop what he was doing either. Jenny could feel her dinner curdling and rising toward her esophagus. She averted her eyes, fighting to keep her food down and her impression of Mr. Renkin somewhat intact.

When they finally left the courtyard, Jenny's nausea abated, but she was sweating, only in her armpits, not from physical activity or nerves but from the intensity of it all. She felt a sense of power that she couldn't wrap her head around. She felt older somehow. If Mallory had witnessed that, she would have made such a big deal about it. Jenny wasn't like that. *It was just sex. No big deal*, she thought, trying to convince herself of her maturity.

Jenny slapped her palms against the window, said a little prayer, and scooted the glass up, confirming it was unlocked. She wriggled her fingers under the opening and lifted the window just enough to crawl her skinny body through and head back to the dance, where she had a date with a slippery cup of soda.

CHAPTER NINE

VIRGINIA

I HAD ONE great love in my life. His name was Mark, and I met him when I was thirteen years old. We shared our first kiss when I was fourteen and it was messy. I didn't know what I was doing; he did. I just tried to keep up. When he pulled away, I ran to the bathroom and threw up. I'd never seen a movie where the heroine finally kisses her hero and then projectile vomits. We were special.

As long as we were together, Mark never made me puke again. The first time he reached inside my underwear, I definitely experienced some nausea, but it didn't last. I've tried for years to pretend that my time with Mark was anything but perfect, to move on, to chalk it up as typical first love. I was a teenager, for Christ's sake. How could it have been real?

It's hard to explain how he opened me up. I had spent years perfecting my curt-little-bitch demeanor after my mother's suicide, something my father, in particular, did not enjoy. I was distant and I was difficult. I didn't even know what I wanted most of the time.

The other girls in my class were equally into Mark and soon forgot about me and my drama. We were at that age when a hot guy, especially one who wouldn't give you the time of day, was infinitely more interesting than anyone else. I could have shown up with both of my arms missing and the conversation still would have been, "What kind of music do you think he likes?"

I had one class with Mark every day from 10 to 11:15, and it became the only hour of my day that mattered. I watched the other girls fawn over him and I was jealous, but I just couldn't do it. I wasn't a fawner. The grown woman in me is extremely proud of that little girl, but trust me, at the time, I hated my defiant self. How would Mark ever register my existence?

Well, he did. Slowly over the course of the year, he began to notice the girl who wasn't noticing him, or so he thought. He chose me. We became infatuated with each other, but we were both too stubborn to say anything.

After nine months of purposefully standing close to each other, brushing against each other when we could, I committed the ultimate feminist sin. I failed a test on purpose and pretended I needed a tutor. Mark was amazing at math. I was a fourteen-year-old girl attracted to a guy's math ability. That's how messed up I was. And what's worse, it worked. Those after-school meetings allowed us the opportunity to finally give in.

It didn't take long, alone, both of us leaning over the same textbook. Things were happening in my body that I thought I might have to see a doctor about. Puberty, holy shit. Two weeks after my first tutor session, Mark kissed me, and I puked.

The next four years were a perfect blur. When I looked back, I couldn't even remember things chronologically. All I had were moments that fired at me, unrelenting, until I had to lie down on the floor, close my eyes, and breathe like I was about to give birth.

That didn't happen as much anymore. I was too numb to let

myself feel like that. It had been eight years since the day Mark ended it. He wanted me to go out and experience what life was like without him, to find myself, to be sure of what I wanted. I will never forget the day; it was my eighteenth birthday. Mark Renkin was thirty-two.

If I had to label it, Mark was a pedophile; it was statutory rape. That fucking depressed me. I didn't like to think about it that way. Pedophiles were gross bald skeeves in vans who raped little kids. Mark played soccer and looked like he could be in commercials. I had tits and pubes already. I'd seen enough TV to know real pedophiles lose interest once that stuff happens. I could tell myself whatever I wanted, but when my almost-fourteen-year-old sister was found raped, I thought of Mark.

He was never violent with me, but when people started asking, "Do you know any grown men who would want to have sex with a child?" I did.

IT WAS A SMALL TOWN. I saw Mark way more than I wanted to, but after years of trying to exchange pleasantries, we had stopped speaking. As soon as I saw him anywhere, I would immediately turn around, walk away, and count to thirty before I could stop and re-enter the world.

I hadn't exchanged a single word with Mark in five years as I approached his front door. He still lived in the same modest house on Sanford Hill that I used to visit for hours after school. It was within a half mile from my own home at the time, but the woods provided enough seclusion for me to feel like I was a world away from my family.

We would sit on his wooden porch swing most nights in the fall. It was my favorite season. He would sit all the way to the right, and I would take up the rest of the swing, leaning against his shoulder. I would cover myself in a warm patchwork blanket and throw a loose corner over Mark's knees, my arm over his waist, my hand tucked behind his far side.

The swing was still there, but had suffered during the eight winters. The wood was splintered in several spots, and it wavered in the fall breeze as I ascended the steps onto his front porch. The days were growing shorter, and daylight was already scarce by five. I raced over to avoid arriving during the darkness. An afternoon visit somehow seemed more manageable to my psyche.

I stood in front of the door and recited my mantra under my breath: "His loss. His loss. His loss." It was my depressing chant to create false self-esteem. It had started years ago as a long self-affirming speech that over time was abbreviated to a sort of slogan. I knocked, three solid knocks that stung my knuckles.

I heard movement inside the house, and my heart sank, my pep talk a waste. I wasn't ready for this. It was too late to run. I could hide, but my car was in the driveway. I heard the lock turning and I thought of my sister. This was about her. I was the only one who would know to ask him these questions. It was not a time to be selfish. This man had made me selfish for eight years.

The door opened and there he stood. Just a man. His green eyes were tired, there was gray in his hair, but otherwise he was just as I'd left him. He squinted at me as if he didn't believe it.

"Hi," I said.

He took his arm from the door and shifted his stance. "Virginia," he stated the obvious. "Hi."

I waited to be invited in. I ran a million scenarios in my head, but they always started with him inviting me in.

"Can I come in?"

He looked over his shoulder into the house. It was more a gesture than an actual attempt to see anything. He looked back at me, uneasy. "Why don't we talk out here?" He motioned to the swing, and I felt sick, not that I would throw up but that I might never eat again as long as I live.

I nodded. Power was everything. In that moment, I was Jenny's great crusader, not a damaged old lover. I took a seat on the left side without thinking. It was muscle memory, I guess. He sat on the right, and we both worked to create as much space between us as possible.

"What's going on, Ginny?" he asked. I hated when he called me that and he knew it. At least, I thought he knew it. I couldn't remember if I had ever told him I didn't like it. In love, I let a lot of things go.

"I . . ." Crap, I didn't know where to start. "I . . . You know about my sister, Jenny?" I barely phrased a question.

"Oh my God, yes, I'm so sorry. I was surprised to see you. I wasn't even thinking. I'm so sorry."

"Did you know her?"

"I had her in class this year, but she was quiet and the semester just started. Hunter knew her better than I did."

Fucking Hunter Willoughby. I hadn't even thought about it. That's why I couldn't go in the house. He was dating fucking Hunter Willoughby. I overheard the news one day about a year ago while I was microwaving a Jimmy Dean sausage biscuit at the gas station. I had abandoned the sandwich and sprinted to my car. I scoured every detail of her limited social media presence until three in the morning. There was no evidence of Mark. It was new. It was fresh. It wasn't serious. It wouldn't last. Maybe it wasn't even true. I told myself a lot of things so that I could continue to function.

Hunter was a senior when I was a sophomore. She was some kind of rich, white, small-town goth. She wore thick black eyeliner under her from-a-box black hair dye and drew anarchy symbols with a Sharpie all over her jeans and backpack. She ran with a small group of other seniors who looked down on everyone else because they had transcended to some higher plane of not giving a shit. Mark and I used to make fun of them all the time. I contemplated reminding him of it. Hunter went away to college and came back like she had gone through some sort of Banana Republic brain remapping. The return of her natural blonde hair must have had a memory-wipe effect on Mark. If he forgot all that shit about her, how much had he forgotten about me?

I was spiraling. I couldn't afford to fixate on his relationship. To go *there*. I was at his doorstep for a reason. "They think they caught the guy," I said for a reaction. It wasn't even true.

Mark's eyes widened. "Really? That's great. I didn't hear anything."

"They haven't announced it yet, so keep your trap shut," I joked, then regretted it. It just came out. I wanted so badly to be cold.

"Is it the guy on the news? The pedophile from the pageants?" He threw the "pedophile" word around a little too easily.

"Yeah, but I'm not so sure. Things don't add up." Why was I talking so much?

"So, you're on the case now?" His sarcasm was insulting. He was trying to assert dominance. To put me in my place. The place I had gladly filled for him in the past.

"She's my sister, and if I think the killer is still out there, I'm not just going to sit around. Is that OK with you?"

He threw up his hands in surrender. "Of course. It just, I don't know, doesn't seem like you."

"Because you know me so well?"

"I'm not trying to be combative. Why did you even come here?"

"Because she was thirteen, Mark. She was thirteen and she was raped." I let my voice waver slightly on the word "raped."

Mark stared forward for a beat, as if trying to follow my logic and make the connection. "What are you trying to say?" His voice lowered, serious, no longer cordial.

"I'm not saying anything. I just know teen girls are your type and maybe you knew Jenny more than you're saying."

Mark jumped to his feet, the force causing the swing to jerk me harshly back and forth. He turned to me, one hand in the air to conduct as he spoke. "You're insane. That's what this is about? You think I'm some pedophile? Is that really what you think? That I preyed on you? That I prey on and rape little girls?"

I had hit a chord for sure, but I didn't know what it meant. I looked away. I wanted him to keep talking. I didn't know if my motivation was for Jenny or myself. I figured it could be for both of us.

He did a slow spin to compose himself, then came back to the swing, stopping the jerking with his feet. He faced me and grabbed my hand, disarming me immediately.

"Ginny, I'm not a monster. I loved you. You have to know that. We were together for four years. You know me." He stared into my deprived eyes.

Show no reaction, I told myself. I pulled my hand away with just the right speed to prove I was unaffected, a lie.

"I have a girlfriend. She's thirty. I wasn't with anyone else after you. You have to believe me. I never even spoke to Jenny outside of class."

I did believe him. I couldn't help it. I wasn't a take-no-nonsense cop, or a hard-as-nails private investigator. I was a useless, floundering girl who, at twenty-six, still didn't refer to herself as a woman. He was the man I had spent my formative years admiring wholeheartedly.

"I shouldn't have come here," I said as I stood. I was gentle. The swing barely moved. My face was showing my entire hand.

"It's OK. It was nice to see you, to talk to you, even given the circumstances." He smiled, and I hated him.

"Yeah," I said, which was more in the affirmative than I would have liked.

I stepped away, and he grabbed my wrist, turning me back. "I'm sorry about your sister. I'm here if you need me."

I pulled my hand back and walked to my car. He would be there on our swing if I needed him. He would be there, waiting for me to run to him for support, to remind him that after eight years, I still needed him. I couldn't be that person. I had to be strong. If he wanted to feel needed, Hunter Willoughby could do it. I had bigger fish to fry. I was solving a fucking murder.

CHAPTER TEN

JENNY

THE SWIMMING HOLE was a twenty-minute walk from school grounds. Jenny wasn't allowed to go to the swimming hole, but not because of one of Linda's overbearing phobias, just good parenting. Most kids weren't allowed to go. There was actually a town ordinance preventing kids under eighteen from swimming there. A rock formation caused the river to pool in one spot, and the rumor around school was it was a hundred feet deep.

Jenny followed JP through the tall grass on a thin path matted down to let them know they were going the right way. The blades tickled her legs, and she couldn't help but swat at them, just in case there was even a chance it was a bug.

They hadn't spoken much since they started on their way. Being new to town, JP had just learned about the spot, and his curiosity dwarfed any attempt at patience. They left right after his lunch period. He waited by her locker and extended her the offer to come along. Jenny exhausted a few subtle attempts to decline. She explained they were both under the allowed age, quickly realizing that only fueled his fire. She tried suggesting they wait until after school, but when he showed zero hesitation in going without her, she gave in.

The river became audible at the same point the flat ground turned to a steep decline and the tall grass gave way to a dark dirt, more defined by the thick and mangled roots dipping in and out of it than the trees they belonged to.

Jenny was methodic in her steps, more like sideways shuffles at this point. The last thing she needed was to trip and fall down the hill, rolling by JP like a total spaz. The first time he reached up to take her hand to help her through a spot of loose dirt that he himself had skidded through, she wasn't sure if she should take it. Would he be more impressed if she waved him off?

"C'mon," he insisted, in one word convincing her she was over-thinking it.

She didn't hesitate again to take his hand, three times total before the dirt ended and the smooth surface of the massive rock began. They walked together to the cliff's edge, laying eyes on the water below. The thin river poured into a still pool, a circumference of roughly fifty feet, before spilling over the back side and continuing on its way.

"It's pretty cool," JP announced, bestowing it with the rare approval of a teenager.

"Yeah," Jenny agreed. It *was* cool. It was beautiful and quiet, and its perfection was only interrupted by several warning signs threatening all sorts of deathly peril.

JP allowed another second of romantic silence before pulling his shirt over his head and kicking off his boots. "It's gonna be cold as shit," he said, sliding his socks off as he undid the button on his jeans.

Jenny looked away as he undressed, unsure of the protocol here. She slowly removed her own boots to feign shared enthusiasm.

He was oblivious. Down to just his boxers, JP took two steps backward, rubbing his hands together, and crouching into a runner's stance. He made eye contact with Jenny, throwing her a wink, before sprinting forward and leaping off the edge.

"Woo-hoo," he hollered out while midair, waving his arms and legs, reminding Jenny he was just a kid too, before hitting the water and slipping below the surface.

The splash subsided and the water calmed. Jenny slid off her sweatshirt, waiting for him to reappear. It was taking too long. Was he messing with her? She moved as close to the edge as possible, staring down at his point of entry. Her breathing stopped. This was her punishment. Rules weren't just to ruin her day; they were in place for a reason and now this guy was drowning.

The water began to ripple, and there he was, coming to the surface. She exhaled. She could see the pale skin of his back and the stripes on his boxers, but something wasn't right. He breached the surface flat and facedown.

Jenny panicked. It might not be as deep as everyone said and he had just jumped right in. Did he break his neck? On instinct she moved to the less severe slope of the rock, sliding on her butt down to the water's edge. She could feel the sharp rocks stabbing her, but she didn't slow down. She crawled over the final rock and into the water, deep immediately and the bottom unfathomable to her searching feet.

The second she started splashing toward him, his body moved.

JP rolled onto his back, then upright, taking in a huge breath through his grin.

"I'm touched," he teased.

"What the heck?" Jenny asked.

"I knew you were gonna be too chickenshit to get in, so I thought I'd give you a little motivation."

"You're a jerk," she said through shortened breaths as she kicked her arms and legs to stay afloat. Relieved and mad, but more relieved.

"Get on your back, you look like you're going to drown."

"I'm not going to drown, I'm tired from trying to save your life." Jenny stopped treading water and swam closer to him. "I would have jumped in. You didn't have to be an asshole."

"Forgive me?" he asked, splashing a little water at her.

"Hey!" she yelled, splashing even more back.

They laughed and splashed like two typical teens, short on words and high on hormones. She was convinced the consequences, whatever they might be, would be totally worth it.

JENNY SAT DIRECTLY in the center of the couch. It was a stiff couch. All of the furniture in her house was. Her parents were trying to impress, but she wasn't sure who. The only houseguest they ever had was Virginia and they couldn't care less what she thought.

She wondered what her father's place in New York City looked like. Small. That was the only detail he volunteered freely. So small it barely fit a bed. Just a flophouse for him to sleep. Jenny had never been; neither had her mother. It had been that way since Jenny was born, and it was only as she got older that Jenny started to realize how unusual it was. Occasionally her mother would make vague comments about her and Jenny visiting, but her father would only tolerate it in the abstract. He would reference "perhaps in the fall" or "perhaps in the spring," whichever "perhaps" was at least three months away. Her mother seemed content just pretending they'd visit. Linda didn't like being out of her comfort zone. She could keep it together enough to drag Jenny to every hotel ballroom in the Northeast for pageants, but she hated strange crowds and might implode if she ever set foot in Times Square. The city was Dad's thing.

Her father pulled his Mercedes out of the driveway before sunrise every Monday and returned the following Friday night so late it was technically Saturday morning. Most of his coworkers worked six to seven days a week, but he worked seventeen hours a day, five days a week, so that he could spend the weekends with his family.

He stood before Jenny, rubbing his jaw, preparing his words. Linda sat on the edge of the chair to the right of the couch, her hands folded across her flawless white blouse.

"I want to know where you went," he finally spoke.

The school had called Linda when Jenny left school to go to the swimming hole. Jenny had anticipated the call, but didn't care. She was desperate for independence. She crossed her arms and leaned back, defiant.

"Please just tell him," said Linda.

"Nowhere," said Jenny.

"Nowhere?" he repeated.

"I didn't feel well, so I left."

Linda perked up. "Are you OK? You didn't tell me."

"She isn't sick, Linda. I don't know what's going on with you, Jenny. Do you think I've been too lenient with you?" He stared hard at her.

"No," she said, looking away.

"I think maybe I have. I let you walk away from the pageants. That was a mistake. I know something unfortunate happened to you, but it's not an excuse to waste your life."

"Nothing happened to me." Jenny shot forward. "Mom is a lunatic." She flopped back down, recrossing her arms and pouting.

Linda sighed.

"So, what's your plan now?" he asked. "To be a degenerate like your sister? Isn't it obvious? It's right in your face what this behavior leads to."

"I'm thirteen. I just want to go to school. Isn't that enough?"

"You don't want to go to school. You want to skip school."

"It was one time. I won't do it again."

"I don't go through all of this . . ." he said, waving his arms to encompass *this*, "so that you can just be a waste. Things won't just work out because you're special. You're not special. No one is special. People work for what they achieve. We're nipping it in the bud before it goes too far. Do you know what happens to little girls with no plan, no motivation, no goals?" he asked.

"They die?" Jenny spat back.

Her father whipped his face toward her, finger pointed. "Don't you ever take that tone with me, do you understand?" His finger remained pointed at her, teeth clenched. This was how he spoke to Virginia, not her. She felt her lip quivering.

"I'm sorry," she said as tears started to run down her face.

"You're going to see the guidance counselor again, figure out something to do with yourself. You don't have to do pageants, but you aren't going to embarrass yourself." His phone buzzed in his pocket, stealing his attention.

Linda used the opportunity to move to Jenny on the couch, throwing her arms around her. "It's OK. You just lost your way a little bit. We'll figure this out and you'll be just perfect again." She rocked Jenny in her arms as the young girl sobbed.

Her father slipped the phone back into his pocket, seeing the tears pouring from his daughter's face. He allowed Linda to continue to bear the brunt of the consoling, but rested his palm on the back of Jenny's head. "You don't need to be upset, honey. I'm sorry I raised my voice."

Jenny heard his words, but they didn't help. The tone of his voice was going to stick with her. She was sick of being compared to her sister, judged like somehow all the strikes Virginia had against her were on Jenny too. People talk about the pressure to live up to the firstborn; no one says anything about how hard it can be to live down to one.

JENNY STAYED IN HER ROOM the rest of the weekend, only emerging for the bathroom and meals she was ordered to attend. With no phone and no computer to entertain her, she managed to finish her homework for the week. She had spent the last twenty-four hours reading about World War I and photosynthesis and felt no more prepared for the world.

At thirteen, she was so far away from having any control over her life. Thoughts flooded her brain until she worried her ears might start bleeding. Could she sit in this room until she turned eighteen? And then what? College? Would her parents pay for an out-of-state school? Somewhere far away that they couldn't drive to? She doubted it. She needed legal and financial freedom, two things she couldn't even imagine on the horizon. She wanted to scream. She wanted to pound her fists against the door.

A KNOCK WOKE JENNY from her nap around six on Sunday night. She walked to the door, opening it a crack. It was Virginia, dressed in baggy clothes that looked comfortable but unflattering. Jenny could never understand her sister. She just did nothing for no reason. She wasn't too stupid to have a real job. She wasn't too ugly to have a boyfriend. She wasn't too boring to have friends. She simply existed. It was maddening.

Jenny opened the door the rest of the way and went back to her bed. "What do you want?" she asked, flopping back down.

"Sunday dinner," said Virginia.

The two sisters didn't agree on much, but in recent months Jenny had developed a similar distaste for the formal family affair.

"Tell them I'm sick."

"No way. With two victims, their powers are dulled. If you leave me alone, it will be too strong. I will be destroyed," said Virginia. There was her sense of humor. Humor that could get her friends. Why didn't she have any friends?

Jenny laughed. "I think I'm going to get it worse than you. They've been lecturing me all weekend."

Virginia perked up at this. She closed the bedroom door behind her and took a seat in a white wooden chair next to Jenny's vanity table. "What did you do?"

"Skipped some classes at school," Jenny said, and shrugged.

"What for?"

"For fun. I don't know. Whatever."

"That does sound fun."

"My mom says you quit another job."

"I bet she did."

"Why did you quit?" Jenny pressed.

Virginia just shrugged.

"What do you do all day?" Jenny asked, rolling to her side and propping her head on her hand like they were two girls at a slumber party.

"What's with all the questions? You sound like Linda and Dad."

"Just curious," said Jenny. "Can I ask you something?" She sat back up and crossed her legs underneath her.

"You just asked me like fifty things," said Virginia.

"Yeah, but you aren't answering any of them."

"Fine, what?"

"Were you always like this?" asked Jenny, keeping it vague and not sure what clarification to provide even if she wanted to.

Virginia tilted her head, staring at Jenny, as if debating whether or not to take offense.

"I didn't mean it, like, mean," Jenny clarified.

"Well, as long as you didn't mean it *like mean*," Virginia mocked her sister.

"Never mind," Jenny grumbled, knowing better than to try to scratch the surface with Virginia. If it was some sort of genetic adult-onset dystopian misery, Jenny would just have to deal with it. Symptoms were already presenting themselves.

Jenny rolled off the bed and past Virginia. "Let's get this over with."

CHAPTER ELEVEN

VIRGINIA

I HAD SOLVED zero murders since I stormed off Mark's porch. I watched three episodes of *Law & Order: SVU*, but they were useless. The reality I had to face was, if Mark wasn't involved in Jenny's murder, did I really care who did it?

Yes. I could care about this. Even if it was rooted in some sick obsession with proving Linda and my father and the whole damn town wrong. The crusade could be noble regardless.

I didn't even know where to start. It seemed going outside would be productive. I decided to drive to the gas station in town and fill my tank. Having a full gas tank, instead of coasting around on fumes like usual, would make me feel adult and responsible.

It takes a long time to fill a whole tank, even in a crappy little car. I stood there holding the pump, watching cars drive by, feeling too exposed. I don't know where I found the ego to think people would want to stop and bother me, but the mind can do crazy things.

After a parade of old cars similar to my own passed by, I saw one hit the blinker. I knew this car. A silver Mercedes that belonged to my father. Even in this tiny town, the odds of being there at the same time as him were so low that the coincidence felt exceptionally cruel.

I could have stopped the pump and left with half a tank, failing at my very first mission, but I didn't. Instead, I ran through the entire conversation in my mind. A back-and-forth of three to four generic questions would be enough for both of us to pretend our relationship wasn't complete garbage. The tank would certainly be full by then, a signal that we were fated to end the conversation there, and it would be over. I swallowed and relaxed my shoulders. Easy breezy.

His car slowed at the entrance and we made eye contact. I want to say I *think* we made eye contact, but I know we did. Then he killed the blinker and accelerated. He kept driving in some world where he had convinced himself I hadn't noticed. It felt hypocritical to fault him for something I had considered doing only two seconds earlier, but he was the parent. It stung. I won't say it hurt—I was too numb to him for that—but there was still a sting to it. A feeling of worthlessness crept up from not very deep, if I'm being honest. Rationally, I didn't blame him. Our interactions sucked; talking with him wasn't my preferred hobby either, but just . . . what a dick.

The gas pump clicked. There. That would have been it, the extent of the conversation. I returned the pump to its home and screwed the gas cap back on.

"Virginia?"

I heard my name coming from behind like a mallet to the back of the head. I turned to see the detective. Holden? Colton? Something I couldn't remember.

"Hi," I said, racing around the car to get to the driver's side door.

"How are—?"

The door sealed out the sound of his voice. I think the timing was gray enough where maybe I hadn't heard him attempt to extend the interaction. Didn't matter much. I turned the key and put the car in drive.

I pulled out into the street, admiring my full tank and seamless escape. My escape from social interaction. Though the detective was probably the exact person I *should* be talking to. Distracted by my father being King of the Assholes, I forgot the whole reason I'd left the house in the first place was to try to figure out more about Jenny.

I turned my car around in a convenient driveway and headed back into town toward the police station, convinced that if I saw that silver Mercedes on the way, I was going to ram it off the road with some sort of '80s action catchphrase like "Ignore this, bitch."

CHAPTER TWELVE

JENNY

SUNDAY DINNER wasn't as bad as Jenny had anticipated. She didn't realize her parents would never be willing to let anyone know Jenny had done something wrong, not even Virginia. They grilled Virginia on her recent unemployment while her sister shot Jenny dirty looks.

Jenny retreated to her room not long after Virginia left. Things felt weird with her parents. Sunday nights she used to curl up on the couch with her mother and watch a movie they could both agree on. Her father would sit in the chair with a book, uninterested but present. It was hard to explain, but Jenny always felt a little extra special to them after an evening with Virginia.

She didn't feel special tonight. Her father had yelled at her. She just wished she could have it both ways. She wished she could break the rules without disappointing her parents. Unfortunately, these things were mutually exclusive, and she had to decide which path she preferred.

Jenny crawled onto her bed with a magazine she had already read and leafed through the pages as if a new picture or article would appear. She had no TV in her room. She had no cell phone. Her room was supposed to be a sanctuary, but without stimulation, it was suffocating. She was almost fourteen; she wasn't going to sit on the floor playing with stuffed animals. It started to feel calculated. Her parents did this on purpose. They weren't letting her grow up.

A knock at the door startled Jenny and felt too on the nose. As she sat on her bed, stewing over how her parents treated her like a child, there was her mother, at the door and ready to smother away any notions of independent thinking.

Another knock.

Jenny flipped the magazine to the next page, waiting for her mother to lose patience and just barge in.

Only she didn't.

Jenny could hear footsteps, soft on the carpet in the hallway but recognizable. She placed the magazine down, the abnormality piquing her interest. Maybe she was being too hard on her mother. Jenny was the one who had quit the pageants. She had changed their dynamic. She could be more tolerant of her mother. Give her the time to adapt. Her mother was sensitive, emotional, and prone to overreaction, but they could find balance. Linda was already improving if she was willing to walk away when Jenny didn't answer the door.

She slid off the bed and made her way across the room. She would poke her head out and tell her mother good night, rewarding her for allowing Jenny some space. She opened the door and looked down the hall, but it wasn't her mother who had been knocking.

"Dad?"

Her father turned around to face his daughter, tentatively, and seeming like he had already mentally committed to her not opening the door.

"Were you sleeping?" he asked.

"Yeah," she lied, not wanting to admit she was just in there being a brat. "It's OK, though."

"I was just going to let you know that I am heading back to work tonight."

"OK," she said. It wasn't uncommon for him to leave late Sunday night instead of Monday morning. Jenny noticed it always correlated with a particularly stressful weekend. Usually Linda or Virginia was to blame. She was pretty sure it was her this time. He had never felt the need to personally notify her before. "Are you mad at me?"

"No," he said, shaking his head but keeping his distance.

"OK," she said, hoping he would elaborate a bit, but at least he hadn't said yes. "I'm going to see Ms. Willoughby again," she offered, to seal the deal. "The guidance counselor," she clarified.

"That's good." He adjusted his stance a bit, clearly uncomfortable. "I'm trying to do things differently with you."

"What do you mean?" she asked, knowing full well he meant he didn't want her to be like her sister.

"I'm not going to let things get out of hand. Do you understand? You have a lot of potential. I don't want you to throw it away."

"I'm *not*, Dad," she spat back in kind to what she felt was at least an insult and at most a threat.

"Watch the attitude," he barked.

"It's not attitude. I just want you to trust me and stop treating me like I'm a freaking baby."

"If you don't want me to treat you like a child, you need to stop acting like one."

"OK, whatever you say. You're always right. You're the best dad who ever existed," she scoffed, not sure exactly why the whole interaction was making her so angry.

The door to her parents' bedroom opened, and out came Linda to insert herself. "Is everything OK? What's going on?"

"Nothing," Jenny muttered.

"Calvin?" Linda looked to her husband, eyes glazed over from the post-dinner glasses of wine.

"Everything is fine. Go back to bed."

"Why don't you stay tonight? It's already so late," she suggested.

"No, we talked about this. Don't even start."

Linda's head fell to the side as if there might be a little more protest left in her, but she couldn't find the strength and just slunk back inside the bedroom. It was gross to watch, and Jenny felt disgusted by both of them.

"Bye, Dad," she said, stepping back into her own room and shutting the door. He wouldn't come in for the last word. She knew he regretted knocking in the first place.

LINDA'S BEDROOM DOOR had been closed for over an hour when Jenny cracked her own door open. She hadn't seen JP all weekend. She had been too scared to try to sneak out while her father was home, but now he was gone, and after their little interaction, she felt even less motivated to do as she was told.

She tiptoed down the stairs, the ritual almost second nature by now. She reached the bottom and went right for the lamp on the end table, no need to feel her way around anymore. As soon as the room lit up, her senses were heightened and she noticed it right away: The door to the alcohol cabinet was wide-open. Someone was in the house.

Jenny turned the light back off to hide in the darkness. She crept toward the kitchen, feeling the floor turn from carpet to tile under her feet. She paused again for any sounds. Silence.

As she reached the kitchen island, halfway to the garage door, she noticed the bottle of bourbon that had assaulted her nasal cavity the first night she snuck out. Things weren't adding up, but time wasn't on her side. Getting out of the house was her only concern.

She reached the door to the garage, and as she grabbed for the handle, the light over the oven switched on. Jenny whipped around to see Linda revealed under the pointed yellow glow. It wasn't an intruder, but her mother, looking like a stranger. Mascara ran down her red face as she stood holding a glass of the brown liquor.

"Mom?"

"Where are you going?" she asked.

"Nowhere."

The lie seemed to cause Linda physical pain. She recoiled into herself, relying on the counter to keep her on her feet.

"Mom?" Jenny asked, taking careful steps toward her.

"Did I do this to you?" Linda whined, alcohol robbing her of any dignity.

"Everything is OK," Jenny argued, reaching a hand to her mother's shoulder.

The touch triggered Linda, who regained her strength and lunged toward her daughter, grabbing her by both arms. "Tell me where you're going! Are you doing drugs? Are you having sex?" She shook her daughter for an answer.

"No, Mom, I promise. Please stop." Jenny was tearing up now. An uncontrollable reaction to being violently shaken.

Linda's eyes widened in a moment of brief clarity, and she

released Jenny's arms, horrified at what she was doing, and collapsed back against the counter.

Jenny retreated one step at a time until she felt the door, reaching behind her back and sliding her fingers around the knob.

"Mommy needs you to be a good girl," Linda pleaded. "You are being a very, very bad girl."

Her mother had devolved into something infantile, a behavior scarier in that moment than any physical harm she could do. Jenny returned to her first plan, yanked the door open, and bolted.

"Jenny!" her mother yelled into the night, watching her daughter sprint down the driveway where she could find cover just beyond the jurisdiction of the house lights. "Come back! I'm sorry!" Her screams faded away with every stride Jenny took.

CHAPTER THIRTEEN

VIRGINIA

I MADE IT all the way to the police station without facing the choice to either ram my father off the road or, more likely, just drive past him scowling.

I parked my car on the street in front of the station, noticing the detective had beaten me there—just barely as he was still in the small parking lot clutching his gas station coffee.

I hopped out and hustled toward him to allow our interaction to occur in the infinite space of the outside world and not in the claustrophobic confines of the station. He noticed me right away as I was the only other human in sight.

"Hi," he said, apparently feeling inclined to speak first but not sure what to say.

"I was just wondering if there have been any breaks in the case," I said, cutting to the chase.

"Oh." He paused like maybe he thought I was there for some other reason. I don't know. To report a stolen bicycle or something. "Yeah," he said to buy more time, scratching at the back of his head.

I didn't think it was a particularly difficult question. His awkwardness screamed the answer was yes, unless he was just ashamed that it was no.

"Did you hear something?" he finally asked.

"Not yet," I quipped, smirking a bit to encourage him to fill the void.

"Well, I can tell you there has been some movement and I promise to fill you in as soon as I can."

"Well . . ." I mimicked, highlighting his delivery. "You *can* fill me in right now."

"Virginia." He smiled like he appreciated my effort, but it wasn't quite enough.

"I promise I won't tell anyone. I don't even have anyone to tell if I wanted to. I just need to know; I need to know there's something going in the right direction. Does that make sense?"

"Yeah, yeah, it makes sense." He rubbed at the back of his head again, clenching his teeth and weighing whether or not to walk away.

"Please," I added, short, soft, and just the right kind of pathetic.

He exhaled. Admitting defeat.

THEY FOUND BENJY LINCOLN at a bus station in Maryland. The police were keeping it under wraps to avoid a media swarm, but now I knew about it.

Detective Colsen led me through the station, staying close, as if he could sense how uncomfortable I became once we were inside. He kept his hand on my back and his pace steady to discourage anyone from asking any questions or daring to stop us.

The preferential treatment was causing the release of some long-dormant endorphins. In that moment, he was giving me something I hadn't realized I wanted. Somewhere inside, I liked it, but I couldn't admit it. For eight years I had told myself I would never, could never, have feelings for someone else. Accepting that I might have feelings now would mean for all those years I was wrong. The darkness I lived in had to be real. It had to be something I couldn't have avoided.

I ALLOWED DETECTIVE COLSEN to hold the door open for me as I stepped into the small viewing room. The space was tight for two. If either one of us swayed, our arms would touch, but we both held our ground.

"Be happy," he said. "We've got him." Colsen tipped his head toward the double mirror, nodded, and excused himself.

I turned to the mirror. Benjy sat on the other side. He wasn't what I'd expected. I'd envisioned a comb-over, thick out-of-style glasses, maybe a van offering free candy and some lost puppy posters. He just looked depressing. He was overweight, egg-shaped, with a quarter inch of buzzed hair. He wore gray sweatpants that tapered off right before his velcro sneakers and a stretched-out light blue T-shirt. The pocket over his left breast was even further stretched out, evidencing he actually used it to carry things.

I was not feeling the vengeful satisfaction of my sister's murderer being brought to justice. I felt lost, unaffected, unable to ground myself in the moment. There was something wrong. Even if he didn't kill her, he was still a grown man overly affectionate toward young girls. Something inside me was broken.

Detective Colsen entered the interrogation room looking down at a folder, just like he had for me. He needed more moves.

Benjy looked up, fear all over his pudgy face.

Colsen took a seat and fanned out the folder. There it was again, Jenny's dead body. Benjy retreated, turning his head to the left as far as he could away from the picture, the skin on his neck bunching and twisting. His eyes closed so tightly deep lines formed across his forehead.

"Oh, I'm sorry," said Colsen. He closed the folder. "It's OK. I put them away."

Benjy opened his right eye and turned back just enough to confirm the pictures were gone. The closed folder brought the rest of his head back around. He waited, wide-eyed, for the detective to say something.

Colsen stared at him, watching him squirm, seeing if he would speak. Benjy said nothing.

"Mr. Lincoln, did you know the victim, Jenny Kennedy?"

Benjy averted his eyes, but nodded.

"Mr. Lincoln, please answer all questions with a verbal yes or no."

"My—my name is Benjy," he stuttered.

"OK." Colsen softened his voice. "Benjy, did you know Jenny Kennedy?"

Benjy nodded again, but then remembered. "Yes."

"And what was the nature of your relationship? How did you know Jenny?"

"I saw her in the pageants. She was very good. She was nice to me."

"And what happened at the pageant in New Hampshire on April 19 of this year?"

Benjy began to rock in his seat.

"Mr. Lincoln . . . I'm sorry, I mean Benjy . . ." Colsen corrected himself with enough compassion to encourage honesty.

"They locked me in a closet. Then I had to go to the police station. I didn't like it. And then Jenny didn't do any more pageants."

"And this upset you?"

Benjy nodded, and I wondered why he didn't have a lawyer. I wasn't even sure he was capable of comprehending he was a suspect.

"When's the last time you saw Jenny?" Colsen asked.

Benjy started shaking his head. "No, no, I didn't see Jenny."

"I asked when the last time was. You have seen her before. When was the last time? Was it last week?" Objection, leading the witness, per every law show ever.

"No, no, not last week. Not for a long long time."

"You were in Maryland, at a bus station. We talked to Mr. Johnson. He said you left your apartment four weeks ago. Were you running away from something?"

Benjy continued to shake his head. "No, no, I was not. I was moving away."

"Why were you moving away?"

"I'm going to live in Mexico."

"Mexico? You just decided to move to Mexico at the same time Jenny was killed?" Colsen flipped back open the folder, revealing the gruesome pictures.

Benjy jumped from the chair and stumbled to a corner of the room, his hands cuffed together. "Stop. I don't want to look. Stop."

"What happened, Benjy? Was there an accident? I know you didn't mean to hurt her, but sometimes accidents happen."

Benjy pressed his face into the corner of the room. "I would never hurt her. She's my friend. No, no, no."

————

WHEN IT WAS OVER, Colsen squeezed himself back into the viewing room. He leaned against the two-way mirror, his arms crossed around the folder and a satisfied smirk on his face.

"We got him. He's going to go to prison for a long time. Does that help, knowing he's not out there?" He uncrossed one arm to put his hand on my shoulder.

"You're acting like you got a confession. Unless this is a trick mirror, all you got was a man to cry and run into the corner professing his innocence."

Colsen pulled his arm back. "Oh, c'mon, he was fleeing the country."

"You said he left his home weeks ago. How does that make any sense? If he was fleeing the country, why did he leave weeks before the murder?" I felt like Nancy Drew.

"He left to come here, then he fled after the murder."

"Then you think the murder was premeditated? He packed up all his belongings to move to Mexico after a quick murder along the way? Look at him. You think he planned this? You think he had the wherewithal to put on a condom so that he wouldn't leave any DNA? He has velcro sneakers for God's sake."

"I don't have to explain anything to you," Colsen said, stepping toward the door. "You know your way out?"

"I don't think it's him."

"Prove it," he said as he walked away, not bothering to hold the door for me.

I turned back to Benjy. His picture would look perfect juxtaposed with Jenny's glamour shot on every newspaper. People would love the justice for that manufactured little girl who was nothing like the teen who had been murdered.

I wondered what Jenny would think about all of this. I didn't know my sister very well. That was obvious. I was on a soapbox telling everyone to stop pretending she was some perfect doll, but that's how I always saw her. I didn't try to get to know her. I didn't take her out for ice cream or go to any of her pageants. To me she was just the epitome of what my father wanted me to be, and therefore my natural enemy. Maybe it wasn't too late to get to know her. Somebody had to.

CHAPTER FOURTEEN

JENNY

JENNY RAN UP the pitch-black hill, panting, her body temperature rising despite the crisp fall air. She couldn't wrap her head around what just happened. It was too fresh. Her mother had snapped again.

She dipped through the trees lining Mr. Renkin's property. JP's front yard shared a hint of forest with Mr. Renkin's backyard, and cutting through saved Jenny ten minutes of following the road around the bend. She hesitated as she reached the tree line, but lights from JP's house spilled through and she focused on the glow to keep herself moving.

She found JP sitting on the steps of the dilapidated front porch, smoking a cigarette and staring into the woods. He stood when he saw her emerge from the tree line and flicked the remaining stub of the cigarette into the driveway. She didn't break stride until she reached him, wrapping her thin arms around him.

"What's wrong?" JP rested his arms loosely around her.

She said nothing, only sobbed into his camouflage jacket.

He placed his hand on the back of her head, rubbing her hair. "It's OK, just tell me what's wrong."

"My mom is crazy," she said into his chest.

JP held her closer and let her cry it out.

After a minute, the tears dried up and she peeled herself off of him. "I'm sorry," she said.

"Don't be sorry."

She wanted to kiss him. She had never kissed anyone before.

"I can't go home," she said. "I want to come with you to Mexico."

JP took a step back and ran his hand through his matted hair. "Why don't we just sit for a minute?"

Jenny was hurt. It was rejection. She was Jenny Kennedy. She was fawned over. She was not rejected. "If you don't want to come with me, I'll go by myself. You can stay here."

"That's not what I said. Don't overreact," he said. "You want to run away? You need a plan. Crying and running is not a plan. You need money, a place to go, something to do when your picture is plastered all over the news. Without those things, you'll just live on the streets for a few nights until they drag you home."

"Is that why you're still here? Why you haven't run away yet?"

"I'm not running away. I don't have anywhere to run from. I'm just going to leave when I'm ready." He pulled another cigarette from his pocket. "I'm gonna smoke, OK? I know you don't like it, but you're stressing me out."

She just nodded. He wasn't impressed with her. She'd thought he would sweep her up and save her. She'd thought he would like her more as a victim. Not JP. She had pushed him away, and it was killing her.

"You're right, I was just acting like a baby." She clenched her teeth together, trying to sell it.

"It's OK, you're just a kid."

The words drilled through her chest. She felt her lip shudder and knew she had to get out of there before she made it even worse. "I'm gonna go." She rose from her seat.

"Are you mad? I didn't mean anything. I'm sorry. You don't have to go. We can watch TV or something."

"No, I'm fine. I'll see you in school." Jenny started to walk away.

"OK, I'll see you in the morning . . ." He phrased it almost as a question, but she just kept walking.

She kept her pace steady as she headed down the driveway, counting the seconds until she would be out of sight and could start running. Maybe she *was* just a kid. How many people had to say it before she believed it? Maybe she should just take up cheerleading and let Mallory pick an appropriate boyfriend for her. Or maybe she should make a plan and get the hell away from these people.

LINDA WAS PASSED OUT on the couch when Jenny got home. Jenny flung a stack of mail onto the kitchen island. She had noticed the overflowing mailbox while standing in her driveway, searching for the strength to go inside. Her mother was incapable of even the simplest tasks lately.

Jenny locked the door to her bedroom just in case her mother had any more crazy left in her that night. She collapsed onto her bed, not even bothering to change into pajamas. Her whole body was tense, a tightness that could only be relieved by bursting into tears, but she found it impossible. She wrapped her arms around a pillow and squeezed it as hard as she could against her chest until, hours later, she fell asleep.

When Jenny woke in the morning, her jaw hurt. She had been clenching it in her sleep. She lay still, delaying the inevitable interaction with Linda as long as possible. For the first time in a long time, she wished her father was home.

A soft knock on the door disrupted her sanctuary. Jenny whipped her head toward the noise like a deer in the woods.

"Jenny, honey, it's time to get up for school," Linda said through the door with a cavity-inducing sweetness to her tone. "Are you awake?"

Jenny flung her feet to the floor and sat up. "Yes," she gargled out with the morning's first words. "I'll be right down."

She heard Linda descend the stairs. Jenny was relieved. She didn't need an apology; she needed it to never have happened in the first place.

JENNY ENTERED the kitchen to find her mother pulling a tray of muffins from the oven. She was going to the cabinet for a granola bar when Linda finally noticed her.

"Muffins." She shoved the hot pan in Jenny's general direction.

"I have to go. I'm going to miss the bus."

"I can drive you," Linda offered over Jenny's dead body.

"It's OK, I have a big day today." She smiled to drive the point home.

Jenny did have a big day ahead of her; it just wasn't going to be at school.

NEW LOFTON WAS nine stops north of Wrenton. Jenny disembarked the bus a little before eleven at a nondescript bench in front of a post office that felt no different from the one in her own small town. The streets were quiet. Her pace was slow, timid. She had been dabbling quite heavily in disobeying her parents, but this took the cake for sure.

Her destination, an uninviting brick building, was three stories high and packed full of efficiency units. She inspected the call box to the right of the door. It was in rough shape. Most of the name-plates were blank, others faded from the sun. She knew he was number five but couldn't find the label for even that much. She was about to start from the top when she heard the lock click.

Jenny grabbed the door as it swung toward her. A musty old woman crept out like it might take her all day to reach the sidewalk. Jenny smiled to acknowledge it was no problem for her to hold the door open. The lady responded with a muted grunt.

The smell from the woman was pungent and carried into the hallway where she left her wake. There were small sconces along the walls, but thick layers of dust dulled their effect.

Apartment five was all the way at the end. Jenny took a deep breath and tapped her knuckles against the door. There were no sounds from inside. She knocked again, a little louder.

Behind her, a door opened and a skinny man in a bathrobe appeared. The robe was open, revealing everything not covered by his yellowed briefs, the most she had ever seen of a man. Jenny tightened her hands around the straps of her backpack, prepared to run.

"You gotta knock real loud for him," the man said.

Jenny didn't react, hoping he would just go away.

The man shoved out of his apartment, pushed right by her, and pounded his fist on the door to number five.

"He's always got those damn headphones on. Hey!" He pounded

again, then listened. Furniture creaked from within, then footsteps. The neighbor nodded and scurried back into his apartment.

The door opened, and Jenny blinked a few times to adjust to the daylight seeping out from the apartment. The man stood before her in a thin, pit-stained white T-shirt and gray sweatpants. His eyes were as warm as ever. "Jenny?" he asked, not trusting himself.

"Hi, Benjy." She smiled.

CHAPTER FIFTEEN

VIRGINIA

THE NEWS OF BENJY'S ARREST broke on all major news outlets at 10 A.M. EST on Saturday. It was four days after he was found. I was sure it was a strategic move to announce right at the beginning of the weekend. Everyone out there could sigh in unison and go back to living life. *Unlock the doors, they caught the monster. Let's go to Applebee's.* People had a real twisted sense of sympathy for someone they never met.

All of the reports were the same, monotone news anchors trying their best to emit emotion, moving stills of Jenny looking like a miniature Dolly Parton, and the same recycled five seconds of footage showing Benjy being transported from the station into a police van.

The announcement had finally cleared my street of news vans. I kind of missed them. Walking outside to silence was odd, almost creepy. I'd forgotten how quiet this town could be.

I MET DETECTIVE COLSEN at the bowling alley in the next town over. He thought the invite was hilarious and charming. I thought it was interesting he chose the only place he knew I didn't like. This was the first thing I'd had resembling a date in years.

He was heading back to Hartsfield now that Benjy was arrested. In other words, they were giving up on other suspects. It blew my mind. I had to meet with the detective even if it meant wearing a color other than black or gray and throwing a few giggles his way.

His first name was Brandon. I hadn't really thought much about it, but after the awkward tea exchange, he made it clear that this was a personal encounter. I found him at the table farthest from the door. His casual attire was slapped over his clean-cut body, his hair parted and gelled the same way as when it accompanied a suit and tie. He had already ordered a pitcher of beer and reserved a lane. What a gentleman.

I headed toward him wondering how long I would have to make small talk before I could dive into some hard-hitting questions. He stood to greet me, going in for a light one-arm hug and a kiss on the cheek. I wasn't sure we were there yet, but it wasn't horrible. He was gentle in his approach.

"I thought you were going to stand me up," he joked. "I was kind of a jerk the other day."

I was twenty minutes late. It wasn't a calculated move. I had sat on my bed watching the clock almost paralyzed. It wasn't a date, but it was a date. Since my meeting with Mark, I'd been cycling through wanting to jump anybody who'd have me and never wanting to be intimate with another soul ever.

"Sorry," I said as he motioned for me to join him at the table.

He poured beer into a clear plastic cup for me. The cups were so small, I wondered if they were meant to deter overdrinking. Judging by a group of loud fat guys at the other end of the alley, the small cups didn't prevent excessive drinking, just led to excessive pouring.

"Cheers." He lifted his cup to mine. We both took casual sips, riding the line between lush and lame. "I got us a lane," he said.

"Maybe later." I had nothing against bowling in principle but I so long ago had lost the ability to be carefree. Stupid really. I knew I was being stupid. I just couldn't. That's the only way to explain it.

"How are you doing?" he asked.

"I'm good," I said, realizing it was the first time since the murder that I'd answered that way. "As good as I can be."

Brandon nodded. "I get it, but sometimes we have to find the silver lining. Try to focus on the positives instead of the negatives that we can't change." He was trying to be sweet. It felt a little rehearsed. I wondered how many victims' families he had taken to bowling alleys.

"And what would be the silver lining I should focus on?" I asked.

"We don't always catch the bad guy. That's something. Some families have to live knowing they got away with it, that killing their loved one had no consequences."

"But you didn't catch the bad guy. Not for sure. You just caught the easiest guy."

"Really? You *really* think he didn't do it?"

"It just doesn't feel right. He's . . . I don't know the right way to say this . . . He seems like a child," I explained the best I could.

"Children kill all the time. Underdeveloped brains lack the ability to understand the consequences of their actions. He'll probably go to some facility instead of prison, but it doesn't make him any less guilty or any less of a threat to society." He topped off my beer like he had rested his case.

"Did you look at anyone else? She wasn't this perfect little angel, you know? She was getting into trouble. Did her parents tell you that? I doubt it."

"What kind of trouble?" He was willing to hear me out, even if it was just to get into my pants.

I wasn't prepared for follow-up questions. "I don't know. Normal teenage stuff, I guess. Skipping school."

"I'm going to tell you something, but I shouldn't. Do you understand? This isn't public knowledge."

"OK."

"I just hate seeing you like this, feeling like justice won't be served."

"What?"

"Benjy was lying. He saw Jenny two weeks before her murder at his apartment. She was there and he told me that he hadn't seen her since the pageant."

"How do you—"

"A neighbor saw her."

I sat back. I wasn't prepared for that. Maybe I was wrong. What was I doing? Fuck.

"I'm good at my job, Virginia. I know you think I'm some schmuck that doesn't care about anything but closing the case, but it isn't true. If there were other suspects, other evidence, I would investigate it. There's nothing. Nothing but a man with history of abuse toward your sister lying about seeing her in the weeks before her death and fleeing to Mexico."

I thought about what he was saying. He was right. I did think he was some schmuck. Maybe I was wrong about him, but not about Benjy.

"I want to talk to him," I said.

"To Benjy? No way."

"Why?"

"Do I really need to answer that?" he asked.

I leaned toward him, hoping my eager face would convince him it was a good idea.

"He's lawyered up now anyway. Some shit-brain public defender. We can't even talk to him anymore."

"*You* can't talk to him. He can have visitors, right? I'm Jenny's sister. Jenny was his friend. He'll probably want to see me. Maybe he'll even open up to me. You're at a dead end." I just kept talking so he couldn't say no.

"That's a real fine ethical line."

"I don't mind." I smiled. "I have no moral compass."

Brandon finished another cup and started pouring. "Well, that's good to know." He grinned. "Let's just try and enjoy ourselves to-night."

"Is that a yes?"

"No, it's not a yes."

"But it's not a no?"

"What can I say other than yes that will make you drop it for now?"

"Maybe."

"Fine, maybe." He laughed, and I did too. The ridiculousness of the exchange allowed us both a second to forget we were talking about the lead suspect in the rape and murder of my sister. It felt good, and maybe he was on to something with this whole *let's just try and enjoy ourselves tonight*.

"Fair enough," I said and motioned for him to fill my cup.

CHAPTER SIXTEEN

JENNY

BENJY GRINNED FROM EAR to ear seeing Jenny in front of him. "Come in. Come in," he repeated while opening the door all the way for her. The apartment was meticulous and sparse—a twin bed, a table with a folding chair, and a dated box television. The aforementioned headphones rested atop the bed.

Benjy hustled to the one chair and pulled it out for Jenny. "You can sit here. I just have one chair. I sit on the bed most of the time."

She sat on the chair, and once she looked comfortable, Benjy took a seat on the edge of his bed.

"You look very pretty. I haven't seen you in a long time, but you still are very pretty."

"Thank you. How are you doing? Are you OK?"

"I can't go to pageants anymore." He stood back up, too anxious to sit still. He shuffled to the window. "I can see the park from here, see?"

Jenny shifted higher in the chair to look out the window. She could see a rusty swing set with a matching slide. Not much of a park, but it wasn't the time for cynicism. "That's great."

The outside world caught Benjy's attention, and he stopped rambling.

Afraid he might never turn back to her, Jenny pressed on. "What happened after I left? Were you arrested?"

Benjy lowered his head and walked back to the bed. "I had to go in the police car and they yelled at me over and over again, 'What did you do? What did you do?'"

"I'm so sorry. My mother shouldn't have done that. She's a monster."

Benjy flinched at the word as if she meant it literally.

"I'm going to leave my home. I can't stay there any longer. I need to get away from my mother."

"You're gonna run away?" he asked.

"Yes, but it's not what you're thinking. I have a plan. It will be OK. I'm just going away until I turn eighteen. Then I can come back. It's only four years."

"Four years is a long time."

"It's not that long and it will be worth it. Do you know anything about Mexico? It's a country right below the United States. They have beautiful beaches and amazing food. It will be easy for me to fit in there, get a job even."

Benjy popped up from the bed again, heading back to the window. "I don't want you to go. I don't think you'll be safe."

"Why would you say that?"

"You're gonna be all alone. You shouldn't be alone. You're a kid." He turned back to explain it to her in the most basic sense. "Kids have to be with adults."

Jenny lowered her posture so that she could look up at him with her best puppy dog eyes and adjusted her tone. "I need your help."

"You need *my* help?"

"Yes, you, Benjy, are all I have."

He came back from the window, repeating a tiresome pattern. "What can I do?" he asked as he sat back down.

Jenny scooted the chair toward the bed until she could reach out and grab his hands. "I need money."

"OK."

"OK?" She was surprised how easy he gave in.

Benjy removed his hands from hers and was back off the bed. She waited for him to head to the window, but instead he dropped to one knee, then both knees, then all fours. He was not a spry man. It was a process.

He reached under the bed and pulled out a shoebox. Reebok. Once he could see it, he shoved it back under the bed and reached for another. Nike. That was the one. He flipped off the top, revealing freestanding bills with the wrinkles of being in a thousand pockets. They were mostly singles, but Jenny could see a few fives.

Benjy began to remove each bill, flatten it over his thigh, and place it onto a stack. Once all thirty-two bills were in a neat pile, he handed them to Jenny to count.

Sixty-four dollars.

"This is it?" she asked.

"It's not enough?" He fell from his knees to sit on the floor against the bed.

Jenny held the dirty money in her hands. She stared at it like she could change the ones to hundreds. What was she thinking? She was so stupid to think she could do this, to think Benjy would have the thousands of dollars she needed. Her breath became short.

"You can get more money," said Benjy.

"No, I can't. I don't know anybody else."

"What about Gil? Gil's got lots of money. He has a boat."

"Who's Gil?" she asked.

"Gil is my friend. He writes me letters all the time. He likes pageants too." He crawled back onto his knees and reached under the bed. This time, the Reebok box was right.

It was full of letters, placed back in their envelopes for safekeeping except one on top that she recognized right away.

"This is the letter from you." He handed it to her. "It's my favorite."

She took it from him, but had no interest in revisiting it.

He dumped the remaining letters on the floor. "These are from Gil. He used to write once a week, but not so much lately, because I don't go to pageants anymore."

Jenny fanned out the letters on the floor, not sure what to do with them. "What do you guys talk about?"

"All kinds of stuff, but mostly about pageants. Gil lives in New York City. He tells me all about stuff there and I tell him about the pageants. Oh, let me show you . . ." Benjy riffled through the letters until he found the one he was looking for.

He pulled a generic picture of the New York skyline from the envelope. "This is where he lives. Isn't it nice?"

"Yeah, it's really nice," she said to please him.

"And I send him pictures too. All the time. He really likes it when I send pictures."

"What kind of pictures do you send?"

"Of you."

"Me?"

"I told him you were the prettiest one in the pageants and he agrees. He says you can be Miss America, but I told him you don't want to do pageants anymore and that you are going to be something else."

"And you think he could help me?" It was a long shot and he was probably a pervert, but there was no harm in gathering the facts.

"Sure. He's my friend."

"I'm going to think about it. Do you think I could take one of these envelopes with his address?"

Benjy separated the envelope in his hands from the letter without hesitation and gave it to her.

"Thanks. Benjy . . . Is there anything bad in any of the letters?"

He didn't understand the question.

"I mean, does Gil say anything weird? Like, about me?" Jenny wasn't sure how to ask if Gil was a raging pedophile. She had to be careful to not worry Benjy or discredit his only friend.

"Gil says lots about you. I say lots too. We like talking about you." He waited to see if that's what she was asking.

Jenny sighed. He wasn't getting her question, but that could also be her answer. If Benjy didn't understand, this guy couldn't be too bad, right? Gil owned a boat, lived in Manhattan, and had a clear interest in her. She was out of options. It was worth considering.

THE COUNTY BUS dropped Jenny off in town just in time for her to run back and catch the after-school bus home.

Jenny jumped off the bottom step, a successful landing capping off her somewhat successful adventure. She checked her watch as she bent down to tighten her shoelaces. She was cutting it close and would have to jog back to the school.

"Jenny?" The voice startled her, provoking a weird panic that somehow Linda knew everything and was waiting there to catch her and send her to reform school.

She stood up to see it was just Ms. Willoughby walking from Stone's Variety Store to her car, holding a small package of four cupcakes. "What are you doing?" she asked.

What could Jenny be doing that would explain her getting off the county bus alone? "Nothing," she said, not one of her more creative lies.

"Were you getting off that bus?" Ms. Willoughby pushed.

"What? No," Jenny said, realizing if she was asking, she didn't know for sure.

"I got an e-mail that you weren't in school today, an unexcused absence."

The door to Stone's opened again, and Mr. Renkin trotted out, on his way to Ms. Willoughby's car. He would 100 percent know Jenny had skipped school. She'd even missed a quiz. She needed an excuse and fast.

Like a miracle from baby Jesus, a car door between them opened and out stepped Virginia—her useless, schlubby sister. Only she didn't look as schlubby as usual, and she was about to be very useful.

Ms. Willoughby turned to see where Jenny was looking, and they both watched as Virginia walked across the parking lot, past Mr. Renkin, past Stone's, and on her way to the post office. They all kind of froze, even Mr. Renkin, watching Virginia glide through the town center. Seeing her sister so presentable was distracting, and it was just the distraction Jenny needed.

"Oh, there's my sister. We had kind of a skip day. My mom knew about it. She must have forgotten to call." Jenny shrugged at

Ms. Willoughby. "See you tomorrow," she said, turning away and running after her sister. "Virginia, wait up!"

Virginia turned around like she'd seen a ghost. She looked from Jenny running toward her to Ms. Willoughby, then to Mr. Renkin, not sure of what to make of the situation, unaware of her role in the events unfolding.

"Hey," Jenny said as she reached her and slowed to a stop.

"Hey," she said, acknowledging Jenny's presence but seemingly preoccupied with her surroundings.

"Can you give me a ride home?" Jenny asked.

"Um . . ." Virginia paused. To say she seemed frazzled was an understatement. She shoved her hands into the pockets of her nicely fitted jeans, almost to bring her arms into her body and make herself less noticeable. "No, not really."

Jenny looked at her watch. She had wasted too much time getting stuck with Ms. Willoughby. "Please," she begged.

"I just can't, OK? I'll see you on Sunday," said Virginia, pulling her hands out of her pockets and rubbing them together like she might start a fire. Her eyes darted around, over Jenny's head. Her mouth flapped open a bit like she might say more, but she instead took a defiant step around Jenny and scurried back to her car. She never went into the post office.

"Fine," Jenny blurted out after her. When Virginia didn't turn back, she added, "I hate you!" before taking off toward the school, praying for the bus to still be there. As she ran by, Ms. Willoughby and Mr. Renkin gave her disappointed looks, witnesses to her outburst. It was childish and she regretted it, but she had done some serious stuff that day and a stupid run-in with her idiot sister wasn't going to unravel all her hard work.

———

SHE CAUGHT THE BUS at the last possible second. It had actually started rolling, but her body darting across the parking lot grabbed the driver's attention enough to stop and let her on. JP sat toward the middle, and she swung into the seat to join him.

"You still mad at me?" he asked.

"Whatever, JP," she said, remembering she was mad at him, or at least supposed to be.

"Don't be mad." He rubbed his knuckles into her shoulder. "We're best friends," he said with his best schoolgirl voice.

She smiled. His effort was appreciated.

"Where'd you go today?" he asked.

"What do you mean?"

"I know you weren't in school, dumbo, so spill it."

"I went to visit a friend. Jealous?"

"A friend? Does it have anything to do with last night? With your mom?"

Jenny shrugged. "More to do with you, I guess."

"With me?"

"You made it pretty clear last night that you weren't going to help me. So I found someone who will."

"In less than twenty-four hours you went out and found someone to help you run away? Who is it, the runaway fairy?"

"It's a friend and he has money. A lot of it."

This piqued JP's interest. "And he's going to give it to you?"

"I think so. I can be pretty persuasive."

JP raised an eyebrow. "Does this friend know what you need the money for?"

"Does it matter?"

"How much money?"

"You have a lot of questions. Are you reconsidering my offer?" she asked.

"What offer?"

"To come with me."

"You mean to take you with *me*?"

"Not anymore." She grinned. "You have the plan. I have the money. Seems even to me."

JP laughed. "Look, you get the money and we'll talk about it."

The bus barreled down Pike Street, and Jenny could see her house up ahead. Panic set in. If Ms. Willoughby got an e-mail about her skipping, Linda had definitely gotten a phone call. She squeezed her brain for what she told herself would be one last great idea. And then it came to her.

"Give me your pocketknife," she said.

JENNY HOPPED OFF the bus at Sanford Hill and promised to bring JP his knife back the next day. He wasn't worried. He was a kid with a lot of knives.

She took slow cautious steps toward her house until the rest of the kids were out of sight; then she ducked into the tree line across the street. She went just far enough into the woods to give her a sense of privacy.

Jenny removed her jacket and tied it around her waist. A branch snapped, and Jenny froze. A dumpy squirrel scurried in front of her, and she sighed, trying to relax. This wasn't going to be pleasant, but it was better than the alternative.

She rolled up the left sleeve of her light green sweater, and once it was two inches above her elbow, she pulled the knife from her pocket.

It stuck a bit when she unfolded it before giving way and flinging open. She was embarrassed how much she flinched. It wasn't a good sign for her tolerance going forward.

Jenny bent her left elbow and peered around to inspect the back of her forearm. She took one exaggerated breath and put the knife to her arm. She pushed hard, knowing she wouldn't be able to go back a second time. The knife plunged into her skin and she pulled it down toward her hand until she couldn't tolerate the pain, leaving about an inch-and-a-half gash.

It took what felt like forever for the blood to come out. The back of her arm seemed like a safe place on her body that wouldn't bleed too much, but it had to bleed enough. Then the blood came, pooling in the wound before spilling over the edge.

She had to move quickly now, dropping the knife, and pulling down her pants with her right hand. It was awkward, and she regretted not pulling them down first. Her underwear caught on the jeans and came down with them just enough. Jenny reached between her legs with her bloody arm, rubbing everywhere, then squeezing her arm against her underwear. The blood soaked in. She separated her underwear from her jeans and did the same to the crotch of her pants. Dark red seeped deep into the fibers.

Twenty minutes later, Jenny burst through the garage door, ready to sell it.

"Jenny!" Linda yelled from the other room. "Is that you? The school called and—"

"Mom!" Jenny screamed with a high pitch reserved for true panic.

Linda stormed into the kitchen to find her daughter.

"Mom, I got my period." Jenny turned toward her mother, alligator tears in her eyes, forearm blood between her legs.

Linda covered her mouth. "My baby," she gasped as she ran to comfort her daughter's fake entrance to puberty.

CHAPTER SEVENTEEN

VIRGINIA

THERE WERE FIVE LIQUOR STORES within a twenty-minute drive of my apartment. I tried my best to mix up which one I went to every time. I didn't want a pattern to develop. I didn't want to be noticed.

I squeezed in between two obnoxiously large cars in front of Delaney's package store on Main Street in Barnmont, the next town over. It was my least favorite of the five. There was no parking lot, and they fancied themselves as selling rare wines.

Inside, to the left, there were six impressive rows of wine. I headed to the right. The second aisle was my mecca, vodka. I grabbed a bottle from the bottom shelf, the cheap stuff. I didn't know any better and I was poor. Plus, I was less likely to hurt myself with a plastic bottle.

I was shuffling off to cash out with my bottle in hand when I saw her and froze. Hunter Willoughby was casually perusing the wine racks, the wine racks that stood between me and the register.

I lunged back into my own aisle. I didn't want to talk to anyone, especially not her. I moved to the opposite end of my aisle and slid out into the back row of the store, lined with refrigerated beer. I inched along, feigning interest in the variety of lagers until I could see her again.

She was attractive. I wasn't so delusional that I couldn't see that. I was pretty too, but somehow not pretty enough. Or not the right kind of pretty for Mark.

I watched her. She would lift a bottle of wine, read the label, then put it back. I didn't know what she was looking for, but she hadn't found it yet, not the right vineyard in France or something. She was looking for a most delicious wine to bring over to Mark's house. He was probably making her dinner, his signature pasta maybe. They would eat and drink until they were full, laughing, exchanging soft touches, building to the moment he would take her in his arms and kiss her. They would both be buzzed from the wine, inhibitions properly subdued. They would make love; then he would ask her to move in, to marry him. They would have four kids and a summer home on the Cape.

I put my bottle of vodka on the ground in front of me and ran out of the store. There were four more places I could get cheap vodka without having a mental breakdown.

I MOVED MY KEYS in my hands like I had lost all motor skills. An act I had done a million times seemed impossible. Pick out car key, put car key in door, think about how shitty and old my car is to have manual locks, open door, drive away, easy. Standing on the side of the road in front of Delaney's, I might as well have been wearing oven mitts. Was this a panic attack? Or maybe just a normal panic? Where is the line that determines if the panic is attacking?

"Hey, Virginia . . ." A voice penetrated my brain in what I determined could only be a hallucination brought on by the attacking panic. It was the voice of the very person I was panicking about.

Hunter Willoughby stood on the sidewalk adjacent to my car. I clutched my keys, turning them from Mexican jumping beans to sedentary rock. I said nothing. My brain was screaming for me to speak so I didn't look like a psychopath, but also maybe I was one. I wasn't feeling particularly well-adjusted in the moment.

"I don't mean to bother you. I just wanted to say I'm so sorry about Jenny. I know you two weren't very close, but she was an amazing girl and it's a real loss."

The SUBTEXT. *I* didn't know her very well? *She* knew that *I* didn't know Jenny very well? Crap, I still hadn't said anything. I was just standing in the road, not moving, not reacting, which, based on what was going on in my head, was maybe a good thing.

Hunter smiled. I would like to say it was a conniving smile, or that of a supervillain, but it was a kind, generous smile. How dare she?

"Look, this is probably really weird of me to ask, but I was in there looking for a bottle of wine and . . . Do you want to maybe just go grab a drink instead?" she asked.

Well, I did not see that coming. It was so far from the realm of possibility that I was incapable of reacting. What was one more minute of awkward silence while I processed? On the one hand, I wanted to run screaming. But there was the other hand. The other hand that society ingrained in unsuspecting women a long time ago. I wanted to know everything about her, every detail that I could twist to prove that I was better—prettier, smarter, funnier—*better*.

"I can't," I said, making my first healthy choice maybe ever.

"Right, yeah, I get it. It would be weird. Maybe another time. Or not." She smiled, her awkwardness making her endearing instead of detestable. But she was still THE WORST.

Hunter headed back into Delaney's, and I was finally able to grasp the right key in my hand.

RIVERVIEW LIQUOR ALLOWED ME to acquire a precious bottle of vodka without incident. I placed the bottle on my makeshift coffee table and took three more steps to the bedroom area of my studio. I pulled a T-shirt, then a pair of sweatpants, from amidst the giant ball of blankets on top of the bed. I flung the blankets back around, knocking the cordless phone off the nightstand. I knocked that stupid thing onto the floor fifty times a day, and half the time I just left it there. I didn't even want it; it was part of some bundle deal with the Internet and cable. The first week it rang a hundred thousand times, all telemarketers, so I turned off the ringer and left it as a decoration.

Comfortably in my pajamas, I sat down on the couch and started my night. Saturday nights were for drinking—heavy, blackout, throw-up-all-morning drinking. It was the Ambien that really made it special, taking away all my thoughts and memories. It was a pattern I'd fallen into over the years. An homage to my mother maybe. Six days a week, I fought my demons, and one night a week, I took a break. I could take the pills and mix them with alcohol, slowing down everything that made me human—breathing, moving, thinking. It was a cheat day. A system employed by thousands of overweight women all over the world, but I didn't want brownies; I wanted vodka and pills.

It was the two-week anniversary of Jenny's murder, and here I was, doing the exact same thing I had done that night. It seemed like things should be different now, but they weren't. I placed a pill on my tongue and took a shot straight from the bottle to wash it down. I didn't enjoy the taste of it. I was drinking to feel fantastic, then horrible, then black out. It was in my genes.

CHAPTER EIGHTEEN

JENNY

THE PAINT IN Ms. Willoughby's office was chipping in several spots, mostly around the vents and door. One of the file cabinets must have been moved a hair recently, revealing a thin strip of carpet brighter than the discolored majority. There was not one but two permanent rings on the desk from sweating plastic cups, and that's just what Jenny could see in the limited space not covered with paperwork. She hadn't noticed the wear and tear the first time she met with the counselor, but now she had little else to do while she waited.

Ms. Willoughby was late for their meeting. The secretary had insisted Jenny wait inside the office. It was quite trusting of the woman; Jenny could only imagine what sort of confidential information about her peers existed in the binders and files cluttering the space. It paid to be labeled a good kid, and Jenny still managed to fall in that category.

"Sorry, sorry," Ms. Willoughby muttered as she shuffled into the office, manhandling a stack of papers and a pen she almost dropped twice before finally dumping it all down on the desk. She looked at Jenny and released a big sigh, a symbolic start-over. "Jenny, it's nice to see you again."

Jenny smiled as the woman took her seat. It was an odd thing to say in the way it would be odd for a judge to tell a criminal that it was nice to see them again.

"Let me just . . ." The woman rotated in her seat to open the top drawer in the file cabinet behind her. She came back around clutching a file.

"Is that mine? Do I have a file?" Jenny asked.

"Yes, it's just a formality. I make a file for everyone who comes in. It's my attempt to stay organized." She smiled. "How am I doing?" Ms. Willoughby used the back of her hand to plow a bunch of other files to the side of her desk to make room for Jenny's.

"Great," Jenny said, laughing.

"Did you get everything sorted out yesterday? Did your mom call and get the skip taken care of?"

"Yeah."

"Good." Ms. Willoughby stared at the open file for a beat, but with just a single sheet of paper that Jenny could tell didn't say much, it was useless. "So, what brings you back to see me?"

"Same as last time. My parents think it's good for me to come see you. I'm sorry, this is probably really annoying for you. I don't mean to be wasting your time."

"Oh my God, Jenny, stop right there. Don't worry about me. You can come in as often as you like. I probably shouldn't say this, but you're the easiest part of my day. I thought we had a nice talk last time."

"Yeah," Jenny said, flattered but skeptical of her sincerity.

"How are you adjusting to eighth grade?"

"It's fine," Jenny responded with a canned teenage response.

"That's good. It's different, though, having multiple teachers every day. Are you handling the workload all right?"

"Yeah, I have to take a makeup quiz after school because of the day I missed, but it'll be easy. Mr. Jacobs uses the practice questions from the book. If you fail one of his quizzes, you're just an idiot."

Ms. Willoughby grinned, not bothered by Mr. Jacobs's inadequacies or Jenny's insults.

"It helps to have an easy class here and there. You won't get much out of it, but sometimes a break is more valuable. Gives your brain a chance to recharge. You're in the advanced math class, right?"

Yeah, with your boyfriend who you have sex with at school, Jenny thought, but certainly didn't say. Instead she nodded.

"See, one easy class and one difficult class, averages out to be two regular classes."

"I guess." Jenny laughed.

"That was a math joke. I knew you could handle it." Ms. Willoughby joined Jenny in laughing until it waned naturally back to silence. "And I'm guessing you're still out on cheerleading?"

"Yeah."

"Have you considered any other extracurriculars? Auditions for the fall play are coming up. They don't usually give the eighth graders the good parts, but you could be a tree or a townsperson or something. It's still fun to be involved."

"Maybe," Jenny said, knowing it wasn't going to happen. Lately she'd felt repulsed by anything with that kumbaya, school-spirit camaraderie vibe.

"Or not." Ms. Willoughby chuckled, seeing right through her. "I'll tell you a secret, but I'll deny it if you tell anyone, promise?"

Jenny's spine straightened. Has anyone in the history of the universe ever said no to learning a secret? "Promise."

"It really doesn't matter what you do this year. Eighth grade is like a free trial. Colleges only care about your four years of real high school. Don't get arrested or expelled and try not to develop any destructive patterns that you can't break next year and you'll be fine."

Jenny grinned. Experiencing Ms. Willoughby's candor and lack of bullshit felt like a privilege. "That sounds good to me."

"Yeah, I thought it would. That doesn't mean go crazy. I just know you're conflicted. Are you feeling a lot of pressure from your parents?"

"I guess," Jenny said, not wanting to talk about her mother. She didn't want to share that part of her life with Ms. Willoughby. If she was honest, her file would no longer be just a formality. She would be another one of those students stressing the guidance counselor out with their problems, and Jenny would be her job, not her respite. She wouldn't be special. She liked things this way much better. "It's fine," she added, tying a big fat bow on that line of questioning.

IT WAS ALREADY after four on Friday afternoon when Jenny finished her social studies quiz. Mr. Jacobs agreed to let her make it up after Linda called him five or six times begging him not to give her a zero. It was a weekly quiz and only about 1 percent of her total grade, but Linda wouldn't drop it.

The halls were completely empty at that hour, and even Jenny's own steps did little to disrupt the silence. There wasn't much ventilation in the back stairwell, and the smells of puberty lingered. She took her time down the first couple steps before she heard a noise; a brief mumbled moan came from directly below.

Jenny pressed her body against the railing and leaned over just in time to witness Trevor Larson's head roll back and let out a much louder sound. When he was done, his whole body relaxed. Jenny thought he might be hurt until a bob of blonde curly hair rose up and revealed itself. She recognized that hair immediately; it was Mallory. Jenny knew enough about the world to know what was going on. Mallory just gave Trevor Larson a blow job in the disgusting high school stairwell.

Jenny turned to sneak back upstairs, but as she did, her backpack brushed against the railing and the zipper scratched the metal, creating a faint noise that shattered the silence. Trevor and Mallory whipped their heads toward Jenny, who stared back long enough for everyone to get a good look at each other.

"Sorry," Jenny muttered as she sprinted back up the stairs.

JENNY HUSTLED DOWN the hallway, not sure where she was headed but knowing she had to get out of there.

"Jenny!" Mallory called after her. "Jenny, wait! I know you can hear me."

Jenny could tell that Mallory was running from the cadence of her words. She couldn't escape without changing her pace and giving away that she did hear her, a lose-lose. Jenny threw her hands into her pockets and spun around casually.

"Hey, Mallory." Jenny stopped and waited for her. "I won't tell anyone what I saw."

"What is it you think you saw?"

"Nothing," Jenny tried to insist.

"C'mon," Mallory scoffed. "I trust you. You won't say anything. I just, like, don't want anyone else to know, OK?"

"Is Trevor your boyfriend now?" Jenny asked.

"Ew, no. He's just good practice, and he knows to keep his mouth shut. He's teaching me stuff so I won't be a total spaz with someone I actually like."

"And you like doing that *stuff*?"

"Jesus, Jenny, don't say it like that. You sound like my little sister. Don't you want to start doing stuff? It's totally normal."

Jenny thought about the question. Did she want to start doing that stuff? Kind of. Well, not putting a penis in her mouth in a dirty stairwell, but kissing, stuff like that.

"I could find someone for you if you want," Mallory said as if it were a new offer and not something she was constantly trying to do to everyone around her.

Jenny was so tired of deflecting everyone's advice and pressure to do stupid crap she didn't want to do.

"Unless there is already someone?" Mallory pressed. The corners of her mouth curled a bit, salivating at the prospect of stumbling onto a secret.

"No, you're so obsessed. There are more important things in the world," Jenny snapped.

"You don't have to be a bitch," said Mallory. "I was just trying to help you, because people are talking about you. There's only so much I can do to protect you, you know?"

"I just want to be left alone," said Jenny.

"It's not that easy. You're making yourself a target because you've gotten so freaking weird."

"Well, if people need something to talk about, I just saw something interesting in the stairwell," said Jenny under her breath, without making eye contact.

"What the hell? Is that a threat?"

Jenny took a deep breath. She wasn't interested in threatening Mallory. It just came out in the heat of the moment. It was maybe a glimpse of the Jenny that she was supposed to be. "No, sorry. I didn't mean that. I'm not going to say anything."

"I swear to God, if anyone finds out—"

"OK," Jenny accepted the threat before it was vocalized. It didn't matter. It held no weight in the grand scheme of things to be nervous about; she had arranged to meet Benjy's friend Gil the next day, alone.

CHAPTER NINETEEN

VIRGINIA

IT WAS AN HOUR drive to the county jail in Hartsfield, where Benjy was being held. I didn't mind the drive, though; it gave me plenty of time to bask in my victory. Brandon was letting me talk to Benjy. I'd remained persistent in my request until he came around, realizing he needed me.

I was on Brandon's turf now, and he was waiting for me outside the four-story cement building right in the middle of a commercial street. Thirty years ago, the shops were booming. Internet, drugs, the economy killed it. Businesses came in and out of the storefronts; nothing but a dollar store stuck. Well, the dollar store and the jail.

The detective leaned against the railing. His sleeves were rolled up, arms crossed, looking as relaxed as ever. He pushed off the railing to stand on his own when he saw me round the corner from the parking lot.

"How was the drive?"

"It was fine." I climbed the six steps and met him at the top. He almost went in for a hug but pulled back before contact. Based on our location and mission, he seemed conflicted over our personal and professional relationship. For me, there wasn't any confusion. I felt like a professional. I wasn't being paid, but he was, and we were kind of working together. That was enough for me.

"Are you ready?" he asked as he opened the front door for me.

I was ready. There wasn't much to lose, and Benjy wasn't scary. It's not like they suspected the leader of the Hells Angels.

Brandon showed me into a small room with one window. There was a wooden table with three matching chairs. Police decor was pretty transparent. Metal was for interrogation, wood for visitation.

Brandon held out a chair for me on the side with two chairs. Apparently I could have brought a friend. He seemed nervous.

"Are *you* OK?" I asked.

He straightened at the implication. "Yeah, why?"

"Nothing."

"I don't know what he's going to tell you," said Brandon, "but remember, this is a murderer who has been caught. He will say anything, and I know you're desperate for answers, so just make sure to be cautious." He touched my shoulder as he backed away. The gentle touch was back.

"I will," I said. "I have no expectations. We just have to try." I wondered if I scared him by referring to us as a *we*. I'm sure the thought of having an unqualified civilian partner was like a kick in the balls of his ego. He was tolerating my curiosity just enough to get into my pants. I was sure of it.

"Nothing he says can be used, remember. This is more for you. I want you to have closure. Even if he confesses, it doesn't matter. We won't be listening. It's the only way the lawyer would agree to this," he explained.

"He could shed some light on what she was into." I just wished he would entertain other scenarios. Isn't it more fun that way? If I were a detective, I would have a huge murder board with every person Jenny ever met. I would stand in front of it long into the night, moving Post-its around until I had an irrefutable conclusion.

"He'll say anything. He's desperate." He ended on that note and slid out of the room.

Three minutes later, a uniformed police officer brought in Benjy. He was in what looked like khaki scrubs. I wondered when and why they stopped using black-and-white-striped uniforms. In this outfit, Benjy could wander into a hospital and start mopping the floors and no one would notice.

The officer guided Benjy to the chair across the table from me. He smiled when he looked at my face. Handcuffs restricted his ability to brace himself, and he landed with a thud.

"You can take those off," I said to the officer.

"Detective Colsen said to leave them on. I'm sorry, ma'am." He nodded and stepped out of the room.

It was just the two of us. No one was watching; no one could hear. If he were a murderer, this would have been scary. I was glad I didn't believe it.

"Hi, Benjy, I'm Virginia." I smiled, not to manipulate him but because I wanted to.

"You look like Jenny," he said, like it was the greatest compliment he could give.

"Thank you."

"You are very pretty." He avoided looking directly at me as he spoke.

"How did you know Jenny?"

He looked back at the mention of her name and beamed. "She

was my friend. I don't have many friends. Just a few. Do you have a lot of friends?"

"No, I don't have many friends at all."

"Oh . . . I could be your friend. I like to write letters. Do you like to get letters?"

"Sure," I said. Mark used to write me notes, slipping them into my backpack so I would find them later. I shook off the memory. It wasn't the time for that.

"OK, I will write you a letter when I get home," he said.

"I don't know if you'll get to go home."

He looked down at his hands, bound together, like he knew.

"Benjy, can you tell me what happened when you saw Jenny a few weeks ago?"

He shook his head. "No, no, no, I did not see her. I haven't seen her since the pageant."

"I know you saw her. It's OK. Your neighbor saw her at your apartment."

He kept shaking his head. His face was pained. "She said I couldn't tell anybody."

"It's OK, I promise. You can tell me. Look at me, Benjy. I'm not a bad guy. I'm not the police."

He raised his eyes to meet mine, and my resemblance to Jenny gave him permission to tell.

BRANDON SLID INTO THE ROOM seconds after the officer took Benjy away, his response time negating any attempts to pretend he wasn't curious. "So? What did he say?"

"Who the fuck is Gil?" I asked as I stood and pushed past him out of the room. I was furious. In twelve minutes, I'd found out my sister had been introduced to another pageant pervert in the weeks leading up to her murder. What the hell had the police been doing all this time?

CHAPTER TWENTY

JENNY

GIL'S LETTER SAID he would be at Roaster's Tavern at noon. It was two towns away and Jenny had to take the bus again. She'd insisted on a Saturday so she wouldn't have to skip school. She told Linda she was going to Mallory's house. Mallory was one of the only friends Linda approved of for Jenny, which was ironic after what Jenny had seen yesterday.

Roaster's Tavern had no windows, and Jenny wondered if that was a calculated move by Gil. She had never been inside. Her parents wouldn't be caught dead there. The only reason Jenny knew of the place was because it was down the road from where she got her spray tans before pageants. Did Gil know that?

She opened the door and took two steps inside, waiting for her eyes to adjust. Once the door shut behind her, mustard-tinted overhead lights were all there was. The hostess stand was abandoned for reasons other than a crowd. The place was dead.

Jenny ventured into the main dining area. It was full of booths with cracked dark navy leather upholstery. Still no sign of any employees. At a table in the corner, a man sat with a young girl sipping on a soda. Jenny's stomach churned at the sight. Was this place pedophile-friendly? What had she walked into?

Maybe it was just a deadbeat dad doing his monthly duty. They weren't talking, so that could very well be the case. She'd always thought of pedophiles as probably quite charming, not prone to long bouts of silence. That's how you hunt animals, not children. Children like attention.

With no visible staff and one potential pervert, she wondered who would help her if things with Gil went south. She had thought a public place would be safe. She'd felt so smart requesting they meet in public. She should have picked the place. Lesson learned.

Before Jenny could fully comprehend the seriousness of the situation and bolt, an arm emerged from a booth across the room, followed by a smiling face as the man stood for her attention.

"Jenny," he said, waving.

First impression was everything. He wasn't old. She'd thought he would be old for some reason. He seemed to be around Virginia's age. He had small glasses and greasy hair that was shellacked over his forehead. Under a patchy mustache, his big grin seemed friendly enough. As she got closer, the acne scars became prominent. He was an oily guy. On numerous occasions Linda lectured Jenny on skin care, never too dry but never, ever oily.

"Jenny." He continued grinning like they were old friends.

"Hi," she managed.

He leaned a shoulder toward her, considering a hug, but when she didn't reciprocate, he yanked it back and motioned for her to join him in the booth.

She slid in across from him and waited. He wrung his sweaty

hands together, leaning toward her, glowing. Benjy used to act like this, but Benjy was special, slow and harmless.

"I'm so glad you wanted to meet." Gil kept grinning, so many visible teeth.

"Sure. Was it a long drive?" Jenny wanted the small talk to last forever. She was afraid of where the conversation would lead if it didn't.

"No, not too bad. What about you? How did you get here?"

"My friend drove me." Jenny wanted a fictional person lurking around who would notice if she disappeared.

"I could have picked you up. It would have been no trouble."

She just smiled. That would never happen.

"Do you want something to eat? The service here is awful, but the food is pretty good." He strained his neck around, looking for the waitress, becoming increasingly agitated when he couldn't find her, and his teeth retreated back behind a scowl. "I'm sorry, it's really inexcusable." He stood to get a better look around.

"It's OK," Jenny said. "I'm not hungry."

"Are you sure?"

"Positive."

He sat back down, returning all of his attention to her. "I forgot, I brought you something." He reached into his messenger bag and pulled out a jewelry box and handed it to her.

Jenny took the box. A present.

"Go ahead, open it."

Jenny flipped it open, revealing a thin gold chain with a heart charm. A heart. What was he trying to say? That he loved her? Her face wrinkled.

"Sorry, I should explain. Benjy told me you didn't want to do pageants anymore. I thought this would remind you to always follow your heart." He barely got the words out. He was nervous. He was trying so hard to impress her. She wished JP would learn a thing or two from this guy.

"Thank you," she said, and she meant it, slipping the box into her pocket.

"Don't get me wrong, I'm so glad you wrote to me, but what made you want to meet? I didn't even think you knew who I was."

Jenny hesitated, but she'd have to speak up sooner or later. It was going well so far. He seemed sweet. Just a lonely guy like Benjy. These men made her feel like a celebrity. She held all the cards. They would do anything for her.

"Benjy thought you might be able to help me," she said, looking down at the table.

"What kind of help?"

"I need money."

He scoffed, forcing her to look up.

"You need money?" he repeated for effect, then rolled his eyes.

"Yes," she whispered.

He smiled, but it was a different smile. It was smug, less teeth. "You're thirteen years old. What could you possibly need?"

"I don't want to say."

"I can buy you presents. We can meet together more, get to know each other. I will make it worth your while."

"No, I just need money, five thousand dollars. I need it soon, but we can still see each other." She scooted forward in her seat, debating reaching out to take his hands. That would work on Benjy, but she was hesitant to make physical contact with Gil.

"I thought you liked me." He shook his head. She was losing him.

"I do."

"I should have known better," he said to himself. "Out of the blue, you contact me. I'm so stupid." He crossed his arms, pouting like a child.

"I'm sorry, this was a mistake." Jenny slid out of the booth, and he grabbed her arm, jolting her back. She could see her own reflection in his glasses. Past her own face, his dark eyes narrowed.

"You want money?" he hissed. "You want five thousand dollars from me?"

"No, it's OK, I'm so sorry."

His hand gripped her forearm. His elbow was locked. He could hold her there forever if he wanted to. "Are you a virgin, Jenny?"

She tried not to answer, but he squeezed her arm, forcing it out of her. "Yes." Her eyes burned in anticipation of tears.

"Give me your virginity and I'll give you the money," he said, holding her there as the horror crept over her face. When a ridge of tears gathered on her eyelids, he changed his tune and released her arm. "Sorry."

It was too late. Jenny didn't waste another second as she turned and sprinted through the empty booths and out of the tavern, praying he wouldn't follow her.

THE BUS RIDE home felt the longest yet. How could she have been so stupid? She was lucky she hadn't been kidnapped, spending the rest of her good-looking years in Gil's basement.

What was she going to tell JP? She couldn't tell him the truth—he would think she was stupid for having gone, and he would be right. Jenny didn't even know if she wanted to run away anymore.

What if this was a sign? A sign of what was out there in the real world? She didn't have it so bad. If she could just get over herself, high school could be great. Her popularity wasn't too far gone, and she had dirt on Mallory.

If she just sucked it up for five more years, joined cheerleading, and got straight A's, her parents would get off her back. She could smile. She could pretend it was everything she wanted. JP would probably leave, but so what? He wasn't the be-all and end-all in her life. She felt weak for letting him get so far into her head. He wasn't even her boyfriend. He was a jerk who had shown her a little attention. Her desire for attention from older men was going to catch up to her someday, and at this rate, soon.

JENNY ENTERED THE HOUSE from the garage. The sun was on its way down and blasted through the kitchen windows, blinding her.

"Where were you?" Her mother's voice came from across the room.

Jenny held up her hand to block the sunlight enough to make out Linda's shadowy figure leaning against the long cabinet, holding a glass of the dark liquor.

Jenny backed toward the door. She wasn't ready for this. She was at Mallory's. It was Saturday. Her dad was home. She'd thought she was safe.

"Tell me where you were." Linda moved into the empty space between them.

"Where's Dad?" Jenny asked, praying for a savior, knowing he wouldn't come.

Her mother stepped toward her. "Your father is staying in New York this weekend. He hasn't done that in six years. Are you proud of yourself? Is it worth being a little shit to drive your father away?" Linda took another step closer to Jenny.

Jenny had no answers. There was no rationalizing with Linda, no explaining maybe it was her he was avoiding. But if Jenny was driving Linda to behave like this, maybe she *was* to blame.

"I'm sorry, Mom. I'll be better."

"Those are just words. What is it that I've done to you? You were such a good girl. Your father was so happy. You're ruining this family and you won't even tell me why."

"Please stop freaking out. I'm not ruining anything."

"You're upsetting your father. We only get two days. I don't want him to be upset when he's here, do you understand?"

"Yeah, I get it," Jenny said, taking a step to the side, looking to get around her mother, but Linda moved to cut her off.

"We were so close. Why won't you talk to me anymore?" Linda hung her head, trying for sympathy. "Tell me where you were today."

"I was at Mallory's," Jenny said. She knew Linda must already know that was a lie, but she didn't have time to rethink her alibi and hoped she'd just accept it. Instead, her mother slapped her across the face.

"You're lying! You are lying to your mother."

It stunned Jenny for a second, looking at Linda, feeling the pain in her cheek, wondering if she was hallucinating. As the reality set in, Jenny reached for her face, but her mother yanked her arm away. "If I can't trust you to leave this house, you won't leave this house." With that, she dragged Jenny by her wrists out of the kitchen, up the stairs, and toward her precious pink bedroom.

Linda shoved her daughter inside, slamming the door behind her. Jenny's stuffed animals stared at her from the floor of the closet as the young girl stood sobbing in the center of her room. She could hear Linda grunting through the wall and the hutch down the hall rattling as her mother yanked it toward her door. It was so heavy, Linda must have been running on pure drunken adrenaline.

The noises came to a stop outside Jenny's door. It was silent for a moment before Linda went barreling down the stairs. Jenny approached her bedroom door and opened it enough to see the antique hutch completely blocking the doorway, trapping her inside.

CHAPTER TWENTY-ONE

VIRGINIA

BRANDON CALLED FOUR TIMES within an hour after I stormed out of the jail before I finally agreed to meet him. I drove down the street and sat in my car, knowing I would have to see him before I went home. I wanted him to squirm first. He suggested a coffee shop a few blocks away via his tenth text, and I agreed with a potent K.

I ordered a small amaretto upside-down latte, whatever that meant, and waited for Brandon on a comfy armchair toward the back. I wanted to get there first. I wanted him to have to walk toward me while I sat in a power pose with a smug look on my face. I felt intimidating and powerful, having dropped a bomb on his case.

He arrived just as the barista brought me my drink, creating an awkward bottleneck between the tables en route to me and ruining my moment. Great start.

He took a seat in the accompanying armchair, and I realized it was a poor choice for a serious sit-down. He adjusted to sit only on the edge, maintaining some sense of an upright posture. I stayed in a lounge position, unable to reposition in the squishy chair without looking like the boat in *The Perfect Storm*.

"Why did you take off so fast? Are you OK?" he asked.

"Who's Gil, Detective Colsen?"

"I have no idea. The first time I heard the name was out of your mouth."

"Your airtight murder suspect introduced Jenny to one of his friends two weeks before she died. Did you know that?"

"Of course I didn't know that," he said. "Benjy wouldn't even admit he saw Jenny."

"Well, he told me. Said that Jenny came to him for money, but he didn't have enough so he told her his friend Gil would help her."

"Money? Why would she need money?"

I threw up my hands. "I don't know! You're the detective."

Brandon forfeited his posture and gave in to the chair. "I don't know, this seems convenient."

"Convenient for who?"

"The man's been arrested, gets caught in a lie, and then all of a sudden there's another man who Jenny contacted."

"You know, it *is* possible you're wrong. I know you can't fathom it, but it might be the case."

"You don't think very highly of me," Brandon said and waited a beat for me to protest, but I didn't. "I'm going to look into it. I'm just not going to go crazy over some unsupported detail from a guy with nothing to lose. It's something you would know if you were a real detective. People lie. All the time. You need evidence, motive, something else to go on."

"Good," I said without giving his dig about real detectives a reaction.

"What else do you know about him?"

Crap. I knew nothing really. A name. A place. A vague connection to Benjy. "He lives in New York City."

"OK, what else?"

I turned my attention to my drink and took a long sip while he waited for more information. When my mouth was full, I was forced to swallow. Distraction over, I shrugged, admitting that's all I knew.

Brandon rubbed his forehead. "Great, Gil from New York City. Alert the media."

He was right. I would need more—some way to find Gil or at least prove he was real. Jenny had to have known something. It was time to do a little less talking and a little more snooping.

SUNDAY DINNER. Normally I dreaded this, even more so now that Jenny was gone, but this Sunday I was happy for an excuse to be in the house. Any other visit would seem suspicious. The news vans were gone. They'd stayed around a few days after they announced Benjy's arrest, trying to illicit a sound bite from someone in the family. My father and Linda made a formal statement in front of the station about justice and remembering Jenny. After that, the vans pulled out. I'm sure they were happy to put the taillights to this snooze town.

I walked through the garage. Linda threw a fit if anyone walked through the formal front door. There was pristine white carpet immediately inside, and she would do anything to keep it that way. When Jenny was three or four, I would open that door as a joke to watch Linda jump from her seat and scream. Little Jenny would laugh hysterically, and I would close the door and walk around through the garage. Somewhere along the way, our little joke faded away and the distance between my sister and I grew.

"Virginia? In the living room," my father yelled.

The kitchen was cold and sterile. There was always something cooking on Sunday. Even if it was store-bought, it was being heated. Not tonight.

I stepped into the living room and found my father gripping his phone, typing away.

I leaned against the doorway, waiting for him to put it down and approve an interaction. "What's up with dinner?" I asked when I thought he'd forgotten I was there.

"Linda isn't feeling well. I thought we could go out to eat," he said.

This had never happened. Not once in eight years of Sunday dinners had we ever gone out. Why tonight, the one night I wanted to stay in the house and snoop around, did he want to go out?

"I could cook something."

"No." He stood from his chair. "We'll go for pizza."

Part of me wanted to believe he was reaching out to me. He had lost one daughter and wanted to shore up his relationship with the one he had left. In reality, I knew, the pizza place was the closest and quickest option.

We drove in his slick silver Mercedes. He got a new car every two years, and this was my first and probably only time in this one. The leather seats were cold and uncomfortable, like our conversation.

"What's wrong with Linda?" I asked.

"She isn't feeling well."

"Is it a bug or something?"

"No, it's from Jenny. She's not the same, as I'm sure you can understand," he said to guilt me away from further questions. It worked.

We rode in silence for the next six minutes. I watched the clock.

"I'll be heading back to work tomorrow. There's no time limit on grieving for your child, but I have to go back. It's time," he said as a fact, not looking for my approval.

I thought about the time he took to grieve for my mother. I couldn't remember. I just nodded. I wanted to ask about Linda, about leaving her, but before I could find a way to ask that wouldn't set him off, he broached the topic.

"Do you think you could look in on Linda occasionally? I know you don't care for her, but she is alone and having a hard time," he said, showing some unexpected empathy. Two wives committing suicide wouldn't look great on his résumé, I suppose.

I really didn't want to, but I didn't have the energy to disobey my father to his face in a confined space. It came in the form of a question, but make no mistake, this was an order. "Sure" was all I said.

Pizza was uneventful. He asked pointed questions about my future, clinical and never personal. "Are you looking for work? . . . Do think you'll ever find a career? . . . Do you have any savings left?"

I gave vague, monosyllabic answers that frustrated the line of questioning.

Then we sat silent for a beat until he tried again. Neither one of us had ever eaten so fast. It was one thing we had in common; we didn't want to be there.

I knew what he saw when he looked at me: He saw all of his perceived failures. I dressed like a homeless person, I was snarky and abrasive, I didn't have a job or much of a life. And when I looked at him, I saw his disgust. Maybe when he looked at me, he saw my mother; maybe when he looked at me, he saw Jenny. He wished it had been me. I wished it had been me. The whole damn town wished it had been me. If it had been me, it would have been something I did, something I got wrapped up in, somehow my fault.

I debated telling him about Gil. He had a right to know, but my father had so little respect for me, he probably wouldn't believe me. I wasn't ready for him to know how involved I had become. Part of me worried he might be proud of me, and this man did not deserve that. He did not deserve anything except guilt over how he had raised his children and the consequences it bore.

As we pulled back into the driveway, I needed an excuse to go inside. I wanted five minutes alone in Jenny's room. We got out of the car, and I followed my father toward the garage. He looked back, puzzled that I wasn't going to my own car, but said nothing.

He flipped on the lights to the kitchen as we entered. Still no signs of Linda.

"Do you think I could borrow a few books?" I asked. "My cable isn't working."

"Fine." He said, walking out of the kitchen. I walked by him in the living room on my way. He didn't even look up. He had done his Sunday duty. If I wanted to stay longer, that was on me. I passed the front stairs and wished I could just run up into Jenny's room instead of playing games.

The back of the house was quiet, a preserved dwelling for a big family or guests, not two grieving parents. I opened the door to the study so the creak would reach him, then slipped off my shoes and held them in my hands. I ascended the back stairs, my socks on the carpet not creating a sound.

There were four doors in the upstairs hallway, a bathroom, the bedroom Linda was boarded up in, my old room that was now storage for crap that should be thrown away, and, lastly, closest to the front stairs, Jenny's room. Her door was open a crack, and I was able to push it the rest of the way without giving away my position. It was untouched. Jenny's jacket rested over the back of her vanity chair. A few schoolbooks were spread across the floor. Her bed was a mess. Linda strictly required Jenny to make her bed every morning, which made the image particularly disturbing.

I wasn't sure where to start. I took timid steps toward the vanity and rested my shoes on the chair. Last year, the vanity was covered with neatly sorted makeup, nail polish, and hair accessories. It had devolved to a makeshift desk where Jenny stored old schoolwork and broken pencils. I leafed through the stack of papers. Her grades were slipping, as noted by red-penned notes like, *Not your best. B-*.

I slid open the drawer of the vanity, discovering the makeup that used to sit on top. A set of eye shadow had cracked open, leaving blue and purple powder over everything. Blue eye shadow for a ten-year-old. How does anyone rationalize that? Five years ago, I would have put an exorbitant amount on my eyelids and gone downstairs, pretending nothing was different. Jenny would laugh, my father would show no reaction, and Linda would plead for me not to waste the expensive makeup. First the jokes died; then Jenny did.

The textbooks on the floor were nothing of note. I slid them apart as if I was trying not to leave fingerprints. Math, history, science, boring and not all that different from the books I had in school. With her books all over the floor, I looked for her backpack. I opened the closet. Several bulky gowns and costumes, wrapped in plastic, were pushed to one side. Jenny's assorted school clothes were spread out along the rest of the rod. A pile of stuffed animals was on the floor. No schoolbag.

"What are you doing?" my father's voice boomed.

I slammed the closet door closed and whipped around to see him in the doorway. He had been as silent as I thought I was being. "I'm sorry," I rushed to say.

"You shouldn't be in here. Linda doesn't want anyone in here touching things, and I can't take anything more upsetting her right now."

"Are you just going to leave it like this? Forever?"

"Don't start trouble, Virginia. I think it's time for you to leave." He moved from the door, creating space for me to exit.

I grabbed my shoes and walked out, feeling as unwelcome as ever. That wasn't new, but the missing bag was. Was anyone looking for the bag?

CHAPTER TWENTY-TWO

JENNY

BY THE TIME Jenny woke up on Sunday morning, the antique hutch was back where it belonged. She slept with her headphones blaring in her ears until the battery ran its course long after she fell asleep. It was something new she was trying in order to drown out the sounds in her head when there was nothing else.

She stayed in her room as long as she could, spending most of the day sitting on the floor, her back against her bed, staring at the door and contemplating her future. She waited for Linda to come to the door. Which Linda, she couldn't know.

The darker it got outside, the more nervous she became. She should just go downstairs and confront her mother. Whatever happened, it couldn't be worse than the suspense of it all, but she was paralyzed. *Just a few more minutes*, she thought. *Then I'll go downstairs*. But she didn't. She just sat there until she heard someone on the stairs.

Jenny scooted her feet toward her body, reached her hands onto the bed behind her, and slowly rose to her feet, unsteady from hours of sitting still. There was a light knock and then the knob began to turn. It played so slowly in Jenny's mind, she half expected the grim reaper to be standing on the other side.

The door opened just enough for Linda to push her face through, as if she was extending some sort of privacy by not opening it all the way. "Jenny . . ." Her voice was quiet and level, and when her eyes met Jenny's, she smiled. "Your sister will be here soon. C'mon downstairs."

Sunday. Sunday-dinner Sunday! Time had escaped Jenny's brain. Her father wasn't home, she hadn't left her room, there were none of the normal markers, but it was Sunday and Virginia was coming over to, without knowing it, force Linda to behave. This was the second time that week Virginia had shown up at just the right time to help Jenny, and she decided she would queue up an apology for her outburst that day in town.

SUNDAY DINNERS without her father were rare. They should have been an opportunity for the three girls to relax a bit, but it never worked out that way. It was always worse when Linda drove the conversation. This time was no different. The first twenty minutes Linda talked Virginia's ear off about nursing school as if she knew anything about it or Virginia would ever consider it. Virginia took Linda's *advice* as long as she could stomach before saying something under her breath about Linda not working a day in her life. Then Linda threw out a patented "I'm only trying to help. That's all I've ever done with you, Virginia."

"Thank you," Virginia said. "From the bottom of my heart."

Linda rolled her eyes and sawed away at the severely overcooked steak strips on her plate.

"So, what was Dad's excuse?" Virginia blurted out.

"It's quarter end. It's not an excuse," Linda said so genuinely Jenny knew her mother was past the point of ever being trustworthy again.

Virginia looked to Jenny for confirmation.

"Don't look at her like you think I'm lying," said Linda. "It's very rude."

"I was just looking at her. Is that not allowed? I thought you loved this sort of thing, people staring at your precious Jenny?"

Jenny buried a smile down at her plate before turning to Virginia with her eyes crossed and her bottom jaw stuck out, her best attempt at ugly.

"Gorgeous," Virginia pandered.

Linda's knife scraped against her plate, and they all winced. "You know, maybe you should worry a little less about getting a laugh and spend a little more time being a positive role model for your sister."

Virginia shoved a forkful of salad into her mouth. "Don't do drugs."

Linda shook her head. "I'm done," she announced, standing with her plate and heading into the kitchen.

Virginia turned to Jenny, wide-eyed and looking for corroboration that Linda's sudden departure was out of character. Jenny just shrugged. Of course it was out of character. Virginia had no idea.

"Sorry about the other day in town," Jenny said quiet enough to keep their conversation private. "I don't hate you. I was just pissed."

"What was going on? It looked like you were mixed up in something with Mark Renkin."

"No, it was nothing. I was just trying to catch the bus from school and was worried I wasn't going to make it."

"Did you?"

"Yeah, it was fine."

Virginia nodded, but bit at her lip like she was eager to pry. Jenny wasn't having it. "You were all dressed up. What were you doing?"

"Nothing . . . And I wasn't *dressed up*."

"Yes, you were. For you. Look what you're wearing right now." Jenny glanced down at Virginia's worn leggings. "And your hair was all nice and you were being really weird. You just got out of your car, but you didn't go anywhere."

"It was nothing."

"If it was nothing, then what were you doing in town and why wouldn't you give me a ride home?"

"I was just running errands."

"But you didn't go anywhere. You just got out of your car, then got back in," Jenny pressed. "And you were all crazy-eyes and manic."

"Jenny, fucking drop it," Virginia snapped. Jenny recoiled, not used to Virginia dropping f-bombs on her.

Virginia slid her chair back and grabbed her plate, the steak untouched. "I think I'm done too."

"Fine, don't tell me," said Jenny.

"There's nothing to tell," said Virginia as she walked off into the kitchen. Jenny had pissed her sister off, but at least Virginia wasn't going to ask any more questions about what Jenny was doing in town that day. Or, worse, mention it in front of Linda.

JENNY LEFT THE HOUSE for school an hour early to avoid interaction with her mother. She headed up Sanford Hill and found JP out behind his house. He was an early riser and liked to brag about it. Marines get up early. She heard the knives whacking into the tree before she could even see him. The knives no longer frightened her. The initial hesitation toward the machete was a distant memory.

Jenny stepped on a branch as she entered the backyard. *Snap*. JP whipped around, raising a knife above his head, ready to defend his land.

Jenny jumped back. "Whoa!"

"Sorry," he said, turning and hurling the knife toward a tree. The knife penetrated the trunk and stuck, vibrating with the leftover force. "You're up early."

She wanted to tell him what had happened Saturday night, tell him that she was a prisoner in her own home, show him the bruises on her wrists from where Linda had held her. But would he comfort her or think she was a baby? How far would Linda have to go for Jenny to get some sympathy from this guy?

JP picked up another knife from the ground. It was small for him, maybe eight inches long, with a dark wooden handle carved with deep swirls. "You want?" he asked.

Jenny approached him and took the knife in her hand. She turned it over and back to inspect the tiny weapon.

"Just pull it over your shoulder . . ." He mimicked the movement for her. "And heave it. Like you're casting a fishing rod."

Jenny lifted the knife over her shoulder as instructed. "I've never been fishing." She grunted as she hurled the knife toward the tree. The handle hit the trunk, and the knife went flying.

"It takes practice," he explained, walking toward the trees. "So, what's up with the money?" he asked, bending down to grab Jenny's errant knife.

Jenny regretted telling him about the money. Now she was going to look like a failure. "It's not going to work out."

"Of course not," he mumbled.

He didn't believe in her. Did he think she'd made the whole thing up? This was bullshit. She wanted credit for finding Gil, for meeting him, for being so brave, for doing something.

"Look, I went and met the guy in Lansville. It's just not going to work, OK? He was a jerk." She wanted him to ask more. Didn't he hear that he was a jerk? Doesn't he want to defend her honor?

"It's fine," JP said, walking back with the knives cradled in his arms like firewood. "I wasn't counting on it anyway."

"You didn't think I could get the money?" He had so little faith in her and it was driving her mad. He was nothing, just a loser. She was Jenny Kennedy.

"I didn't say that." He dropped the knives at his feet. "I'm just not going to rely on anyone, especially you."

"What do you mean *especially* me? At least I had an idea. You're just talk. You probably don't even know anyone in Mexico. You just made that up so you can sound cool. Well, forget it. I'm gonna go wait for the bus." Jenny turned and stomped away.

She heard him running, but didn't turn back until he grabbed her arm and whipped her around. It wasn't the way Linda grabbed her. Or Gil. It was firm but soft, and as soon as she was facing him, he loosened his grip almost completely.

"It's not made up, OK? I'm gonna go. I'm gonna get out of here and do something," he almost whispered. His face was different: There was no grin; his eyes were wide. He leaned in and kissed her. It was a straight face-press, no tongues, no moving heads back and forth, a direct delivery for the count of five. He pulled back, looked at her for a beat, then walked away.

Jenny touched her lips as if he had left something behind. Her first kiss. She thought she liked it. She liked that *he* had kissed her instead of some asshole like Trevor Larson, but the act was weird, like walking into a glass door. Wasn't this where he told her she was pretty, or that he loved her? Instead, JP went back to throwing knives.

She took two steps back toward the driveway, enough to regain his attention.

"Was that your first kiss?" he asked.

She debated lying. A lot of girls in her class had boyfriends. Mallory was giving blow jobs in the stairwell, but JP once told her she didn't have to pretend around him. "Yes," she admitted.

"Nice." He nodded without looking at her. "I figured. That's why I didn't use any tongue. It can be a lot." With that, he let another knife fly.

Was he being considerate or judgmental? Why was he so hard to read? How many girls had he kissed? Any combination of words seemed like a gamble, so Jenny stayed quiet and waited for him to decide the next move.

JP threw three more knives before gathering them up and placing them back in his hiding spot behind the flat rock. She followed him to the back porch, where he grabbed his backpack. She wondered if they'd ever speak again.

"Do you have a passport?" he asked, breaking the silence.

"No, but my sister does."

"Good." He quickened his pace and they headed for the bus. "We'll need it."

CHAPTER TWENTY-THREE

VIRGINIA

JENNY'S BODY WAS found in the woods bordering one of the Emersons' cornfields. A quick thunderstorm in the early hours of the morning had washed most of the scene away. Mitch Emerson's black Lab found her body before anyone even knew she was missing. She was left in the open, a flower tucked in her hands, which were folded over her dirty, damp, bruised, bloody body.

The nearest houses other than Jenny's own were on Sanford Hill, a half mile through the woods. One of those houses was Mark Renkin's, and as I stood in the place they found her body, I knew my trajectory would take me there.

The edge of the cornfield was about a hundred yards from the road, so the body was assumed to be a dump job by someone who hadn't anticipated the farmer's morning walk. A small radius around the body was searched for evidence. No one combed the woods. They were out of the way between Jenny's house and the body. It didn't fit the narrative they wanted.

As I thought about marching toward Mark's house, my motivations became mush. My confidence imploded. If I found something near his house, could I go to the front door? Could I demand he tell me what he knew? Would he invite me in, convince me he wasn't involved, and then we would just talk? Talk until it was dark and then he would ask me to stay?

I shook my head at my own insanity. I hated him, right? I wanted so bad to find something in those woods, but I didn't know why. Part of me wanted to show Brandon up, prove I was right. Part of me wanted justice for Jenny. Part of me, a growing part, wanted something to point to Mark. I wanted him involved. I wanted to see him, to talk to him, to have him plead his innocence to me. More and more, though, I wanted him to be guilty, guilty of something unimaginable that would cement his status as a bad man so I could finally let go.

I meandered through the woods for over an hour. I was expecting a dark, scary, unforgiving forest that wouldn't think twice about allowing a murder inside, but at that hour, with the sun rising through the trees, it was so peaceful. The leaves were changing into shades of orange and red, the pine trees green as ever. Squirrels and other wildlife I didn't want to think about were busy preparing for winter, creating just enough of a soundtrack to keep my mind from wandering to a dark place.

I didn't find her backpack like I'd irrationally expected. I didn't find much of anything other than some empty beer cans that had been there for a lot longer than a few weeks. The trees began to thin, and I knew I was close to Mark's. I had no real navigation skills, so the first house I reached was actually the home of the Castletons, a well-known family with a handful of kids. I had been the same year as the oldest, Billy—a short-tempered wrestling star with the worst bacne. The Castletons lived a few houses before Mark's, so I stayed in the woods and wandered uphill.

After a few minutes, I saw the log siding. I loved that Mark lived in a log cabin, or at least a house manufactured to look like one. It was the perfect escape for me for years. Smoke billowed from the chimney. He was proud of his fireplace and the money he saved on heat. He fired that thing up at the first sign of winter. I remembered sweating in the afternoon with the house like a sauna. We'd laugh, strip down a few layers, and talk about going to the beach.

I inched toward the edge of the tree line, still disguised by a massive oak. It was after seven, but both cars were still in the driveway. Mark's green Blazer and Hunter Willoughby's navy Accord. I guess she stayed there a lot. I didn't know. I didn't want to know. The man who ended it with me so we could both live our lives before settling down had settled down. It felt like a lie, a great hoax to dispose of me. When we were ready, we were supposed to get back together. He hadn't come back for me.

The front door slammed shut, but I couldn't see it from where I stood. I waited until I saw Hunter stomping into the driveway toward her car.

"Hunter!" Mark shouted from where she had emerged.

My body tensed.

"I'm going to be late and so are you." She hustled to her car as he came into view, jogging from the front of the house.

"Wait!" he yelled, but she ignored him.

As she reached for the car door, he caught up and grabbed her arm. It was a firm, aggressive grip that stopped her in her tracks before he yanked her body around to face him.

From the woods I could see panic cross her face. His voice was calm, but his body language was intimidating. He never acted that way with me.

"You're overreacting," he said to her, possibly the worst thing anyone could say to someone.

"What's it going to take for you to fully commit to this? To us?" she asked.

"Is this about moving in?" he said, dismissing her feelings by citing a topic that must have been a sore subject for her.

"I don't know why I'm even with you. You make me hate myself. You do horrible things to me," she said, trying to turn away from him.

What had he done? As he held her arm, I couldn't help but wonder if he hit her, maybe once, maybe all the time. I couldn't process what I was hearing or seeing. This man I was watching wasn't my Mark. The only explanation was that they didn't have what we had.

Hunter held back tears and tried to hold her ground. After a beat, Mark released her arm with a violent shove that made her whole body fall back. She went with the motion and continued to spin away from him, climbing into the car without another word.

He moved closer to the vehicle. "I'm sorry, OK?" he said as she slammed the door in his face. He rested his arm on the roof and leaned down to her level, inches apart but separated by the glass. "Do you hear me? I'm sorry. Can we talk tonight?"

Hunter reversed with abandon, and Mark slammed his fist down on the top of the car before it slipped from his reach. I watched Mark watch her leave. He crossed his arms over a small stomach that had developed in the last eight years. He stayed in the driveway even after she was gone. He was just staring, a man admiring his property.

The world was silent until my phone screamed out a repetitive screeching ring that could be heard on Mars. It broke Mark's tranquil moment, and he spun around toward me. Of all the places to have perfect reception in this town. I ripped the phone from my pocket, but my grip was overaggressive, and when it caught on the edge of my pocket, it flew through the air, landing in a pile of leaves. I dropped to my knees, crawling toward the ringing, begging for it to stop.

I lunged forward, swiping across the screen, stopping the sound, answering the call. The screen lit up: BRANDON COLSEN. I grabbed the phone and crawled behind a tree, praying Mark had gone back inside.

"Virginia?" Brandon's voice projected from the phone in my hand.

"Shhh," I whispered, finally placing it to my ear.

"What's going on?"

"Sorry, I didn't mean to pick up. I'm busy. I'll call you back later, OK?"

"OK—"

"Don't call back," I said and hung up.

I peeked around the tree just in time to see Mark step into the woods, the leaves crackling under his feet. I whipped back behind the tree and said a small prayer to anyone who would listen.

Beep. Beep. Beep. A text message. I lifted the phone to silence it. It was from Brandon, that asshole. Across my screen read: GIL ANDERSON. 28 W. 47TH ST. NEW YORK, NY. Brandon had found him. From a name and a city, he found him in less than three days. I was a little impressed.

"Well, this is awkward," Mark said to my back as I stared at my phone, lost in the land of Brandon and Gil.

I turned to face him, having to look up from my desperate positioning among the leaves. "Great reception here," I joked, holding up my phone. What else could I say?

CHAPTER TWENTY-FOUR

JENNY

IT WAS BECOMING almost impossible for Jenny to sneak out. During the week, Linda had taken to sleeping downstairs on the couch, on guard and poised to catch Jenny in the act.

When her father came home, things went back to normal. Linda played doting housewife to an indifferent man and a terrified daughter. Jenny knew Linda wasn't telling him anything. Ever since he hadn't come home the previous weekend, she had completely changed her demeanor around him. Things were perfect; no need to stay in New York.

Jenny knew her only chance to sneak out would be on the weekends now. She laughed thinking about how her father used to be the one she was afraid of. The escape route was the same as it always was. Jenny slipped into her brown boots and was out the garage door without incident. Inside the garage, she found her old bike behind the unused recycle bins. It was pink, of course, with tassels on the handles. Jenny was proud of her independence, her defiance, and her persistence; she was not proud of traveling by princess bike. She walked it to the end of the driveway before mounting it. Her knees tapped against her elbows as she pedaled toward the center of town.

JENNY KNOCKED ON the door to apartment six. It was almost eleven. She had no idea if it was too late. She didn't know much about her sister other than what could be gleaned from Sunday dinners and the crap her parents would say after she left.

Virginia opened the door a crack in flannel pants and an old T-shirt. She looked like she had been woken from the dead. "Jenny?" she asked, opening the door all the way. "Is everything OK?" Her words cut in and out, and she coughed to wake up her voice.

"I was at Mallory's house and we got in a fight. Can I come in?" Poor Mallory, always the star of Jenny's lies. This time it was just geographically convenient; Mallory's family lived down the street. If she told Virginia she rode her bike all the way from her own house in the middle of the night, she would have a lot of explaining to do.

Virginia stepped aside to let her sister in. "Do you want to call Linda?"

"No, can I just hang out here for a little bit, then I'll go back? I don't want Mom to freak out," Jenny said, knowing Virginia had no idea what it meant for Linda to freak out. It sounded like typical teenager talk.

"I guess," Virginia said, less than enthusiastic. Jenny threw her coat off and plopped down on the couch while Virginia shut the door. She had never been inside before. It was nothing special, but it was Virginia's private space, free of Linda's knickknacks.

"Did I wake you up?"

"I sleep too much anyway," Virginia yawned, joining her sister on the couch.

"I, like, never sleep anymore," Jenny said, which had the benefit of sounding edgy while still being honest.

"How's school?" Virginia asked, like every adult asks a child they know nothing about.

"It's fine."

"Are you still skipping?"

"No, not really. I'm on thin ice at school and Mom and Dad are flipping out."

"They don't want you to turn into me." Virginia smiled. She accepted her standing in the family.

"What did you even do to make them hate you so much?"

"Who knows. I didn't become president of the United States."

"Is it because my mom isn't your mom?"

"I don't know, Dad gave up on me long before he even met your mother."

"When your mom died?"

"Jeez, a lot of hard-hitting questions. Is that your thing now? A million questions?"

"Sorry." Jenny ended that line of questioning. She scanned the apartment. It didn't look like Virginia had many guests. "Do you have a boyfriend?"

"Does it look like it?"

Jenny shrugged. "I don't know. I only see you on Sundays. It's not like you would bring a guy there. I wouldn't bring my boyfriend there."

"Do *you* have a boyfriend?"

"No, I just mean if I did . . ." She trailed off and reconsidered where she wanted this conversation to go. "Tons of girls in my class are having sex," she blurted out.

Virginia's eyes widened, caught off guard. "Good for them." It wasn't the reaction Jenny had expected. She'd thought she would get a lecture about being way too young to even think about sex.

"How old were you when you first . . . you know?"

Virginia thought for a second. "Fourteen."

Jenny considered the answer. It seemed like a good age. Younger than JP, older than her. "Was he your boyfriend?"

"Yes," Virginia answered, clearly not caring to elaborate.

"I don't know, having a boyfriend is a big deal. It seems like a lot of work. Wouldn't it be better to just have sex with a friend or something?" Jenny asked.

"You make it sound like you have to have sex. You don't have to have sex, you know?" Virginia clarified in her best role model attempt.

"I know. I'm just saying, it's not really that big of a deal, right? Like everyone makes such a big deal about the first time, but who ends up with the guy they first have sex with? No one. You're lucky if you even make it through high school together."

"How old are you?" Virginia looked at the young girl as if trying to match her face to her words.

"Thirteen," Jenny said. It didn't bother her that Virginia didn't know how old she was. The ignorance was mutual.

"You have some pretty profound thoughts on sex for thirteen."

"Do you think it's a big deal?" Jenny asked.

"Honestly, the sex isn't a big deal. *Love* is a big deal. I think they should warn kids about falling in love. That's where you really can get into trouble. Try not to fall in love until you're older. That's my advice."

It was actually kind of nice talking to her sister, and Jenny regretted screaming that she hated her that day in town. This was a nice memory to leave on, and maybe someday they could reconnect, when Jenny came back from Mexico. She would be older and happier; maybe Virginia would be too.

"Can we watch a movie?" Jenny asked, refocusing on the mission at hand.

Twenty minutes into some TV movie, Virginia passed out.

Jenny had a lot of practice sneaking around by now, and she took her time getting off the couch, practically rolling off so as not to disturb her sister in the slightest. She stood for a moment, making sure Virginia stayed a corpse.

There was really only one place someone would keep important documents in that apartment: a small desk pushed against the wall near the kitchenette. Jenny took light steps in its direction, flexing her calves and staying on the balls of her feet. The apartment had hardwood floors that begged to creak, and she missed the silence of socks on carpet.

She paused again for signs of life from Virginia once she reached the desk, but there were none. She slid open the thin drawer along the surface of the desk first. It was full of plastic takeout utensils and dipping-sauce packets, a result of its proximity to the kitchen. There were two larger drawers to the side, and the first was home to a potpourri of bills, junk mail, and receipts. It was like a catchall for adult responsibility. Jenny leafed through it a bit, but it was obvious the passport wasn't in there.

There was one drawer left. She pulled it open, panicking she wouldn't find what she was looking for, but there it was, right on top. She knew Virginia had a passport. Her parents still complained about a school trip they let her go on to Spain, something along the lines of if they had known she was going to need money from them for the rest of their lives, they would have saved on the trip, but to have actually found it . . . She couldn't believe it. Something had finally gone right.

Jenny flipped open the little blue book. Virginia looked young, seventeen or eighteen. She stared at the picture, worried about passing for her sister, but when she used her finger to cover Virginia's brown hair, the similarities were almost eerie, their father's dominant bone structure erasing their mothers' identities.

She slipped the passport into her back pocket. She couldn't wait to tell JP. All of a sudden, it felt real. There was a way out and she held the ticket—finally, something tangible. This was a turning point, a sign. She knew it.

Jenny was about to close the drawer and hightail it out of there when something caught her eye. Peeking out from underneath Virginia's high school diploma sat a stack of neatly folded lined notebook paper. The notes were destined for her attention because of their meticulous presentation, contrasting greatly with the contents of the previous drawers.

She glanced over at her sister—still breathing heavily, eyes closed, drool forming. There was a little time to snoop. Jenny grabbed a few off the top of the stack, Virginia's name written in identical handwriting on each one. She wasted no time opening the first one, guided by the weathered, permanent creases from being refolded a million times.

Ginny,

I love you to the moon, my little snail. School is so boring today. I can't wait until this day is over. I'm going to smother you with snuggles until you can't breathe and kisses are the only thing that will save you.

Love, Mark

P.S. I can see down your shirt when you reach under your desk. :)

Whoa, Jenny thought. Scandalous. This must be who Virginia lost her virginity to. Someone worth saving notes from for all these years. Who was this Mark? What had happened? With all the crap on the Internet, who knew a stack full of handwritten notes could be so intriguing?

Jenny unfolded the next one.

Virginia,

You did great on your test. Derivatives are nothing to joke about and you've mastered them. I felt weird about giving you the highest grade, but it isn't favoritism, I promise. Of course, that doesn't mean I'm not going to reward you. Tonight I'm going to show you how proud I am. I hope you can stay the night. You might be too tired to walk home.

Love, Mark

P.S. It was so hard not to touch you in class today.

Holy shit. Mark was her teacher. Mark was Mr. Renkin. Gross! Jenny's head was swirling. Virginia was sleeping with Mr. Renkin. He was her teacher and they were doing it. Was it still happening? That day when they were all in town and everyone was being weird.

Were they there together? He was with Ms. Willoughby, though. What was going on?

Jenny buried the three letters she had plucked off the top into her other back pocket, threw on her coat, and ran out the door. This was something she could use. She just didn't know how yet.

CHAPTER TWENTY-FIVE

VIRGINIA

I STAYED SITTING in the wet leaves. I knew once I got up, it would be real. Mark stood four feet away, hands on his hips, looking down at me. It was hard to read his expression. Maybe I was going to find out if he was capable of murder today after all.

I knew if I started talking, I was only going to dig myself into a hole. Once I started talking to Mark, I couldn't stop until I had admitted every feeling, thought, and secret in my head. I fought the urge to speak as long as I could, mere seconds that felt like hours. There must have been some story I could tell, some reason I was in the woods behind his house.

"I . . ." I opened my mouth emitting some sound, hoping a concise, reasonable story would come out once I started.

"Virginia!" someone shouted through the woods, and we both turned toward the voice. A young boy in a ratty camouflage jacket stomped through the leaves and branches toward us. The crunch of his footsteps was loud; we should have heard him sooner. He must have been standing still—and close—for a long time, but he was acting as if he had just discovered us. I wondered if Mark realized it too.

"Virginia," he repeated, now close enough to stop walking and talk to us. I didn't recognize him at all, but he knew me. "I told you not to take the shortcut through the woods. The leaves are wet and all over. It's hard to stick to the path." He extended his hand to mine and pulled me to my feet.

"JP, right?" Mark asked the boy.

"Yeah."

Mark was trying to process the information. He looked to me for answers. "You know him?" he asked, which felt accusatory after JP's greeting, whoever JP was.

"Yes," I said without hesitation.

JP took over again before I could get myself in trouble. "Virginia is my tutor."

A tutor. That was a nice thought, that someone would hire me to have influence over their child.

"In math," I added, to be part of the lie and hit Mark where it hurt.

He just nodded, having no choice but to believe it. "She was always great at math. I had Virginia in my class a long time ago."

Not that long, I thought.

Mark looked at me like he was replaying footage of our past. I wanted him to stop. The way he was looking at me, it was nostalgic. It was warm and it let hope creep in—not the flawed generic hope that kept me going but the specific Mark-and-me hope that kept me from moving on.

"We better get started," I said, turning to JP and breaking Mark's gaze and its power over me.

"See you around, Mr. Renkin." JP turned back toward his house.

I stepped to follow him, looking briefly up at Mark as I passed him, a small smile escaping that I quickly sucked back in. He stood there watching us walk away for what felt like an unusually long time. *Go back in the house*, I thought. Finally, I heard leaves crunching behind me where we left him. I didn't turn back. I looked forward at the back of the lanky teenager who was a mystery all his own.

I FOLLOWED JP onto his front porch before it seemed safe to address reality. Calling it a porch was generous. It was some rotting elevated wood slats in front of the doorway. He opened the door, content with me following him inside.

"So, I'm going to go," I said, unsure if that was rude. Did I owe him something for saving me?

He turned back to me. "Oh, yeah, sorry. I knew your sister. That's how I knew who you were."

I just nodded, still not sure if it was OK for me to leave yet.

"You were spying on him," he said, nodding toward Mark's house.

"No, I wasn't."

"Then what were you doing in the woods?"

"I don't have to explain anything to you."

"Whatever, I guess I should have just left you there then," he said.

"Sorry, no . . . I appreciate it. It's personal, OK? But I wasn't spying on him. I was just in the woods and that's where I ended up. It was bad timing I guess."

"You mean because he and Ms. Willoughby were fighting?"

"Who's the one spying now?" He was standing still in those woods too, taking in a show. "Do they fight a lot?" I asked, hoping my savior knew more about their relationship.

He just shrugged. "I don't know. I try to stay out of people's business."

"Except mine."

"I guess. You can go now."

"OK," I said, backing off the porch. "Thank you."

"No prob," he said as he walked inside and shut the door.

THE QUICKEST ROUTE back to my car was through the woods, but I was feeling less adventurous. I walked down JP's driveway toward the road. The day had just started and already sufficiently sucked. Then I remembered Brandon's text. He'd found Gil. I quickened my pace, not a run but more than my morose tromp.

One more bend and I would be at the bottom of the hill. That's when the car pulled up. A green Blazer that decimated my eager, proactive mind-set and left me empty. The passenger window slid down as the car slowed next to me.

"You need a ride?" Mark asked, leaning over from the driver's seat.

"No, it's fine," I said, trying not to look directly at him.

He drove away, and I thought I had dodged a bullet until he pulled over on the side of the road ahead of me. He turned the car off and climbed out. He was waiting for me.

I had few options to get away from him, but it didn't matter; this was what I wanted deep inside. I kept my pace as steady as possible until I was almost at him. "What are you doing?" I asked.

"That was a quick tutoring session."

"What do you want me to say?" I said as I reached him.

"I knew you weren't his tutor. It's seven in the morning. He has school soon, and you aren't an early riser." His voice softened on the last part, emphasizing he knew something about me.

"Things change."

"They do."

"He knew my sister. That's why I was going to see him. I don't know why we lied."

"I don't need an explanation," he said as he stepped toward me. I curled my hands into nervous fists, but I didn't retreat. "I like seeing you. I don't like it when you ignore me in town." He took another step closer.

He didn't elaborate on the last time I had ignored him in town. It wasn't like most times. I had been caught. He caught me, and we had looked at each other in an unavoidable way until I had to flee. It was his birthday and I *was* trying to be seen, but not like that. Not in front of Hunter and not in front of my sister. Not me panicking. Not me running.

His birthday. I always found a way to be seen on his birthday. Every year, I told myself it would be the last time. Every year, I failed. When we were together, his birthday was a big deal. I planned it for months. I would cook; I would arrange surprises; I babysat tiny Jenny like crazy for weeks to earn enough money to pull it all off. That night in mid-September, he could do anything to me. He didn't have to ask; he didn't have to be cautious or ease into things, testing the waters. He could do anything. It made him so happy.

The weight a school-age girl gives to a birthday is almost inexplicable. At that age, they're so rare. You can count them on your fingers and toes. Birthdays still seem so very special, and that's how I treated his birthday even though he'd had plenty. I knew it was an attention he would never get elsewhere. It's an enthusiasm that only an adolescent brain can generate.

That's why, once a year, I found a way to be seen. I showered and did my hair; I put on real clothes; I applied makeup, all just enough to look fucking banging without appearing like I was trying to. Just more like, maybe I looked like that all the time because I was so successful and well-adjusted without him. Then I would plant myself around town, waiting in my car until I saw him, jumping out with perfect timing to cross his eye line. I didn't make eye contact. I could never know if he ever even saw me, but believing he did filled me with such endorphins that I thought maybe I would be all right after all.

By midnight, when I realized he had not been so enraptured by memories and my success-oozing beauty that he was at my doorstep begging to have me back, I would crawl into bed, cry to the point I might have an aneurysm, and vow not to do it the next year. This year, though, I knew he saw me and I knew why he didn't show up on my doorstep. Jenny appeared out of nowhere and I was unprepared. The fragility of my act was not structured for flexibility in the face of the unexpected. I reacted like a freak, ten times more so in my head than anywhere else. The crying that night was worse than any years in recent memory. But now, now Mark was standing in front of me, telling me he liked seeing me, telling me he didn't like when I ignored him. It was a tempting redemption I struggled to fend off.

I turned my head away. I wasn't strong enough to say anything. He entered my space. His hot breath cut through the fall air. I could smell his scent, and with it came memories. I felt like I was sixteen again, when we were at our absolute best.

"What about Hunter?" I asked as I turned to face him again.

"Fuck Hunter," he spit out as he lunged toward me, putting both hands around my face. The force pushed me back against the Blazer. Before I could react, he was kissing me.

I knew I should push him off. I knew he didn't deserve me. He was an asshole, a pedophile, a cheater, but I wanted it and I let him kiss me.

His hands left my face and slid into my jacket, cupping my waist. Every second I let him kiss me undid years of healing. I didn't want to go back to that dark place he had left me in. I was finally feeling alive. I was hunting Jenny's killer, outsmarting Detective Colsen, leaving my apartment regularly. I couldn't go back to that place.

I put my hands on his chest and pushed him back. He seemed shocked. I'd never said no to him before.

He inched back toward me, but I slid off the Blazer, allowing for more room to evade him.

"This life I made after you . . ." He shook his head. "It's not what I want. I'm miserable. Ginny, please . . ."

"I hate when you call me that."

"Isn't this what you want?"

I honestly didn't know. Part of me wanted to let him screw me right there against the Blazer in the middle of the road. Part of me wanted him to take me back to his place and hold me as we sat on his swing, talking about the future. Part of me wanted him to have a heart attack and drop dead at my feet. But the largest part of me wanted to walk away, to not look back, to cry alone in my apartment that night but never give him the satisfaction of knowing how I felt and what the past eight years had been like for me.

"No," I said.

I started walking away before he could respond. I was walking away from Mark Renkin. For eight years, all I'd wanted was the power to say no. To have the last word. For him to regret ever letting me go. I was done with Mark Renkin, and I hoped he would never affect my life ever again.

"Then stop fucking calling me," he yelled at my back.

I stopped in my tracks. I turned, looking at him like he was crazy. "What are you talking about?"

"The calls, almost every Saturday. I know it's you. I have caller ID."

"I call you?"

"Jesus, how messed up are you? You don't know you're calling me?"

I choked hard on the emptiness in my throat. Is this what I was doing when I was blacking out? I was embarrassed, ashamed, and afraid of myself. I didn't want to hear any more. I started walking away again, as fast as I could without actually breathing.

CHAPTER TWENTY-SIX

JENNY

THE FIRST CHANCE JENNY GOT, Monday afternoon, she stomped up Sanford Hill in her well-worn brown boots. She was trying not to get ahead of herself, but the letters in her pocket felt as good as currency. Information is power, and she had her hands on one hell of a bombshell. There were a million reasons Mr. Renkin wouldn't want this getting out. He would lose his job, Ms. Willoughby would leave him, he could even go to prison.

She climbed the stairs onto Mr. Renkin's front porch and took a deep breath before knocking on the door. The woods were silent, and she could hear Mr. Renkin skipping down the stairs inside. This was it. It didn't have to be complicated. It was a straightforward deal.

He opened the door, expecting an adult but finding a teenager.

"Jenny?"

"Hi."

"What are you doing here? Are you OK?" He looked out behind her like he expected to see someone chasing her.

"We need to talk," she said like she planned. Short, direct sentences that would command his attention.

"Is that so?" He wasn't taking her seriously.

"About my sister."

He released the door and tucked his hands into the pockets of his khaki teacher pants. He rocked on his feet, waiting for her follow-up statement.

"Can I come in?" she asked, not wanting to conduct serious business on the front porch like a Girl Scout. She was selling secrets, not cookies.

He backed up, leaving his hands in his pockets but pushing the door open with his backside. Jenny entered the rustic living room. It was bigger than it looked from the outside. The whole floor was an open layout with high ceilings lined with wooden beams.

He closed the door behind her and stood in the entranceway as she took in the house. She had never been in a teacher's house before. It was just a house, but a teacher-student relationship was so complicated and regimented that it felt almost forbidden to be in there. If kids at school knew, her popularity would skyrocket. Mallory would die.

She took the step down from the entranceway, now officially in his living room. "Mr. Renkin, I have a proposition for you."

"Let's hear it," he said, too jovial for her liking.

"I know about your sexual relationship with my sister." She crossed her arms as a symbolic mic drop.

His green eyes shrank in a way that made Jenny uncomfortable, like he was zooming in on her. "Did she send you here?"

"No, Virginia has no idea." She hadn't really considered the repercussions for her sister. Would he tell her? She didn't want her sister to be mad. "I found something . . . notes."

Mr. Renkin finally removed his hands from his pockets and mirrored her stance. He looked unamused and anxious to see where this was going. His unique eyes were no longer his best feature; instead they suddenly seemed the wrong color for his face, as if he had become possessed.

In her heart, Jenny felt the foundations of fear. She had walked in holding all the cards, but standing in the shadow of an agitated adult man, she felt her power dwindling. She soldiered on. "The notes are from you to my sister, when she was in high school and you were her teacher. You were having a sexual relationship. I have nothing to gain from telling anyone and you have a lot to lose. All I am asking for is five thousand dollars and I will give you the notes and we can forget this ever happened."

Mr. Renkin laughed, a nervous and guilty laugh. "I don't believe you. I barely knew your sister. There were no letters." He left a sloppy grin on his face, waiting for her next move.

"Five thousand dollars," she repeated.

He broke his stance and breezed past her into the kitchen. Only a small island separated him from the living room, where she remained. Jenny didn't know how to react. Was this a break from negotiations? Did he need a snack or something?

"Can I get you anything?" he asked like he hadn't heard a word she said. He grabbed an apple from the fruit bowl and slid a large knife from a wood block that housed an array of smaller knives more appropriate for the apple.

Jenny took a defiant step toward the kitchen, not wanting him to take control of the situation but keeping the island between them just in case. "No," she said.

He drove the knife into the apple, separating it into two halves. "Look, this was very brave of you coming here, but it's not going to happen. What's going to happen is you're going to give me the notes, you're going to leave, and you are never going to talk to anyone about this ever again." He split one of the halves again, and Jenny flinched at the wet snap of the knife hitting the cutting board.

She rested her hands on the island, supporting herself as she leaned in. "Five. Thousand. Dollars." She was going toe-to-toe with this man, and it was empowering. Fuck Linda and her dad. Fuck Gil. Fuck Mark Renkin. She was young, but she was savvy, and if they wanted to underestimate her, they would pay.

He placed the knife down on the counter and glared at her for a beat. This was not the face of everyone's favorite teacher. This was the face of a proud man who was being threatened. He stepped back around the island, removing the barrier between them.

"I don't think you understand," he said, seizing Jenny's arms, a jolt that decimated all the courage she had gathered. "Where are they? You're going to give me whatever it is you think you have."

His hands on her and the threat of violence that carried was not a line she could handle him crossing. "OK," Jenny choked out, appropriately terrified.

He released her, shaking his head as if to scold her, justifying his actions as necessary to combat this nuisance. He backed away, convinced he'd won, but the space allowed for Jenny's instinct to flee to take over. She waited for him to turn his head, and when he did, she ran for the door.

He had no choice but to chase her, to stop her and try to de-escalate the situation. Jenny had miscalculated everything, especially the time it would take her to get to the door. She knew he was close, and when she turned to see just how close, she forgot the step. Her foot met a dead end, bringing her crashing down, the side of her skull slamming against the hardwood floor.

She reached for her head, the sharp pain pulsing from one side and spreading to the other in waves. Her eyes were heavy, and she fought to keep them open as she rolled onto her back. A second later, Mr. Renkin stood over her.

He dropped to his knees. He unzipped her jacket and she tensed all over. Everything was cloudy, muffled. She felt him at her pants. His hands were all over her. She tried kicking, but it was no use. Her head was throbbing, her eyelids closing. His hands crawled back into her jacket. She wanted him to stop. Was this what happened with her sister? What had she done?

Suddenly, his hands were gone. All she felt was the cold floor and the fire in her head. She fought to open her eyes one more time and saw his blurry body stand. In his hand were the letters. Her eyes closed. She couldn't feel the floor. She couldn't feel the fire. She felt nothing.

CHAPTER TWENTY-SEVEN

VIRGINIA

I SWUNG MY ARMS, trying to get back to my car as quickly as possible. I knew I was blacking out—that was the point—but how could my unconscious self build such a wall from my conscious self? Was I insane? Was I on the verge of a mental breakdown, or was I just a raging addict? I didn't feel like an addict. I didn't crave alcohol or drugs. My Saturday-night drinking binge was more of a ritual. If I was out with friends, no one would bat an eyelash. Being alone in my apartment was giving it a stigma. Whatever the reason, I could never do it again, just like all the other things I told myself I would never do again.

I opened the outgoing call log on my cell phone, scrolling and scrolling. I didn't see his number anywhere. Was he lying? Did he make it up to mess with my mind? Why would he do that? Then it clicked. I wasn't allowed to have a cell phone in high school. I had Mark's number memorized. That fucking landline in my apartment. Sometimes I knocked it off the table, and sometimes, I guess, I picked it up.

I felt nauseous. All these years, I'd thought I was doing the right thing. No contact with Mark. That's what every book, every website, said to do. Was it possible these phone calls that I wasn't even conscious of making were setbacks? Every Saturday resetting the clock? Was that why I was still dressing up on every birthday? Was that why after eight years I was still alone, still pining, still afraid to go to sleep without the TV on? So stupid. So weak. I was disgusted. This was not who I wanted to be, but wanting just wasn't enough.

ONCE I WAS safely back in my car, I called Brandon. I needed a distraction. Brandon was my distraction. Solving my dead sister's murder was my distraction.

"Hey," he answered. "Are you OK? What was that about?"

"Nothing."

"I made some calls. Gil's in the wind. Hasn't been to work in weeks. Mail was overflowing. It's a dead end."

"I wouldn't call it a dead end. I would say it's pretty suspicious, no?" I barked at him, at a breaking point and worried he was relapsing back into his myopic crime-solving self.

"I didn't mean a dead end—that was the wrong expression. I just mean, sending cops to the apartment was a dead end."

I relaxed. *Stay with me, Brandon.*

"So, what now?" Police work was slow. I wanted to start kicking down doors.

"Well, we have a few problems." His use of "we" wasn't lost on me. "People like Benjy, I mean as 'the guy.' It was easy. It makes sense. This poking around I'm doing is drawing attention. My superiors aren't exactly thrilled that I'm making noise on a closed case."

"Don't tell me these are excuses, tell me this is setup for a big *but*."

"*But* . . . I can't just turn my back on this. You would never forgive me."

"And *you* would never be able to live with yourself?"

"That too," he said with a stifled laugh. "I took tomorrow off. Told the guys I needed a little rest and relaxation. I was thinking about taking a trip to New York City."

Finally, my annoying, lazy, by-the-book detective was becoming the renegade I was looking for, but I had to remain calm if I wanted to stay in the *we*.

"I hear the city is lovely this time of year," I said.

"You could join me. We could do dinner or a show or something."

"Just to be clear, we're going there to follow up on Gil, right?"

He broke into a laugh. "Yes, Virginia."

I smiled and for almost four full seconds forgot about my interaction with Mark.

I GOT BACK to my apartment after running every errand I could possibly think of. I didn't want to be home. I didn't want to be alone, but I didn't have much of a choice. I set my bag down by the door. That spot on the floor seemed as good as any other. The loneliness gathering in the pit of my stomach was confusing. I had been a loner for years, but was it all a lie? Deep down, did I know I still had Mark? Is that what was getting me through the days?

That was gone now. It was my choice. I tried to find power in that. It didn't work. I didn't have friends. When I was with Mark, I didn't need friends. In hindsight, a huge mistake. I thought about calling Brandon again. Was he my friend? No. People who have romantic feelings for you aren't your friends. Like everyone else, they just want something from you. I would see him in the morning anyway. I just needed a distraction until then.

Then I remembered Linda. I'd promised my father I would check on that mess, make sure she wasn't lying in the bathtub with her wrists slit because her favorite toy was dead and her husband didn't like her enough to spend more than two days a week in her presence.

I COULDN'T REMEMBER the last time I'd gone to the house on a day other than Sunday. Even the day they found Jenny was a Sunday. It was like church, a place you go to feel horribly judged out of forced ritualistic obligation.

I flipped on the light, revealing the kitchen in shambles. There were dishes in the sink, mostly glasses, very few plates. The stools against the kitchen island were pulled out and askew. Any other house and I wouldn't have thought much about it, but this was Linda's kitchen. She always kept it immaculate. Was that all an act for my father, or was this evidence of her unraveling because of Jenny's death?

"Linda?" I yelled out into the sleeping house and waited for her obnoxious voice to call back.

"Linda?" I said again as I entered the living room, letting her name bounce off the walls. I pulled the chain on one of her colorful Tiffany lamps, illuminating the room. It was in an equal state of disarray. Two blankets were bunched up on the couch, an empty glass without a coaster on the table. Anarchy. Still no sign of Linda, and I was starting to worry what I might find.

I grabbed the banister and hoisted myself up the first few steps, repeating the action until I reached the top and spotted the first evidence of life. A small glow came from the crack under the upstairs bathroom door.

"Linda?" I put my ear against the door and listened. Nothing. I knocked gently without removing my ear. A barely audible moan came from inside. It didn't sound healthy. Was it too late to leave? Could I resist the temptation of what was behind mystery door number one? Never.

I twisted the knob and pushed the door open to collect my prize.

Linda was sprawled across the bathroom floor in just her underwear, more than I ever wanted to see of my stepmother. A strong stench of vomit slapped me in the face. It was on the toilet seat, it was ground into the rug, it was congealed to her hair. She didn't turn to look at me, keeping her face toward the base of the toilet, but she moaned again to prove she was alive.

"Jesus, Linda." I suspected she had helped herself to a bottle of Drano, but as my nose adjusted to the strength of the smell, the stench of alcohol presented itself. I knew the fusion of hard alcohol and vomit all too well.

I turned the shower on full blast and lifted her into the tub, not caring much about the temperature. She let out a weak scream when the cold water hit her body, but I didn't care. She wouldn't remember. I squirted bodywash on top of her, anything to mask the smell as I waited for the vomit to wash away.

Once she was clean, I turned the shower off and patted her down with a towel. I left her in the tub. The chances of her puking again were high, and I wanted to save myself the effort later. She slumped to the side, eyes closed, and started breathing heavily. She was out for now.

———

AFTER WATCHING SITCOM reruns for a couple of hours and eating about six granola bars since Linda's last in-tub puke, I felt confident enough to put her to bed and head home.

I turned left onto Main Street without coming anywhere close to a complete stop at the sign. Ten o'clock was late for a small town and I was more than alone on the road.

The only business between Linda's house and my apartment was the town pub, and as I passed it, I caught a glimpse of something I couldn't ignore. It was obstructed by the dumpster in the back of the small parking lot where it escaped nearly all of the moonlight. I don't know why I was even looking, but I was and I saw it. A navy Accord was in the parking lot, Hunter Willoughby's navy Accord.

The pub was devoid of any charm, not a place you would expect to find anyone short of a full-blown alcoholic. The best thing the pub had going for it was that it seemed immune to town gossip. Gossip craved scandal, people looking for cracks in their friends and neighbors to tear them down with. A bunch of drunks living in a constant state of rock bottom wasn't interesting to anyone. It made the building invisible.

Fueled by the possibility of Hunter having a fraction of the damage I saddled myself with, my car full-on Herbie-the-Love-Bugged into the parking lot. It couldn't have been *me*. Clearly going into that pub to talk to Hunter Willoughby was not something *I* wanted to do.

When I stepped through the rotting wooden door frame, the lights were so weak, I thought the place might be closed. This was possibly a watering hole for raccoons, there was so little light. The bar was directly in line with the entrance, and behind it was Monty, the man in his late sixties who owned the place. He wore a beautiful stained gray T-shirt and was filling a beer from one of two taps. There were four men at the bar, all with comparable portly body types and blotchy red faces. The only one I knew for sure was Boomer, the famed town drunk. I wondered if the other drunks were jealous of his notoriety.

Monty looked up from the tap at the sound of the door closing behind me. "Must be ladies' night," he said, laughing. "I didn't prepare anything, so first one's on the house."

I took the glass he slid toward me and scanned the room. There were a handful of no-frills tables along the right-side wall that must have been remnants of the year the pub tried to serve food. Hunter sat alone at one of them, peering over her bottle at me, my entrance an unavoidable distraction in the small space.

I approached her, and she watched me the entire way.

"Hey," I said.

"Come here often?" She smiled like we were sharing a similar shame.

Was it too soon to ask what Mark had done to her? Ask if they were breaking up? Probably.

"I'm not even drinking." She laughed and pointed at her nearly full bottle of beer. "I don't know what I'm doing here." She seemed chatty and vulnerable for someone not drinking, but she was having trouble making eye contact.

"Honestly, I saw your car in the parking lot," I said, sliding into the chair across from her.

She looked up at me at that point, but held it for only a second.

"Why did you want to get a drink with me the other night?" I asked. After everything with Mark, I was dying to know.

"Ridiculous, right?" She smiled. "I know we weren't exactly friends in high school." That was an interesting way to put it. The only direct interaction I could remember offhand was when I had the misfortune of being alone in the bathroom with her. She was having some sort of embarrassing stomach issue and clearly thought she was by herself. When she realized there was a witness, she demanded to know who I was, so I lifted my feet up and hid in the stall for over an hour. Not exactly friends.

"I was hoping, maybe, you would want to talk about Jenny," she said, looking almost ashamed to be asking.

The cartoon physicality of my reaction would have been to flip backward over my chair in shock. Like a true asshole, my brain had been 100 percent Mark since seeing him in the woods. Even the prospect of hunting Gil had been only momentary relief. Hunter was thinking about my poor dead sister while I was moping around like some kind of jilted Juliet.

"OK," I said.

Hunter picked at the label of her beer bottle, a rumored sign of sexual frustration, but I was reaching. "It's just really, really fucked up," she muttered.

"Did you know her?" I asked. I knew she did from Mark, but I played dumb. I wasn't really sure what was happening. I took a generous swig from my beer while I waited for her answer. Drinking would be fine as long as I laid off the pills, a justification I could live with.

"I did," she said as she brushed her hair behind her ear. "I'm a guidance counselor at the school, did you know that?"

"Yes," I said, forgetting almost immediately that I was worried about revealing I knew more about her than I should.

"I was seeing Jenny a lot. About once a week." Hunter's voice cracked, and I was seized with fear that she would start crying or something. She recovered. "I think maybe . . . I don't know . . . This is hard to say . . . but I feel guilty."

What was I supposed to say to that? It was my role to feel guilty. She was my sister, and I was the one who had fucked up when it came to her. I wanted to hate Hunter, but the prospect of someone possibly understanding the way I was feeling, and handling it just as poorly, brought color to my cheeks.

"Why would you say that?" I asked.

"It was literally my job to help her and . . . It's just crazy. I thought she was fine; I envied how fine I thought she was. Did I miss something? Could I have prevented this? Intervened before it was too late?" She swallowed, trying to pull back from the deep.

"I think about that too." I paused. "I was such a shitty sister."

She shrugged. I enjoyed the space we were in where neither one of us felt it necessary to convince the other that her guilt and fears were wrong.

Hunter put her beer to her lips and committed to drinking instead of just staring at it. I did the same. The chugging gave me space to think. What was I doing? There were a thousand reasons to get the hell out of there, but I was kind of into it. I wanted to live in the dark space for a bit. I wanted company in the dark space.

"Did Jenny ever say anything . . ." I debated about confidentiality or whatever, but I wasn't a cop. "Anything about a man named Gil?"

"Who's Gil?"

"No one." I shook my head. Her answer was enough to know that was a dead end. "Can I ask you something?"

"Obviously." She laughed while motioning to the bartender for another round.

"What was she into? What did you guys talk about? Are you allowed to say?"

"Fuck it, I don't care. I don't know what she was into. We mostly just talked about what she *wasn't* into. Pageants, cheerleading, she really hated this little brat Mallory Murphy."

Fuck, fuck, fuck, why was Hunter Willoughby so likable? When did this happen? Or was she only unlikable in the first place because she had what I wanted? Just like Jenny.

"Do you know her?" she asked. "Mallory?"

"Not really, I know of her. I try not to get mixed up in high school drama."

"High school drama is my life," she joked. "Fuck . . . Fuck, I'm swearing a lot."

"Must be the ambiance," I said as Monty brought us two more beers.

"In high school I knew you were hooking up with Mark," she blurted out, bringing the new beer to her mouth to steady her bottom lip, which quivered as the words unfolded. People had a habit of doing that to me, blurting things out that for most would require a preface and a bit of sugarcoating. I don't know why. I was used to it, but I didn't like it. Was it flattering in that it seemed like I could take it? Or did they just not care?

"What?" I asked, shocked. Was Hunter Willoughby really the type of person who could have kept that a secret? Did Mark know she knew? Could I ask that question?

"I saw him rub your butt once," she explained.

"Rub my butt?" I couldn't help but find humor in her words, a humor I assumed was intended to mask the weight of the confession.

"Mm-hmm. It was after school and no one was around, but I

forgot a book under my desk and I went back to the classroom and looked through the little window and you were sitting there and he was leaning over you. You dropped your pencil, and when you reached down to pick it up, he put his hand on your ass. You smiled all googly-eyed like that was a very welcome and common practice."

"Shit. Why didn't you say anything?"

"Because I wanted it to be me, and if anyone found out, they would have fired him or arrested him or something," she tried to explain. "I don't know. It made sense at the time. It's less digestible now that I'm saying it out loud."

"Well, I guess it all worked out."

We both fell silent for a beat, imagining the fantasy that things really had worked out for the better.

"Does Mark know?" I decided to go for it.

She took a swig from her beer. "Yeah, it sounds stupid now, but that's kind of how we got together . . . This feels weird. I should stop."

"No, keep going. It's all in the past," I lied.

"I got too drunk at the faculty Christmas party last year. God, it already sounds so pathetic." She shook her head. "He invited me back to his place, and I ended up admitting what I had seen all those years ago. Pillow talk. I thought it would be sexy to have this little secret between us. So fucked up. I'm sorry."

"Don't apologize to me." I smiled. "Christmas parties are pretty wild."

She laughed hard at that, and it actually felt kind of good to make her feel better. Don't ask me why it made her laugh and don't ask why it made me feel good. Nothing was going as planned.

"You like to drink, don't you?" she asked out of nowhere.

"I guess so." I wasn't sure if she was trying to insult me. Was this all an elaborate setup to go Jerry Springer on me for my past with Mark? Scream at me to leave her man alone? Did she know about the phone calls? Was I a complete idiot for embracing the camaraderie?

"I've never been good at it. I pass out or fall asleep before I get to have any fun. But let's try, huh?" Without waiting for an answer, she motioned to the bartender for shots.

I *was* a good drinker, and many drinks later, I was comfortably buzzed and Hunter was hammered. As I entered the euphoria of the buzz, I was able to let go of the baggage between us. I was even able to let go of the thought that I was technically having a girls' night, which was not something I had ever done as an adult.

"Do you know what I hate about this town?" Hunter asked, leaning across the table at me now. "I hate that I think that I like it. How lame do I have to be to want to live here? Why don't I want to go to Europe and meet a man with a mustache or live in a bustling city where I have to hail cabs in the wind?"

"It's not for everyone," I offered.

"What do you want?"

I thought about what I wanted, what I would do if I weren't crippled by a broken heart and had a passion for any part of life. "Maybe to live in an RV and drive around exchanging pleasantries with strangers, but never actually having to get to know anyone."

Hunter leaned back in a full-body laugh at my pathetic hopes and dreams. "Maybe I'll join you."

"That kind of defeats the point." I laughed, denying every thought that maybe it wouldn't be the end of the world.

"How do you know if there's something better out there?" she asked. "The grass is always greener on the other side, right? But that just means stick with what you have. That can't be right. It's kind of a fucked-up saying. Like, if you think maybe there is something better out there for you, then you're some asshole who will never be content. It's like the universe has to give you an undeniable sign that there could be something more for you out there to make it OK to pursue it."

She was talking about Mark maybe? "Are you content?" I pushed.

"Who the hell knows? Are you content?"

"No," I admitted without reservation.

Monty appeared in my periphery for the first time without drinks in hand. "Closin' up, ladies."

"Boo," Hunter protested in jest.

"It's been great having ya. Give me a warning next time. I'll get some curtains or something."

"You don't have any windows," I reminded him as he headed back to the bar to push the drunks out with a stick.

Hunter swung her legs out from under the table and rose to her feet with the grace of a Weeble. I followed, looking much better in my own head at least. I watched her shuffle, pause, resteady herself multiple times from our table to the parking lot, and as she fumbled around in her purse for her keys, the anxiety of doing the right thing had me instantly regretting ever stopping at the pub in the first place. An entire night of enjoyment could easily be erased by one awkward moment.

"I don't think you should drive," I said.

"I'm fine," she insisted.

"Look, I live right down the street. See that blue building? Right there."

She looked up and squinted to see it.

"Just come over. Have some tea or something. Sober up a little bit."

Hunter fumbled for her keys for a few more seconds before giving up. "Fine." She smiled and hooked her arm through mine for balance and warmth. This was SO weird.

Inside my apartment, I sat her on my tiny couch and headed to the microwave. A fresh box of tea bags sat on the mini fridge.

While the mug spun in the microwave, I watched her lift her legs onto the couch and roll to her side. This was what Mark liked to look at. Did I get it? I guess so.

I placed the mug down on the coffee table as she fought to keep her eyes open.

"You can stay," I offered, giving her permission to stop the fight. I pulled a blanket from my bed and covered her. I didn't even have the urge to suffocate her with a pillow.

I crawled into bed and drifted off to the sounds of Hunter fucking Willoughby's drunk breathing. It was kind of nice.

CHAPTER TWENTY-EIGHT

JENNY

"JENNY . . . JENNY!"

She heard her name. She felt the hand on her shoulder, tossing her awake. Her eyes fluttered open. Above her were dark mahogany beams. She stared at one of the knots. As she focused on the perfect imperfection, she found clarity and shot up into a sitting position. Her head was pounding.

Jenny was on the leather couch in his living room with a blanket over her. Mr. Renkin sat on the coffee table next to her, his hand retreating from her shoulder.

"Are you OK?" he asked as if he had just found her there.

She was anything but OK. She nodded anyway.

"You need to go now," he said, reaching his hand out to help her up. She took it, not wanting to. "It's OK."

Had she been dreaming? Because he seemed completely unaware of the horrible things he had just done to her. Did he hope maybe she didn't remember?

"C'mon," he said. "Hurry up."

In a fog, Jenny walked to the door. He opened it for her and she stepped through.

"Don't come back here. It's not appropriate," he said.

Jenny nodded and he shut the door in her face. Her throat was closing and she couldn't speak. She found her footing as she climbed off the porch; then she started running as fast as she could. She made it to the end of the driveway before stopping, keeling over, and sucking for breath. It wasn't coming.

A car coming up the hill announced itself with the rev of its engine around the bend where the incline built. Jenny pulled herself together and jumped over the ditch, scrambling up the small bank into the edge of the woods. She ducked behind the first tree as the navy Accord drove past and pulled into Mr. Renkin's driveway.

No, Ms. Willoughby, Jenny thought. *Stay away from him.* She could do so much better. She needed a Mallory in her life to point out his inadequacy and find her someone worthier.

Jenny slid back down the bank into the ditch. She had no idea what time it was. The sun had nearly set. How long had she been out? Whatever it was, it was too late. She couldn't face her mother now. Wasn't one assault enough? Jenny was playing dangerous games. Why couldn't she stop?

JENNY BURST THROUGH the front door of JP's house. He came out of his room to investigate the noise and she met him in the hallway, throwing her arms around him. She didn't care what he thought. She needed comfort. Before he could push her away, or call her a baby, she reached up and kissed him. She expected him to pull away, but he didn't. He stayed still, their lips stuck together.

Jenny guided his mouth open. She wanted more. She hated that he thought she was too inexperienced to be kissed for real. He followed her lead and then took charge. It was new, it was scary, and it washed away her pain. She completely lost control. The euphoria turned to nerves, and she pushed against his chest until their mouths were apart. She stepped back while JP held his ground, grinning at her like he was in on a secret she wanted no one to know.

"You aren't my boyfriend, you know?" Jenny said, trying her best to regain control.

"OK."

"I just wanted to, that's all. It's not a big deal." Jenny was talking too much, but she didn't know how to stop herself. "I'm sure you've done this a thousand times and I don't care."

JP moved toward her and put both hands on her shoulders to calm her down. "It's cool," he said. "It's very cool."

Jenny smiled. It might have been the nicest thing he'd ever said to her.

JP BROUGHT BLANKETS and pillows from his room and added them to a pile of couch cushions on the floor while Jenny did her best to turn them into a bed.

"Are you sure you want to stay?" JP asked. "What if your mom calls the cops?"

"She won't." Linda was probably drunk and wouldn't risk having the cops involved. "Will you sleep out here with me?" Jenny watched his reaction. He fidgeted, delaying a response. "Just in case Boomer comes home," she clarified.

"Yeah, whatever."

The makeshift bed was wide enough to allow two inches of space between them, but the electricity coming off their bodies seemed to fill the tiny void as if they were touching. Jenny felt the safest she had in a while.

"JP . . ." she said into the silence.

"Yeah?"

"I think we should leave soon. I don't want to argue about it or just talk like it's a fantasy. I want to make a real plan." She stared at the ceiling thinking about Mr. Renkin, her mother, Gil. "I don't feel safe here."

"OK," he said without a fight.

She smiled, glad they were both staring at the ceiling and he couldn't see her. "When's the last time you talked to your cousin?" she asked.

"Couple months ago. He's working for a fisherman. He guts fish for him or something. Gets paid in cash and fish. Do you like fish?"

"Yeah." Jenny hated fish, but it seemed important to him. She could grow to like it. "Is that what we would do? Gut fish?"

"That's what I would do, but maybe we can get you a different job if you don't like it. It will just be for a few years anyway."

"For you. What happens when you turn eighteen, but I'm only sixteen? Are you going to leave me?"

"I don't know. I don't want to lie to you. I don't want to trick you into coming. Two years is a long time. A lot can change."

Jenny's heart sank.

"And maybe it would be better for us if I came back and joined the military as soon as possible. That way I'd be done with basic training and be more settled for you when you came back."

Talk of their future together was intoxicating. She couldn't turn back now even if she wanted to. They lay silent for a moment under the pretext of thinking, but Jenny was ecstatic.

"The problem is the money," JP said, snapping her back to reality. "We'll need a couple thousand each to get there, get set up with a little place. We can't stay with my cousin. He already lives with a bunch of guys and there isn't room."

Jenny sighed audibly, and JP turned his face toward her for the first time since they'd lain down. "What?" he asked.

She wasn't sure if she should tell him, share what had happened with her attempts to get the money. Mr. Renkin wasn't an option. He had the notes and wasn't afraid to hurt her to keep his secret safe. Gil was still in play. "I have a way to get the money, but it's awful and I don't want to do it."

"What is it?"

Jenny turned her face toward him, biting her bottom lip, nervous to speak. He met her look with encouraging eyes.

"There's a man who wants to pay me to have sex with him. Because I'm a virgin and he knows me from the pageants." She felt ashamed even saying it. Gil was the pervert, but the offer alone had tainted her, stolen her innocence.

"No way," JP said without hesitation.

"He'll give me five thousand dollars."

"He could give you an island, it's not happening."

Jenny smiled at the boy. He smiled back for a beat, then composed himself and rolled onto his back. "We'll find the money a different way."

"How?" Jenny demanded, unhappy he had turned away.

"I don't know."

"That isn't a plan, JP. That's just fantasizing."

"What do you want me to do? Rob a bank?"

Jenny didn't respond to his sarcasm. Why could he only show his soft side for fifteen seconds at a time before turning back into a tough guy? It was so frustrating. If he wanted to be such a tough guy, it was about time he proved it. "What if there was a way to get the money without having sex with him?"

"I'm listening," he said.

"What if I agree to it, have him come here, and then we rob him? He's not a big guy. You can use your knives and surprise him. Actually, my dad has a gun that I can get. We'll take the money and leave that night."

They both stared at the ceiling again, searching for holes in the plan, neither coming up with anything worth vocalizing. The longer the silence lasted, the more of a reality it became.

CHAPTER TWENTY-NINE

VIRGINIA

I HEARD HUNTER sneak out around six. I woke to the sound of the door closing and thought for sure the time had come for me to be murdered by ninjas who were not even good at being ninjas. Then I remembered my night and my houseguest. I couldn't afford to over-analyze it. Brandon was coming at seven to head to New York on a Gil hunt.

"GOOD MORNING, sunshine," he said as I sank into the passenger seat holding a large mug of tea. "Rough night?"

He was fishing to see what my social life was like. I wasn't about to tell him, especially since I'd made Hunter the tea he so coveted. "I'm not used to getting up this early."

"You can sleep if you want," he offered, and I accepted.

BRANDON WOKE ME up three hours later, whispering my name and patting my shoulder. I rubbed at my crusty eyes until I could keep them open. The sky was littered with tall, brown uniform apartment buildings. Wrenton was smack-dab in between Boston and New York City, but I had barely spent time in either place. A couple field trips when I was a kid, but as an adult, I had just sunk into the town. It had that effect.

"Where are we?" I asked.

"The Bronx."

I knew only one thing about the Bronx, and then there it was: Yankee Stadium. I was in awe as we cruised by. It was majestic. A gigantic pristine structure in the midst of its dirty brown surroundings. It looked like an escape, a place for people to go and look at a big green field and forget about their life outside those towering white walls. The idea of an escape, even a temporary one, sounded so tempting.

I sat up in the seat and wiped a small dab of drool from the side of my mouth.

"Can we play car games now?" he asked, and I turned to glare at him. "I'm joking."

"Did you bring the file?" I asked.

"It's in my bag, behind the seat."

I contorted my body around and flipped open his leather mansatchel. I pulled out a manila folder from inside and flopped back into my seat.

"Be careful, there are pictures in there," he warned.

Right on cue, I opened the folder to the picture he loved to keep on top, Jenny's dead body. I didn't turn away this time. I was starting to get used to it. The more I dug around and the more time had passed, the less real she seemed. I looked closely at it, closer than I ever thought I could.

"You OK?" he asked.

"What do you think is up with the hair?" I said.

"I don't know. Some kind of fantasy?"

"But why would a pedophile want to cut her hair? Wouldn't he be into her long blonde hair?"

"I don't know what pedophiles are into."

"Aren't you supposed to profile the murderer?"

"Fine, he cut her hair because he was stealing her innocence and wanted it to show," he said off the top of his head. It wasn't the worst theory.

"Which *he* are you referring to? Benjy? Or Gil?" I asked.

"You tell me."

I let it go and went back to the picture. Such care went into placing her body. I saw this on TV plenty of times. The murderer really loved her and somehow rationalized killing her for her own good. No one wanted her to grow up, so maybe it was about immortalizing her at this age. Her nightgown was bloody and covered in dirt, but you could still make out how childish it was—pink, ruffles, ribbons.

"I don't think she would wear this on her own," I said out loud, but more to myself than trying to convince Brandon.

"Why's that?"

"Real teens don't wear these things. This is a fantasy. She slept in a T-shirt and pajama pants like the rest of the world."

"Makes sense. He dressed her up like he wanted."

Brandon was right. All signs were pointing to a pedophile, the real kind. The nightgown, the hair, the flowers, and, of course, the rape. I hoped it was Gil. I couldn't stomach thinking Jenny was in contact with any more grown men.

I LOOKED AT the file for the rest of the drive. Pictures, statements, forensics with no answers. I was sure I wasn't allowed to see this, but I wasn't about to say something. I read my father's statement, then Linda's. They were home together. Both claimed Jenny went to her room around eight and they never heard her leave. Neither thought she had ever snuck out before, but had no explanation for how she could have been taken without them hearing. They just seemed in denial.

My statement was in there. I sounded difficult. I had no alibi, but now I knew if I really needed to provide one, Mark could probably corroborate a drunken phone call that night. Not much weight was given to my statement. I wasn't the only one who thought it was unlikely I raped my sister.

When the stop-and-go traffic of the city started to make me nauseous, I put the file away. "I haven't been here in forever," I said, staring out the window. I felt small. My world felt small. This seemed like a place where one could start over. No one in Wrenton could ever start over.

"Doesn't your dad live here during the week?" he asked.

"Yeah, but he doesn't let us visit. Not that I would want to. Maybe when I was a kid. Now, I like the idea of him being far away."

"My father is an asshole too. Some guys just don't have the dad gene."

I liked that. It wasn't anyone's fault; my dad was just born that way. I wondered about Brandon's dad, but didn't want to pry. If he was abusive, it would be a real mood killer, and we had the whole day ahead of us.

———

GIL LIVED ON the seventh floor. The hallway was narrow. I guess if I lived there, I would rather the space go toward my apartment, but still, this seemed like it should be a building code violation. I walked behind Brandon, not sure we would fit comfortably side by side.

We stopped in front of Gil's apartment, number 713. Brandon pounded his fist against the door before we could even stop and discuss what could be on the other side. This was a reminder of how, no matter how much I wanted to deny it, he was a cop and I was not.

"I doubt he's here," Brandon said.

"We knew that before we left. Do you know how to pick a lock?" I asked, knowing I might be turned on if the answer was yes and wanting to know that I was still capable of it.

"Kind of, I'll be right back."

Brandon returned ten minutes later. I heard the keys coming down the hall before I could even see him. He dangled them out in front to taunt me. "These might work," he said.

"Where did you get those?"

"I asked the building manager. I showed him my badge, but he didn't really give a shit. Probably would have given them to you too." He stuck the key in and unlocked the dead bolt and then the door knob. He twisted the knob and pushed the door forward. "Voilà!" he teased.

We both stepped inside. We were officially trespassing, and it was awesome.

The apartment had an open layout with hardwood floors and two bedrooms. "Nice place," Brandon said, and I thought he was joking, but he didn't sound like it. I guess for New York City, this was a nice place. There was a large flat-screen TV mounted to the wall. I couldn't see the wires, so I accepted it was a classy place.

"Where do we start?" I asked.

He didn't respond and instead drifted into the master bedroom. The bed was made, no sign of a hasty exit. Brandon reached into his pocket and pulled out a rubber glove. He put it on, and it immediately turned me on in a weird *oh my God, this is what they do on TV* way. He pulled out another glove and tossed it to me. All of my dreams were coming true.

The euphoria ended as soon as I opened the drawer to the bedside table and saw a picture of Jenny in one of her over-the-top dresses, posing onstage. "Brandon . . ."

He came to my side and followed the trajectory of my stare. He pulled the picture out and put it on the bed. Below it was another, a different dress, a different stage. There were five pictures total, enough to be haunting in that tiny drawer. Underneath the photos was a piece of notebook paper folded into thirds. Brandon put on a second glove and lifted the letter.

I repositioned myself close behind him to read over his shoulder. The handwriting caused me to tense up all over. It was sloppy. It was girly. It was Jenny's.

Hi Gil,

My name is Jenny Kennedy. I think you know who I am. Benjy told me you are a fan. I was wondering if you would like to meet me. We could get to know each other. I live in Massachusetts, but maybe we could meet somewhere in between. Please write me back if you are interested. You can send the letters to my friend's house, 425 Pike Street, Wrenton, MA 00334, and she will bring them to me at school. I look forward to hearing from you.

Sincerely,

Jenny

Brandon turned his head to read my reaction. "That's her address."

I backed away from him and the letter. "But she didn't want him to know that." What was she thinking? Why would she do this? I sat down on the bed, and Brandon lunged to pull me up.

"Don't sit on the bed. No one can know we were in here or none of this is admissible." He folded the letter and put it back in the drawer, placing the pictures on top. "We have to get out of here and hope the manager forgets my face. Make sure everything looks exactly like you found it."

I considered protesting. I wanted more answers, but he was already on the move.

SEEING THE SIGHTS seemed foolish to both of us after being in that apartment, seeing those pictures, and reading that letter. We decided to grab lunch and call it a trip. Brandon led me into a café in the bottom of one of the million towering skyscrapers. All the way to New York to order a cold sandwich at the counter, but I didn't care anymore.

We sat at a small round table that we were lucky to find during the hectic lunch hour. Neither one of us had spoken much since we left the apartment. I knew Brandon was panicking. He had to point the investigation toward Gil, but he couldn't tell anyone what we had done.

"How's your sandwich?" I asked.

"Tastes like plastic."

"Do you want half of mine? The tuna overpowers the plastic."

He smiled but declined. I wanted to help him. I didn't like seeing him like this. He was always so cocky and confident. I didn't love him like that either, but this was worse. Catching Benjy had garnered him a lot of praise. This was going to turn him into a pariah. The media would go nuts, and someone would have to take the fall. He didn't say so, but we both knew it would be him. He arrested the wrong man. It's a hard thing to swallow.

"It's funny," he said, almost like he could read my thoughts. "I'm going to have to work my tail off to get this sorted out, only to be punished once the truth comes out." He laughed the saddest laugh I ever heard. "But what am I going to do? Nothing? Let Benjy rot in prison while Gil is out there preying on other girls?"

"If you catch Gil, don't you think people will forget?"

"I guess we'll find out." He took a large bite of his plastic sandwich, and neither of us spoke until he swallowed.

"Do you want me to get more out of Benjy?" I asked. "If he says more, admits specifics about Gil, won't that be enough to officially open the investigation?"

"You'll have to convince him to tell me or another detective, and his lawyer will be there. He can't just tell you things in private."

"I think I could. I mean the lawyer would welcome another suspect."

"But she won't let him admit to sending any illicit materials, like photos or letters talking about inappropriate things."

"I don't think he did. I really think he believes they were just friends. I think Gil took advantage of him."

Brandon threw the last bit of his sandwich down, admitting defeat. "This is the beginning of the end," he joked.

I laughed for his benefit. I was happy to play such a pivotal role going forward. I was like a secret weapon. I was the dead-sister-look-alike slow-man whisperer.

I was considering what else I could say to cheer Brandon up when several middle-aged businessmen, practically clones, entered the café. They talked among themselves with the volume of men who thought very highly of themselves. Each one held an identical, thin computer briefcase that I recognized. The embroidered letters glowed at me, *Gilders & Pendergast Investments*.

"Those men work at my father's company," I said. "Is his office in this building? Why would you bring me here?" I glared at Brandon. I wanted to run back to the car. This felt like a betrayal.

"I just thought, we came all this way, and you said he never let you visit . . . Maybe you would want to see him in his element. And maybe he could see you, here on your own. He might be impressed."

"You think I want to impress him? I've spent my whole life trying to disappoint that man. The pressures he put on me, the rules, the abandonment—" I stopped. Why did I just say all of those things? And why to Brandon? I sounded childish, spilling my guts out like that. I sounded insane.

He just stared back at me, equally surprised at my confession. "I'm sorry," he said. "I didn't know. I projected my own shit with my dad onto you. I shouldn't have assumed—" He cut himself off, shaking his head, embarrassed.

"Do you think he has a picture of Jenny in his office?" I asked without expecting an answer. "I bet he hated when she died. I bet they brought him flowers and a condolence card signed by people who he can't stand. He wouldn't like that. I bet he regrets ever having children." I wished I could just stop talking.

"I'm sure that's not true," he said, reaching out and placing his hand on top of mine. I didn't know if I should pull away, so I left it there, letting him believe he was comforting me.

"If I went up there, what would I say?" The idea was growing on me. He would hate that I showed up. I would introduce myself to his colleagues. I would leave my mark and then people would ask about me to be polite going forward. I would infiltrate his place of escape from us.

"You don't have to," he said. "It was a bad idea."

"It was a bad idea for *you*, but for me, it might be a good idea."

He had overstepped severely and for all the wrong reasons, but the result was the same. I was sitting at the base of my father's New York office building.

I thought about Jenny. I thought about my mother. I even thought about Linda. I would do this for them. I would walk in there as a representative of the silent Kennedy women, demanding the attention he refused to give. Don't tell us to stay home, waiting for our allotted two days a week. We were his family, and we existed every single day.

I LEFT BRANDON in the café without an invitation or an explanation and marched myself into the adjacent lobby. It had been a long day and night, and I was fueled by adrenaline and tuna.

I stepped off the elevator on the fifteenth floor, the farthest I could get without a badge, and faced two well-groomed security guards behind the reception desk.

"Good afternoon," the older of the two greeted me.

"Hi, I'm here to see Calvin Kennedy."

"Is he expecting you?"

"Yes."

The guard typed into his computer. It was taking too long for my liking. I watched men and women in fancy suits swipe badges in and out of the adjacent doors, and I considered making a run for it behind one of them.

"I don't see that name in here," the security guard said. "Do you know what department he's in?"

I didn't. I knew nothing about my father's job. "He does investments or something, obviously. He's been here forever, like thirty years," I said, like that would help find a name in the database.

The security guard picked up the phone and dialed an extension. "Hi, this is Arnold from security. I have someone here to see Calvin Kennedy, but I don't see him in the system." He paused while the voice at the other end spoke. "She said she has a meeting." Pause. "Well, I assume a meeting here, she's standing in front of me." Pause. "OK, thanks." He hung up the phone and turned to me. "Someone will be out in a minute."

"Is everything OK?" I asked. I was worried that I was about to be arrested or knocked out and dragged into an interrogation room. Was this a front? A top secret government agency? Was my dad a spy? It would explain so much.

The door opened, and a woman in a well-fitting dark purple skirt suit walked straight toward me, owning her very tall heels. "Hello, I'm Natasha McCarron, director of human resources." She extended her hand with a practiced smile.

"Hello."

"You have a meeting with Calvin Kennedy?"

"Yes."

"There must be some confusion. Mr. Kennedy doesn't work in this building. He works from home. Are you a client?"

My father does not work from home. He hates his home. "Are you sure?" I asked.

"Yes, he works remotely. We pride ourselves on flexibility here. Are you a client?" she repeated herself.

"No, I'm sorry," I mumbled. "This was a mistake." I backed away from her and pushed the elevator button like a maniac. The doors finally opened, and I pushed myself through some exiting suits.

My knees weakened, and I steadied myself against the back of the elevator. I couldn't even process the information, let alone react to it. If my father didn't work in the office, where did he work? Where did he go? Why would he lie? What else was he lying about?

THE RIDE HOME was long and silent. I stared out the window most of the way. I was annoyed at Brandon for setting me up and scared of what I didn't know about my father. I didn't want to talk. I didn't want to share. I just wanted to go home.

Three and a half hours later we passed the pub by my apartment. The navy Accord was there.

Brandon parked in front of my building. When he dared to turn the car off, I shot him a look. He stared down at the steering wheel as he collected his thoughts. It was such a human moment for him. I found power in his nervousness.

He made eye contact before he spoke. "I'd like to come in. Just for a little bit, if it's OK with you. I feel really bad for overstepping. It would be nice to hang out for a bit and see if I can fix it."

I wasn't sure what to say or even think. I was thinking about Hunter's car. If Brandon left, would I go there? I wanted him to come up and I wanted him to leave. What happened to the good old days when I could trust myself to sit alone in my apartment? I was so mad at him, but in the face of the choice I knew it was the saner option.

He followed me inside. I had tea this time, but I also had wine.

We took our drinks to the couch, and I tried to convince myself that it was just two friends hanging out. Human interaction two nights in a row, what a twist.

"Is this awkward?" he asked.

"A little, I don't have a lot of guests."

"I show up at people's places all the time, just barge in. So I'm pretty comfortable." He smiled and I laughed, but I didn't want to. After our day, after what we found and after what he did, we weren't there yet.

"What's it like to always be trying to solve some crime, some murder, just waking up every day and thinking about some horrible thing?" I asked, turning the lighthearted banter in the other direction, where I felt more comfortable.

It was a drastic turn, and he took the appropriate length of time to consider it. "It's not all the time. Hartsfield isn't exactly New York City. This is the worst one for me, your sister. I had another big case once. Three years ago a woman was killed in her home. It was a real mess. Just blood everywhere, right out of a horror movie. I'm sorry, is this too much?"

"No," I promised.

"I had just become a detective; I think a dirty beat-cop uniform was probably still on my closet floor at the time. I was just supposed to follow and observe. The lead detective had been doing this for forty years. They arrested the ex-boyfriend right away, but something wasn't right. The boyfriend had a new girlfriend and a new job out of town. The motive just wasn't there for me."

I wanted to ask a million questions, but I let him continue. It seemed therapeutic for him to be rehashing this.

"I started looking into it after work. Nothing too intense, just rereading interviews and looking at the pictures. I didn't have much of a life, so it was easy to poke around here and there. Eventually, it really started to bother me that her parents had died in a car accident just two weeks earlier. I mean, at first I just accepted what a tragedy it was, but the more I thought about it, the more I couldn't sit with the coincidence. It was her fucking brother. Killed her for the house—she wanted to sell it and he couldn't afford to buy her out. That was it. That was reason enough for him. And he really fucked her up so that it would look like a crime of passion. Can you believe it?"

"People are shit," I said.

"They really are. It messed me up for a little while, just the cold, calculated nature of it, but I didn't have to be a junior detective anymore. Got to be the lead on the very next case."

"Which was?"

"Liquor store robbery."

I laughed and he did too. I was OK with it this time.

"I told you, they aren't all this bad. This one is as bad as I hope it ever gets for me."

"You don't have to tell me," I said.

"Sorry, you're right. I can't even imagine what it's like to know the victim. It's hard enough as it is to come in after the fact."

"Aren't you supposed to be detached? Doesn't that affect your ability to do your job?"

"I try to stay objective, but I'm not a monster," he said.

"I remember the first day we met at the police station. Chief Garrety said you were some big hotshot from the city and that I should smile a lot to give a good impression."

"You left an impression all right."

"What does that mean?"

He took a long swig of his wine. "Nothing."

"Fine," I teased.

"What are you going to do when this is all over?" he asked, leaning back and resting his head on the back of the couch.

"Like, in life?"

"Yeah, in life."

"I don't know. What I'm doing right now. Am I supposed to do something different?"

"Not if you don't want to. It just seems like you live under a dark cloud."

"I'm not fucking Eeyore."

"I didn't mean it like that," he said.

"I know you think finding Jenny's killer is going to be some great catharsis for me."

"Maybe. What do you think?"

"I think you're being awfully deep for your first glass of wine."

Everything was getting too comfortable and I was getting uncomfortable. It's amazing that as a human you can recognize all of your own flaws and psychoses but can do nothing to alter them. It was OK to feel comfortable. It was OK to feel attracted to him. It was OK to share things. Brain, mouth, body allow it.

I finished my wine for no reason other than to have the liquid prevent me from continuing to talk. I rose from the couch and went back to the bottle on the desk near the kitchenette. He followed.

He came to a rest next to me. We both stared down at the table, feigning ignorance of the proximity of our arms. I waited for him to move. He didn't at first. Our hands just rested around our drinks, our faces staring forward.

Nothing in the world was happening in that moment other than his arm and my arm being a centimeter apart. My cheeks flushed, and my heart pounded in the most irrational way. I wanted to go back to the couch, but I couldn't move. In order to not say or do something I would regret, I had to stay perfectly still.

Brandon finally moved. He turned around and rested against the table. The space previously between our arms was now the negligible distance between our hips. He held his glass in front of him, something for him to look at other than me.

His movement broke my focus enough for me to engage in the normal human behavior of grabbing the bottle of wine and refilling my glass. Neither of us did anything to threaten the proximity of our hips. I put the wine bottle down and he looked back up at me.

"What?" I asked, trying to be coy, but it came out so soft, it held no power.

"Nothing." He smiled. He took his right hand from the glass he was clutching and brushed my forearm. The hairs stood up on end to match the visceral reaction of my flushed cheeks. He watched the trail of his own hand as it slowly grazed up and down my arm. I glared forward, fighting the urge to react and just let the moment be. Should I have gone to the pub instead?

After a beat, his hand retreated to his glass and waited for validation. I let him sweat for a second before I turned and made the eye contact that had been eluding us since he followed me from the couch. I moved my hand to the far side of his face. I could feel stubble that wasn't visible to the naked eye.

"What are we doing?" I asked. I needed to know. I let my hand fall from his face to suggest it was his turn for a move.

He held eye contact as he reached across my body, wrapping his hand around the far edge of my waist and pulling me in front of him with an exhilarating jerk.

We were at another standstill. I had never experienced anything so intense while also so timid. There was a line we were about to cross. Each step left us with another second to think about what we were doing and call it off.

I reached behind him and put down my wineglass. It was the best *yes* he was going to get. He followed suit and abandoned his wine. He moved the hair off my shoulder, and I closed my eyes just long enough to focus on his fingers brushing across my collarbone. He leaned forward and kissed my neck, three innocent kisses along the ridge. He pulled back again, but I was over the pauses and the stares. I wrapped my hands around his head and kissed him, nothing innocent about it.

That night I didn't think about Jenny or Gil. I didn't think about Mark, or Hunter at the pub. I didn't think about whatever lie my father was living. That night was an escape. It wouldn't last.

CHAPTER THIRTY

JENNY

JENNY'S EYES sprang open as JP's elbow nudged her rib cage. She could hear raindrops tapping against the thin roof as she focused on the scenery and then JP next to her.

"You gotta get up if you want to go home and change before the bus," he said.

Jenny sat up, simultaneously patting down her bedhead and wiping drool from the side of her face.

"Are you worried about your mom?" he asked. "I could come with you."

Like a typical teenager obsessed with a boy, Jenny had forgotten about Linda. She hated these little moments that made her feel just like one of her peers and not the mature, beyond-her-years girl she saw herself as.

"That's OK," she said as she used the couch behind her to leverage into a standing position. "You would only make it worse." Jenny could handle Linda. She was getting used to it now, the heartbreaking language, the violent attacks, the unrecognizable woman who lived in her house.

JP stood and followed Jenny to the door, where she slipped her small feet into her boots. Was he going to kiss her good-bye? Or hug her at least? This was uncharted territory. They were running away together, but in that moment, her focus was on how to leave his house.

"We'll make a plan this week," she said. "It'll take at least a week to set it up, and that's only if he responds immediately. I think we should try to get a letter out as soon as possible." Jenny wished she had his e-mail address or even his phone number. The waiting was impossible.

"I don't know if I've ever sent a letter." JP laughed. "Maybe to Santa." The thought of JP writing a letter to Santa made Jenny happy. Would they have kids someday? JP in his military uniform, taking them to see Santa. She had to rein herself in. That was a long time away. Robbing a pervert and years of gutting fish would come first.

JP opened the front door for her, pulling it as far as he could, creating maximum space between them. There would be no hug or kiss. Jenny was relieved. The kiss last night was amazing, but it was passion in the moment. Anything now would be forced. They would have plenty of time for real moments. It was better they stayed focused. Jenny threw the hood of her jacket over her golden hair and ran out into the rain.

JENNY TIPTOED THROUGH her house. She was grateful Linda wasn't waiting in the kitchen for her like so many times before, stalking in the dark, ready for a fight.

The living room was empty. She made her way up the stairs, weightless, silent. At the top she found her mother's door ajar. Jenny poked her head in. No Linda.

Her mother rarely left the house anymore. She couldn't risk slipping up in public and alerting the town that she had cracked. She had to be somewhere.

Every empty room Jenny found increased the suspense. She wanted to get this over with, take her punishment and get to school. If she prolonged the meeting until the afternoon, Linda would surely be drunk again and it would be much worse.

Jenny made her way through the whole house, even the rooms they never used, until she finally spotted Linda. Her mother sat slumped over in a chair on the back deck. The rain was pouring down on her.

Jenny slid open the glass door, expecting her mother to react to the noise, but she didn't move. The young girl walked around the chair to face her mother, whose chest rose and fell to its own beat. Drops fell from Linda's nose, catching on her upper lip before running off her face. An empty glass sat on the table next to her. Such an obvious disease lacking any charm.

"Mom," Jenny yelled, feeling crazy for trying to wake the beast. Jenny reached for her shoulder and shook it. "Mom!"

The woman stirred and murmured incoherently. Jenny released her shoulder and backed out of reach.

"Mom, it's me, wake up. You're getting soaked."

"Where were you?" Linda muttered, still not opening her eyes.

"I was at Mallory's house. I told you I was sleeping over there last night."

"You're lying," Linda slurred as she lunged forward, trying to grab Jenny and falling to the wet, rain-sealed boards of the deck. She paused on all fours, unable to stand, unwilling to collapse.

"C'mon, let me help you." Jenny locked her arms under her mother's armpits and hoisted the woman up. It was clear Linda wouldn't be able to do any real damage to Jenny that morning; she had reserved all the damage for herself.

JENNY WALKED THROUGH the hall after second period like a zombie. Students pushed past her, but her pace remained plodding. Gil was weighing on her mind. She didn't want to see that man again. After a fight with Linda or a kiss from JP, the plan sounded easy. When she was just a girl walking to class, it seemed insane. She would talk to JP after school. It was time to circle back down to reality.

As she rounded the corner toward her locker, a chorus of girly giggles rose over the typical soundtrack of the hallway. Between Jenny and her locker stood Mallory, immersed in a group of popular high school girls. Christine Castleton held the group's attention, and Mallory stood by her side as the dutiful protégé.

Past the girls, the sea of students seemed to part as Mr. Renkin rounded the corner into view, the one person she wanted to interact with even less than Mallory. Jenny froze. Surrounded by fifty witnesses, she was still scared.

"Mr. Renkin!" Christine yelled down the hall. She grinned at the man as her girls fell in line against the lockers.

"Hello, girls," he said without altering his stride.

As he approached, Christine grabbed Mallory's sleeve and yanked her off the locker and into Mr. Renkin's path, timing it perfectly.

"Whoa," he said as he jumped to the side, trying to avoid her, but hitting her with his elbow at the last second. "Are you all right?" he asked Mallory.

"Yeah." She smiled. "I'll just have to rub it a little." Then she winked, and the girls behind her snickered.

Mr. Renkin glanced over at Christine, not naïve to her part in it all. She just grinned before turning her attention to her locker.

"You girls should be more careful," he said.

"We will," teased Mallory.

Mr. Renkin nodded before continuing down the hall in Jenny's direction. Christine turned back from her locker to whisper something to Mallory. The way Mallory watched the older girl, she might as well have gotten out a pad and pencil to take notes. Jenny wondered how long it would be before Mallory showed up at school with matching magenta hair.

That was what Jenny was supposed to be doing. In a way, she was. They were all toying with older men, exploring boundaries without any comprehension of the consequences.

Jenny inched back against the lockers, hoping she would become invisible, but Mr. Renkin, fast approaching, locked eyes with her. Jenny swallowed hard, praying he would just keep walking.

"Good morning, Jenny," he said, stopping in front of her. He stood close and lowered his voice. "I hope everything is OK between us?"

Jenny nodded, too nervous to use her words.

He reached toward her, and she flinched. "Relax, it's just your collar." He untucked the corner of Jenny's jacket. "See you in class," he said.

Jenny forced a smile, which gave him the confidence to walk away.

"Jenny!" Mallory yelled down the hall.

She turned to see Mallory and the other girls staring, having watched the entire interaction. Mallory put her hands up, craving an explanation, but Jenny couldn't stomach it. She didn't want to stand and giggle about Mr. Renkin, the man who had slept with her sister and left Jenny unconscious, even if Mallory demanded it.

JENNY SAT AT the end of the cafeteria table with her cold pizza, so immersed in her social studies homework that she didn't notice a boy sit down across from her.

"Hey," he said. It was Kevin Neary. Everyone knew Kevin Neary. He was a senior with 0 percent body fat and a boy-band face.

"Hi," Jenny said, entirely unsure why he was talking to her.

"You're Jenny, right?"

"Yeah."

"Cool, I'm Kevin."

"I know," Jenny said, hoping he would just get to the point. He was gorgeous and popular, and she could feel her cheeks getting red.

He looked down at her homework. "Is that from Mr. Jacobs?"

"Yeah."

"Cool. I had him."

"Cool," she said, speaking his language.

"I was going to walk to Stone's during study hall for a sandwich. Do you want to come? It'll be better than that crap," he said, pointing to her pizza.

"I don't have study hall. I'm only in eighth grade." Why did she say that? What a loser. Jenny cringed.

"Right," he said.

"I can skip, though. It's just health class," Jenny course-corrected. She was too flattered by the invitation to consider the consequences of her actions, or the motives of his.

"Really? That's badass."

Jenny beamed.

"Meet me behind the shed by the soccer field. Do you know where that is? Where the losers go to smoke."

"I know where it is."

"Cool, see you there." Kevin smiled like even his face had perfectly toned muscles. He pushed off the table as he stood, causing his arm muscles to flex. Jenny couldn't fathom taking another bite of cold pizza. Her heart was beating out of her chest.

JENNY MARCHED PAST THE DOOR to health class and into the bathroom. She looked in the mirror. She had stopped wearing makeup and regretted it. Her face looked plain. She looked young and washed out from lack of sleep. At least she had her hair, soft blonde waves that didn't suffer at all from her neglect. She ran her hand through, fixing the inconsistent part that rested just off center. This was what she looked like. It would have to do.

She hustled across the parking lot. There was no one in sight. The last thing she wanted was to be caught. She didn't even know what she was getting into. Did Kevin Neary actually like her? She thought about JP. Was she cheating on him? No. They weren't even anything official, and she wasn't doing anything anyway. Just going to get a sandwich.

If Kevin Neary was her boyfriend, she would be the most popular girl in the entire school, but that's not what she cared about, right? What was she even doing? She and JP finally had a plan to get the money; things were in motion, and now she was second-guessing her life strategy. She couldn't even think straight. She was acting exactly like a teenage girl, but that awareness wasn't stopping her; it was Kevin Neary.

She reached the shed and walked around to the back. There was no one there, just a lot of cigarette butts mixed into the wood chips. She had really hoped she wouldn't get there first. She didn't want to seem desperate. She debated running back to the parking lot and hiding behind a car, but before she could decide what to do, she heard footsteps.

Mallory Murphy stepped around the corner. Then three more girls: Nora, Liz, and Laura. All four were at Jenny's birthday party last year.

"Hi, Jenny," Mallory said, coming to a stop right in front of her.

"Hey."

"What are you doing out here?"

"Nothing," Jenny said, kicking at the ground.

Mallory looked back at her three groupies, and they snickered. "That's not what I heard. I heard you came here to meet Kevin Neary."

It was a trap. The whole thing was a trap because Jenny had rejected them, abandoned their plans for lifelong friendship without explanation. She didn't respond. She'd let them have this. It was the least she could do. Soon she would be gone. They had to live this life forever.

"What did you think? He liked you? He asked me to homecoming, you know? Christine set it up." Mallory had cool high school friends that she was desperately trying to fill the void with. Jenny could see the pleasure in her eyes when she said Christine's name.

Jenny stayed silent. She had no desire to be a part of this.

"Say something," Mallory demanded. "You're so weird now, Jenny. What happened? Did you get, like, molested or something?" The girls all laughed at the most distasteful joke ever made.

Jenny rolled her eyes at their stupidity, which did not sit well with Mallory.

"You aren't even pretty anymore," Mallory felt the need to point out.

"I don't care."

"Of course you care. No one wants to be an ugly slut."

Jenny went to walk away, but the three other girls had circled her, forcing her to turn back to their leader. Jenny had had it. Mallory had no idea who she was messing with. Jenny had to deal with Linda. Did Mallory really think she would be afraid of her? "Fuck off, Mallory," she suggested.

"Excuse me?"

"Fuck. Off."

Mallory stepped forward and shoved Jenny on the shoulder. Her stocky little gymnast body packed quite the punch. Jenny wanted to punch her in the nose, but she was outnumbered. She stared into Mallory's eyes for a hint of what she was thinking.

There were footsteps before there was an answer.

"You all better get the fuck out of here," JP said, stepping into their view from behind the shed, then flicking his cigarette to the ground and stomping it out.

Mallory hesitated, weighing her options. JP didn't play by the rules and she couldn't risk it. "Whatever," she muttered, stepping away from Jenny.

The girls filed past JP one at a time until it was Mallory's turn.

She brushed past him, making contact in an attempt to maintain the upper hand, but JP grabbed her arm, halting her steps and her nonsense.

"You are a twisted little fuck," he stated as a fact.

Mallory's face contorted and landed somewhere between disgust and fear.

"Let go of me," she demanded.

"Why? Am I making you uncomfortable? Do you have a crush on me, Mallory? Do you want me to touch you?" He moved his other hand to her face.

"No." Mallory swung her arm around to slap his hand away. "You're disgusting!"

"I wouldn't touch you with a ten-foot pole," he said, releasing her with a shove that set her back a few steps. "Mess with her again and you won't like it." He lifted up the front of his shirt, revealing one of his precious knives.

Mallory's eyes stung with tears against her will.

"Grow up," JP said and walked away. He said nothing to Jenny. He had done enough.

CHAPTER THIRTY-ONE

VIRGINIA

MY BRAIN SHOOK inside my skull; then it stopped. I was asleep, but I was awake. Then it was shaking again. As the last veil of sleep lifted, I realized my phone was vibrating across the bed.

I brushed my arm around in a wide sweeping motion. I was alone in the big bed. It had been two days since Brandon was there. I hadn't washed the sheets and could still smell the disruption he'd left to my own natural scent. He'd called a handful of times, but I didn't pick up. I was nervous. I didn't know where to go from there.

As my hand made contact with the phone, I assumed it was him again. When I lifted it to my one barely open eye, I saw who it was. The screen read: Dad.

My father never called. Literally, it was possible he had never called my cell phone once. Did he know I went to New York? Was he calling to explain himself, beg for me not to tell Linda? Was it possible my father would finally need something from me?

"Hello. Hello. Hello," I practiced until my voice woke up. Then I answered the phone for real. "Hello."

"Virginia, this is sick," he said. "What were you thinking? Do you know how bad this looks for all of us?"

I forced my tired body into a sitting position. "What are you talking about?"

"The detective. This is so inappropriate. He's going to lose his job, and people are going to think you don't even care about Jenny. How could you do this?"

"Dad, just slow down. What about the detective?"

"You're sleeping with the lead detective in charge of finding your sister's killer. You see nothing wrong with that, I suppose? Well, that's not how everyone else feels. It's everywhere. Have you left the house, turned on the TV?"

"Just, hold on." I put the phone on speaker and used it to search the Internet for my name. My father sounded frantic. There were no pauses in between his sentences. I had never heard him like this.

The search engine shot a million results at me, all of them explaining what my father was talking about. "Shit," I said as grainy pictures of Brandon kissing me good-bye at my front door filled my screen. I wasn't even wearing pants, just a long T-shirt that was a tad too short when I extended onto my tiptoes to kiss him, revealing the edge of my underwear.

"Virginia?" my dad said, sick of waiting on my silence.

"I'm here," I said as I scrolled through the pictures, all taken within the twenty seconds I was outside. "I don't even . . . How? The reporters left weeks ago."

"It could have been anyone with a cell phone, but don't worry, they'll definitely be back now. They'll be back on all of us. They're going to question what kind of family we are. They'll start digging again. I can't believe you could stoop to this level."

"I'm sorry, Dad. It isn't like it seems." But it was how it seemed. I thought a lot about the consequences of lying in bed with Brandon that night, but they were all personal, selfish consequences. I didn't even think about Jenny. Brandon was supposed to be helping her, not *me*.

THE PLAN WITH BENJY had to move forward regardless of my public image or Brandon's. He left me a message saying to come to the station at noon on Friday. I still wasn't picking up the phone. Every good feeling he gave me triggered the memory of opposing heartbreak courtesy of Mark Renkin. When you burn your hand on the stove, you tend to avoid touching it again.

There were some lingering news vans waiting for any official or unofficial comment from the police or at least a sighting of Brandon so that they could swarm him and ask him about sleeping with me. I parked in the loading zone of the alley to the side of the building as instructed. I was out of sight and could slip easily into a door marked *Exit Only*.

I flipped down the visor and judged my appearance in the mirror, pulling the elastic from my messy bun and letting the long hair fall past my shoulders. I felt a foreign need to look presentable. I riffled through my bag until I found an old crusty tube of mascara. I applied a couple coats to my neglected eyelashes and was amazed by the exponential improvement. I wanted to be taken seriously. I had been branded a selfish slut by the media, but I was the one they needed. I was the one Benjy would talk to.

A YOUNG FEMALE COP manned the front desk. "How can I help—" She paused against her will as she glanced up and recognized me.

"I'm here to see Detective Colsen." I used his formal title even though the whole world knew we were past that.

"Just a minute." She jumped from her stool.

The officer didn't return with Brandon. Instead, she brought a tall gray-haired man in a loose suit that did little to flatter his Lurch-like stature.

"Hello, Virginia." He extended his hand. "I'm Sheriff Franklin Sharp." He put weight behind the inflection of his title and paired it with a forceful handshake.

"Hello."

"Detective Colsen has filled me in on the situation. He thinks Benjy has information on another suspect and that you might get him to share."

"Where's Bran— Detective Colsen?"

The side of the sheriff's mouth curled up, and he shot a glance at the young cop, who didn't reciprocate his judgment. "He's not here today. I'll be handling this myself. It's a sensitive situation, as I'm sure you can understand."

I just nodded. I didn't want to talk to this man anymore. I just wanted to get it over with. All of it.

BENJY SPILLED ON Gil just as I'd known he would. I told the sweet man that Gil may have killed Jenny, and he completely broke down. Benjy had a simple mind, but he comprehended guilt.

A press conference was held on Saturday. Brandon called several times that morning, but I ignored him. I watched the press conference alone in my apartment, the way I did most things. Sheriff Sharp walked to the podium, posturing with his shoulders back and his head held as high as it would reach. He had ditched his loose suit for a fancy official-looking sheriff's uniform adorned with lots of pins and whatnot. Camera shutters filled the silence as he waited a dramatic moment before speaking.

"Ladies and gentlemen, I am Sheriff Franklin Sharp and we have called this conference to announce that the investigation into the murder of Jenny Kennedy has been reopened."

Murmurs of shock rippled through the crowd. The sheriff waited for the chatter to subside before he began again. "At this time, we are only prepared to share that in light of recent events, Detective Brandon Colsen has been removed from the case. A viable suspect who was previously overlooked has emerged, and we are dedicating our full resources to investigating this further."

I couldn't believe it. Without Brandon, they wouldn't even know Gil existed. The same man who chastised him for continuing to investigate a solved case stood in front of the cameras blaming Brandon for arresting the wrong man. I felt a strange tug at my stomach muscles. Was I somehow responsible for this? The least I could have done was answer the poor guy's calls.

Members of the press began a barrage of overlapping questions. Some boomed louder than others.

"Who is the new suspect?"

"Did Detective Colsen ignore evidence?"

"Was he distracted by the victim's sister?"

"Does she have other motives?"

The sheriff's face reacted with a twitch in the direction of each question, but he didn't answer any of them. "That's all we're prepared to share at this time, thank you." With that, he stepped off the podium and back through the line of people that stood behind him.

I reached for my phone. It rang and rang and rang. My mind went to a bad place. I was sure Brandon had shot himself or was just lying in the bathtub crying and debating dropping an appliance in with him, ending it all.

"Hello?" he answered, pulling me back into the light.

"Hey, it's me."

"I'm guessing you just watched the press conference."

"How are you doing?"

"Great," he said.

"Do you want to come over?"

"Do you have alcohol?"

"Kind of."

He laughed, which made me feel better. "What does that mean?"

"I have vodka, but I've sworn off the stuff. You can have it, though."

"I'll bring some beer, or wine, or turpentine, something."

"And food, bring food. I have nothing," I said. "I'm not being dramatic, maybe some ketchup packets, that's it."

"I remember."

"OK."

"OK," he responded in kind, and we paused at an awkward phone impasse.

"I'm hanging up," I announced and then did.

I OPENED THE DOOR to find a Brandon I didn't recognize. His boyish face was the same with his big dumb smile, but his hair was all kinds of bedhead, poking out from a fitted baseball hat, and he wore jeans and a thin T-shirt that showed off definition in his arms that I hadn't really noticed before, even the other night.

"You look rough," I said.

"Thank you," he said, making me feel only a little bad.

There were two news vans parked outside, and when I heard their doors open, I grabbed Brandon by his shirt and yanked him inside before they could snap any more pictures.

He set a six-pack of an amber beer down on the coffee table. There was something sweet about it only being six beers. He didn't come over to get shit-faced and forget his problems. He didn't come over to get me shit-faced so that he could fuck me. He was just a decent guy who was going through some stuff and needed a friend.

I flopped down on the couch and he joined me. "Any news on Gil?" I couldn't help myself. It was just what we were comfortable talking about.

"I'm kind of out of the loop," he said.

"Then what am I doing hanging out with you?" I joked.

"This young deputy, Paulson, is supposed to let me know if anything happens. He's my little spy."

"They said you're off the case. What does that mean?"

"I'm suspended."

"For how long?"

"I have to go through the review board. I guess I didn't really think how it would look, you and me. I guess I wasn't thinking about much of anything else that night."

"I get it."

"Or for a while, really. I can't deny that you've been a distraction. I told you a lot of things about the case that I shouldn't have. I even took you to Gil's apartment. That was stupid and dangerous."

"Do you think it hurts the case?"

"What case? There's no one in custody. Just a phantom pedophile that no one's seen in weeks." He sighed and twisted the bottle of beer around in his hands. "I don't want to give up. I want to figure this out. I can't just walk away."

"Then don't. I don't want to give up either. I like this, feeling productive, having something to think about when I wake up in the morning, even if it's a really fucked-up thing to think about."

"Then we won't give up."

"I always liked you better when you were being a nervous renegade anyway. When you're cocky, it's really off-putting," I admitted.

"You don't have to tell me everything you think about me, you know? Just the compliments are fine."

In that moment, I wanted to confess what I'd learned about my father. I wanted to vent all of the horrible memories I had, and I wanted to tell him I'd realized my father was lying, not just to me and to himself, but to the police.

When my father had called me that morning, he was freaking out. He didn't want the police or the media looking at us again. It was obvious he was hiding something, but was he hiding something about Jenny? I couldn't say anything to Brandon, not until I had more information.

LATER THAT NIGHT, when Brandon suggested he leave, I knew he wanted me to protest, but it was bad enough he was at my apartment again. More pictures of him doing the walk of shame in the morning would have been the nail in his coffin, and so I let him go.

I crawled into bed, praying for sleep. Tomorrow was a big day, Sunday dinner. That night I would follow my father to see where he really went during the week. As an added bonus, I would get to listen to him berate me all through dinner about my dalliances with Brandon, win-win.

I tossed. I turned. Sleep was not for me. That's when I realized it was Saturday night and I was sober. I was proud of myself. I hadn't even had one of Brandon's beers. I wasn't about to crawl to the freezer and pull out a bottle of vodka, but surely a celebratory drink was in order.

In hindsight, it was just an excuse to see if Hunter was at the pub again. Things with Mark had to be bad. It's not that I wished her ill anymore, but I'd wanted this forever. I think I still wanted it. If Mark was single, what did that mean? I wouldn't take him back. Never, right? But he could apologize and beg me to take him back and that would feel good and then I would say something like, "No, Mark. You suck." It would be poetry.

I went straight to Monty at the bar and ordered two tequila shots. Not a lot of tequila flowing in that place based on the thickness of the dust that dispersed as Monty wrapped his fingers around the handle.

"I'm celebrating," I whispered to Monty. He winked, acknowledging it was a secret.

I brought the shots to Hunter at the same table. She looked remarkably good for someone spending multiple nights a week at this pub.

"Hey" was all she said.

"Hey, shots," I responded, presenting them to her.

She took hers down with spirit as I sat.

"What brings you here tonight?" I asked.

"The fucking ambiance," she joked, calling back to our first night. She was quick and witty and too likable even during her downward spiral.

"Shouldn't you be home calling my boyfriend?" she asked, answering one of my lingering questions. I could tell she'd already had a few drinks. It wasn't a malicious question. It had the air of a person who was giving up.

"I'm so sorry about that," I said. It was genuine. I was sorry I had done that, mostly because I didn't enjoy finding out how pathetic and sick I was. "I didn't even know I was doing it. I promise, it won't happen again."

I felt a ping in my chest warning me it was finally time for her to smarten up and treat me like the garbage I was. They were breaking up, and it was my fault. It was not a good feeling, but it felt good and that was not a good feeling.

"Does it have anything to do with the new guy?" she asked.

"Maybe," I said honestly. She had the right to ask me as many invasive questions as she wanted to.

"You guys looked good in the paper. It was kind of hot really. Scandalous."

"It was a mistake," I said.

"I met him. He came to the school and talked to everyone who knew Jenny. He seemed nice. Well, he seemed kind of full of himself, but he was polite." She laughed, then fell silent for a beat. "I don't think I am coping well. Do you think I'm coping well?"

"With what?" I asked, begging for all the juicy details of her crumbling relationship.

"Jenny."

Shit, how did this happen again? I was such an asshole. She wasn't thinking about Mark. She was thinking about the vicious murder of a little girl who she felt a sense of responsibility for. I was thriving in the wake of Jenny's murder like some sort of demon. My lip started to quiver. Oh my God. Oh my God.

"Are you OK?" she asked, not sure what was happening.

"I'm an asshole. I'm just really a selfish asshole. I'm not even thinking about Jenny. Honestly, I think I'm over it." My voice cut out at the end as tears started streaming from my eyes. "I didn't even know her, not really. And now, now I'm trying to act like some crusader that cares more about her than anyone else. It's bullshit. I never even cried once and not because I was trying to be strong or because I was in denial. I think I didn't cry because it didn't mean anything, not really. It was just another shitty thing to happen in a long line of shitty things that happen." I wiped tears from my face and sucked in my bottom lip to compose myself. What just happened? I was embarrassed, and I stood to leave.

"Don't leave," she said, taking my hand until I agreed to sit back down.

Monty brought another round of shots that we both threw back. It was going to be a long night.

"Do you feel safe?" she asked, picking at her beer bottle again. The question was somehow disarming, as if I needed to be further disarmed. "I think all the time, what if it wasn't just some pedophile from out of town obsessed with Jenny? What if it's someone who lives in this town and he's going to do it again?"

Shit. I hadn't really thought about it like that. I was the champion of *it could have been anyone*, but I'd never considered what that would actually mean. I always assumed Jenny would be the only victim in this town, that somehow she was so perfect she had a monopoly on tragedy.

"I have a gun," she said like she'd been building up to it, like maybe I would judge her. "I've had it forever. My father bought it for me when I graduated college. I keep it in my nightstand now. Not that I even know how to use it," she scoffed. "Pull the trigger, I guess."

"If I had a gun, I would probably just end up shooting myself," I said in a way that left it vague whether I meant by mistake or intention. She didn't push. It made me so happy.

Many shots later, there was no pretense that Hunter would drive home. We would both be lucky to stay on our feet back to my apartment. At some point soon after my little breakdown, I began outpacing her, enough for both of us to enjoy the same level of intoxication without her dying.

The gravel along the road crunched beneath our feet as we shuffled down the street. "The rape is the hardest part," Hunter slurred out. "I don't like to think about it, but it just pops in my head all the time. I haven't had sex since, you know? That's how fucked up I am. See, not coping." She tried to laugh.

I thought about Mark being so aggressive the day I went looking for Jenny's bag. It made more sense now, but screw him for holding it against her. And super screw him for the things he said before kissing me in the road. He didn't care about me. It was just primal horniness.

We stumbled into my apartment, and I made a mad dash to the bathroom. The amount of urine that had gathered in the five-minute walk from the bar defied the laws of science.

When I emerged, I found Hunter lying in my bed. She was still conscious, but didn't look to be capable of movement. I looked at my small couch. It was a good little couch that I had napped on a million times, but I didn't go there. I went to my bed and lay down next to her. We both stared at the ceiling. I wondered if it was spinning as violently for her.

"What if Mark could see us now?" she whispered.

"We deserve so much better than him," I admitted, finding a hint of clarity.

"Maybe we don't," she said.

She reached over and grabbed my hand. We stayed there for what could have been hours or seconds, but it was enough time to reflect on the fact that I was attracted to Brandon and obsessed with Hunter. Two people. Two people I could feel. Together, they might be enough to free me from Mark.

CHAPTER THIRTY-TWO

JENNY

THIS WAS THE first time Jenny wasn't looking forward to her scheduled meeting with Ms. Willoughby. She was still shaken by what went down with Mallory, and now she had to deal with the Mr. Renkin thing. Was she obliged to say something to Ms. Willoughby? Should she just mind her own business? They seemed happy enough. Maybe it was a side of him only reserved for the most desperate of situations. Maybe it was her fault for pushing him to that point. Maybe it was her fault for pushing Linda too. Maybe Jenny just had to stop. Maybe it had all gone too far.

Jenny waited patiently for her turn, keeping her hands together, a combination of rubbing and clenching to keep them from shaking. When the door finally opened, Mallory Murphy's smug face and annoying curls stepped into the waiting area.

This wasn't a thing. Mallory didn't see the guidance counselor. Mallory didn't need guidance. She was invading Jenny's one safe space. Why? Was she in there telling on Jenny? JP's threats hadn't scared her; they'd inspired her. Mallory wouldn't rest now until she'd turned everyone against her.

There was no scenario in which Jenny told the truth and things got better, and she was stupid for even entertaining the thought. She got up and walked out of the guidance office. She had a plan. Her own plan. The only one that would work.

JENNY WAITED behind the bleachers in the upstairs balcony of the gym, arriving first and leaning up against the locked cage that held all the broken gym class equipment.

"Get back to class," a gruff voice yelled from behind the bleachers. Jenny seized before JP stepped out, laughing.

"You're an idiot," she teased.

JP moved next to her and joined in leaning against the cage. He loved positioning himself next to her instead of in front. It made conversations awkward, but kept them on topic instead of looking into each other's eyes and wondering if they should act on their feelings again.

"Thank you . . ." Jenny said under her breath. "For the Mallory thing."

"No big deal. What was all that about Kevin Neary?"

He must have been lurking nearby, watching and listening to them before stepping in. How long was he there? Was he jealous? Or mad?

"It was nothing. Just people being stupid."

"Do you even know him?" JP wasn't so eager to let this go, and Jenny was enjoying the attention.

"Not really. He was talking to me at lunch today." She didn't feel it necessary to let JP know that she had intended on skipping school with Kevin. If she regretted it enough, it was like it didn't happen.

"You like him?"

"No."

"Yeah, right."

"I don't. I swear. He's an idiot and he's, like, old. He's eighteen."

"Whatever," he said.

"What was that about with Mallory? Do you really think she has a crush on you?"

"No, I was just saying it to mess with her."

"She might have a crush on you, you never know."

"No, thank you," he said, and Jenny tried to hide how happy that response made her. JP made her feel different. It wasn't like Kevin had made her feel earlier that day. It was more than that. The idea of being with Kevin was about everyone else. Being with JP was just about her and him.

"I don't think we should wait," Jenny thought aloud.

"What do you mean?"

"I don't want to do all this back and forth, writing letters to Gil and waiting for him to respond. It could take forever. Let's just send one letter . . . today, telling him I changed my mind and when to show up."

"Are you sure about this? The whole thing, I mean."

"It's worth it," she said.

"Where are we gonna do this?"

"Your house?" she suggested.

"Yeah, that could work. I don't really want this guy knowing where I live, but we'll leave that night anyway. If he comes back and kills Boomer, he'd probably be doing the man a favor. When do you want to do it?"

"It has to be a Saturday. Those are the easiest nights for me to sneak out because my dad's home and my mom behaves."

"That's probably best for him too. You know, if he has a job."

Jenny laughed.

"What?"

"I'm glad you are being so considerate of his schedule." She laughed again and JP cracked a smile.

"OK," she said, back to business. "Let's say this Saturday. If he doesn't show, we can try again next week, but I don't want to wait any longer than we have to. And I think if he has to decide right away, it won't give him any time to think really. Like, you know, make a plan about hiding the money, or change the details or something."

"That's smart," JP said, making Jenny proud of herself. "I can hide behind the couch. I don't want to be in another room because it's too far; he could hear me coming. You just gotta keep him in front of the couch. Get him to sit down and I'll pop up and scare the shit out of him."

"You have to wait for him to show the money. He might lie if he's scared, so just let me get him to show it first or this will all be for nothing," she said.

"Duh."

"Should we tie him up? I mean, I don't want him to follow us, but I also don't want Boomer to come home and find him."

"He could die if he had to wait for Boomer to come home," said JP. "I have some handcuffs. We can handcuff him and put the key across the room. It would take him a while to get free."

"But we can't leave until the morning, because of the bus."

"We just gotta get out of the house. He won't find us. We'll walk to town, then wait till morning. Bring warm clothes."

Warm clothes, she thought. *Sure, that will thwart any potential disaster.*

CHAPTER THIRTY-THREE

VIRGINIA

THERE HAD BEEN so many intolerable Sunday dinners in the past, but this one was by far the worst. There was a trifecta of horrible things weighing on my mind that I had to ignore to get through it. There was finding Linda puking all over herself earlier in the week, the reopening of Jenny's case, and my father being a sociopathic liar. At least Linda had finally cooked something.

The three of us sat at the table set with the good china and candles that flickered against the wallpaper. It was a far cry from the previous week's pizza party. Everything my father ever said or did needed to be reevaluated under a new lens. Nothing stood out, thinking back on it. I didn't even know what to look for. If I didn't know the reason for a lie, it might as well be the truth.

"Now that you've drawn all this attention back to us, you can't be talking to the media," said my father. "No more outbursts. We don't need to give them any more reasons to look at you."

I hated every word that seeped from his mouth, but he had a point. Now that the case was reopened, would I be a suspect? The evil half sister who had seduced the lead detective. What kind of world do we live in that I could be among a list of suspects who were all pedophiles?

"They like your face on the cover," my father continued, trying to flex his knowledge of the world. "You look innocent, but with nothing to show for yourself, you could be perceived as suspicious, someone with nothing to lose." He spoke as if he weren't aware he was insulting me. "The sheriff from Hartsfield called us," he continued. "He wouldn't tell us much about this new suspect. They're keeping the details out of the media so they don't spook him. They can't find him, you know?"

"Yeah, I know," I said.

"Do you know anything else?" Linda chimed in.

"No."

"Not even from that other detective? You know—"

"No," I cut her off. *Butt out, Linda.*

The next twenty minutes were unbearable. Conversation ceased, and it was just a chorus of silverware scraping against the china. Finally, my father removed his napkin from his lap and placed it on the table, signifying the end of the meal.

I left with little theatrics, backed my car out of the driveway, pulled around the corner, and killed the lights. My father wouldn't leave for hours, but I would be waiting.

I HAD NEARLY nodded off when I heard a car approaching. I pulled myself up in my seat, clenched the steering wheel, and waited to see if it was him. The car passed in front of me, and in the split second between when its headlights were blinding me and when it slipped into darkness, I recognized the silver Mercedes.

He rounded the bend, and I turned on my car. I did my best to keep a comfortable distance, and within ten minutes I could tell we weren't on our way to New York. Pulling onto Main Street, he turned right, north, and away from the city.

An hour and a half into the drive, I worried that I should have brought snacks, or at least water. He stopped only once at a gas station in New Lofton. He was back on the road in five minutes, and any hope that we were close faded away.

Another hour past the gas station, he began navigating side streets and I knew we were almost there. A sign a few miles back told me we were in Rutland, Vermont. It was very New England, with trees lining the streets and quaint houses with swings in the front yard. I'm sure it was a lovely place, but it made no sense.

The farther we got from the main street, the more nervous I became about getting caught. I pulled over and cut the lights. The neighborhood was a simple grid, and I was confident I could find his car in one of the driveways ahead.

I waited five long minutes, fidgeting with the radio, putting my hair up, then letting it back down. Unable to bear the anticipation any longer, I fired the car back up and crept through the streets, turning one way, then looping back when I didn't find him.

I finally spotted his car in the driveway of a single-story yellow house. The landscape was well manicured, with two rocking chairs on the front porch that gave it character. I drove to the end of the street and parked my car. I'd done it. I found him.

I had no plan. What was I going to find? A secret family? A serial killer's lair? Just a stupid house he went to because he hated us? I thought about him sitting on that porch, rocking back and forth as my mother hung from a tree. How could he be so selfish?

Whatever I was going to find inside, it was going to destroy him. This was even better than marching into his office. I was going to corrupt his private space. Infect it with memories that he could no longer lock outside. I pressed my finger against the doorbell, alerting those inside to my presence and setting off the high-pitched yaps of a dog.

The door opened, and a man in his fifties who was not my father stood in front of me holding the tiny dog. I didn't recognize him. His face was warm, and for a second I dreamed he was my father and inside this magic house he transformed into the pleasant-looking man in front of me.

"Virginia?" the man asked. He knew who I was.

I said nothing. I had no theories.

"What are you doing here?"

"Who are you?" I asked.

"I'm Charlie," he said, providing zero useful information. His forehead wrinkled behind his soft tone, nerves battling his desire to be hospitable.

"Do you live here?" I asked.

"I do."

"Is my dad in there?"

Charlie hesitated. He looked behind him into the house, then back at me. His legs twitched like he might have to go to the bathroom. "Can you give me a minute?" he asked, shutting the door in my face.

I stood on the doorstep, trying to make out any noise from inside. The dog started yapping again, almost on cue, and any voices were drowned out.

Three minutes later the door opened again. This time the man in his fifties who greeted me was my father. "Virginia, what are you doing here?"

"I followed you."

"Why?" he asked, like a good reason could erase what I was seeing. His voice was loose, not the stern delivery I was used to.

"I went to New York. I know you don't work in that office."

My father swallowed hard. He was caught with no time to prepare a story. "You shouldn't be here," he said, like I would just leave.

"Tell me I shouldn't call Detective Colsen."

"Detective Colsen? Why would you call Detective Colsen?"

"You are living a secret life! Did she find out about it? Did you do something to Jenny? Do you know what happened to her?"

"No. Please, calm down."

"Tell me," I demanded.

"Come inside," he beckoned, surveying the neighborhood to see if my voice had triggered any reaction. "Let me explain."

Inside I found Charlie sitting on a fabric sofa, failing to look comfortable. The fireplace was roaring, and a bottle of wine chilled in a bucket on the coffee table. My father shut the door behind me as I drifted toward the mantel and a row of framed pictures. The first three were pageant photos of Jenny. The third was a picture of me holding Jenny when she was only a week old. Whatever this place was, we weren't secrets here.

The fourth picture answered all my questions, then created more. It was my father sitting on a large rock, smiling to the point I almost didn't recognize him. Behind him, with comfy sweater arms wrapped around his waist, was Charlie.

"Dad . . ." I turned to face my father as he bit his lip. He couldn't say anything the picture didn't already say. My father had a boyfriend.

———

I SAT THROUGH A LONG STORY, spanning nearly thirty years, told mostly by Charlie as my father sat in a chair with his legs crossed and his hands folded. Charlie was a good storyteller. He almost made me forget about my family too.

The two men worked together at the New York office, successful investors making money and names for themselves within the company. The futures they planned on imploded one night twenty-five years ago when they gave in to feelings both were denying. The office was a boys' club, and not the kind that would welcome two gay men. My father was married with a one-year-old and told Charlie he would never come out. Charlie was ready to tell the world, but understood.

My father promised Charlie it would never happen again. Charlie was devastated and a month later approached management about working remotely from home. He was a top earner and the company didn't want to lose him. A week later, Charlie bought this house in Vermont.

The two men didn't speak for over a year until my father showed up on Charlie's doorstep with a proposition; they would be together, but it would be a secret and my dad would keep his family, forever his cover story. They argued at first. Charlie didn't want to be in the closet, but the more he pushed, the further my father retreated. It was a compromise that Charlie insisted was worth it, and I added Charlie to the list of people my father mistreated.

I wanted to give Charlie a hug. I wanted my father to leave and I wanted to talk to Charlie all night. Instead, the opposite happened. After an hour of storytelling and a genuine attempt to get to know me, Charlie stood. "Well, I'm going to head to bed and give you two a chance to talk without me hogging the conversation."

He stopped and gave me a hug. He whispered in my ear as he did, "Forgive him. He's a good man." Then he kissed my cheek.

He walked behind my father toward the bedroom, stopping to kiss him on top of his head. My father reached up to touch Charlie's shoulder, a gentle apologetic touch that was unrecognizable. Then Charlie left us to silence.

One of us had to speak first. I didn't know what to say. Did I hate him less knowing the truth, or did I hate him more? Living in the closet all those years, stuck in a loveless marriage, it was sad and it explained so much, but *he* did this. He dragged all of us down with him because he was too afraid to be different, to seem anything less than perfect. He was already too far in with me and my mother when it happened, but he chose to marry Linda knowing. He chose to have Jenny as some sick cover.

I didn't want to talk about his pretend life anymore. Or I guess *we* were his pretend life. Either way, I didn't want to partake in this fantasy where my father was a loving, happy man. I'd rather talk about perverts.

"I told you it wasn't Benjy," I said.

"I knew it wasn't him."

"What do you mean? You said it was him a million times. You yelled at me for firing up Linda with my theories."

"Virginia, please. There's no need to yell." He lowered his voice to compensate for mine.

"You should have said something to the cops. Do you know how much time they wasted on Benjy? And now they can't find the other guy. It's probably too late—"

"I didn't tell the cops because I'm afraid of who did it," he said.

"You know who did it?"

"I'm not afraid *of* who did it," he clarified. "I'm afraid *for* who did it."

I wasn't understanding. He was being cryptic, and I couldn't keep up. There was so much information to process already.

"Just tell me," I begged, exhausted.

He finally uncrossed his legs. He had sat in one position for over an hour, and whatever he was about to say needed his feet to be grounded. He rested both elbows on his thighs and leaned toward me.

"You called me that night. I was driving to meet Charlie in Hartsfield and you called my cell. You were incoherent, yelling about Jenny." He waited for my response.

I had none. There was no memory. It was a Saturday night. "What did I say?"

"Nothing. All I could understand was her name. You were slurring, yelling, then whispering, then you just hung up."

What did I know about Jenny? Why had I called my father, of all people?

"Why didn't you call the police?" I asked. If I knew something, if I had done something, maybe he could have stopped it before it was too late. Then he said something that made an unbearable situation worse.

"It wasn't the first time I got a call like that from you."

My eyes started to flutter, blinking back tears.

"Usually on Saturday nights, you'll call. You never say much, at least nothing I can really understand. Sometimes, you just hang up as soon as I answer, but that's why I didn't think anything of it. Not until after, of course."

Tears poured down my face. I was embarrassed. I was scared. "Dad . . ."

He rose from the chair and joined me on the couch. He put his arm around me, and I cried into his chest. There was no time to make a pros and cons list about letting him comfort me. I just broke down.

I cried and cried forever, and he stayed, rubbing my head until I stopped. "I didn't hurt her, I couldn't have," I choked out.

"Shhh," he whispered. I pushed myself off of him and swallowed to compose myself, my face drenched in the tears that hadn't soaked into his shirt.

"Dad, I swear I didn't do anything to her. I drank too much and I took pills and I don't remember anything, but I woke up in my bed, in my pajamas, when the police called the next day. I wasn't in the woods and I certainly didn't rape her."

"But you called. You were saying her name at the same time she was being killed. You knew something."

I closed my eyes and tried to focus, tried to revive dead brain cells. What did I know? There was nothing there. There never was. Eight years of calls to Mark Renkin. Eight years of calls to my father. One night with my sister. They were all lost.

Instead, I had a realization. "You were going to meet Charlie?"

He sighed, ashamed. "I try not to see him on the weekends, try to let that be family time, but I just needed to get out for a little while."

"You lied."

My father looked around the room, everything a lie, and waited for me to justify making such an obvious statement.

"No, you lied about your alibi. You said you were home. What about Linda? You were her alibi too. You said Jenny was asleep in her bed. You said you and Linda were home all night and didn't hear anything. What if she did hear something? What if she did something and she's covering it up and you gave her an alibi?"

My father's head tilted, an instinctive reaction to the implausible thought of Linda's involvement. After a beat, he came back to center, opening his mind to the possibility.

CHAPTER THIRTY-FOUR

JENNY

THE NIGHT OF their plan arrived. JP had brought the letter to the post office on Tuesday and paid extra to have it sent overnight. There was no way to know if Gil got it or if he was still interested in the deal. They just had to wait.

Jenny called it a night around nine o'clock. She gave her dad a huge hug that he wasn't expecting but accepted. It was her good-bye. She hugged Linda too. The woman had no hesitation returning the embrace, in full denial of what their relationship had become. Jenny closed her eyes as she wrapped her arms around her mother and tried focusing on fond memories of their distant past. That was the mother she owed a good-bye hug to, not the one in her arms.

Jenny climbed the stairs toward her room, taking her time and running her hand along the wall. This house was the only home she'd ever known.

Her backpack was loaded and leaning against her vanity chair. She climbed into bed with her iPod and pulled the covers to her neck. Jenny stuffed the buds into her ears and started a playlist she had made just for that night. It was two hours of her favorite songs, enough time for her parents to go to bed and fall asleep. She nestled into her pillow as the first song started. She wasn't worried she would fall asleep. This was the most exciting night of her life.

THE PLAYLIST ENDED right on cue. Two hours and five minutes later, Jenny slid her arms from under the covers and yanked out the ear-buds. The rest of her remained still, listening. The house was silent. She flipped off the covers and swung her feet around to the floor.

Her socks slid across the carpet as she made her way to the door. She touched the knob, causing a shock from the friction. She yanked her hand back. Once recovered, she reached back and opened the door a crack, just enough to see her parents' bedroom door was closed, no light glowing from underneath, no light reflecting from downstairs.

Jenny took two steps to her vanity and stepped over her backpack to slip into the chair. She reached down and pulled her hairbrush from the front pocket. She drew the bristles through her golden hair several times, each stroke causing the hair to fall perfectly back in place. Jenny untwisted two hair bands from the handle and set them on the table with the brush.

She parted her hair down the middle, tying it into symmetric pigtails that made her look years younger in an instant. She placed the brush back into the backpack and opened the top vanity drawer.

Inside sat carefully organized stacks of makeup that she hadn't touched in months. She took a moment to stare at the mascaras, the lipsticks, the fake eyelashes, before pushing the top layer of bold blues and reds toward the back of the drawer. The next layer of makeup was more of the same. She dove both hands in, digging through, making a mess and more noise than she should. An eye shadow set caught against a lip in the drawer and the top popped off, dumping blue dust everywhere—a mess she would never have to clean up.

Under the next bronzer compact, she found what she was looking for. She pulled the small rectangle out of the drawer and opened it. It was light pink blush with a tiny brush inside for application. She brought the brush to her cheeks, making small circles that grew with each rotation until she had the rosy cheeks of a doll.

She had decided to look as young as possible. It was important that she fit Gil's fantasy and didn't seem threatening. She looked in the mirror and felt ridiculous. She dropped the blush back into the vanity drawer and closed it.

As she stood, she reached for her backpack, slipping her arms through the straps. Jenny hesitated once more at the door to make sure the house was asleep. With nothing to give her second thoughts, she slid out the door and crept down the stairs.

SHE DIDN'T MAKE IT halfway through the living room before a glass smashed into the back of her head, sending her to her knees. Shards of glass rained down on the carpet, her hands narrowly missing them as she threw her arms out to catch herself.

She wanted to reach for her head, but didn't trust her balance. Her hands in front of her were blurry and multiplying. She tried to blink her mind clear as she heard someone approaching. She wanted to look, she wanted to stand, but she needed time, a minute for her brain to recalibrate.

Before she could move, her head jerked back. Someone had

grabbed her by the pigtails, whipping her neck and flinging her backward. Her backpack hit first, then her tailbone. Pieces of glass dug into her skin.

She could hear footsteps leaving the edge of the carpet and hitting the wood flooring down the hall. Jenny moaned as she rolled to the side, reaching behind her to pull out the glass that was stabbing her. The pieces weren't in deep, but they stung. She twisted her head toward the hall. It was dark, but she knew who it was.

Linda stormed back from the study, gripping a pair of severe metal scissors.

"Dad!" Jenny screamed. Her eyes darted between her fast-approaching mother and the stairs she prayed her father would come running down. "Dad!" she screamed again, her voice piercing even her own ears.

Jenny tried to stand, but her mother was already coming down on her. Linda grabbed a pigtail and yanked Jenny onto her stomach, the pull of her pigtail in Linda's hand jerking her face to a stop just before it could make contact with the slivers of glass in the carpet below.

"You're a little animal," Linda spat at her daughter. "Why did you do this to us?"

Jenny could hear the scratch of the worn scissors as they parted.

"This is what you want? To be a little whore?"

The scissors clamped shut and Jenny's face crashed to the ground, tiny bits of glass slicing thin cuts on her rosy cheeks.

Seconds later, her head was yanked up again by the remaining pigtail.

"You're a bad seed just like your sister. I'm a good mother." The scissors closed again, and Jenny's face slammed back into the carpet, causing another batch of cuts. Linda dropped the scissors on the ground, where they landed in front of Jenny's wet eyes.

Her mother stepped away and Jenny could finally reach for her head. The pigtails were gone. She pinched a chunk of hair at the root and followed it to the tip, inches from where she started. Tears rolled down her cheeks. She lifted her head and watched her mother walk toward the liquor cabinet. Without thinking, Jenny's small hand reached over and gripped the scissors. She took them in her palm and crawled to her feet.

Linda bent down into the cabinet, stumbling a bit. She wouldn't be conscious much longer. Linda grabbed a bottle and stared out the bay window, swaying from side to side.

Jenny stood, feet planted, hands clenching the scissors, eyes bearing down. Her mother didn't turn back. Instead, she brought the bottle to her mouth and took a long swig. Jenny could kill her mother. It would be easy. The woman was barely staying on her feet. She was a crazy drunk and she needed to be put down.

Jenny dropped the scissors at her feet. She waited another second for Linda to turn and acknowledge her, and when she didn't, Jenny left. In a way, she was grateful. After this night, she would never miss her mother again.

CHAPTER THIRTY-FIVE

VIRGINIA

THE SUN WAS BARELY UP when my father backed his car out of the driveway and turned away from the inviting Vermont home. I shifted my car into drive and coasted from the curb. I was following my father again, but this time my presence was welcomed. We were headed home to confront Linda. It was only Monday, and he was leaving Charlie for the week. He was choosing us in that moment, and it wasn't lost on me.

I had no idea what kind of Linda we were going to find. My last unexpected visit had found Linda hammered beyond recognition, lying in her own puke, but the night before she had been an over-the-top Stepford wife. Which one was real? Probably neither.

I hadn't seen a soul for the last few miles, and as we approached the house, I longed for a neighbor walking the dog or a kid on a bike. I was anxious and uncomfortable, and the postapocalyptic vibe wasn't helping. I got out of the car and slammed the door before our footsteps became the only noise in earshot.

I followed my father in through the garage. He didn't speak. I could tell from his frigid mannerisms that he was back in his disguise.

I would have to return to Vermont if I wanted to see the other Dad again.

The kitchen was clean and barren. The drawn curtains didn't let either one of us forget we were unexpected guests. We moved silently through the house. I contemplated bumping into something to let a sound ring out, announcing our presence, but I followed my father's lead. I wanted Linda to come running down the stairs. I didn't want to *find* her.

We climbed the stairs. He knew where he was going, and I had no reason to argue.

I felt like I no longer knew a single person in my life. Everything was a lie. Everything was an act. I craved seeing Linda come out of the bathroom, hair and makeup perfect, yelling at us for tracking dirt onto the stairs and complaining what an inconvenience it was to have the carpet guys come to the house even though she never had anything better to do. I hated that Linda, but it was the Linda I had always known and understood how to deal with. I wanted that Linda.

The door to the bedroom my father shared with Linda in what I can only imagine was a cold, frictionless bed was closed. He opened it and stepped through. I followed, empowered to consider myself welcome inside.

The bed was made and empty. We both stood there a moment, staring at the bed like she would manifest if we looked hard enough. My father broke first and headed toward the bathroom. An idea came to me and I backed out of the room.

Jenny's door was closed to the point I couldn't see in, but not shoved the extra inch to catch the handle. I placed my right hand against the door, eye level in an unconscious effort to obstruct what

I was about to see. I pushed forward and stepped into a room I had now been in more times since her death than in the whole year before.

Linda looked like a bag of bones. Only a faint rise and fall in her chest kept me from screaming. She was on her back, on top of Jenny's bed, one arm above her head, one tucked behind her. Her head hung to the side in a position someone in a right state of mind would never choose.

"Dad," I said somewhere above a whisper. I heard him coming from the other room, but I kept my eyes on Linda, panicking in between each of her labored breaths. There were pills. It wasn't dramatic like in the movies, just one pill bottle on the nightstand. It wasn't even knocked over, but I knew it was empty.

My father pushed the door farther to accommodate his larger body as he entered. He stopped behind me, looking over my shoulder at his wife. After a brief pause, he pushed me aside and ran to her. He knelt down and touched her arm.

"Linda," he said, quietly at first. She didn't react. He was being too gentle. "Linda . . ." he tried again, this time shaking her shoulder and causing her head to bounce a bit against the pillow. She moaned and flipped her face away from him.

The moan awakened something in my father, and he seized her other shoulder. He yanked her up and down, grasping for consciousness. "Linda, wake up! Linda!"

She moaned again as she moved her head back and forth, trying to make him stop, but it was like her head weighed a hundred pounds.

He released her shoulders and put his hand around her jaw, holding her in place. He was close to her face now, within inches. "Linda, you need to wake up. What do you know about Jenny? What happened that night?"

Linda groaned from somewhere deep inside that caused me to grimace and my father to release her and fall back onto his heels. She rolled to her side, revealing the hidden hand clutching Jenny's pigtails.

I whipped my face toward the back of my father's head and waited for him to turn his eyes to me. We communicated without speaking; we had discovered something horrible.

Linda's eyes fluttered open. Then closed. Then open again, struggling to stay that way. "I'm sorry," she whispered.

"Are those Jenny's?" my father asked, coming off his heels a bit.

"I attacked her," Linda mumbled like her tongue was too big for her mouth. "I hit her and I cut her hair off . . . She ran away."

Her eyes closed and her body went limp. My father attempted to shake her awake again, but she just flopped around like a doll. Those were the only words we were going to get from her in that room.

"Call 9-1-1," he said, and I pulled my phone from my pocket. This was going to be ugly. Did she do something? Did I do something? What about Gil?

I TEXTED BRANDON on the way to the hospital. There was too much to talk about and I didn't want to do it over the phone. By the time I parked and got inside, they had wheeled her off and left my dad in the waiting room. He was typing like mad on his phone, and I now knew that what I used to think were work e-mails were in fact texts to Charlie. I wondered how many times I was furious with him for dealing with work when in reality he was talking to his true love. Christmas mornings, birthdays, every other ordinary day?

I slunk into the seat next to him, and he stopped typing.

"She's going to be fine. They're letting her sleep it off," he said without eye contact. Then we sat in silence. He wasn't on his phone; it was a real, mutual silence.

"I won't tell," I said so he wouldn't have to ask.

My father shook his head. He was embarrassed, which I loved.

"It wasn't like it is now," he said. "I sacrificed what I wanted so that you and then Jenny could have a normal life."

"Are you serious? You definitely didn't do this for me or Jenny. You don't even really like us."

"Is that what you think?" He looked up at me.

"Don't ask that like I'm overreacting," I said, trying my best to keep a calm tone.

"We would have been ostracized. School would have been a nightmare for you."

"School *was* a nightmare because my mom fucking killed herself," I threw back at him.

His head fell.

"I'm sorry," I said. I wasn't really sorry; at least, I don't think I was.

"Do you blame me now? For Jenny?" he asked, begging me to let him off the hook.

"Hard to tell. I don't know what happened to her. I'll reserve blame for when we have answers," I said, jaded to the max.

"Hindsight is twenty-twenty, Virginia, and I want you to know I'm sorry. Every time I thought about telling someone, the fear was too much. After your mother—" He closed his eyes for a beat.

"Logically, it made sense to tell the truth, but when my body was physically ill from the thought of it, I convinced myself it must be wrong and then I shut it out. I didn't weigh the pros and cons, I just tuned it out." He spewed vulnerability in his same dry, weighted tone. I guess that's just how he sounded all the time, his disguise so ingrained into who he was now, so trained to become cold and distant whenever he left Vermont.

My defenses were skyrocketing. I was thrilled about this other Dad, but I was too exhausted to rely on my judgment that it was for real. It was better not to risk it. When in doubt about matters of the heart, best to think about murder, facts, murder facts. "Do you think Linda killed her?" I asked. "Is it possible? I mean, anything is possible, but is it reasonable?"

He sighed, accepting I wasn't ready to forgive him. "I hope not. I really hope not. She said Jenny ran away."

When he glanced back at his phone, I welcomed the opportunity for a break.

I stood up like I wanted to stretch my legs and really just moved to another seat on the opposite side of the waiting room. I sat still, alone with my thoughts with no way to act on them. It kept coming back to the rape. Anyone could have killed her, but Linda didn't rape her. I didn't rape her. I realized in that moment I was relieved that Jenny had been raped. If she hadn't been, would I actually entertain the idea I was involved? No. I had to believe in myself. I had no reason to kill her. If I wanted her dead, it would have been back when she was Little Miss Perfect. It made no sense now. A drunken phone call. That was it. It had to be.

"Virginia," Brandon snapped me out of my head.

"Thanks for coming," I said, standing up and letting him hug me.

"Of course, what happened?"

"I don't know. We came home and found her passed out in Jenny's bed. She said a few words, but she was definitely messed up. She's fine, though."

Brandon took a seat next to me, and we both stared out into the waiting room. My father hadn't even looked up from his phone enough to notice Brandon was there.

"What were you doing with your dad? I thought you hated him."

"I don't know," I mumbled, hoping he would drop it.

He turned in his chair to face me. I kept my face forward, sneaking glimpses of him in my periphery that begged him to turn away. "I know something happened in New York. I don't know what, and you don't have to tell me, but you can if you want."

"Just family stuff," I said.

It wasn't my secret to share. Not with the detective, even if I was sleeping with him. He would think the same things I did. The lying, the cheating—better to just keep him focused on finding Gil. We were a group of wretched people, it turned out, but Gil was still the most likely suspect. Gil, the missing pedophile.

"Any news on Gil?"

Brandon sat back in his chair, consenting to not talking about my father anymore. "Paulson says they can't find him. He's a ghost."

I didn't know what felt worse, them arresting an innocent man or being unable to catch a guilty one. I guess in either scenario, Gil was on the loose. At least now Benjy could move on with his life, whatever life was for him.

"Let me ask you something," he said perking up. "Do *you* think it was Gil?"

"What do you mean?"

"I mean, you had a big hunch it wasn't Benjy. You thought it was too convenient and that your sister had grown out of her pedophile-bait phase. I'm just checking, with all signs pointing to Gil, do you think he did it?"

I didn't answer right away because I didn't really know what I thought. Benjy was different. You could tell Benjy was harmless and people were overreacting. Gil was bad news, and I'd fought tooth and nail to uncover his mere existence, so why couldn't I commit 100 percent? Could everything I'd learned in the last few weeks about my family and myself just be coincidence? Or was there something shadier there, something twisted and growing, something just about to crack the surface?

Rape, I thought. The linchpin in all my theories. But that night, if it had all started with Linda and not the actual killer, any forensic timeline the police were using could be wrong. A thought that was both relieving and horrifying crept in. The night Jenny came to my apartment. The questions she was asking about sex. I didn't think anything of it, typical teenage curiosity, just another bout of her annoying rapid-fire questions, but . . . "Could it have been consensual?" I asked. "The rape, could it have been consensual sex masked by unrelated trauma to her body?"

CHAPTER THIRTY-SIX

JENNY

JENNY DIDN'T WAIT FOR JP to answer the door; she busted in while one of her trembling hands was still knocking.

The boy was sitting on the couch, just sitting, waiting for her. He jumped to his feet in sync with the front door. His eyes widened at the sight of her, cuts on her face, her hair chopped beyond recognition. "Jenny?"

She took four steps toward him, tears in her eyes, and let him wrap his arms around her.

"Did he do this? Is he here?" JP looked around as if Gil were somehow in the room.

"No, my mom," she said, swaying, eyes darting around.

JP moved his hands to her face to focus her. He held her cheeks in his palms while he wiped her tears away with his thumbs. "Does it hurt?" he asked, brushing his right thumb just below the most obvious of the cuts.

"Not really. Look at my hair," she pouted, allowing herself some teenage vanity in the moment. "What am I going to do? Gil is going to hate this."

JP released her face. "Jenny, you're beautiful, so beautiful."

She didn't believe him. How could she? "I have to go to the bathroom."

JP backed away.

She sniffled in an attempt to compose herself, then brushed past him. She closed the bathroom door and set her backpack down on top of the toilet. There wasn't much room to maneuver inside. The bathroom was gross—mold, tiny hairs, brown buildup under everything balancing on the sink.

Atop the small radiator was a folded cotton nightgown. JP had lifted it from a clothing donation box in town. It was white with pink cuffs and a pattern of pink bows. It was for a much younger girl, but Jenny was skinny and would have no problem getting into it. It would have gone well with her pigtails.

She turned from the radiator and caught herself in the mirror. She looked like a public service ad for something horrible. She unrolled a handful of toilet paper squares and ripped them from the roll. She ran the water and didn't wait for it to warm up before dipping the thin paper underneath. Once wet, it compacted to the size of a cotton ball, and she brought it to her face, dabbing the cuts. The blood was dry, and after attempting to be gentle, she gritted her teeth and scrubbed at the red crust. Eventually, only the actual cuts remained. They weren't particularly deep or menacing, but a glaring and obvious disruption to her otherwise smooth skin.

Jenny pressed her palms against her hairline in an attempt to flatten the chunks of various lengths that stood at attention. When she removed her hands, the hairs bounced right back. She slid her hands under the water and used it to slick back and finally tame the hair. She unzipped the front pocket of her backpack and pulled out a handful of barrettes. She had such little hair left, but it took seven barrettes to leave her confident that it would stay put once dry.

Jenny grabbed the nightgown from the radiator, held it by the shoulders, and let it unfold to the ground. She had worn so many things like this as a child. The perversion of what she was doing finally set in. In that moment, she wasn't thinking about the courageous plan she had unfurled to seize control of her life; she was thinking about putting on that nightgown to turn on an older man who was sexually attracted to children. She swallowed hard, then laid the nightgown over her backpack and lifted her sweatshirt above her head.

The nightgown was comfortable, a thought she couldn't believe she was having. Her purple-striped cotton underwear was slightly visible if she pulled the gown tight across her backside, and she debated changing, but it seemed futile. She had only a few other pairs with her, and they all had patterns too.

She slipped her hand into the front pocket of her backpack for the final touch, crawling her fingers around the passport until she felt the thin gold chain in the crevice of the pocket. Jenny reached around her neck and hooked the small clasp. The heart charm rested just above her nightgown, on prominent display now that there were no long pigtails to crowd the frame.

She stuffed her clothes into her backpack. It was completely full now. These were the worldly possessions she was taking with her to Mexico. Nothing else would fit.

JP WAS STILL STANDING when she came out of the bathroom. He seemed nervous, but it made her feel more comfortable. He should be nervous. What they were doing was scary.

He turned to look at her. His expression was searching for a way to make her feel better. "You look . . . young," he said, neither one of them knowing if that was a compliment.

Jenny set her backpack down on the chair and used her free hands to fan out the nightgown in front of her. "Kind of creepy, isn't it?"

JP smiled. "I like what you did with your hair. I don't know what the pervert will say, but I think it's hot," he joked, and Jenny relaxed a bit. In the grand scheme of things, she cared much more about what JP thought.

"How long do we have?"

JP looked down at his watch. "About a half hour if he's on time . . . if he even shows."

Jenny moved to the couch and took a seat. He stayed stationary, unsure how to act around her now that she was in uniform.

"Sit with me." She didn't bother to ask. She had all the power now. She was making the sacrifice. She was going into the line of fire. For the next half hour, he would have to do whatever she said.

He tried to leave space as he sat, but the weak cushions had too much give and he came to a rest directly next to her, their thighs pressing against each other.

"Do you have the gun?" he asked.

"Oh my God," she said, and cringed. "I forgot, I'm so sorry, but my mom—"

"It's OK," he said. "I'm better with my knives anyway."

Jenny lifted his arm and put it around her shoulders. She leaned against his chest and he didn't fight her. "Tell me more about Mexico," she said, wanting to put her thoughts anywhere else.

"It's really warm there. We can swim all year if we want. The water is blue; it's not polluted or anything."

Jenny reached her head up and kissed him on the cheek. She pulled her lips back, but left her head close. He turned to face her, and she kissed him on the lips, a closed-mouth kiss that lasted enough time to be more than a peck. She pulled her face back again. He stayed. He stared into her eyes. He said nothing. He did nothing. She was the boss.

Jenny placed her hand on the back of his neck and bent her finger just enough to create pressure and move his head toward hers. They kissed again, intensely this time. The back-and-forth was enough to sit Jenny up and off of his chest. Their bodies seesawed back and forth before she finally pulled him on top of her.

JP pushed his chest up off of her and their lips separated. "Jenny . . ."

"Please, I want to." She guided his hand down her thigh to the bottom of the nightgown, wrapping his fingers around the pink ruffled edge.

CHAPTER THIRTY-SEVEN

VIRGINIA

I HAD LEARNED something in the past few weeks, something I didn't realize was relevant until that moment, about Mallory Murphy. Hunter told me Jenny hated her. What is the most likely cause of the end of a childhood friendship between two teenage girls? It pained me to think with such bias, but it was probably a boy.

I sat in my car outside of the school, waiting for Mallory. I'd seen just enough pictures of her in my life to pick her out in a crowd. Eventually, she emerged from the building flanked by two lackeys. I got out of my car and met them at the edge of the parking lot.

"Hey, you're Mallory, right?"

Mallory smirked as if I should know for sure who she was.

"I'm Jenny's sister, Virginia."

"I know."

"Can I talk to you for a minute?"

"Sure." She dismissed her friends with some sort of flippant hand motion that was almost too stereotypical to stomach.

"Do you know if Jenny had a boyfriend?" I asked once we were alone.

"Why?"

"I just want to know. I'm her sister."

"We already covered that. This is weird." She looked around like she might need backup. "Is that all you wanted to ask?"

"I know you two were fighting."

"How do you know that?" she said, asking me to prove it.

"Does it matter? Is it true or not?"

Mallory scoffed, not feeling any obligation to respect her elders. "I have to go."

She turned, and I grabbed her arm, probably harder than I should have.

"Let go of me," she said, and I released her immediately.

"Look." I lowered my voice. "I don't want to have to tell the police you know something. I don't want to have to tell them you were fighting with Jenny over a guy."

"We weren't fighting over a guy," she spat back at me. "We were fighting because she was being a bitch and then her psycho boyfriend attacked me."

"What are you talking about? Who was her boyfriend, and what do you mean he attacked you?"

"Never mind, it was nothing."

"What's his name?"

"You can't tell anyone I told you. You have to promise because that psycho will seriously kill me."

"Oh my God, Mallory, did you tell anyone this? Jenny was literally murdered. Why didn't you tell the police?"

"JP didn't kill her." She rolled her eyes at me like I was mentally challenged. "It was a pedophile. Everyone knows that."

JP. I knew that name. Why did I know that name? Mark's face flashed in front of me. I was sitting in the woods, and Mark was looking down at me. That was the name of the kid hiding in the woods, JP.

I turned away from Mallory and ran to my car.

"Where are you going?" she yelled after me, but I couldn't look at her stupid, stupid face any longer.

I CALLED BRANDON, and he left the hospital to pick me up at my apartment. We were going to see JP, Jenny's boyfriend, whose name hadn't made the police file once. There was no question I would go with Brandon. His days of feigning resistance to being accompanied by a civilian on official police business were over. I mean, he wasn't supposed to be investigating the case anyway. If anything, I was letting him accompany me on official civilian business.

"Are they all like this?" I asked.

"What do you mean?"

"I don't know." I searched for what I meant. "So many different people who could have killed a thirteen-year-old girl."

"I don't know. I hope not, or I should just retire now. If I even still have a job." Awkward. "So, you think JP might be involved?" he asked.

"What? I didn't say that."

"You said *so many* people. I wouldn't call Gil *so many* people."

I didn't even realize what I was saying. In my mind, there were a lot more suspects. The things I now knew about Linda, my father, and myself, the thought of the rape being off the table. And Mark. Mark—Jenny's teacher. Mark—the secret pedophile. The morality of keeping all of these thoughts to myself was tricky. Was I protecting my family, myself, or a murderer? If I told him everything I knew, would it help? Would it explain anything?

"I don't know. What do you think?" I asked.

"You're the one who's met him."

"He's just a scrubby kid." I thought about how JP had saved my ass with Mark. Throwing unfounded suspicion on him based on the word of that dimwit Mallory seemed like a shitty way to repay him. "It's hard to give anyone more weight than Gil. That would be an insane coincidence."

"I guess. The kid could have been jealous, though, if he found out she was talking to Gil. Jealousy is a good old-fashioned motive."

"Well, *now* I think he might have done it," I said, and smiled at Brandon.

"Your parents' house." He pointed as we turned onto Sanford Hill, as if I didn't know.

"Would you like to stop and say hi?"

"Maybe if they were home. Awfully close, though."

"Everything is close in this town."

The road became densely packed with trees not much past the driveway to my old house. Brandon drove so slowly. He wasn't used to roads like this with no streetlights and barely enough room for two cars.

My stomach dropped as we approached Mark's house. I was practicing *out of sight, out of mind*, but now that his house was in front of me, he consumed my mind. I'd survived the past two Saturdays without a phone call. Did he notice? Did it upset him? Why did I care?

There is an instinct so human and uncontrollable where you want to be loved wholeheartedly by someone even if you don't, or won't, love them back, even if you know they are the worst thing on the planet for you. *I can move on, but you can't*—that's the rule. I was the strong person who didn't care anymore, the one who was moving on. It was his role now to be paralyzed without my love.

I looked for Hunter's car in the driveway, but only Mark's Blazer was there. Of course I was happy she wasn't there with Mark, but also, lately, the sight of her car, the thought of seeing her, brought an odd sense of comfort. She was my new drug. She was what I turned to late at night when I couldn't be alone with my thoughts.

"Are you OK?" Brandon asked. Apparently I looked as uncomfortable on the outside as I felt on the inside.

"Yeah, JP's house is up here around the corner."

He steered the car around the bend like an elderly woman.

"That one," I said.

IT TOOK FOUR knocks for someone to answer the door.

"Why hello," Boomer said, showing no concern over our presence. His face was red and puffy, his thin hair pointed in different directions across the top of his head.

"Boomer, I don't know if you know me, but—"

"You're the Kennedy girl," he cut me off. "People in this town got a lot to say about you. Should mind their own business, though, if you ask me."

"I'm sure they do," I said.

"Do you think you all could give me a ride to town?" he asked, making clear he couldn't care less about why we were at his doorstep.

"Does JP live here?" Brandon asked.

"The kid? Yeah, he's out back, I think."

Brandon turned to go find JP.

"I'll grab you before we head back to town," I said. It was a long walk for an old drunk, even if he did it every day.

I shuffled my feet quickly to catch up with Brandon and match his stride. He was like a hunting dog who'd caught a scent, nose to the ground, charging forward.

I spotted JP as soon as we rounded the corner revealing the back-yard. He was about thirty yards away near the tree line in the same raggedy camouflage jacket, which wasn't doing its job since he was so clearly visible among the trees. His back was to us, and he appeared to be doing something with the thick tree trunk in front of him. Brandon slowed his pace, letting his footsteps become silent, and I followed his example.

As we got closer, I could make out what JP was doing with the tree. He was working a knife back and forth, trying to loosen it from the bark's hold. It was a pretty big knife, but JP was being careful not to yank on it too hard and break the thing.

He heard us before we could say anything and whipped around in a defensive stance like any rational human being who is being snuck up on would. "What the fuck?" barked JP.

"JP, I'm Detective Colsen, and I'd like to ask you a few questions."

"OK," he said. He looked at me for approval and I nodded to reassure him.

"Did you know Jenny Kennedy?" Brandon asked.

"Yeah."

"Care to elaborate?"

"You asked a yes-or-no question. If you want more, ask an

open-ended question." He turned away from us and started pulling on the knife again.

"Listen," Brandon said. "It's completely your right to act like a punk, but I can tell you it won't help. This is serious. A girl was murdered. A detective is at your house asking questions. I'm not someone you want to piss off."

"Are you even a cop anymore? I saw the news. Let me see your badge." JP crossed his arms and waited. Brandon scoffed, feigning that the request was ridiculous even though his badge was currently sitting in the desk of Sheriff Sharp.

"JP," I said before things got any uglier, "we're just trying to find out what happened. You told me yourself that Jenny was your friend. We're just trying to find out if you were more than friends."

His eyes narrowed, glaring at me. "Why?"

"Someone told me you were her boyfriend."

"Let me guess, Mallory Murphy? I'm sure that little psycho had some really nice things to say about me." JP thought Mallory was a psycho. Mallory thought JP was a psycho. Were we just wasting our time here, caught in the middle of some inane teenage drama?

"Look . . ." JP paused to look around like he was about to tell a secret someone would overhear. "Jenny was helping me with some of my classes and I was embarrassed, so we would meet in private and I guess someone saw us and thought it was more than that. Once Mallory hears a rumor about anyone else on the planet, she gets jealous. Everyone knows that, even me."

Brandon took the information in and relaxed his shoulders almost in relief at the explanation. For me, a sharp pain dug into my stomach. I had heard about this kid's tutor before, when it was a lie about me.

"When's the last time you saw her?" Brandon asked.

"The Friday before, on the bus home from school."

"Did Jenny ever mention a man named Gil?"

"I try not to associate myself with greasy perverts," he said.

"What about Jenny? You think she would associate herself with him?" asked Brandon.

JP shrugged. "I don't know. I didn't really know her. The world's a weird place, though." He smiled, and Brandon reciprocated. Were they best bros now?

WE LEFT JP to his knife and headed back to the car. The whole interaction left me uneasy. JP's performance gave me questions, and Brandon's gave me concerns. I reached for the car door and remembered my promise.

"I'm gonna grab Boomer."

"Really?" Brandon asked, annoying me further.

"Don't be an asshole."

He threw his hands up to surrender.

The front door was open a crack, and I pushed it the rest of the way. "Boomer, we're heading to town if you want a ride."

A hacking cough echoed from inside the bathroom. "One second, hon," his voice came through the door.

With a minute to kill, I moseyed around—snooping was becoming my specialty. There were two bedrooms off the back of the living room. The one on the left was Boomer's based on the extra-large cargo shorts and yellowed T-shirts all over the floor. The door to the second room was closed.

Out the window I could see JP still hard at work on getting the knife out, and Boomer was busy hacking away in the bathroom, so I opened the door. The room was bare, a twin mattress on the floor with a wool comforter on top, no sheets. A pile of T-shirts and underwear leaked out from the closet. The wooden slat door was closed as much as it could be with the clothes in the way.

I stepped over a few schoolbooks that weren't being properly cared for and reached for the closet handle. As the door opened and the light snuck in, I saw what I hadn't even remembered I was looking for. Something was not sitting well with me, and something had called me to that room. Underneath two hanging sweaters I could never see JP wearing was a stuffed-to-the-brim purple L.L.Bean backpack. Jenny's backpack.

CHAPTER THIRTY-EIGHT

JENNY

JENNY SAT STILL on the couch while JP went into the bathroom to throw away the condom. She didn't even know where he had pulled it from, but she was glad he was thinking when she so clearly wasn't. She didn't know what to think now that it was over.

It wasn't regret or glee or satisfaction. She just felt the same, worried about Gil, worried about robbing him, and worried about running away. It was fast and awkward, and JP seemed ashamed when it was over. He kissed her once on the forehead and hustled into the bathroom.

In some sick way, this was the last thing she needed to absolutely convince herself she was doing the right thing, that she loved JP and he loved her, that she was mature enough for this and everything would be OK.

JP came out of the bathroom, but didn't make eye contact as he walked behind the couch, got down on his knees, and reached underneath. Jenny twisted her upper body around so that she could watch him.

He slid a flattened military-green canvas bag out. On top of it was his collection of knives. The machete rested in the middle, dwarfing the others. He lifted one of the smaller knives and handed it to her. "Here, put this between the couch cushions."

Jenny took the knife in her hand. It was the one she'd held before, with the intricate swirls on the handle. "Do I have to?"

"No, but it's good to have a backup, take all precautions. If something goes wrong, I don't want you to be unarmed," he said.

She knew he was right, but even the *thought* of something going wrong was terrifying. She didn't know how to fight or be intimidating. Her one attempt with Mr. Renkin had gone so horribly. If this operation ended up in her hands, there's no telling what would happen.

She slid the knife in between the cushions, pulled her hand out, then stuck it back in, making sure to note the exact placement of the handle. If things went south, reaching in and grasping the sharp blade would be a crappy way to start her fight.

JP lifted the machete and hooked it into a homemade belt loop made for just that. Two of the smaller knives had sheaths, and he stuck those directly into his pockets. It all seemed so old-fashioned. Jenny would have felt so much better if she had remembered the gun.

"How much longer?" she asked, hoping time could somehow move backward.

"Ten minutes," he said as he walked around the couch to stand in front of her. "I'm going to be behind the couch, so whatever you do, keep him in front."

"OK," she said, unhappy with her escalating responsibility in the plan.

"I'm just going to say this, so tell me if you don't want to do it, but I think it will be easier if you let him get on top of you." JP looked down. He didn't like saying it as much as she didn't like hearing it.

"Why?"

He looked back up at her. "I just think if he's lying down, it will be easy for me to jump up and push him off to the floor. Then I can run around and put the machete to his throat. If he's sitting, he'll be really alert and hard to knock over."

It made sense to her, but it also made her nauseous. JP had just been on top of her, something she had wanted and asked for and still didn't particularly enjoy. Now, within the hour, she would let Gil do the same.

"OK," she said.

"Hey, we can still turn back. This is really fucking twisted. We don't have to do this. We can save up money, get jobs, whatever it takes."

"No. We're doing this. It's just a few minutes for the rest of our lives. I don't care if some gross asshole lies on me for two seconds." She did care, but she had to keep JP's head in the game. This had to work. She had no home to go to anymore. Linda had almost killed her.

JP nodded. He took a seat next to her on the couch. They both faced the door. Jenny wanted to keep talking, but what was there to say?

"Are you OK?" he asked, turning his head to look at her but keeping his shoulders facing ahead. "You know, OK about the other thing?" He was asking about the sex, but in the vaguest way possible. Was he asking if she enjoyed it? If she was OK that it happened? If she was physically all right?

"Yeah," she said, not knowing which question he was asking and knowing it didn't really matter.

"Good," he said. "I just want you to be comfortable, about

everything." He was being so sweet, and in different circumstances it would have melted her heart. In this moment, she wanted him to stop being so sensitive and to act like a guy who was going to have no problem overpowering a grown-ass adult and stealing his money.

"If all else fails, just kick him in the balls," she said.

JP couldn't help but laugh, and it broke the tension. "What? Where did that come from?"

"I don't know. I just know, like, guys don't kick other guys in the nuts when they fight, but I don't want you to worry about being a man. I want you to do whatever you have to."

"I'll lick his nuts if that's what it takes for this all to work," he said.

"That's gross!"

They both laughed, but it waned quickly. She looked at his face as he stared at his knees, the machete resting adjacent to his left thigh. His skin had a natural smoothness buried under soft pubescent stubble. His sparse hints of facial hair followed no rules on appropriate places to grow, and she appreciated that he did nothing to maintain it. His eyes were deep, and the whole package was just something so different, so appealing to her. This boy was everything to her in that moment. She wanted so badly to reach out and touch his cheek, but before she could, headlights cut through the windows and across his perfect face.

Gil was there, five minutes early.

CHAPTER THIRTY-NINE

VIRGINIA

BRANDON AND I rode in silence back to town. Boomer sat in the back, happy to stare out the window, nodding off occasionally before snoring himself awake.

The backpack. Was it the smoking gun? Why would he keep it in his room if he'd killed her? I guess he was just a dumb kid. Did he rape her? Was it consensual? Was he smart enough not to leave any evidence?

Maybe he found her bag in the woods. A fifteen-year-old boy who thinks he's a badass walks through the woods behind his house and finds a dead girl's backpack. It didn't seem that exciting. Maybe if it was the murder weapon, but a little girl's bag full of . . . I don't know . . . What was in the bag? Boomer had come out of the bathroom before I could look, but I needed to know.

I was in a familiar situation. I knew something, something big, something Brandon didn't know but probably should. There was no way to prove I'd ever seen the bag, and deep down, I just didn't want to tell him. If I told Brandon about the bag, the police would swarm the house, arrest JP, and relax the search for Gil. Their crime solving was so shortsighted, something I had criticized Brandon for from the beginning. If they had one suspect, the rest of the world became innocent by default.

I was feeling selfish and stubborn. Every step of the way, I had been the one solving this case, shedding light on a new angle, pushing harder for answers, while Brandon just reacted. I didn't trust anyone but myself. She was my sister. I was going to find answers. When I needed Brandon for something, I would let him know. What was the harm in keeping a few things to myself? Jenny wasn't going to get any deader.

Brandon pulled over in front of the pub. "I assume this is where you're headed," he said to Boomer.

The parking lot did not contain a navy Accord, and I hated that I was so concerned with looking. Irked by Brandon after his feeble interrogation of JP, I craved my other person.

"Perfect," Boomer said, reaching for the door handle. "Thanks again." With that he was out the door and shuffling toward the pub.

Brandon pulled the car back onto the road. "What did you think about JP?"

"I don't know," I said without inflection.

"Whoa, what's wrong?"

I didn't know exactly what was wrong. I just thought of him buying JP's excuse so easily. I thought about him being kicked off the case. Was I finally seeing the real Brandon? An incompetent cop promoted too soon after one lucky break?

"It's just frustrating," I said. "It feels like we keep moving side to side and never forward. Do you think we're any closer to figuring anything out?" I meant it as an accusation, but I hoped he'd have actual answers.

"Virginia . . ." He gave himself a weighted pause.

"What?"

"He knew who Gil was. The name hasn't been released, but he knew that Gil was the 'greasy pervert,'" he said with a smirk, and I equal parts loved and hated him again. Just like it should be. "And the knife, not the right size, but where there's smoke, there's fire. We have to get a search warrant for that dump."

"Fuck," I said, cringing.

"What?"

"I saw something at the house." I regretted not telling him immediately.

"What?"

"Jenny's backpack was in his closet." I braced for impact.

"Are you shitting me?"

"No, it was there. I just . . ." I searched for an excuse.

Brandon slammed on the brakes and veered off the road. Pausing any follow-up discussion, he whipped the car around and we were headed back to JP.

CHAPTER FORTY

JENNY

JP JUMPED FROM the couch at the first sign of their guest. He grabbed his coat off the nearby chair and flung it on over his worn black T-shirt. He pulled two leather gloves from the left pocket and slipped them over his hands. He moved fast, but Jenny could see his hands shaking ever so slightly.

She stayed still, sitting on the couch with perfect posture, watching JP and listening to the car approaching outside.

"Relax," JP whispered to her as he moved behind the couch. "Everything is going to be OK." Then he disappeared.

The headlights cut out, and the outside world went silent again. Jenny curled her hands into tight fists at her sides. She stared toward the front door, wishing JP was still sitting beside her. She knew he was close, but she felt alone.

Footsteps hit the front porch and echoed through the house. The wood was old, and each step from outside unleashed a piercing creak.

Jenny's heart was pounding; each beat made her whole body twitch. She had never felt this way before, even with Linda. It was the suspense, the waiting.

Their guest knocked twice.

Jenny could throw up if she allowed herself to. The line between voluntary and involuntary body movements was blurred. Three more knocks came, same rhythm but with more force. Jenny didn't budge.

"Answer the door," JP said from behind the couch with little volume but a lot of pressure. She could hear him, but his words didn't penetrate her fog.

"Jenny!" He punched his fist against the back of the couch, the force pushing through the cushion and reaching her. It jolted her enough to snap the trance.

The skinny young girl in the white-and-pink nightgown and hair full of barrettes pushed her tight fists against the couch, giving her the leverage to get to her feet. She stood for a moment, her surroundings clouded, all sounds dulled.

She walked toward the door, the floor inside providing its own soundtrack. Jenny wrapped her hand around the knob. Her nail polish had chipped at some point during the night, but this was the first time she noticed. Linda hated chipped nail polish. She said there was nothing trashier. The image of her mother hit Jenny hard. She had already been through so much.

She could see his car in the driveway through the window, but he was hidden behind the door, obstructed, invisible, maybe somehow not actually there. She twisted the knob and pulled open the front door. There he stood, uglier than she remembered. His hair was greasy, but combed backward like every hair was fleeing his face. He wore a yellow button-down shirt that looked two sizes too big for him tucked into straight-leg jeans. He was holding a teddy bear and a carton of six dark pink drinks, straight out of a nightmare.

"This is for you," Gil said, extending the teddy bear toward her.

"Thank you," Jenny managed.

"May I come in?" he asked when Jenny failed to offer. She nodded and stepped backward, allowing him space.

Gil looked around the living room. "Is this your house?"

"No."

"Are we alone?"

"Yes," she said, watching his movements carefully. She had to keep him in front of the couch.

"Would you like a drink?" He lifted the six-pack of wine coolers in the air.

"No, thank you."

"They're really good and will help you relax." He started moving toward the kitchen, the counter in direct view of JP.

"OK," Jenny blurted out to stop him. "But bring them over here to the couch."

Gil seemed pleased with her change of heart and altered his trajectory like she'd hoped he would.

Jenny sat on the couch first. She clenched her legs together and rested her hands on her knees in an attempt to keep herself guarded.

Gil sat down next to her as he placed the drinks on the coffee table. He pulled a bottle from the carton, twisted off the top, and handed it to her. Then he did the same for himself.

"You cut your hair," he said as he relaxed back into the couch, placing his right arm along the back, his hand resting just behind Jenny's head.

"Yeah," Jenny said, lifting the drink to her mouth but using her tongue to prevent any liquid from going into her mouth.

"And your face." He examined the cuts. "Is someone hurting you?"

"No. Just an accident," she explained.

He waited a moment to see if she would admit to a different tale, but she was striving to say as little as possible and remained silent.

"The necklace." He noticed it, taking the heart charm between his two fingers, his knuckles brushing against her chest. "I'm so glad you kept it."

Jenny tried her best to force a smile.

"I'm happy you reached out to me again," he said, releasing the necklace and returning his arm to the back of the couch. "I really hated how our first meeting went." He slid his hand forward just enough to run his fingers along Jenny's short hair. She cringed, and he frowned.

"Sorry," she said. "I hate my new haircut."

"You look beautiful." His eyes traced from her face to her knees as he said it. He drew his arm back down and moved it toward her legs.

Jenny spread her fingers across her knees, ready to hold them together with all of her strength.

He pinched the pink ruffled edge of her nightgown between his thumb and forefinger, moving them together to feel the fabric. "This is cute," he said. "I really like it."

Jenny stared down at his fingers, praying for them not to get any closer.

"I wasn't sure what to wear," said Gil. "How did I do?"

Jenny moved her line of sight from his hands to his face. His big brown eyes looked young and innocent, which was so deceiving. His eyebrows were thick and unruly and looked like two mini versions of his mustache. Gil's acne scars were so pronounced, even with his dark complexion. His adolescence must have been torture.

"You look nice," she said, almost pitying him.

Gil smiled and released her nightgown. The immediate relief Jenny felt disappeared almost as quickly as it came when his full palm landed on her thigh. He rubbed it back and forth, soft at first, then firmer. Each back-and-forth pushing a little farther.

"Do you have the money?" she blurted out as the base of his palm reached the edge of her underwear.

His hand paused. "Jenny . . ."

"We had a deal, and I just want to make sure you're going to hold up your end," she said in the longest sentence she had strung together since he arrived.

Gil removed his hand and sighed. "You are sounding like a little prostitute."

"This was your idea. Why are you getting upset?"

"Do you think I am proud of this? I don't want to think about it. Can't we just pretend this isn't a transaction? You will get your money, just don't make me think about it, OK?"

Jenny didn't know what to say. He had a sick and pathetic point, and she was nervous to push him further on the issue. But what if there was no money? She had to see the money.

"I'm really sorry, but I need to see the money. Just show it to me and then I won't say another word. We can enjoy our drinks and our night together."

"Why are you doing this?" Gil raised his voice. "Just stop." He put his wine cooler on the table and turned his body toward her. He grabbed her drink and slammed it next to his. Hers was still so full that liquid sloshed out of the top.

He put his hands on her knees and scooted toward her. "It's up to you how this goes. I want this to be special and gentle. It will be better that way."

His hands jumped to her hips, and he pulled her close. Jenny didn't fight back or give in. Her body became an inanimate object. Her chest was near his, but her head hung back. He leaned forward and kissed her.

Jenny stopped breathing. His mustache was rough, and tiny hairs stabbed her upper lip. It was nothing like JP's soft face. He pushed her down onto her back. His hands slid up her sides, and just as he was about to reach her breasts, she flung her head to the side.

"JP!" she screamed.

Gil froze. He looked to her for an explanation. His eyes grew. His lips closed to form a word, but before he could speak, the weight of him on top of her was gone.

JP was above her for an instant before he ran to the other side of the couch, machete tightly gripped in his hand.

Jenny raised herself up onto her elbows to get a better view of the action below her.

Gil rolled to his side in an attempt to get up, still processing what had happened. JP threw his leg over Gil's midsection, driving his knee into his rib cage, preventing him from lifting his upper half.

JP shoved the machete toward Gil's throat, leaving half an inch of wiggle room. Gil's eyes crossed as he tried to focus on the sharp weapon capable of ending his life.

"Where's the money?" JP demanded, but Gil didn't respond.

JP slapped him across the face with his free hand. "The money, you fucking pervert. Where's the money?"

Tears welled in Gil's dopey brown eyes. He was scared. Jenny didn't know what to think. She hadn't expected him to be so human. Monsters are supposed to be monsters. He was just so pathetic, everything about him. She wanted him to hand over the money and get the hell out of there, having learned a valuable lesson.

JP clenched his hand around Gil's neck, steadying the man so that he could move the machete closer to his throat. There was fire in JP's eyes, a mix of rage and fear. Jenny had never seen that in him before. There was a hint of it when he grabbed Mallory, but not like this. He was usually so calm, like he knew the secret to life.

JP touched the machete to Gil's neck. It was too close for Jenny and, in her opinion, the worst way to get Gil to talk. She eased forward on the couch, closer to them but not enough movement to startle either one. She raised her right hand and stretched it in slow motion toward JP. He twitched slightly to catch her in his periphery, but said nothing.

She guided her hand the rest of the way until it touched JP's forearm, inches from where he grasped the machete. His gaze remained on Gil, but he didn't resist her touch. Jenny wrapped her fingers around his arm, pulling it back and allowing breathing room between the blade and Gil's throat.

JP continued to tremble. Jenny slid from the couch to her knees on the floor next to him. She placed her other hand on JP's shoulder as if she could transfer a sense of tranquility through her fingertips. With both of her hands on him, she felt his shoulders relax. Jenny sighed. Now they could negotiate and get what they needed from Gil.

Or not.

CHAPTER FORTY-ONE

VIRGINIA

BRANDON DIDN'T ASK me any more questions about the bag, and he was driving so fast I didn't dare distract him. He hugged the dark, winding curves on Sanford Hill. We were there in under ten minutes.

Brandon took large strides toward the front door, and I did my best to keep up.

"What's the plan here?" I asked.

"You distract him. I'll go to the bathroom and accidentally stumble upon it."

"It's in the closet, not much of an accident."

"Who's going to say something? You?"

We were moving so fast. On the hunt. It was exhilarating.

Brandon reached the door and extended his hand to knock in one fluid motion. Then he stopped, adjusted his jacket, and composed himself.

JP answered the door without much suspense. "Back so soon?" His attitude was repulsive now that he might have killed her.

What a pathetic ending. Bad guys are supposed to be scary, not prepubescent. I couldn't even find comfort in the thought of a punishment. He was just a kid, but all bad men were once kids, I guess.

"I apologize," said Brandon. "There are a few things I forgot to cover. Don't tell, but I'm kind of new at this. May we come in?"

JP backed up, signaling his permission to enter. He lacked any hosting skills, and we all just stood in the middle of the living room.

"Do you mind if I use the bathroom?" asked Brandon.

"Whatever." JP nodded toward the back of the house.

Shit, this was my moment. What was I supposed to do? Was I standing with a murderer? I stared at my feet until Brandon was out of sight and JP was over the quiet game.

"What's up?" he asked. "What's he want to know?"

"I don't know. Something about the timeline, trying to figure out the last time everyone saw Jenny."

"I already told you that."

"I don't know. I'm not the detective."

I heard Brandon walking back. JP seemed calm, and a part of me felt bad. His whole life was about to come crashing down. Brandon rounded the corner, a gloved hand holding up the backpack.

JP's eyes blew up. "Where'd you get that?"

"You know where I got this," said Brandon.

"It's not mine." He took a couple steps backward.

"Don't do it, kid."

Brandon's words fueled the opposite reaction, and JP turned around, breaking into a sprint, throwing the sliding glass door open like it wasn't even there. Brandon dropped the backpack on the floor and took off after him.

It was just me and the bag. Alone at last. It stared at me, begging me to look inside.

———

THROUGH THE GLASS DOOR, I saw Brandon tackle JP to the ground. The kid stood no chance. I pulled off my scarf and wrapped it around both of my hands, connecting them like polyester handcuffs. Who knows what forensic tests the backpack was going to go through, and I didn't need my fingerprints all over it.

I unzipped the main compartment using my hand in an awkward pinching motion to keep the scarf from falling off. It was stuffed to the brim with clothes. I did my best to dig through it given my constraints. There were just clothes, a hairbrush, a toothbrush.

I twisted my head back to glance out the door. Brandon pulled JP to his feet and turned him back toward the house. I shoved the clothes back inside the bag and pinched the zipper closed. I went for the front pocket next. The zipper was horizontal and easier to open. I reached my scarf paw inside and felt something.

The object was thin and firm. I pinched it and slid it out enough to get a look at it. It was a passport. A bag full of clothes and a passport. I didn't even have to be a junior detective to know this meant she was running away. Where were all the answers? I just had more questions. Why was she running? Because of Linda? Was that JP's motive? Was it just a coincidence? What if Linda found out? Or our father? Was there someone she was going to see? Gil maybe? What if she and Gil were running away to some deplorable country where you can have child brides?

I pulled the passport out into my hands. I hesitated a moment. I wanted to see her face. I missed her face, the real face, not a glamour shot or a crime scene photo. But would it hurt to see? I couldn't afford to be sad now. We were so close to ending it all. Cops would swarm the house. JP would break under interrogation. The news vans would multiply for a week then leave forever. My father would send Linda to some fancy rehab—the longer, the better. Maybe he would come out. Maybe he would become Vermont Dad.

I palmed the passport until I caught my fingers under the front flap. I flipped it open and then I saw it: my own indignant teenage face. It was *my* passport. My passport that I kept in a drawer with the only things I didn't want to lose. Mark's notes were in that drawer.

CHAPTER FORTY-TWO

JENNY

JENNY PULLED JP back onto his heels, trying to defuse the situation, but Gil seized the opportunity to thrash his whole body to the left, disrupting JP's balance enough to free his arms. Before they could realize what had happened, Gil shoved his hands into JP's chest, separating him from Jenny and launching him onto the floor. Gil was on his knees in an instant, an agility Jenny never saw coming.

He dug his right knee into JP's wrist with all of his weight until the pain became unbearable and JP released the machete. Gil reached for the knife, but as his fingers felt the handle, Jenny whipped her leg around and kicked it across the room.

Without looking, Gil swung his extended arm until it collided with Jenny's face and sent her to the floor. She made eye contact with JP as she fell. What had they done?

With his right arm still immobile under Gil's weight, JP violently thrashed his knees and left arm against Gil. He caused little damage, but won Gil's full attention. The man, who moments ago had looked so helpless, was in full control. He pulled back, balling his hand into a fist. He aimed above JP's head, but hesitated and grabbed onto JP's hair instead. Again and again, he bashed JP's head against the floor until the boy lost all the fight in him. JP closed his eyes, life escaping.

Jenny gasped, emitting a pained noise. This was her idea. She'd thought she was so smart.

Gil reacted to the noise and turned toward her. His tone shifted as if he were ashamed of what he'd done to upset her.

"I'm sorry. I was just defending myself." He rose to his feet, looking again like the insecure loser in baggy clothes.

He moved toward her. Jenny used her arms to scoot backward, retreating from his approach. Her movements were no match for a man on his feet. He was upon her in seconds.

"Jenny, please," he pleaded, dropping to the floor beside her. He placed his hand on hers, and when she jerked it away, he seemed surprised. How could a man who had just won the battle for his woman be rejected?

This time he reached out for her shoulder, aggressive, no longer asking permission. He pushed her back. She fell flat against the hardwood floor as he climbed on top of her.

Jenny wanted to fight. She wanted to make it stop, but his weight was so forceful against her. The blows to her head, the fear, it was too much. She went limp, closed her eyes, and pictured the waves crashing against the beautiful white sands of Mexico.

Jenny concentrated on making her body go numb, anything she could do to not feel Gil on top of her. She squeezed her eyes closed as hard as she could, or so she thought. At the sound of his zipper, she found the strength to press her eyelids even closer together. She took one more breath, the last she would take before everything changed.

Jenny opened her eyes when she felt Gil lurching backward. JP's arm was in a chokehold around his neck, yanking him off her. Gil crashed to the floor, and JP pounced on top of him. JP didn't take his eyes off the man as he landed his first punch right below Gil's left eye. Gil flailed underneath the boy and JP landed another punch in the same spot. His fists picked up speed. Over and over again they landed, narrowly avoiding Gil's glasses.

Jenny would not calm JP's rage this time. She scrambled to her feet and raced to the cordless phone resting on the kitchen counter. She dialed 9-1 . . . then stopped. She couldn't call the cops. It would ruin everything. She pressed the cancel button over and over until a dial tone returned. She dialed one of the few numbers she had worked to memorize before they left, her sister's.

It rang over and over. The young girl danced in place, watching JP punch Gil, who was still squirming to deflect the blows. Finally, she heard a click.

Jenny could hear breathing on the other end, but no words. "Hello?" Jenny half asked, half begged.

"Who . . . this?" Virginia slurred, barely coherent.

"Virginia," Jenny screamed, "please, I need your help." She spoke fast with the high pitch of panic.

"What?" A groggy response.

"Virginia, please, it's Jenny. I don't know what to do. A man attacked me. Can you come get me?"

"Jenny?"

Jenny turned the receiver away from her mouth to address JP. "Something's wrong with her." JP didn't react; his hands were full with Gil, who was managing to land his own punches into JP's side. There was no one to help her.

She went back to the phone. "I can't call the cops and I can't go home, what do I do?"

"Mark," Virginia whispered.

"What?"

"Mark."

"Are you at his house?" The question met silence. "Are you at Mr. Renkin's house?" she begged for the answer she wanted. The breathing on the other end became labored and uneven. Then Jenny heard a click. "Virginia? Are you there? Are you OK?"

All that met her on the other end of the phone was a dial tone. Jenny clenched the phone, unwilling to accept that her sister wasn't going to save her. JP and Gil struggled on the floor, neither one able to land a punch to end it. She didn't know what to do. She was a helpless observer.

JP went for the kill, a vicious full-body swing at Gil's face. The man turned his head at the last second, causing JP's fist to just graze his nose and completely throw the boy off balance.

Gil launched his knee between JP's legs. It connected, sending an almost visible shock through JP's whole body. The boy grabbed himself with both hands and rolled to the floor.

Forget it, Jenny thought and grabbed the phone to dial 9-1-1.

Gil scrambled to his feet and lifted his gaze to Jenny. There was something different behind his eyes. Somewhere, between the attempted rape and the fight, he'd found confidence. It was terrifying.

Jenny dropped the phone and sprinted for the sliding glass door. Gil reacted on cue and lunged after her. The three-step advantage was just enough to get Jenny out the door before he reached her. The rusty floodlight lit up the backyard as far as the tree line. She sprinted, barefoot, toward the darkness. Her only hope was to hide.

The grass was cold and damp under her feet, but she had no time to process the feeling. Jenny could hear Gil behind her, the damage

JP had caused slowing his pace just enough. She reached the end of the light and jumped over the rock wall at the edge of the yard. The wet grass was like walking on clouds compared to the twigs she landed on. She grimaced for a beat before swallowing hard and running full speed again. The darkness was her advantage. She only had to hide. He had to find her.

She ran until his steps were muted; then she slowed and went quiet. Ahead was a fallen tree, one of many that littered the old woods. Every step toward it was a potential alert to her position. A loud stick, a disturbed animal, any noise would rock the silence.

Even on its side, the tree was half her height. The last signs of innocence on her soft cotton nightgown disappeared as she crawled over the mossy trunk. She scooped a chunk of leaves and dirt from underneath and then wedged her body into the crevice as best she could.

Once she finally lay still, she realized how cold she was. She fought hard not to shake, but couldn't stop. How long would she have to stay there? How long could she survive there?

CHAPTER FORTY-THREE

VIRGINIA

I WAITED AT JP's with Brandon until more cops showed up. None of them seemed concerned with Brandon's suspension. In a case with so little evidence, the backpack had everyone buzzing with excitement. Jenny's murder had the attention of the nation, and the local cops beamed with the idea they were there for the big arrest. Even Brett, the funeral bouncer, couldn't help but smile as he searched through the drawers in the kitchen for the murder weapon.

JP didn't say a word. He sat on the couch, his hands cuffed behind him, with his head hanging low. The only reaction Brandon could get were involuntary blinks when he raised his voice unexpectedly.

I wanted out of there. I was disappointed. I didn't want it to be JP. It was a depressing answer that made the world seem somehow darker. I felt sick to my stomach. Not about the murder or JP. It was where my own thoughts were trying to go that nauseated me.

Seeing my passport tore open old wounds that I'd hoped this experience had brought closure to. I saw my young face. I thought about Mark's notes. I needed to get home.

I snuck out once Brandon was surrounded by uniformed cops hanging on his every word. My car was back at my apartment and I made a choice that showed my desperation. I walked down the road almost to the end, then cut through the trees once my father's house was visible. Only one small light glowed from inside.

My right shoulder slammed into the door next to the garage. It was locked, and I wasn't expecting it to be. Even after Jenny's murder, they never locked the doors. Locking the doors now would be admitting their actions might have contributed to her death. I didn't know what had changed.

I had no choice but to knock. There was no doorbell, and I pounded my fist, hoping the sound would echo throughout the large house. Eventually, I heard footsteps.

My father opened the door a sliver, not expecting any guests. When he saw me, a relief came over his face that was almost nice. "Virginia," he said, opening the door all the way.

"Hi, Dad. Can you give me a ride home?"

He didn't answer right away. Instead he wrinkled his forehead and tried to figure out what set of events since I'd left the hospital had brought me to his doorstep on foot. "Where's your car?"

"I was with Detective Colsen. We found him." I hadn't planned to share the news until it was already coming out of my mouth.

"The pervert?"

I shook my head. "It wasn't him. It was a kid from school. I don't really know what happened. They were dating maybe." I wasn't trying to be vague. I really didn't know the answers. The more I thought about it, the less sense it made to me too.

"Who?" He adjusted his stance. His shoulders seemed to widen, and his chest puffed out.

"JP," I said, seeing if the name registered with him. It didn't. "He lives up the hill."

My father turned back into the house and grabbed his coat. "The cops are there now?"

I nodded, not sure what I was witnessing.

"Where exactly?"

"Boomer's place."

"You should have called me. What were you doing there anyway?"

I followed him into the garage and watched as he flung drawers open, looking for something.

"Are you going to give me a ride home?" I asked.

He pulled a key from the drawer, slammed it shut, and glared at me. "You always were so selfish. Even as a child." He crossed the garage toward a locked metal cabinet.

His words ripped through my body. "Are you fucking kidding me?" I said.

"Watch your language."

"What do you think you're going to do? March up there and strangle the kid? Some kind of vigilante justice to make you feel like you weren't the shittiest parent on the fucking planet?"

"Your dramatics are not charming."

"Dad, you fucking thought I had something to do with it. Did you forget that? Because I'll never be able to forget. Do you get that?"

"I know!" he shouted, in a way that sounded like he was about to explode. It was a tone only ever reserved for me, to paralyze me from pushing it one hair further. He opened the cabinet and pulled a small lockbox from one of the drawers. It was like he couldn't even see me anymore.

"What is that?" I asked.

"Charlie's on his way here," he said, brushing past me. "He can give you a ride." My father stomped down the driveway, and I knew in that moment I *was* jealous. I was jealous of how much he cared about Jenny. I was jealous of the poor little dead girl.

CHARLIE WAS ALL too happy to see me when he pulled into the driveway ten minutes later and all too eager to give me a ride home. It was obvious he wished he had children of his own, even a bitter adult child. There was too much going on, and we both struggled to find small talk that would be appropriate given the circumstances.

"Why are you with him?" I asked.

"I love him."

"Doesn't seem worth it. He's embarrassed by you. He keeps you hidden up in Vermont like a mistress."

"He's not embarrassed by me. He's embarrassed of himself."

"Well, I think we'd all be better off if he just got over himself and moved to Vermont with you. Maybe he wouldn't be such an asshole."

"You should let him know," Charlie said, and smiled. "He doesn't believe me."

I pointed Charlie toward my apartment, and he pulled into the shared driveway.

"Are you going to be OK?" he asked. "I could come up for a little bit."

I enjoyed Charlie almost too much. I wanted to talk to him more. I wanted him to make me feel better about everything. I wanted to travel back in time and have him come to my school plays. I wanted him to put me on his shoulders and run through the park with me. I felt like a crazy orphan kid who attaches to any adult who walks through the door.

"Maybe another time," I said as I opened the door. "It's been a long night."

"I understand."

"Plus, I need you to go back and make sure my father doesn't murder anyone," I joked before realizing it was in horrible taste.

"I'll take good care of him, sweetheart."

ONCE CHARLIE PULLED AWAY, I let the fake-daddy euphoria leave with him. I raced upstairs and into my apartment. I wasted no time, dropping to my knees and yanking open the bottom drawer of the desk.

It looked different right off the bat. My life was a mess, but that drawer was always organized. In darker times, I would pull each letter out, read them chronologically, trying to figure out where things went wrong. Then, with meticulous precision, I would place them back inside, in the same order, from largest to smallest. I would place my passport and diploma on top, souvenirs from the time.

My passport was in my pocket, its absence justified. Underneath my diploma sat the neat stack of letters, but I knew right away something was wrong. Three were missing.

CHAPTER FORTY-FOUR

JENNY

IT WAS WHEN she stopped shivering that Jenny really began to worry. Her eyes were heavy, and her mind was slipping. She could barely feel her feet, and there had been no signs of Gil in what felt like at least a half hour. She emerged from her hiding spot, crawling out just enough to sit up and let her eyes adjust to the moon.

She rose to her feet and started walking. Her legs were slow to work again, but she fought through it. Where was JP? Why wasn't he looking for her? She had just left him there. What if Gil went back for him? What if JP was dead and the whole time she was just hiding?

She could see the floodlight ahead, but there were no frantic footsteps, no screams, no one calling out her name, no hints of what was in store for her. With the rock wall in front of her, her nerves became overwhelming. Was it too late to run home and crawl into bed? She shook the thought away and stepped over the rocks in the same spot she had jumped over earlier.

The light engulfed her as she looked toward the house. The sliding glass door was closed. Someone had gone through the door after she and Gil ran through. Did this person go in, or did someone come out? Either option could be good or bad, a clue with no value.

Answers wouldn't come from the door. They came when Gil leapt from the darkness and wrapped his arms around her from behind. He squeezed her tight, like she was his greatest carnival prize. The force took her breath away, and she coughed out the last bit of air.

He kissed her cheek close to her ear, then released her, daring her to run even though he was close enough to grab her before she could flinch.

"Jenny," he said with a sigh. "This has turned into a mess." He shook his head with what seemed like genuine regret. "Can we just start over? I'll give you the money, don't worry about that."

"Where's JP?"

"I don't want to talk about him. This is about us," he said.

"Did you kill him?"

He reached forward and grabbed both of her arms. "He was trying to kill me. Didn't you see that? He's crazy and violent. He could hurt you too if he hasn't already." He brushed the back of his hand against the cuts on her left cheek.

Jenny's eyes began to well up. He had killed JP, and now he wanted to change the subject. Her lip quivered to complement the welling tears.

Gil leaned forward and kissed her on one cheek, then the other, as if his affection would help.

"Stop," she whispered, but he didn't listen.

He kissed her more, all over her face. Jenny stared at the ground, replaying every moment in her head, every move she made to get her here, alone with this monster and JP gone forever. "Stop," she yelled, pushing Gil back a few steps.

His compassion disappeared, and his eyes narrowed to slivers. His slimy tongue poked out to run over his bottom lip; then he charged toward her.

Jenny hunched over, bracing for impact.

As the tip of his fingers reached her chest, he stopped on a dime. It was as if he'd hit an invisible wall protecting her.

Jenny looked down to see the bloody tip of the machete poking out from his stomach.

Gil's eyes locked on hers, then rolled backward. The tip of the blade retreated, and she jumped back to avoid his body as it fell.

JP stood behind him, grasping the machete. Blood dripped to the ground. He stared down at his kill like a warrior. He didn't run to hug Jenny; he didn't even look at her. His chest rose and fell like a young boy changed forever.

"Help me get him to the hose," he said, allowing no time to breathe or think. He moved behind Gil's head and wrapped his arms under the dead man's armpits.

Jenny grabbed his feet, afraid to argue.

They carried Gil across the yard. He wasn't big, but he was dead and heavy. JP dropped the shoulders by the hose without warning, and the force ripped the feet from Jenny's hands. JP jumped onto the deck and slipped through the sliding glass door, disappearing into the house and leaving Jenny alone with Gil again.

His eyes were open. A small amount of blood gathered at the corners of his mouth. He was dirty, scratched, bruised, and still. So very still.

JP burst back outside with the sheets from his bed rolled up in his arms and a gallon of bleach in his hand. He threw them onto one of the chairs and went for the hose. He still said nothing. He still didn't look at her.

He cranked the hose on full power. Jenny scooted toward the house to avoid the chilly spray deflecting off the ground. JP took the hose to Gil's body. The force caused Gil's skin to ripple as he moved the stream back and forth, from head to toe.

"What are you doing?" asked Jenny.

"Getting rid of any evidence."

She watched him spray Gil with water for a full two minutes before he was satisfied and turned off the hose. JP grabbed the sheets and spread them out on the ground.

"Help me put him on the blankets."

She took her place at the feet again. She was scared and everything felt wrong, but she was glad that he was in control. All night she had been begging for someone to tell her what to do.

They placed the body in the center of the blankets. This time Jenny was aware of JP's movements and released her hold in sync with his. JP left his eyes on the body while he pushed Jenny out of the way. He folded the bottom of the sheets over Gil's calves, then moved to the side and tucked the edge completely over the body. He rolled the man up like a burrito until he ran out of blanket.

JP grabbed the bottle of bleach from the chair and tucked it in on top of Gil's head. He gripped the edge of the blanket with both hands, twisting it and regripping to ensure he had it. Finally, he looked up at Jenny. "Get out of here," he demanded.

"But—"

"Jenny, leave here right now. Don't come back. You were never here, do you understand?" He took his eyes off her, end of discussion. He stepped backward, dragging the blanket and the body with him toward the driveway.

He was leaving her. She was alone.

Jenny slipped back into the house. She stood still for a moment in the gritty, disheveled living room. She found her boots and slipped her aching, mud-coated feet into them. Her last action in that house was to slide her trembling hand in between the couch cushions and retrieve the knife JP made her hide as a precaution. Gil was dead, yet she felt anything but safe. She put her head down, slipped out the front door, and took off for the only place she could think to go.

CHAPTER FORTY-FIVE

VIRGINIA

I WAS AT MARK'S DOOR before I could process what I was doing. Jenny took those notes. I had no doubt. Jenny knew about us, and I was sure Mark knew something he wasn't saying.

It was sickening. Just when I had finally found a crack, a small opening to squeeze myself through and escape the hold Mark had had on me for years, I was at his doorstep. I was breathing, but it didn't feel like it. It felt like someone was feeding my sternum through a meat grinder.

The door opened. I thought he would be surprised to see me. This was an ambush. Instead, he elongated his neck and unfurled a smug grin across his face. "Hey," he said, waiting for me to explain myself.

My eyes darted around. If I could just avoid looking at him, he couldn't pull me back in.

"Do you want to come in?" He stepped back, leaving room for me to follow. I kept my head down and slid past him.

I loved him, and that wasn't going to change. I had to change. I turned around to face him. This time I let my eyes land on his. Once they locked, it was a relief. I let myself really look at him. Was I happy to hear he was miserable without me? Did I want him to be that man who sat on the porch with me after school? Of course, but he wasn't the same guy. He was violent, evasive, and a liar.

He wasn't interested in exchanging pleasantries. When I didn't speak, he stepped toward me, extending his hand toward my waist. I retreated before he could make contact. He paused a moment, then tried again, his reach more aggressive. I lunged backward, guiding his hand away with my own.

"C'mon, Ginny," he said, moving forward with every step I took back.

"I know you lied about Jenny," I blurted out.

He stopped following me. "What are you talking about?"

"She took the notes, Mark. The notes you wrote me. I'm fucking pathetic and I kept them and she found them and she took them."

"So what? I don't know why that changes anything. What are you trying to say?"

"Why would she take them?" I asked. "She wanted them for something and I highly doubt it was to keep them a secret. Only one of us had something to lose. Did you know she had them? Did she try to blackmail you?"

"Jesus, Virginia, are you trying to be some fucking detective or something?"

"Just tell me the truth. Did she come to you? Did she tell you she knew about us?"

He put his hand to his forehead, massaging around and over his eyes. "Fuck it," he said as he lowered his hand. "Yes, she told me she had the notes."

My mouth fell open, but my jaw tightened and I had nothing to say. I guess I never really thought I could be right. I was just keeping busy, trying to be smarter than the cops, trying to find an excuse to talk to Mark, trying anything to distract me from my life. Now I had uncovered something. Something that could connect me to the murder and absolutely destroy me.

"Did you hurt her?" I asked, demanding an answer I wasn't sure I wanted.

CHAPTER FORTY-SIX

JENNY

IT WAS A STRAIGHT SHOT past the driveway, through a thin line of trees and into Mr. Renkin's backyard. Jenny ran across, anticipating a motion-sensor light that never came.

The house was dark and empty. It was late. No sign of her sister. At this point, her only option was to turn to the man she knew would keep her secrets. Jenny went for it, banging on the glass door. She pounded and pounded until she thought the glass might break.

The stairs lit up first, then the entire living room. Would she tell him the truth or just enough for him to let her stay the night? She could figure things out in the morning, stumble back to Linda and beg forgiveness, or call her dad and expose the truth about her mother, or forget them both and go to Virginia. There were options. She was just too tired to figure them out now.

Mr. Renkin skipped down the stairs in his boxers, throwing a dark gray T-shirt over his head.

Seeing his face, Jenny felt one fleeting ounce of fear—the reaction a reminder of what she used to be afraid of, the good old days when all she had to fear was a little concussion from the school's favorite teacher chasing her. She reached behind her back and slipped her hand under her nightgown. She planted the knife sideways into her underwear, freeing both her hands for whatever was to come.

He squinted in her direction, but the night on the other side must have just projected his own reflection back. He walked over, stopping once he was close enough to reach the glass. He put his hand up and pressed his face against it, finally getting a glimpse of what was on the other side. He smirked ever so slightly before flinging open the door.

"Well, this is quite the surprise. What are you doing here?"

"Is my sister here?" Jenny asked, knowing the answer but hoping for a miracle.

"Why would Virginia be here?"

Jenny shook her head, unsure herself why she thought there was any chance her sister would be there for her in this moment.

"Are you OK, Jenny?" He looked her up and down. She was covered in dirt and scratches, clearly not OK. "Come in," he said before she had to answer.

She stepped onto the hardwood floor. To the left was the kitchen island where she had threatened him; in front of her was the couch she had regained consciousness on.

"Have a seat," he said. "I'll get you some water." There was no urgency in his words or actions. He didn't press for an explanation. He didn't mention calling the cops or her mother. He was just who she wanted him to be.

Jenny didn't take a seat. She moseyed to the couch, but stayed on her feet, afraid to sit with the knife in her underwear. The coffee table was littered with empty beer bottles. Jenny imagined them shattering over her head if she said the wrong thing.

Mr. Renkin brought the water and sat on the couch, unaffected by her standing. "What are you doing here?" he asked again, this time expecting a real answer. "I didn't think we were on the best of terms."

"I thought maybe Virginia was here. I tried calling her and I couldn't really hear her, but she said your name, and with your history and stuff, I just thought maybe . . ."

Mark leaned back on the couch, apparently bothered to be revisiting the subject of his relationship with Virginia but understanding the tone wasn't threatening. He kept his eyes on Jenny, an unrelenting gaze.

The girl shifted her weight between her toes and her heels. She knew she couldn't just stand there forever. Should she leave? Should she sit down? When she looked up at him, she felt like she should say something. When she looked down at the floor, she felt like it was his place to speak.

It was uncomfortable and too drawn out. She was longing for a place to feel safe, to just close her eyes for the night. Thinking it was in this house might have been one of her larger missteps.

"You look like her, you know . . . your sister," he said.

Jenny looked up, instantly regretting letting him take in her full face.

"Even more without your hair," he added. "A bold choice."

It wasn't a choice, she thought.

"Look, Jenny," he said, crossing his legs and becoming somehow even more relaxed. "I know you think I'm a bad guy, but I'm really not. It bothers me what I did to you that day. I shouldn't have done that."

"It's OK," Jenny muttered, not wanting to forgive him, but understanding she was in no position to be confrontational.

"Seriously, what can we do to fix this?" he asked.

Jenny didn't know what to say. It *had* an easy fix. That day he could have just given her the money. It wasn't a solution anymore; maybe it never was. Was the plan ever real, or was it just something she and JP did to pass the time? A fantasy that helped her escape her reality?

Her eyes began to water. Tears were coming.

Mr. Renkin jumped to his feet. "Hey, hey, hey, look at me," he said, reaching out and putting his hands just above her elbows.

Jenny looked at his hands to avoid his face. He was just a symbol of everything bad that had happened to her in the past few weeks. He didn't start it and he certainly couldn't end it. He was just a weak man standing there, thinking he was the reason she was crying.

Jenny took one power sniffle and wiped the wetness from her eyes before any tears could fall out.

Mr. Renkin reached up and moved a piece of Jenny's choppy hair that had escaped one of the barrettes behind her ear. "That's better," he whispered, landing his hand onto her shoulder and staying all too close. "You really do have her eyes." Pervert alert. Jenny could not catch a freaking break.

"Please, Mr. Renkin, just let me go home," Jenny begged with a vulnerability she couldn't control.

He took a defensive stance, hands up, head tilted to make her seem insignificant. "Whoa, of course. I'm not keeping you here," he said, backing away.

Jenny took two subtle steps toward the door, waiting for him to be lying and to lunge at her. He didn't, so she took a few normal steps. Then a few more and she was at the door. He drew in his arms, letting them cross. She reached for the handle. He puffed out his chest and grinned as if somehow he was rejecting her, kicking her out.

The sound of a car turning into the gravel driveway broke the standoff. Jenny couldn't move. She stood behind the door, frozen by the memory of Gil pulling into the driveway earlier that night.

"Jenny!" Mr. Renkin yelled. "Get away from the door."

The volume of his voice gave weight to the fears she was trying to suppress.

"I'm serious," he shouted, lunging forward and grabbing her by the arm, tossing her toward the staircase. "Go upstairs and don't make a sound."

"I . . ." Jenny fumbled over her words and her footing. She had been so close to getting out, and now she was retreating farther inside.

"I'm not fucking around," he said, stepping toward her.

Jenny flinched and inched back, catching her heel on the bottom step and falling backward. Her wrists burned as she threw them out to catch her fall.

"Are you OK?" he asked, as if he actually cared.

Jenny nodded as she crawled her body around and up the stairs, returning to her feet after the first few.

"Don't snoop around up there. Stay in the hall. Be smart."

She glanced back once, enough to regret it. He glared from the bottom of the stairs, his eyes piercing, only turning away when the front door behind him opened.

CHAPTER FORTY-SEVEN

VIRGINIA

"DID YOU KILL HER?" I shouted when Mark didn't respond immediately, letting my voice crack with insanity.

"No, I didn't fucking kill her," Mark snapped. "How could you even think that? Jesus Christ."

He turned away from me, forcing me to bark at the back of his head.

"Prove it. Convince me you didn't do it, because the cops are next door arresting some kid and I want to know they aren't making a mistake."

He turned back. It felt like slow motion the way his face revealed itself to me. "JP?"

I nodded.

He grimaced, alerting me that there was more to say. "I didn't kill her, but I did see her that night. She knocked on my back door. She looked like shit, but wouldn't tell me anything. She only stayed a minute," he scrambled to downplay his confession.

"Are you serious?" My eyes widened and stayed that way. "Why didn't you tell anyone?"

"I couldn't. You know I couldn't. How would I explain why she was here? I didn't kill her. I don't have any information. It would have just opened up a can of worms. What if it led back to us? Would you like that? For everyone to find out the truth?"

"Yeah, I pray every day for everyone to know that my fucking teacher raped me."

"What the fuck, Ginny? Don't say it like that." He moved toward me, almost jovial, desperately seeking to change the mood. He ran his hands down my arms until he could hold mine. We stood holding hands like he was about to propose. His touch felt like nothing but desperation.

"It makes no sense," I said. "None of it makes any sense. Why would JP kill her? Taking our notes, writing to that fucking pervert, stealing my passport . . . she was up to something and she stepped into something she shouldn't have. All of these things can't be a coincidence."

"How would I know?" Mark offered, frustrated and not at all helpful.

I turned away from him so I could better concentrate. Someone got really lucky that Jenny had so many perverts lusting after her. Pretty fucking convenient. Did someone like JP know about Gil and see an opportunity? Where was Gil? Was it him after all and he just happened to prey on Jenny while she was simultaneously doing all this sneaky shit?

I turned back. He was waiting for me, hoping I was ready to move on, like somehow looking away for ten seconds was enough time to get over it. I was anything but over it. "Maybe if the truth came out, some sense would finally come of everything. The *whole* truth," I emphasized, and waited for him to pick up what I meant.

When his nose scrunched up, I knew he got it. "You aren't

thinking clearly," he said, stepping forward to tell *me* what *I* was thinking. "You know we can't tell anyone about us. You know it's better this way. It would ruin everything." He paused to see how I would react.

I didn't react. At least, I don't think I reacted. It wasn't enough to garner a reaction.

He leaned in and lowered his voice. "It's not too late for us," he whispered, tilting his head and coming for my lips.

Time stopped, a sort of freeze frame. Too much needed to be thought about and said in that moment, but there wasn't time. Three weeks ago, I would have killed for those words. I would have been leaning in, but I wasn't leaning in, not now.

CHAPTER FORTY-EIGHT

JENNY

THE SECOND FLOOR was dark and quiet, the only light and sound coming from the living room. Jenny inched up against a small patch of wall between the staircase and an open door to another room—staying in the hallway as instructed. She closed her eyes to focus her senses on hearing the conversation downstairs.

"What are you doing here?" Mr. Renkin asked whoever it was.

"Seriously? That's how you're going to greet me?"

Jenny recognized the voice immediately, and honestly, she should have known the houseguest was Ms. Willoughby. Not every person out in the night was a scary bad guy.

"Sorry," Mr. Renkin said, the insincerity making it all the way up the stairs to Jenny. "We talked about this. You can't just show up."

"You know, that sounds really fucking shady. Is there someone here? Upstairs?" Ms. Willoughby asked, footsteps moving toward the stairs.

Jenny seized before slipping into the first open door. She stayed near the door, out of sight but close enough to listen.

"You can't always jump to that," Mr. Renkin scolded her. "Every time you don't agree with me, you can't accuse me of cheating. It's immature."

The footsteps halted. Ms. Willoughby scoffed, "I'm immature? I'm your girlfriend, and not only will you not let me move in, I have to schedule appointments to come over. You want to live this bachelor fantasy, but you're old and it's a really pathetic look."

"Oh, now you're really changing my mind."

"Well, something is going to change, because I can't. I can't with this. Not again."

"What are you saying?" he pressed.

"You'll see," she said.

Jenny braced herself for things to get really ugly. Mr. Renkin didn't love being threatened. Would he yell? Would he hurt her?

"Hunter," he whispered, doing a compete 180. "I don't like when you get upset. You know you're my everything."

"It doesn't fucking feel like it," she shot back, but softer and already cracking.

"Come here," he said. Jenny wished she could see them. Where was this going? She thought of the night in the courtyard at the dance. It felt like a lifetime ago.

"Babe, I made one mistake. I know I hurt you, but it was over ten years ago. I regret it every day," he insisted.

Ten years ago, Jenny thought. These people were freaking old. Jenny was barely out of diapers ten years ago. *Ten years ago.* Jenny was three years old ten years ago. When Jenny was three, Virginia still lived at home. Virginia was still in high school when she lived at home. Ten years ago Virginia was still in high school having sex with her math teacher. Even in her exhaustion, and with the horror of what had happened tonight still threatening to crush her, Jenny's mind led her to the only possible conclusion: Virginia was the mistake, the mistake that had hurt Hunter.

CHAPTER FORTY-NINE

VIRGINIA

AS HIS LIPS MADE CONTACT, not enough to even squish mine yet, there was a noise outside. A car was pulling into the driveway. Then headlights came through the windows, temporarily blinding me.

I lunged my whole body away from Mark, getting my face the hell away from his.

He was too concerned with the car to notice my rejection. He looked to the front door, then back to me. "Shit, not again. You have to get out of here."

"What?" I said, not even sure of the question I was asking.

"I'm serious," he said, pushing me toward the back door. "It's Hunter. She'll be pissed if she sees you here."

"She should be," I said, twisting away from where he was leading me. "You just tried to kiss me."

"Virginia," he grumbled. "Just go and we'll talk about this later."

"Are you kidding me? I'm not your mistress and I'm not going to sneak out and hide in the woods."

"Is this your thing now? Sabotage? I didn't kill Jenny, so now you're going to ruin my relationship?" With that, he grabbed my arm, squeezing it and hurling me toward the back door. It sent a shock through my entire body. He had never touched me like that. I dug my heels into the ground, which only caused Mark to tighten his grip, laying the foundation for tiny fingerprint bruises. I didn't know why I was fighting him so much. All I knew was that he wanted me to leave and I didn't want him to get what he wanted.

If I went out that door, nothing would change. He would go right back to Hunter while making passes at me whenever the opportunity presented itself. It was time for it all to be over with.

My hands hit the glass. I could see the blue and red lights of the cop cars through the trees, scattered around JP's driveway. Everything so close. Everything so confusing.

Mark pressed his body against mine to keep me pinned against the sliding door while he let go of my arm and reached for the handle. I could feel his stomach. I could feel his hips. I could feel what I didn't want to think about.

I elbowed him in the chest and broke away. I ran back through the living room, around the leather couch, and toward the front door.

I stopped in my tracks as the door opened and I found myself face-to-face with Hunter.

She started to smile, a reaction to seeing me before processing the context. Then the smile was gone. "Virginia?"

I looked over at Mark to gauge his intentions. He slunk closer, not toward either one of us in particular, just getting into position for what was to come.

"What is she doing here?" Hunter asked him, not interested in talking to me directly.

She had been drinking. Not a ton, but enough for her eyes to be glazed over and her cheeks to redden as she processed what she was seeing.

Mark took a deep breath and slid his jaw back and forth. He was stalling.

"Mark!" she shouted, his silence driving her paranoia.

"Nothing's going on," he insisted.

"How stupid do you think I am?" she asked, barging into the house and throwing her keys down on the kitchen island.

I was happy to no longer be directly in between them and was content to just take in the show.

Hunter rested her palms on the island, leaning aggressively as if she were too weak to hold herself up. From behind, I watched her back rise and fall with each heavy breath.

"I don't understand," she muttered before pushing off the counter and spinning back to glare at Mark. "Explain it to me, please."

"Calm down," said Mark.

"I'm not going to fucking calm down," Hunter yelled. "Why is Virginia in your house?" She turned to me before Mark could answer. "Virginia, why are you here?"

"She was just leaving," Mark offered.

"Oh, I see." Hunter nodded. "Then I guess everything is all right." Her sarcasm was completely transparent, and I knew better than to react in any way. Apparently Mark did too because we both remained silent as Hunter walked around the kitchen island and opened the freezer.

Once her face was obstructed by the freezer door, Mark looked back at me again. Each time he looked to me for help, the sadder it got. Not sad like a lost puppy, sad like an absolutely pathetic excuse for a human.

I squinted with disgust, and he turned back in time for her to close the door and reveal the bottle of vodka she was reaching for. I would have killed for a shot or ten, but I wasn't about to speak without invitation.

Mark was becoming increasingly fidgety. I gathered Hunter wasn't prone to uncomfortable silences, and I could attest that it was, in fact, uncomfortable.

"I think you should go," he said to me.

"Why?" Hunter interjected. "Don't leave on my account. Do you two want to go upstairs and fuck or something? I could start dinner." She poured the chilled vodka into a glass she probably should have rinsed out first. I could tell from the shadow there was a film covering the bottom. There was no way she could have missed it. She just didn't care.

This was the Hunter I was always worried would show up. The one who had a deep, unwavering resentment toward me. The one who blamed me for any trouble she was having with Mark, and clearly there was trouble. The one who belonged drinking alone at the pub.

"There's nothing going on," Mark insisted. "I get it. It looks bad, but I promise it's nothing."

Hunter sacrificed the sip of vodka nearing her lips to hurl the cup across the room at him. He ducked at the last second, the glass barely missing his head and making contact with the sliding glass door instead, causing it to shatter.

Mark and I cowered at the piercing crash. It was loud, and I wondered if the cops had heard it and if they would even care if they did.

Once we regained our composure, I looked back at Hunter, who stood still, waiting for us to get over it.

"Jesus Christ, Hunter," Mark yelled. "You're going to pay for that."

She glared at him—the irrelevance in that moment of who would pay for the broken door, his misguided concern almost unfathomable to her.

She finally let her eyes leave Mark and move to me. "Is he telling the truth? Is it nothing?"

Her gaze was intense, and it impeded my ability to reason. What did I want in that moment? What did I want to say? What did I want the outcome to be? It felt like that night outside the liquor store when I couldn't find the words to speak to her.

"Well, your silence speaks volumes," she scoffed.

"Virginia!" Mark yelled. "Tell her the truth."

Of course, by "the truth," he obviously meant *not* the truth. He wanted me to give some plausible explanation for being there. I'm not sure what that could even be. I was there because Jenny found out about us and was blackmailing him. Was that the truth he wanted me to share? Was I supposed to just leave out the hand-holding, the attempted kissing, the *it's not too late for us* part?

I had done it again. I had betrayed Jenny. Like so many times before, it started in the guise of helping her and ended with me completely submersed in self-serving, destructive behavior with Mark.

"Hunter . . ." I swallowed hard and stepped closer to her, getting Mark out of my periphery. "Mark saw Jenny the night she was killed. I found out that she knew some things, and I came here to confront him. He admitted to seeing her, and I don't know what it all means, but that's why I'm here."

"'Don't know what it all means'?" Mark shouted from behind

me. "Don't phrase it like that. Hunter, I had absolutely nothing to do with Jenny's death. I swear to fucking God."

Hunter shook her head. She was past ever believing another word out of his mouth, but she also seemed reluctant to listen to me. I wouldn't listen to me either.

CHAPTER FIFTY

JENNY

JENNY STAYED PERFECTLY STILL, listening to Mr. Renkin spin Ms. Willoughby's anger into forgiveness, convincing her how irrational she was being.

"I'm sorry," she finally said, completing his work and making Jenny want to run down the stairs screaming for Ms. Willoughby to leave this monster, but she didn't move. She was too afraid.

"It's OK, baby," Mr. Renkin offered, so generous.

"Can I stay?" she asked.

"Why don't you come back tomorrow? I'll make dinner."

She didn't respond right away, and Jenny wished so badly that she could see them. Were they touching? Was Ms. Willoughby looking at him or down at the floor?

"Hey, hey, hey . . ." Mr. Renkin said. "Get out of your head. I can see you spiraling. Don't overthink it, OK?"

Jenny heard a kiss, not sure if it was on the lips, the cheek, the forehead.

"I'm just tired and I want to get up early," he explained.

Bull. Shit, Jenny thought.

"OK," Ms. Willoughby said with the minimum volume possible for the word to still reach Jenny.

There were steps toward the door. It opened. Another kiss; then it closed again. Ms. Willoughby was gone and Jenny was alone.

She turned her head from the dim light reaching the hallway and tried to make sense of her surroundings. There was a window. A thick curtain was shielding most of the moonlight, but a thin strip of light at the bottom was enough to interrupt the pitch black. If she climbed out, how far was the drop? Was that even necessary? Mr. Renkin had been letting her go the first time. What's to say this time would be any different?

Jenny tiptoed across the room. She didn't need to hide anymore, but she hoped maybe he had forgotten about her and she wasn't eager to make any noises that would remind him. She pulled back the thick curtain just in time to watch the headlights from Ms. Willoughby's car reverse down the driveway, abandoning Jenny there.

The drop from the window to the ground was severe. Trying to escape that way would surely result in at least a broken ankle, maybe as much as a shattered skull.

She could hear Mr. Renkin moving about downstairs. She didn't want him to come for her, but every step he took increased the suspense and made her thoughts more frantic. Would he hurt her? What if he tried to rape her? Was he capable of that? He could have done something to her that day she was unconscious. Or did he? Did he do something and she just couldn't remember? Maybe he wasn't interested in her at all. Maybe she just had too many perverts in her life and now she couldn't see anything else. Was there permanent damage to her brain?

Jenny turned from the window—the curtain pulled to the side, bunched in her hand, a triangle of exposed glass welcoming a bit of moonlight into the room. It was Mr. Renkin's bedroom. She could make out the foot of the bed—a comforter half tucked in, half tugged up somewhere out of the light, a dresser with two drawers partially open, a pile of dirty clothes next to it.

Mr. Renkin moved again downstairs, reminding her he was still there, and she looked back to the window, as if a ladder could have appeared, or maybe the house had shrunk, neither a reality. She turned back to the door. Should she run? Her head ping-ponged back and forth, a breakdown building, her heart beating so fast she could see the fabric of her nightgown twitching along with it.

Mr. Renkin went silent downstairs. Jenny's heartbeat was an unrelenting repetitive thud, starting in her chest and splitting at the back of her head to pound through each ear canal equally. It was getting louder and faster. It was building to a crescendo. Just as she thought her head was about to explode, spitting brain matter from any available orifice, something moved in the bed.

It was human movement, hidden in the darkness, in a silent house where she thought there was only one person to fear. With the curtain still bunched in her fist, Jenny lifted her arm, slowly increasing the visibility of her surroundings.

First she could see the untucked portion of the comforter snaked around a set of bare legs, one on top of the other. Then there was a hand, indistinguishable, no rings, no nail polish, attached to an unremarkable arm that led to an exposed collarbone above the edge of the blanket. And then . . . flat, messy, bright magenta hair.

Jenny took in one unforgettable memory of Christine Castleton's sleeping face, passed out drunk in Mr. Renkin's bed, before she released the curtain and bolted for the door. She took the stairs so fast that she had to grip the railing and catch herself every time she slipped and took a few faster than expected. She hit the living room floor and sprinted for the door. Nothing would stop her. As she flung it open, she caught a glimpse of Mr. Renkin at the kitchen island. His only movement was to bring his beer to his lips while he watched her. It was eerie, but Jenny couldn't care less once she felt the fresh air on her face and slammed the door behind her.

JENNY SPRINTED DOWN the driveway. She was going to Virginia's. Even if it took an hour, two hours, even if she had to crawl, her decision was made. If Virginia wasn't there, she would sit outside her door and wait. She wasn't going home to her insane mother, and she wasn't going back to help JP bury a body.

Before she reached the end of the driveway, music started blaring from inside Mr. Renkin's house. It made her stop and turn around. She couldn't see him in any of the well-lit windows. Her legs started moving again as she looked over her shoulder and watched the distance from his house grow. Jenny was done getting in other people's business. She was done knowing other people's secrets. She was done having her own secrets.

SHE DIDN'T NOTICE the car until she ran smack into the bumper. A sharp pain pulsed from her left shin, and she threw her weight to her other leg. Applying pressure to the soon-to-be bruise, Jenny looked up at the car. It was dark, silent, and appeared abandoned, but there it sat, not parked, just stopped dead in the center at the end of Mr. Renkin's driveway.

The overhead light came on inside illuminating a long arm as it lowered from the roof. Jenny's eyes met the driver's. They held eye contact, neither blinking, neither moving.

CHAPTER FIFTY-ONE

VIRGINIA

"LOOK, I DON'T know what he's told you about me," I said to her. "I know that I've called the house over the years. I know I'm a mess, but he's not innocent. He's not faithful. At least he's trying very hard not to be."

She closed her eyes. Then she smiled. The smile was devastating to me. Those nights at the bar, I liked to make her smile. This was not that.

She peeled her eyes open and sighed. "You know, I always said to myself, if we could just get past this Virginia thing . . ." She trailed off for a second before coming back. "I mean, Jesus, in high school you were nothing. I guess that's what he liked, what made you vulnerable. That and your age."

Mark rolled his eyes and pouted like he had any grounds to stand on, like somehow playing the pedophilia card should be off the table.

"When he left me for you, I went fucking nuts. I was seriously going to be one of those girls setting houses on fire and spray-painting 'cheater' on the front lawn, but he had this way, you know? Where he convinced me that if I told anyone, it made me pathetic and immature. Like if I couldn't handle the breakup maturely, of course he wouldn't want to be with me. That was what I thought about. Not that he was fucking another freshman."

It suddenly made so much sense, and I felt like I had been whack-a-moled down a hole I might never climb back out of. He was with Hunter first. He did the exact same thing to Hunter. Then he came back to her, and now he was trying to get back to me. There was not a comparable feeling in the world to what it felt like to learn that what I'd thought was a unique and perfect true love was actually a pattern of abuse.

I turned to Mark. He wouldn't even look at me. It seemed obvious now. He didn't end things so that I could find myself. What part of me ever thought he would do something selfless like that? We were young and vulnerable, and without us realizing it, he made himself the center of our worlds. He cut us off from everyone, distracted by the excitement of the secret and the feeling of being special. I was trying so hard not to hate myself in that moment.

It seemed like I should say something to her, but she was monologuing, and what could I contribute? I always thought she barely knew I existed in high school. It was jarring knowing that a part of her had fixated on me and it had brought her a misery matching my own. Maybe it's why I felt such a connection to her.

"Just get past this Virginia thing," she repeated to no one in particular before turning her attention to me. "I prayed for you to move away. I wanted so badly for you to get your act together and leave town. I watched and waited. I judged you for not doing something—textbook projection," she scoffed, finding humor in her own devastation.

"This is the only life I have," she continued. "And he just did it again. Like it was nothing." The vitriol in her voice was palpable now. There was nothing for Mark or me to do but let her continue to build. The acid in my stomach was crawling up my esophagus. I was putting the pieces together; I just didn't know it yet.

She glared at Mark. "There's no getting past the Virginia thing because it's not Virginia. It's you. I finally figured that out the hard way," she said, staring into his soul.

"He was fucking Jenny," she blurted out as she turned back to me.

There it was again, devastating news delivered to me without preamble. It came out so fast and blunt, I was still processing the previous blow and had no window to prepare. I never thought it could really be true. Even when I stood on his front porch ready to confront him. Even when I stalked around in the woods outside his house looking for Jenny's backpack. Even when he admitted she was in his house and knew about us. Never did I really believe he could be fucking her. Hunter, me, Jenny. Three fucking teenagers.

"Well, I guess it was only once," Hunter clarified. "That's what they said, right? That she was a virgin before that night? All your hard work finally paying off and then, what? She regretted it? She freaked out? Were you too rough?"

"What the fuck?" Mark protested. "I didn't touch that girl."

I just couldn't believe him anymore. The lie that broke the camel's back.

"It was so obvious," Hunter retorted. "You think you're so smart, but I knew immediately you were having an affair. I've already lived through this once, remember? Your charm is also your downfall. To be the center of your universe is so all-encompassing and addicting that it's so, *so* obvious when something changes," she spat at him with such conviction she could convince any jury. Of course, I already knew exactly the feeling she was talking about.

Maybe Jenny discovering my notes wasn't about blackmail. Maybe the notes were just about her finding out Mark had been with me too. Maybe Jenny took those letters to confront him because she loved him and this was devastating. Maybe my letters told her she wasn't special, not to him. What would I have done if I had found love letters between Mark and Hunter?

"I thought it was Virginia. I was sure of it." Hunter shook her head, disappointed in herself. "With your history, the phone calls, the way you ogled at her in town, but I should have known it was another kid. And I waited and I saw Jenny come running out of your house that night, so you can just save your energy. It makes sense now. You had been so distracted. She was basically a brand-new teenage Virginia."

"It's not what you think," Mark pleaded, hoping to deescalate the situation.

"I thought it would be Virginia," she repeated, this time more insistent, and it was clear that mattered. It mattered that she thought it was me. It was an explanation. An excuse. That night. That night she saw Jenny leave Mark's house.

"Hunter." I let my volume build as I spoke. "You saw Jenny that night? After she was here?"

"Jenny left . . ." Mark blurted out. "And then I saw you in the driveway." He pointed at her like he was on the witness stand.

"Shut up!" I whisper-yelled. He was in no position to contribute to the conversation, and I wanted him to fucking evaporate into thin air.

"Hunter . . ." I spoke as carefully as I possibly could given the context. "What happened that night?"

CHAPTER FIFTY-TWO

JENNY

JENNY HELD HER SHIN, staring at the driver, not capable of reacting first.

Ms. Willoughby finally reached for the door.

"Jenny?" She rose from the car, the interior light still the only source of light between them.

"Ms. Willoughby!" Jenny exhaled, running to her and throwing her arms around her waist. It wasn't something she planned; it was just something she had to do once she heard her voice. Ms. Willoughby held her close, and Jenny felt such a relief her legs almost gave out. She knew a million questions were coming, but Ms. Willoughby let her have these precious seconds to just exist.

"Oh, Jenny . . ." Ms. Willoughby let Jenny stay resting against her, the girl so desperate for her touch. "This isn't happening," she muttered. "It's not you. It can't be you."

"What?" Jenny asked, trying to push back and create enough space to look up at Ms. Willoughby, but the counselor held Jenny tight, not ready to look her in the eyes.

"Ms. Willoughby?" Jenny asked, concerned and confused.

The woman maintained her hold on Jenny. It was enough time

for the cuts on Jenny's cheek to register as uncomfortable, pressed against her jacket.

"Ms. Willoughby!" Jenny yelled to snap her out of it. She jerked her arms out and broke Ms. Willoughby's grasp. Jenny didn't trust her groggy brain enough to know if the aggressive move was justified.

Jenny inched backward, slow movements disguised as adjustments instead of a retreat. She needed guidance more than ever and waited for Ms. Willoughby to tell her what to do in the moment . . . that night . . . in life.

Ms. Willoughby stepped forward and rested her hands on Jenny's arms. Jenny allowed it. It wasn't threatening; it was intended to be comforting. She bent at the waist to match Jenny's eye level. "Come get in the car, OK?" Her expanding eyes waited for an answer.

"OK," Jenny whispered.

"OK," Ms. Willoughby echoed, robotically standing back up and breaking physical contact. "Come on."

This didn't feel right. Jenny glanced down at her nightgown, tattered, covered in dirt, drops of blood from where she had wiped away the scratches on her face. She reached to her hair, what was left of it, with cold mud clumping the short pieces in groups, nothing like the blonde waves she'd had only hours earlier. Nothing about this felt right. Why didn't Ms. Willoughby ask her what happened? Why wasn't she calling the cops?

"Come on," Ms. Willoughby insisted as she stood at the driver's side door.

Jenny stood still. She clenched her jaw, begging her brain to wake up, but when she tried to think, to figure out why it all felt so wrong, her thoughts just evaporated and she had to start over. It was enough to keep her from stepping toward the car, but she didn't know why.

Was it just paranoia? She had been through so much. Was she crazy now? The whole world wasn't out to get her. She wasn't that special.

Jenny swallowed the saliva that had pooled in her mouth while she stood paralyzed.

"Jenny," Ms. Willoughby insisted. "Let's go. C'mon." She walked back to Jenny once she realized her words weren't working. "Jenny!" she shouted, as if the problem was that Jenny couldn't hear her.

"I . . . I . . . I don't want to," Jenny managed to stammer.

Ms. Willoughby reached out and grabbed the girl's wrist, tugging her toward the car.

Jenny yanked her arm way. "Stop," she pleaded. "Ms. Willoughby, you're scaring me."

Ms. Willoughby rolled her eyes. "I didn't want it to be you. This is making it harder for me, you know? This isn't easy for me."

"What are you talking about?" Jenny asked. How could Ms. Willoughby know anything about what was going on? She hadn't asked her one question.

"I know it feels like you're special. He does that, but he doesn't mean it. He doesn't love you. He's your teacher. What he is doing to you is not OK. This is not your fault. Do you hear me?"

It finally clicked with Jenny's dulled brain what she was talking about. "No," she mumbled, shaking her head. "I'm not . . ."

Ms. Willoughby grabbed Jenny's arms again, holding her body still and pointed at attention. "I don't blame you. I'm not mad at you. This is his fault, not yours. He makes mistakes."

That was putting it mildly. *Mistakes.* Virginia was one of his mistakes. Ms. Willoughby was one of his mistakes. Now his mistake, Christine Castleton, was passed out in his bed. It would be easy to make Ms. Willoughby understand it wasn't Jenny. March her back to his house and show her Christine, but how would Mr. Renkin react? What he had done to Jenny over a few notes from ten years ago could pale in comparison to being caught red-handed with an underage girl drunk and naked in his bed.

"I just want to go home," Jenny whispered.

Ms. Willoughby closed her eyes and took a deep breath, internalizing something Jenny couldn't understand. "All right, sure," she said, letting go of Jenny's arm. "C'mon, I'll give you a ride."

"I'm going to walk," Jenny said, attempting a smile that she was sure came out crooked.

"No, that's ridiculous. It's late." Ms. Willoughby took a few steps closer to Jenny. She rubbed at one of her arms—nervous, twitchy.

"Are you OK?" Jenny asked. The question just came out. It was an instinctive reaction to this unrecognizable behavior from her previously reliable confidant. It was a question Ms. Willoughby should have asked Jenny a hundred times by now. It was as if she couldn't even see Jenny.

"You have to know I didn't want it to be you," Ms. Willoughby insisted. "I didn't think this of you. Even when Mallory tried to warn me, it didn't click. I trusted you; you're good," she said, shaking her head. "Or I'm just so, so stupid. Jesus Christ, you look just like her. A fucking reboot." She smiled at Jenny with big empty eyes, like her whole face was glitching.

"I didn't do anything!" Jenny pleaded, starting to back away but not quite pushed to flee yet. There was something intoxicating about seeing Ms. Willoughby like this. Her vulnerability, her madness, it made Jenny feel the maturity she so craved. In that driveway, in that moment, she wasn't a student or a child. She was another woman, *the* other woman.

Ms. Willoughby shook her head. "No use in lying. I've told them all before, and they won't work on me anymore."

"I'm not lying! Look at me," Jenny begged. "Look at my hair. Look at me!" She reached for the knife in her underwear and pulled it out, an escalation she didn't plan, but Ms. Willoughby was blinded and she needed to make her see.

"Mr. Renkin is horrible," Jenny yelled, holding the knife in front of her as insurance to make sure she could get her words out. "I'm not having sex with him. All those things you're saying are true, but it's not about me. It's about you! *You* are the one he doesn't love. He's a jerk and he's a liar and you shouldn't like him anyway. He did this to you. He was your teacher too and now you're all messed up just like Virginia."

Ms. Willoughby's face hardened, her lip quivering. "And so are you! You're just like Virginia. It was supposed to be her. I came here for her and it was you. Save me your speech. You have no idea." She paused to be alone with her thoughts for a beat, her eyes glued to the ground. "The damage is already done. You're already ruined," she whispered, much softer than anything else she had said that night.

Ms. Willoughby moved closer. Slowly.

The knife became irrelevant. Jenny wasn't going to hurt her. She let her arm drop.

With every step Ms. Willoughby took, she morphed back into the lady who sat behind her desk listening to Jenny, chatting like a confidant, acting like Jenny was special. Jenny could see a way out of this, a good night's sleep, a lot of therapy for them both. Then she was slapped—fast, across her face—stinging the cuts from the glass her mother had thrown at her. Jenny turned and ran.

It was difficult to run on her shin.

It was difficult to run in that nightgown.

It was difficult to run toward the pitch black.

JENNY COULD HEAR footsteps behind her, propelling off the gravel driveway. Ms. Willoughby was gaining on her. She had to get out of the open driveway, so she veered to the left and her feet barely entered the woods when a force hit her from behind. She plummeted toward the ground, releasing the knife in order to brace her fall with both hands.

Twigs and acorns dug into Jenny's back as she rolled over to see Ms. Willoughby over her, crouched and grabbing the knife. She stood back up, looking a hundred feet tall to Jenny on the ground. She looked crazy. And sad. Mr. Renkin made her like this, but Jenny still felt guilty. Ms. Willoughby was nice to her. She was the one who listened to her. The one who wanted to help her. If she could go back, she would never have talked to JP. She would have gotten in the car with Christine Castleton. She would have had her mother call the school and change her to Mallory's block. It sounded cool to say you have no regrets, but Jenny regretted everything as she looked up at Ms. Willoughby, completely ruined.

A part of Jenny never thought Ms. Willoughby would actually hurt her. Even when she was waiting in the driveway, hidden, stalking. Even when she wouldn't let her go. Even now that she stood over her with a knife. To Jenny, they had a bond. Ms. Willoughby cared, she listened, she understood Jenny wasn't like the other kids. It was naïve. She was beginning to see that now.

It was then that the muffled music from Mr. Renkin's house became clear. He had opened the front door. The porch light shot down the driveway, illuminating the navy Accord but doing nothing to the darkness of the woods. Ms. Willoughby whipped her face toward the sound. Impeccable timing. Life-saving timing.

No clever plan would help. It was time to scream, scream at a level of bloody murder only a teenage girl was capable of. A scream that would pierce through Mr. Renkin's loud music and ripple through the woods and down the hill.

A second to part her lips, a second to inhale the necessary air, then one more to release the inescapable scream. It took too long. Just as Jenny began to exhale a sound, Ms. Willoughby lunged to the ground, driving the knife into Jenny's abdomen, cutting off the scream like she had pulled the plug.

Complete shock drove Jenny to try to scream again, but she couldn't inhale, not on her back, not with the knife in her.

Ms. Willoughby yanked the knife out. "Shit. Shiiiiit," she whispered to herself, sitting back on her ankles and staring at the wound as the blood started to show through Jenny's nightgown.

Jenny took short disjointed breaths, trying to process what was happening. She had finally pushed it too far. She wasn't invincible.

Ms. Willoughby glared at the knife in her hand, as if this were its fault.

Jenny rolled on her side. That's as far as she got.

Ms. Willoughby, gripping the knife with both hands this time, plunged it into Jenny's side.

Jenny fell back with the momentum of Ms. Willoughby pulling the knife out again. She pressed her hand against the new wound. The pain was unbearable, and her hand fell to the ground.

Ms. Willoughby rose to her feet.

Jenny couldn't even see her face. She was just a silhouette, adorned with a knife and accented by pointed trees that filled the space behind her as if they were her accomplices.

Jenny stood no chance. She closed her eyes and waited for the knife to find another entry point.

"Hunter?" Mr. Renkin yelled into the night, disrupting everything.

Jenny opened her eyes as Ms. Willoughby turned toward the house.

"Is that you? What are you doing?" He couldn't see. The light didn't reach them.

Ms. Willoughby looked back to Jenny, then back to Mr. Renkin, then back and forth again, unsure of her next move.

Jenny wished she had options. There was only one thing she could think of. A pointless plan maybe, but she couldn't just give up. When Ms. Willoughby looked back to the house, Jenny took in as much air as her failing body could hold. She closed her eyes, making sure not to squeeze them, just let them rest. It took every ounce of self-control to lie still through the pain. Being motionless was easy for actual dead people. They couldn't feel anything; Jenny could feel everything.

She heard leaves crunch as Ms. Willoughby's attention came back. The sound moved closer, so close the leaves tickled at Jenny's legs. Jenny held her breath, her body, her mind. It felt like forever. Ms. Willoughby was silent, but she was there.

"Hunter! What the hell?" Mr. Renkin yelled out again.

Ms. Willoughby finally stepped away.

When the soundtrack of her steps switched from leaves to gravel, Jenny inhaled. It was so forceful her upper body rose off the ground. Pain originated at her wounds and shot to her extremities.

She turned her head to the side, watching Ms. Willoughby step onto the driveway and into the light. Jenny couldn't think even if she wanted to. She crawled to her knees, then somehow back to her feet. She leaned against the closest tree and watched Ms. Willoughby walk back to her car.

"Sorry," she shouted out to him. "My car was giving me trouble."

"Do you need help?" he yelled back.

"No, it's all good," she answered. "Everything is all right now."

She slipped into her car and closed the door.

Mr. Renkin went back in the house.

That was it. Like Jenny was never there. Like no one was dying.

Jenny turned away. The blood was spreading over her nightgown, turning it a dark red. She wouldn't make it far, but she was still on her feet. It was something.

JENNY STUMBLED THROUGH the trees, following the light from JP's front porch. She pressed her hand against the first wound. Her nightgown was surprisingly absorbent; the blood soaked around her hand, but didn't drip.

The air was cold and bitter, but her torso was emanating heat. Sharp pains pulsed through her body. If she could just get to JP, everything would be OK.

As she stepped through the tree line, she noticed the empty driveway. Gil's car was gone. Jenny shuffled toward the house, each step led by her left foot, dragging her fading right side after it. She tried to yell, but all that came out were weak, inaudible sounds. There was a metallic taste in her mouth that she tried hard not to worry about.

JP was gone. He'd taken the car, and probably the body, and left her there. Jenny had few steps left. Each one covered less distance than the one before. She placed her hand on the side of the house to steady herself. Her last eight steps brought her to the backyard. She fell to the ground next to the hose.

Jenny lay on her back, unwilling to move ever again. She stared at the sky in between heavy blinks and tried to find beauty in her last moments, but the stars gave her no hope. They were not romantic. There was no poetic ending. She was just a body next to a hose that her first and only love would use to wash away any evidence of what had happened to her.

CHAPTER FIFTY-THREE

VIRGINIA

"HUNTER, PLEASE," I said, stepping forward and begging for an answer.

She wouldn't look up, and when I got close, I could see tears in her eyes. "It wasn't supposed to be her," she muttered before finally looking up at me. "I thought it was you," she said one more time and three too many times for my liking.

It was the answer I wanted so badly, a true confession from the killer. It wasn't Benjy or Gil. It wasn't JP or Mark or my father. I figured it out when no one else could. I won, but it didn't feel like it. It felt like shit.

I didn't know what to do. Yell for the cops? They were just through the woods. Was I in danger? It didn't feel like it. I wasn't scared. It should have been me, I guess. It was supposed to be me. That would have been better. Mark and I having a torrid affair. Hunter exacting revenge in the night. Jenny still alive, out there engaging in delinquent behavior that was just safe enough to keep her alive until she outgrew her rebellious years. I should have been in Mark's bed, not Jenny. She should have let me have this. This was my thing. She knew; she saw the notes. She didn't need to take this from me. She would still be alive if she hadn't.

Hunter reached across the kitchen island until her hand made contact with the knife block. Mark regained his posture, but we both stayed absolutely still. She slid a knife from the block and set it down on the island in front of her. She took it in. It was a large knife. Maybe she could see her own reflection. Maybe that's why she was staring.

"Hunter," I inserted myself. "It's OK," I whispered, then repeated, "It's OK."

I thought of her in my bed holding my hand. I thought of how well I slept that night. She was somehow my friend, or at least someone who meant something to me. Was any of it real? All the lies she told me. Were they lies, or were her words only untruthful in the context I assumed for them? She was torn apart by Jenny's death. She felt guilty. She felt responsible. She thought she should have done something to prevent it. She couldn't have sex after she found out. She was worried it would happen again. Far from lies, they were all almost *more* authentic now that I knew the truth.

Her eyes fixed on to me like we were having a staring contest. Her face was impossible to read. I couldn't tell if she wanted to hug me and beg me for forgiveness or stab me five hundred times.

Mark took advantage of her momentary distraction and charged toward her, lunging over the island and seizing the knife. It seemed to me like she just let him take it. He slithered back over the island, gripping the knife. Back on his feet, he held it out in front, pointed at Hunter.

"Call the cops, Virginia," he ordered without looking, still glaring at Hunter, almost begging her to try something.

I didn't move.

"Virginia!" he yelled, turning his head only a millisecond to look at me, then back to Hunter.

I still didn't move.

"Goddamn it, Virginia," he barked as he whipped around to scold me. The knife came with him, but before he could point it all the way around . . .

"STOP!" a familiar voice came from outside.

Through the missing glass of the shattered back door, I saw my father crossing the backyard, extending a gun toward us. His presence was unannounced and unexpected and what he would do next—unpredictable.

I looked at Mark and then over to Hunter. I made a decision in that moment that would haunt me forever.

"He did it, Dad!" I yelled. "He killed Jenny!"

Mark never saw it coming. He spun toward me, venom in his eyes and the knife in his hand.

My father pulled the trigger. Just as I'd hoped he would.

The bullet ripped through Mark's chest. The knife fell to the floor.

That was all I needed from my father.

Mark dropped to his knees and rolled onto the hardwood floor. "I didn't kill her," he whispered to me, pleading with his last words as if he still needed to convince me, as if he didn't want to accept what I had just done. That was always his problem. He could never fathom what we were capable of.

The patch of trees separating the property from JP's flooded with cops sprinting toward the sound of the gunshot. A few uniforms emerged from the tree line first, then Brandon. Their guns drawn.

"Put the gun down," one yelled, and my father obeyed. He raised his hands into the air. He was done.

I let Mark look at me as he went. I wanted to kneel down, to grab his hand and give him something to hold on to, but I couldn't let anyone see that. He was Jenny's killer now as far as anyone ever needed to know. Letting him keep my attention was the hardest thing I ever had to do. There was nowhere else I wanted to look, but every second that we stayed linked would be with me forever. I loved him so much and I hated it. I did this for me. Mark and I would never get back together now.

I smiled—one of those smiles to let him know everything would be OK. I had pulled the plug on all of it. He could let go.

Hunter stumbled out from behind the island, reminding me that I was not alone in the house or the lie. She collapsed to the floor a few feet away from Mark and started crying, bobbing in and out of lucidness as he bled out all over the hardwood floor. I stared down at the two of them. I couldn't react. I couldn't even speak. The line between right and wrong was decimated. Was she up for this?

"Call an ambulance," Brandon shouted as he stepped through the broken glass.

An ambulance wasn't going to help. He was gone.

"Are you OK?" Brandon asked, filling the space behind me.

I just nodded without turning to look at him.

He brushed past me and dropped to the floor to uselessly apply pressure to the wound.

I stared at Hunter, alone on the floor. The cops kept a reasonable distance. None of them knew what I knew. Did I make a terrible mistake? I couldn't take it back now. She just stared at Mark. She didn't speak. I prayed she wasn't too crazy to live this lie. I needed her now.

I walked over to her and reached for her shoulder. She grabbed my hand. Our entire friendship was built in the time after she had murdered Jenny. That darkness I found so alluring in her was the killing-a-little-girl kind of darkness. Was any of it genuine? I couldn't ignore how much of myself I saw in her. Had I just been lucky? All those nights that I was blacked out, out of my mind, obsessed with the severity of my worthlessness. Was I lucky to be so passive? Not driven to find a cure like she was? I was no less sick, crazy, broken than she was. It was what happened to us. We were plucked from our peers. We were chosen. We were special. Then we weren't.

It was happening to Jenny too. Maybe Hunter had saved her. Maybe that just made me feel better about what I had done. I could forgive Hunter for what she had done to Jenny because that's the only way I would forgive myself. In hindsight, it was a forgiveness I afforded to us too easily.

I RODE TO the police station with Officer Brett. Brandon had offered, but I insisted he take my father. Brandon was too comfortable and would expect me to talk. Brett was shy and nervous and was content taking the ten-minute drive in silence so that I could think.

I didn't know who Hunter was riding with. I needed to talk to her. We needed to get our stories straight. It was a problem I needed to solve. It was something for me to fixate on instead of any of the horrible garbage thoughts lying just below the surface.

Our story was good. It ticked all the boxes. It would give everyone the pedophile they were looking for. It had everything: motive, a dead perp who couldn't deny it, and enough scandal to satisfy those strangers who filled the pews at her funeral.

No one had to know about me. No one had to know about Hunter. No one had to know it happened to us first.

I WASN'T THE first person brought to the station. JP sat in one of the dated wooden chairs in the waiting area, slouched, hands in his pockets. No one was paying him much attention.

"Have a seat here, will ya?" Brett asked, void of any authority.

I nodded and took a seat next to JP. There were two chairs on each side of the reception desk, and it seemed cold to not sit next to him.

Brett walked through the swinging gate to check in with the chief, and JP and I were alone to talk.

"Hey," he said, casual, a reminder of how young and simple he seemed.

"You all right?" I asked.

"Yeah, now that they know it wasn't me. Did you think it was me?" he asked, looking over at me and trying to read my face.

"Not really," I said, regardless of if I meant it, and that seemed to make him feel a little better.

"Why did he do it?" he asked. "Mr. Renkin?" he clarified unnecessarily.

This was my first performance. No time for rehearsal. House lights were lowered. Curtain drawn. "Something was going on between them and she was threatening to tell, to expose him, I think."

"What do you mean?"

I didn't know how to say it. It would sound so gross out loud.

"Just tell me," he pleaded.

"They had a relationship. They had sex and something went wrong. Or something like that. I don't know the specifics," I explained, then backtracked. I had to stay removed from proprietary details.

His face scrunched. Bothered. "He raped her?" His wheels were spinning.

"I don't think it was like that, but I don't know. I mean, they said she was raped when they found her, but it could have been consensual," I said, not sure if that would make him feel better or not. "As consensual as that sort of thing can be," I clarified.

He didn't say anything. He stared at the floor and reflected on what I just told him. It wasn't sitting well, and I began to panic. Was I this bad at lying? I had lied my whole life. I had to be good at it by now.

I needed to change the subject. I needed more . . . layers . . . a pattern. Page two of the articles soon to be written.

"What do you know about Gil?" I asked as I remembered that gaping hole in the whole thing. "And I know you know something, so don't lie."

I saw his hands clench as he chewed at his bottom lip. "It was nothing. He was just a loser she was messing with. Trying to get things out of him like money and presents and stuff. She never met him in person. She said he was harmless, just mailed her shit when she asked."

"He's missing," I added, thinking he might stumble.

"Guess it doesn't really matter anymore," he said, turning to look at me in a way that felt like what I said next was important. I honestly had no idea if he was lying to my face. It wouldn't be the first time. He was right, though; it didn't matter anymore. What mattered was my lie.

"True," I said. "Who knew she was up to all this shit? Getting mixed up with these men? And why did she need money so badly?" I asked rhetorically, putting questions in his head to regurgitate unconsciously when interrogated.

"She wanted to get out of here," he said. "She didn't like it here."

I just nodded, the kind of nod that goes on way too long and says, *I understand what you just said so deep to the core that I can't find words to express it.*

"But it doesn't make any sense," JP muttered.

I couldn't even convince this kid. Was it possible that a plan this severe made in a split second might not work as I imagined? I had made a fatal miscalculation. Lying about yourself and lying about someone else are two different animals. I couldn't control everything people knew about Mark Renkin. I couldn't control everything people knew about Jenny. I could only control what people knew about me.

"He's very good . . ." I said. "At lying, at hiding, at making others do the same."

JP looked at me, confused and hungry for further explanation.

"Don't feel guilty you didn't know. Mark Renkin had years of practice. It was truly his gift." I rubbed my thumbs together. Was I doing this? "I know, because it happened to me."

"What?" he said, mouth falling open a bit.

I just nodded. "When I was in high school." There it was. Out of my mouth.

The door to the outside swung open before I had to further elaborate. It was Hunter. She was led in by a cop I didn't know, one of

Brandon's. There were no cuffs or fanfare. She wasn't a suspect. She was a witness. Her face was red and puffy, but she was done crying. She looked at JP and then me like we could have been anyone.

The officer held his hand out to direct her into one of the chairs across from us; then he left too, through the swinging gate, back to the boys' club.

JP glanced over at me like I should say something. I had a lot to say, but not out loud across the police station and not in front of JP.

I didn't know what else to do, so I stood up and walked over to her. She straightened her posture, nervous at my approach. I extended my arms and wrapped them around her. She stayed in her seat; I bent over. My arms wrapped tightly around her shoulders. My cheek pressed against hers.

I didn't expect the emotions that came when we inhaled in sync. I had to loosen the embrace to get a grip. I brought my lips as close as I could to whisper in her ear without choking on the wisps of hair.

"They were having an affair and she was going to expose him. He got mad and killed her. He admitted it to us both. Just now. Right before. You don't know anything else. When they push you for more, cry. Break down. Refuse to eat or drink. You're too upset. In shock. Don't say anything else. We will figure this out together." I waited for her to acknowledge my words, to agree to the plan. My mouth stayed close to her ear and hers close to mine.

I felt her inhale again before she spoke. "Someone moved the body," she whispered.

I pulled away from her just as the front door opened again.

"What's going on?" Brandon asked as he marched in with my father. Finally, someone in handcuffs.

I pulled back from Hunter, standing upright and moving to the center of the void between her and JP.

Brandon pushed my father forward, not looking at us but for the other cops. Brett and Brandon's guy hustled toward the gate.

"Why are they all sitting out here?" he asked. "They shouldn't be out here talking to each other."

"We don't have enough rooms," Brett explained.

"Put one in the damn bathroom if you have to," Brandon ordered. He was right. We should have been separated. He was just too late.

ADMITTING IT TO JP was a lot easier than to the cops. If I hadn't already told his dumb young face, I might have chickened out. It wasn't easy sitting in front of two detectives I had never seen before, knowing Brandon was watching on the other side of the mirror, admitting what, up until a few hours earlier, had been my biggest secret.

I struggled to make eye contact, but I didn't worry if it made me look guilty because I wasn't lying about this. I was telling the truth and I had the notes as proof, so whatever I did or didn't do was natural human behavior not to be questioned.

I stayed as clinical as I could. Yes, we had a relationship. Yes, it was sexual. I was fourteen. Yes, he was my teacher. All the parts that mirrored what happened to Jenny. They pushed for more salacious details, curiosity masked as procedure, but I merely asked if that question was necessary whenever I felt it wasn't and they rephrased.

When my statement was deemed enough for the night, given the circumstances, I was allowed to go home. I walked past Brandon like I couldn't hear him until he grabbed my arm to stop me dead in my tracks.

"Virginia, are you OK?"

"Super," I said.

"Let me give you a ride home."

"No, I have a ride. Thanks." I lied. I walked. It wasn't far.

I PULLED THE bottle of vodka from the freezer, an unhealthy swig, three swallows, then crawled into bed and waited for it to hit my bloodstream.

If I had said something sooner . . . I couldn't think about that; it wasn't fair. What happened to Jenny was not my fault, just as what happened to me was not Hunter's fault. It was nice to imagine, just for the night, that's how the world would see it.

MARK RENKIN KILLED Jenny Kennedy.

It was so easy.

No one would want to believe this horrific crime could have been committed by a woman. A young woman. A beautiful woman. A smart woman.

The hair will not rise on anyone's arms if they cross paths with Hunter alone in a dark alley. No one will hesitate to stop in the rain and help her change a flat tire. No one will text Hunter's address to a friend as insurance before going home with her after meeting one night at a bar.

No one would think to believe a woman like me would lie for her.

A jealous woman. A lonely woman. A woman with nothing to gain from it, instead forced to reveal her deepest, darkest secret.

Hunter was with the man I loved. Hunter killed my sister. Hunter had planned to confront *me* that night outside Mark's house.

Yet here we were. There was no going back now.

CHAPTER FIFTY-FOUR

Three Weeks Later

I WENT TO visit my father in prison. He was denied bail. His ability to have a secret life in another state for nearly twenty years didn't bode well in a hearing to decide if he was a flight risk. It was unexpected, and Charlie fired the lawyer immediately.

Maybe I went because of the guilt. Maybe it was because Charlie was so convincing. Maybe it was because, with both of our secrets exposed, prison Dad seemed a little like Vermont Dad.

I sat in a room full of tiny tables and loved ones, waiting for my father to join me. It was so fascinating and surreal to be around real-life criminals. I was a criminal, Hunter was a criminal, my father was a criminal, but it wasn't the same as a guy with tattoos crawling up a neck with the circumference of a basketball. He probably just sold drugs while we were out there killing people, but somehow he was scarier.

The door buzzed, and an officer opened it so that my father could enter. He was growing a bit of a beard, slow and steady, gray and even. He joined me at the table, and I had to give him my full attention.

I studied his face and took note of what memories came first. Him pulling the trigger, obviously. It was recent, traumatic. The night they found my mom, when he told me so matter-of-fact, his affection a hand on my shoulder, not a hug. The day Mark ended things and I went home, unable to save the tears for my room, and he said nothing as I ran by him blithering and incoherent. I tricked my father into killing someone. It certainly wasn't taking the high road, but seeing him in that prison jumpsuit, it felt like a road I could live with.

"Thank you for coming," he said with kind of a smile.

"Sure," I said. "How's it going?"

"It's not horrible. It *is* prison, but I've had a lot of time to just be alone and think. The guards treat me well. I haven't had any issues other than the inherent restrictions of incarceration."

I was OK with that. Prison was enough of a punishment to satisfy my sick brain. I didn't need him shanked or something.

"Have you heard from Linda?" I asked.

"Not really. She's in a facility in Florida. She has a cousin there. I don't suspect she'll be visiting anytime soon."

"No, I imagine not," I said. Poor Linda. To my father and me, Linda died with Jenny. It was all so artificial. If she had any chance of getting better, it was away from us, and neither my father nor I had any desire to argue that point.

We both fell silent. Small talk was never our specialty.

"Why didn't you say anything?" he whispered.

There it was. He couldn't hold it in any longer. That was the question. Of course that was the question. It was the same question everyone had. Why didn't I say something when my teacher kissed me? Why didn't I say something when I grew up and could really understand how wrong it was? Why didn't I say something when Jenny was found? It just felt extra rich coming from him.

I shrugged like a child.

He waited for me to say something, but nodded when he accepted I wasn't going to.

When I did speak, I went in a different direction. "It was crazy when you came charging through with that gun. I didn't really think you were capable of that. I guess Jenny was special. You'd do that kind of thing for Jenny." I delivered my point with all the jealous inflection I intended.

"I would do that for you too," he said. "If I had known . . ." He trailed off.

"First of all, we know that's not true," I said. "I came to your house that night asking for a freaking ride home. A ten-minute ride. You called me selfish or dramatic or some bullshit. You know, if you had just given me a ride because I was your daughter and I was asking, you wouldn't be sitting in here right now."

He inhaled, ready to double down on me being dramatic—old Dad reasserting himself. Then, as if under the guidance of some prison life coach, he exhaled calmly before he spoke.

"You're right. I don't know how to explain it. It was like someone took Jenny from me, stole her right from under me. Just one day she was gone. No more. It drove me mad. I went up the hill that night, and they wouldn't let me anywhere near the kid, thank God. I was pacing, I was out of my mind, and then I heard that glass shatter." He stared down at the table, shaking his head. "And I saw that man holding a knife to you and you told me it was him. That grown man. That man we trusted with our children. I snapped." On that he lifted his eyes to meet mine.

"Virginia, I lost you over a long period of time. The result was the same, but it caused a different reaction in me. Things were hard after your mom, and then when you started high school, it just became unsalvageable, you and me."

"That's so fucked up," I couldn't help but say. "You wiped your hands of me when I was fourteen? Teenagers are supposed to be intolerable. Did you ever think maybe I needed you then more than ever? You realize that now, right? That maybe I was a nightmare because there was something going on with me? Something maybe parents should have fucking noticed?"

"Do you really blame me for what happened to you?" He stared at me, not being combative, just truly asking.

I sighed and leaned back in the chair, letting the intensity calm a bit. "Fuck," I grumbled, rubbing my hands over my face. "I don't know. Not completely. Obviously not completely. Do you blame me for what happened to Jenny?"

It caught him off guard, to be thrown right back at him like that. "I know I shouldn't," he answered. "Not even a little bit."

"But you do," I admitted on his behalf.

"I think we're all to blame," he settled on.

I nodded. He was right.

"I would like to work on this," he said. "Me and you. If you're interested. I know it's not a quick fix, and I know I'm stuck here in prison without much to offer, but it is an offer."

"OK," I said. "I'll think about it."

I WOULD THINK about it. I was his only child again; he cared again. Somewhere along the way, I had to decide if I was entitled to profit from Jenny's death. It seemed wrong, but that had never stopped me before.

———

I PULLED INTO a parking lot conveniently shared by a hair salon, a pharmacy, an ATM, and a pizza place. It was about halfway between Wrenton and Hartsfield and had become a regular meeting place for Brandon and me. By "regular," I mean we had met there a few times since the "truth" came out. The dynamic had changed, but not enough for either of us to walk away completely.

The pizza place looked like every other pizza place I'd ever been in, red counters, boxes stacked to the ceiling, a cash register from the early '90s. It had a vaguely Italian name, the menus were laminated and had turned a shade of yellow from being in endless greasy hands, and customers drank from those thick ruby-red tumblers with free soda refills.

Brandon was there first, waiting for me like always. He greeted me with a kiss on the cheek. "Hey," he whispered right before his lips made contact.

"You smell nice," I said, peeling away and grabbing the seat across from him. I always loved catching Brandon in the window of time post-shower before his bodywash wore off. They say when you're in love with someone, you can smell them, a secret scent that you unlock. I could smell Mark. It wasn't a describable smell. It wasn't lilacs, or cotton, or body odor. It was more of a marker. I couldn't smell Brandon, not in a consistent way.

"How's your day going?" he asked.

I shrugged. "They canceled the winter formal," I said, sharing a story I had overheard at the gas station.

"That's interesting," he said, and I knew he wasn't interested at all.

"Everyone around town is on high alert. They brought in a state counselor to meet with students. They're doing a complete deep dive," I continued.

"I didn't know you were so invested," he said, coming across as insulting despite his intention.

A waitress came to take our order at the perfect moment to prevent me from snapping. Of course I was invested; it had happened to me too. It was not really something I could apply my patented dissociation to.

Brandon was a good guy. He really was, but he was struggling with my past. It was a lot. He felt betrayed that I didn't tell him before I told the world. He knew he shouldn't hold that against me, but it didn't change how it made him feel.

It was hard for me too that he knew. Anytime I was moody or difficult or lazy or anything he didn't enjoy, I knew he was thinking it was because of the Mark thing. I could tell because he would get annoyed and short with me; then something would click and he would change his demeanor and become super affectionate. I hated it. I was allowed to be difficult because that's just who I was, and he was allowed to be mad at me for it. In my mind, getting a free pass on being a bitch because my teacher had sex with me in high school was the most offensive way of him saying he thought my life was completely defined by Mark. It wasn't necessarily fair that I analyzed all of Brandon's intentions that way, but it was how my brain worked and it was the only brain I had.

The waitress finally left, and Brandon turned back to me. "So, I have some news." He lifted his arms onto the table and leaned toward me, smiling so big the news must have been Powerball related.

"What?"

"I got an offer from Boston PD. They want me to come work for major crimes."

"OK," I said before realizing my reaction wasn't reflecting the gravity he had applied to his announcement. "Congratulations," I added, then smiled because I thought I was supposed to, reminding me of the first day we met. I didn't understand why I was supposed to be excited. Boston was far. Not airplane far, but no-meeting-halfway-for-pizza far.

"I want you to come with me," he said, reaching forward and placing his hands on top of mine. "Let's do this together."

Ehhhhhh. I didn't know what to say. He wanted me to say, "Oh my God, yes, of course!" I think that's what I was supposed to want to say too, but I couldn't. To be swept away by Brandon, whisked away to some fresh start—it was unrealistic and a cheap way out that I could never stomach. I wanted to leave Wrenton; I had wanted to for a long time, but not like this. Following Brandon, living through his accomplishments? None of my packing-the-car-and-leaving-town fantasies included a knight in shining armor who had to show up because I couldn't do it without him. I was overanalyzing. Sometimes good things just happen to a person. It was OK. It didn't make me weak. Still, it felt unearned. It felt gross.

"Say something," he said, his excitement level having dropped significantly at my silence and probably my face.

"Where did this all come from?" I asked. "I didn't even know you were looking to move."

"I wasn't, but someone retired, and I've been getting some attention because of Jenny's case so they thought of me."

"Glad to see you are profiting so much from her death," I reacted. "Sorry, I know you didn't mean it like that."

"You're deflecting. What's going on? You don't want to go. I can tell," he said, defeated.

"Not really," I admitted.

He slid his arms off the table and into his lap as he leaned against the metal chair back.

"Is this ever going to work?" he asked.

"I think it is working." I smiled and he reciprocated. We really did like each other.

"Don't throw up in your mouth when I say this, but I want more," he said.

I mocked dry heaving for him, then softened because I appreciated the sentiment he was masking with humor. "I know," I said. "You just asked me to move away with you. That part was obvious."

He laughed, and I hesitated on my decision. Sarcasm-infused sexual tension was where we thrived. I could stay in that forever, but he couldn't. If I hadn't framed Mark, if my secret hadn't come out, would I be saying yes? Or, if I hadn't said those words, would I be saying no because Mark was alive and single and I could never let that go, even given everything I had learned about him?

"Think about it," he said. "Come with me. Leave this all behind. I want more for you."

"Ew, don't say that," I said. "That makes you sound like a dick."

"Really?"

"Yeah, you're saying I'm not enough, but don't worry, you can fix me."

"No, no, no," he said, leaning forward again, smiling, and begging for forgiveness. "I think you're the best. Seriously, I enjoy you so much."

"You enjoy me?" I grinned.

"Yes." He laughed. "I enjoy you."

"I enjoy you too," I admitted.

He reached for my hands again. This time, I turned my palms over and let it be mutual. We made dramatic Romeo-and-Juliet eyes at each other for a hot second. It was a momentary escape, but I knew what I was to him now: a victim. Someone to save; someone who needed to be coddled and shielded from the outside world. I understood now more than I ever did before that it wasn't a way to build a relationship and, frankly, wasn't a way to exist as a person.

Before I could say something twisted to end the quiet, heartfelt moment, he spoke up. "When you're ready to leave, no matter where you're headed, will you let me know? Just let me know you're leaving?"

"Sure," I said. "I'll send you a tit pic."

I DIDN'T GET HOME until after 10:30. Brandon and I had stayed at the pizza place for over two hours, talking and laughing like we hadn't just broken up. I guess it meant we weren't that into it in the first place. I was forever grateful to him nonetheless. It was nice to know I could have a relationship other than with Mark. That seemed important.

I pulled the bottle from the freezer and brought it to the couch. My phone buzzed with an unknown number, and I turned it off before setting it facedown on the table. I was back to drinking on Saturday nights. I'd said I wasn't going to do that anymore, but all things considered, I allowed myself the indulgence.

THINGS HAD CHANGED between Hunter and me. Go figure. We met up a few times, cementing our stories, pretending everything was fine, but we couldn't get back to those nights in the pub. She cried a lot at first, apologizing with every fourth sentence until I begged her to stop. Apologies meant nothing; they were just words, and words between two liars are even less potent. It sounds ridiculous, but Hunter and I could trust each other with our fate, just not our feelings. To be emotional or vulnerable with each other now seemed dangerous, but she never questioned I would keep her secrets. I struggled with the morality of keeping what she had done to Jenny a secret. I should hate her. I should blame her and want her punished, but I knew better than anyone that she *had* been punished. Most of her life had been a punishment, and there was no on/off switch. Living with what she had done was going to be punishment for the both of us.

I never wavered on keeping the secret that Mark had preyed on her as a child too. It was not my place to share. I knew firsthand what it was like to hold on to that secret and what it was like to let that secret out. I would never deprive her of the choice.

It had been cathartic to tell at first, just getting it off my chest, but it was short-lived. I had replaced it with new secrets that left me with all the same fears of being found out, anxiety over what people would think, constant questioning of my decisions, and a guilt that could always find a way to taint any happy thought I had—business as usual in my brain.

What was worse was it didn't help to have people tell me how gross it was or to feel sorry for me; it didn't make me feel any better. The truth was that everything horrible about Mark was foreign to my own experience of being with him. Those were the memories that wouldn't change no matter what I learned after the fact, and without him around anymore to remind me of what he was truly like, those memories prevailed. That's what people couldn't understand.

What I wanted was for someone to tell me it was OK what had happened, not what Mark did but my part. I wanted to hear that they understood, that it could have happened to anyone, that I shouldn't be embarrassed. Telling me over and over again how disgusting and wrong it was did nothing to heal me because I was a willing participant. I wasn't locked in some shed for sixteen years. I was in love—a twisted, manipulative, predatory love, but I was there. I had agency. I made choices—choices that contributed to Jenny's death in more ways than one.

The thing that left it particularly unsatisfying was that telling my secret did nothing to bring justice to the world. There were no other little girls to protect with my confession. Mark Renkin was already dead. I had already taken care of that.

Death was the easy way out for him, but I didn't do it for him. I did it for us.

A KNOCK AT THE DOOR somehow stirred me from my drunken slumber. Thus far, I was still refraining from the pills, knowing I couldn't trust what I would say or do if I blacked out.

It was after midnight; there was no way it was a reporter or a nosy neighbor. My inebriated brain didn't consider who it was or if it was safe to answer; it was proud enough to understand a knock on the door means go answer it.

"Hey," the lanky teen in the camouflage coat greeted me as I opened the door.

"Hey," I said, rubbing at my eyes and trying hard to will myself to sobriety.

"Can I come in?" he asked.

"Sure," I said, backing away, less interested in letting him inside as much as desiring to no longer be standing.

He eyed the vodka on the table, and it seemed unjust to judge someone else's choices after showing up unannounced in the middle of the night. JP took a seat on my tiny couch, and I knew better than to join him and instead sat at the foot of my bed.

"What are you doing here?" I finally realized I should ask.

"I'm leaving," he said.

"You just got here."

"No, town. I'm leaving town. Are you drunk?"

"Probably," I confessed.

"I just . . ." He rubbed his hands along his thighs, building up to say something. "I wanted to get something off my chest."

"OK . . ."

"Jenny wasn't having sex with Mr. Renkin. She did lose her virginity that night, but it was with me. We were running away and she wanted to. We were going to have a whole life together. I know it happened to you, so I'm not saying he was innocent, but you said they were having an affair and it just isn't true." He shook his head, looking down at the floor and not at me.

"Are you sure?" I asked.

"Positive," he whispered.

Had Hunter been wrong? Or did she lie on purpose? She didn't seem like she was lying, but it was laughable that I thought I would be able to tell. No, she saw Jenny leave his house that night. What else was she supposed to think? She had no motive if she didn't believe it. She saw Jenny with her own eyes; she had an excuse for believing it to be true.

Did *I* just believe it because I wanted to? Because of course Mark would be cheating on Hunter. Of course he had to be abandoning her like he had done to me. Of course it would have been Jenny who replaced me. What Hunter said had to be true. That night, when she said so much, it had to be true.

If I had known Jenny wasn't having an affair with Mark, if I weren't so eager to believe the accusation, would things have played out differently? Would Mark still be alive? Would Hunter be in prison and my father in Vermont? What would I have done? These were questions I could never know the answer to, but would never stop asking myself.

"I'm not looking to start a whole thing. I just thought you should know," JP explained, trying to reassure me once he realized my silence was creating a mounting tension. He seemed so genuine. I was happy Jenny had had him in her life given everything else, every other self-motivated monster in her circle, including me.

"But if they weren't together, why did he kill her then?" he asked, flirting back on the edge of maybe looking to start a whole thing.

Why *did* he kill her? It was a rational question, one I hadn't prepared for, but it was all so fucked up, a backup motive rolled right off my tongue. "Jenny knew about me and Mark," I admitted. "I found out way after the fact that she found something in my apartment—evidence. It didn't seem relevant to bring it up, given everything else, but if she had tried to blackmail him . . . if she had threatened him . . ."

"Yeah, she was really ballsy. She might have. We got into some trouble that night. We had a plan to get some money, but it didn't work. I don't know what happened, but I told her to leave and his house is so close. If she thought that was an option . . . I don't know. When I came back later that night, her body was just there, on the ground, in my backyard." His voice was breaking up a bit, and I could tell he was picturing her in his mind, whatever she had looked like then.

"You moved her body?" I asked.

He nodded. "No one would believe me. I didn't know what happened to her, and I just . . . Something really bad happened before that and I couldn't call the cops. If she went over there and did something stupid, maybe he lost it. I don't know."

He started to tear up at that point. It didn't make me uncomfortable. I liked that someone was crying for Jenny, authentically crying over the loss of her.

"I didn't want to move her," he insisted. "I just had to because no one would believe me. I tried to be gentle. I promise, I really did." He looked to me for forgiveness, and I nodded.

"What happened earlier that night?" I asked.

He just shook his head, an obligation to keep the secret to himself. It wasn't much of a secret. I had a good guess.

"Was it Gil?" I asked. "Did something happen with Gil?"

He turned, eyes wide, like my awareness was impossible. It seemed obvious, but maybe the alcohol just dulled my surroundings and made everything clear in my brain. I slid off the bed and joined him on the couch so that he could speak at whatever volume was comfortable for him.

He told me everything. At least, I have to believe it was everything. It was a pretty candid admission. It helped knowing a whole horrible set of events had taken place that had nothing to do with me or my past. It helped knowing Gil wasn't still out there. It helped knowing I now held JP's secret—an insurance policy against him telling anyone else the truth about Jenny and Mark or digging further into that night. It helped that I was still drunk.

What didn't help was when JP told me that Jenny tried to call me that night for help. He breezed over it—merely a bullet point as he rattled off how the night with Gil played out. "She tried to call you, but there was something wrong with you and then . . ." There was something "wrong" with me. The understatement of the century. Jenny needed my help and I didn't deliver. Hell, I didn't even remember. Maybe that's why I called my father. Maybe I was trying to help her. Stretching to that conclusion was too generous. I just had to accept that no matter what I learned about my involvement in that night, no matter how much time passed, there could be more, and it could get worse.

JP stayed the night on the couch just like Hunter did that first night. In the morning, he left without a word, just as she had—the door waking me up as it closed. My head throbbed, and when I never saw him again after that, a tiny part of me always worried that I had just made it all up.

CHAPTER FIFTY-FIVE

EPILOGUE

THE ATTENTION AROUND town was intense and unrelenting. Even when it wasn't, even when it was just a glance over the top of a magazine, it was suffocating. I had to change my phone number. I barely went outside. I watched entire seasons of television in the span of a day. I was drinking a lot, more than I should, more than anyone should.

Hunter left me. She took a job in Connecticut and moved away. A fresh start for her and an excuse for communication between us to become even more infrequent. She told me she didn't want to waste this opportunity for a second chance. I wanted to be happy for her, but I was bitter and I was jealous. I never told her the truth about Jenny and Mark. I considered it, knowing it would derail her "second chance" and keep her close, but I didn't. It would be petty and selfish, even for me. Instead, all I could think when she wouldn't return my calls was a very sarcastic *You're welcome*.

I should have moved away. I knew that's what I should have done. I always said I would, even before Jenny's murder. I just had to figure it all out. This town was impossible for me now. I didn't have to move far, just far enough to not be the story—just far enough for my own fresh start.

I think I was close, close to actually taking action. I'm not sure what I would have done or where I would have gone, but I'm convinced I was on the verge of doing something, finally, without help, just me, doing something to change.

THEN IT ALL RELAXED. There was a new story and I was overshadowed in an instant. A popular senior girl from one of the town's notable families had committed suicide—Billy Castleton's little sister. No one knew why. A new mystery. A new dark cloud over the town. A fresh tragedy that had absolutely nothing to do with me. I could go outside again. I could stay a little longer—just until I figured things out.

ACKNOWLEDGMENTS

FIRST, I HAVE to thank my manager and friend, Emma Ross, who in the corner of a crowded party where we barely knew anyone, convinced me to let her read this little book I had written. Channing Tatum was there; that seems relevant. I can always count on her for a good meal, an unexpected experience, and unfiltered, honest feedback.

Thank you to my agent, Brandi Bowles, for helping me navigate this crazy process with patience and support throughout, and to Addison Duffy for putting this book into Brandi's hands.

I'm so grateful for my editors, Jessica Renheim and Lindsey Rose, and the whole team at Dutton who believed in this book and answered all of my dumb questions in the nicest way possible.

Of course, without my family(s) I would never have done this. To my parents, John and Kathy, and my grandmother, Louise, thank you for always thinking I could do anything. And to my "friend families," the Kews (Meredith, Sherman, Nolan, and Matilda) and the McGlynns (Caitlyn, Andy, Maggie, and Cora), thank you for always opening your homes to me and only judging me a little when I eat Takis for breakfast.

And last, but not least, thank you to all of my early readers who gave me the confidence to keep going.

ONE PLACE. MANY STORIES

Bold, innovative and
empowering publishing.

FOLLOW US ON:

@HQStories